SHADOWFAE

AETHEAON CHRONICLES: BOOK FOUR

LEONARD D. HILLEY II

For my wife, Christal, our two children, and our two grandchildren. My love always.

Aetheaon
Misty Seas of Reus
Isles of Welkstone
Highvale Plains
Brevefar
Icebourne
City of Helfwang
Nagdor
Cronos point
Glacier Ridge
Vale of Frozen Tears
Jamus River
Glasslyn Lake
Methalla
Bridgethorpe
Vylan
Raybourne
Falls Lake
Rivendale
Black Chasm
Woodmog
Bylisanthem
Westwynn
Spellhaven
Taurum
Kingdom of Lagelasid
Shadeport
Kingdom of Ovaloth
N
W E
S

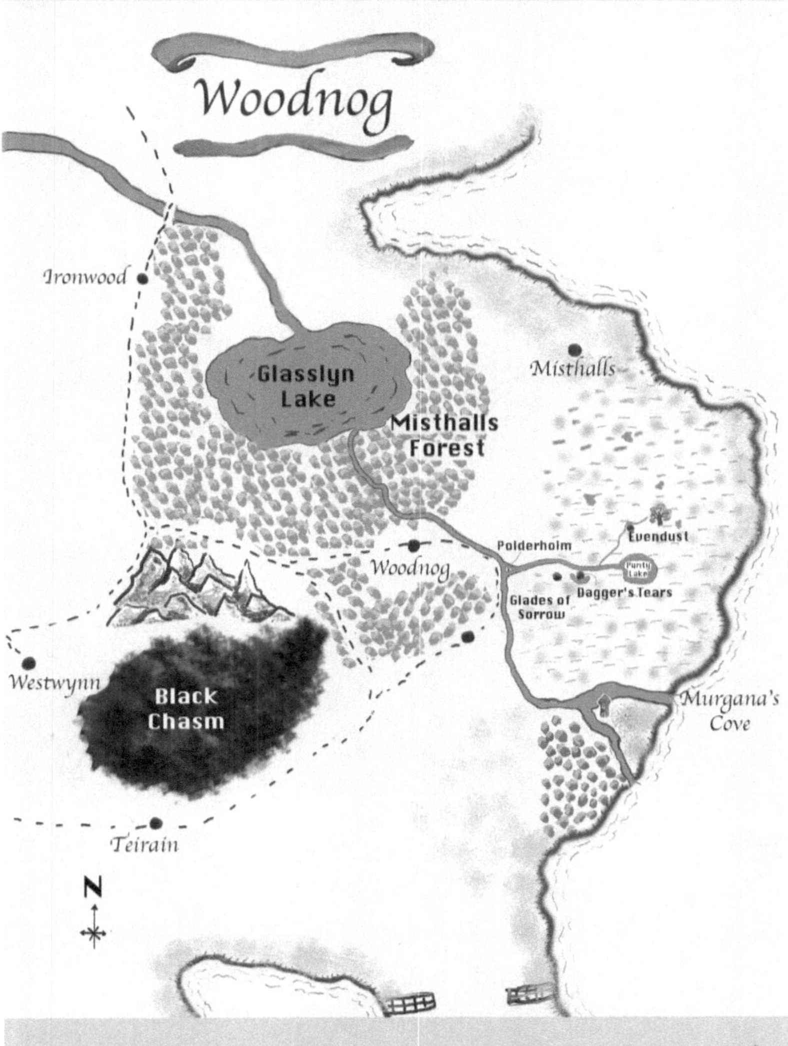

Woodnog
Ironwood
Glasslyn Lake
Misthalls Forest
Misthalls
Polderholm
Evendust
Purity Lake
Woodnog
Glades of Sorrow
Dagger's Tears
Westwynn
Black Chasm
Murgana's Cove
Teirain
N

*R*oble rode his horse, Bleys, while Lehrling followed close behind on his new steed, Patch. In her faery form, Shawndirea sat upon Roble's shoulder and zapped pesky buzzing mosquitoes with little green bolts of magic. The crippled mosquitoes spun and spiraled in clumsy descents before crashing to the ground while she giggled with triumph.

Roble shook his head. "I never thought you'd take pleasure in harming other creatures."

She crinkled her nose and grinned. "I rule and protect the butterflies as their Queen. My charity does not extend to troublesome mosquitoes. Besides, the farther into Woodnog's Quagmire we travel, the more we will be exposed to greater risks of disease. Mosquitoes are prone to deliver such pestilence in our realm."

"I'm not offering complaint," Roble said.

Roble glanced at Lehrling. Beneath Lehrling's blonde beard, his rotund cheeks dimpled a smile and he nodded. He laughed heartily and his plump stomach jiggled.

"What she says is true," Lehrling said.

"How about in your realm, my dearest?" she asked, placing her tiny hand against his cheek. "Do you have pests similar to these?"

Roble nodded. "The same ones, actually. Millions of people have died due to insect vectors and mosquitoes are the primary culprit. Ticks are equally dangerous for spreading disease."

The path ahead twisted and narrowed. A large polished wooden sign hung from a post. A yellow Elfstone embedded at the base of the sign illuminated the elegant lettering, 'Woodnog Swamps: Dangers Unknown.'

Roble studied the sign and shook his head while chuckling. "That's supposed to fill travelers with fear?"

Lehrling frowned. "It should."

"Such a sign only builds my curiosity," Roble replied.

"The fool-hearted—"

"Is that how you view me, Lehrling?" Roble asked. "Fool-hearted?"

"N-o-o-o," Lehrling said in a teasing tone. "None whatsoever. What I meant is that the sign is truthful in its mere warning. It's the unknown dangers that poise our greatest risks. In a day or so, you'll understand."

Shawndirea crinkled her nose and laughed until she snorted. "I'd say within a few hours, Roble will understand."

Beyond the sign, the lush green trees and vines became sparser. The ground was dull brown, almost barren except for the black acrid pools of water, as though the land had been cursed. Absent of grasses, sprigs of sharp-tipped sedges clumped the edges of the stagnant pools. The horses huffed their disdain as biting flies buzzed and crawled along their necks. Finding a place for the horses to graze might prove impossible in these swamps.

Compared to the Woodnog Forests where all flowers, trees, vines, and mosses were touched by the magical blessings of the Fae, Roble could understand how anyone that had left those woods would be overcome by apprehension when entering the toxic bogs and miry land. Anyone except an Overlander who loved science and studied fauna and flora like himself.

No sooner had they rode past the sign than did the sun quite suddenly shun the path before them. The gray sky held no hint of sunlight. A constant dusk shrouded them.

Roble thought it odd and glanced back to see rays of sunlight breaking through the forest canopy on the *other* side of the sign. Chill bumps tickled his arms. It was like they had crossed an unseen dividing barrier, somewhat equivalent to good vs. evil, day vs. dusk, or Heaven opposite Hell.

Thunder rumbled in the distance with a brief, faint shimmer of cloud-to-cloud lightning. Insects chummed and strange birds cried from their hidden places in the thick clumps of yellow-brown grass. Dragonflies darted with winged pixies riding their backs. At first glance, Roble failed to notice the pixies, but after two pixies jousted against one another, his eyes became keener, and he marveled at things he had never seen in the Overlands. Or, had he simply been blind to their existence?

A dark cloud of gnats swarmed the path ahead of them. Roble cleared his throat and pulled his tunic up to cover his nose and mouth. The stench of the acrid air tightened their throats as they rode. Their eyes itched and burned. The quagmire displayed every unwelcoming invitation possible, seemingly hopeful outsiders did just that—stayed out.

An occasional drop of rain spat on the dark swampy mire and browning fauna. Some plopped a loud *Blip!* on the dark water pools. Yellow haze floated like a thin vapor with outreaching tendrils that resembled searching ghostly fingers.

"It'll rain soon," Lehrling said.

"Soon?" Roble said, holding up his palm and watching several large raindrops strike his glove. He grinned. "Seems it has already began."

"It always rains in these swamps," Shawndirea replied.

"Doesn't look like it's rained here in quite some time," Lehrling said.

"How can you tell?" Roble asked. He studied the sticky black mud, which was tacky enough to grip a horse's hoof, suck it down, and prevent the horse from galloping away during a dangerous encounter.

Lehrling laughed. "Because you wouldn't see *any* mud."

"Ah."

"I still think we should have gone with Reise and aided in the overthrow of King Obed," Lehrling said. "That'd be the best retaliation for the destruction the Vykings heaped upon Hoffnung."

"That's ambitious for an old man, don't you think?" Roble said, chuckling softly.

"Old?" Lehrling pointed a stern finger at Roble. "I might be old—"

Roble laughed. "You know I'm only having fun."

Lehrling found no humor in the statement, though he shook his head and shrugged it off with a slight grin. Lehrling's hand involuntarily went to his ribcage, his eyes grew distant, and Roble figured Lehrling was remembering his fall from the horse that had nearly killed him at the slippery entrance to Icevale.

Roble held a fondness for Lehrling, much like his uncle he remembered from his childhood.

Lehrling kept a jolly smile and offered kind advice. Any advice the man gave, Roble took it to heart since he was a stranger in Lehrling and Shawndirea's world. Lehrling never had to take Roble under his wing, and he could've easily dismissed Roble's ignorance as too bothersome to educate. Such, however, wasn't Lehrling's nature. Lehrling had accepted Roble like a son. Perhaps this affection had only begun due to Bausch's untimely death or that Roble had saved Lehrling's life from certain execution at the hands of the invading Vykings? But regardless of the true reason, Roble was thankful to ride with Lehrling. Roble doubted few humans in Aetheaon would have bothered, except to perhaps find a way to rob him.

Lehrling held his ribs for a moment, glanced toward Roble, and apparently realized Roble questioned whether Lehrling was experiencing pain again. Lehrling lowered his hand and offered a slight grin, before looking away with slight embarrassment.

"I must say that I'd rather be doing a million other things at this moment," Roble said with a frustrated sigh, changing the subject. "The swamp's the last place I care to venture."

"As opposed to the Black Chasm?" Lehrling asked.

Roble half grinned and shook his head, recalling how he'd almost died inside the Black Chasm. If not for a magical portal somehow opening nearby and a stranger pulling him through, he'd have never survived. Thus, this was a part of the reason for why he was wandering into the quagmire. Fate was not to be ignored. Deep down, Roble expected he'd return to the Black Chasm in the future, and he'd need to be wiser and better informed in what enemies he might face in battle.

Roble sighed. "Okay, the swamp is the *second* to last place. But I can't ignore Lez'minx's invitation."

"I don't view it as an invitation. Lez'minx wasn't *suggesting* you should find and visit his temple," Lehrling said with a furrowed brow. "I'm more under the impression that the consequences are quite severe, should you decline to meet him."

"I'm under that impression myself," Roble replied. His hands tightened around the reins. "His request was more a threat than hospitality."

Lehrling sighed. "I'm afraid Bausch's fate might've occurred because he had chosen *not* to seek him out."

"You think he was supposed to?"

Lehrling shrugged. "He never mentioned anything about it to me, but he seemed more apprehensive about death after we left Icevale on our journey to Glacier Ridge. He never told me much about his armor, either, though I did ask him."

"I didn't wager any agreement for this armor," Roble said softly. "Finding it was by chance and due to an unfortunate circumstance that I happened upon it. I regret Bausch lost his life. Perhaps if Shawndirea and I had arrived earlier than we had, we could've prevented his death."

"No matter. We cannot change the events set behind us," Lehrling said. His eyes saddened. He cleared his throat. "I have to believe that fate brought you to rescue me. Your timing and arrival were no accident. Bausch's time had come, for reasons I'll never understand, and given the circumstances, Bausch would've wanted you to have his armor."

"I hope so," Roble said in a low whisper.

"I know so," Lehrling said with a forced smile of confidence. "It's a shame you never met him. I sorely miss him. A void has hollowed a place inside my heart. Sometimes I awaken from a dream and immediately look for him, hoping his death was nothing more than an extended tragic nightmare. He's gone in spirit but he lives in my heart and mind. The pain of missing him, however, won't easily go away."

"I imagine not. Such losses never fade quickly. But me wearing his armor doesn't oblige me to serve Lez'minx. I plan to make that clear whenever, or *if*, we find his altar."

"I warned you not to take that dead wizard's rings, remember?"

Shawndirea said. "Lez'minx might insist on more obligations from you because of that."

"I'll outright deny his requests," Roble said firmly.

Shawndirea and Lehrling responded with silence and surprised expressions. Quietness hung in the air for several long seconds.

"Even if it requires your death?" Lehrling asked with his brows raised.

Roble's eyes narrowed. "What life would I have if I'm bound to a deity I don't know or one that I don't trust?"

"That's quite selfish. And what about me?" Shawndirea said, pouting her lips. "Us? There's no *us* if you're dead."

"Are you saying I should worship a strange god?"

Shawndirea beamed a slight grin. "*Who* ever said he's a god or that he wants to be worshipped?"

Roble frowned. "Isn't he a god?"

"He *proclaimed* himself to be a god, but that's entirely different than actually *being* one. For all we know he's a deranged wizard or mage," she said. "Most likely, he's a demigod."

Lehrling's eyes widened and he nodded. "I never considered that. Faery, you may be right."

"What's a demigod?" Roble asked.

"Offspring born from a god and a mortal," Lehrling said.

"That's possible?"

Lehrling nodded.

Roble was silent for several minutes, taking in the information. "Why would a mage or wizard pretend to be a god? That'd be impudent."

"How so?"

"Placing him or herself to be a god when he isn't?"

"You think someone will punish him?" Shawndirea asked.

Roble shrugged.

"Who could?" Shawndirea asked.

"Someone with more power. Maybe one of the real demigods?"

"Sorcerers with great magical abilities tend to think themselves invincible and godlike, often torturing others into submission," she replied. "Demigods tend to think differently. They crave adulation through seduction rather than absolute control. They'd never force others to worship them, but they would bless those who freely do."

"Lez'minx doesn't act like a demigod," Roble said.

She shook her head. "No, he doesn't."

"True loyalty is never gained through manipulation," Roble said.

Lehrling chuckled. "No, but people suffer oppression sometimes in order to eat or live another day."

Roble's jaw tightened. "That's true. Folks under duress get their wills bent and broken, but I'd rather die fighting a tyrant than live my life as a mindless puppet."

"Aye. Not something I'd expect an Overlander to say."

Roble faced Lehrling with a broad grin. "Some of us fight to the death without cowering or flinching, not only to defend ourselves but those we love and hold dear. Those of us with a spine and heart, that is. But about half the population from my realm bleat like mindless sheep following whomever shouts the loudest, regardless of the lack of rationality or common sense. There should be a moral outrage by people, but seldom does it arise."

"Seems those people are like a lot the ones in most of our peasant villages," Lehrling replied. "The longer you live among us, the more you'll see that people tend to be the same regardless of city or race or realm."

"I suppose that shouldn't surprise me," Roble said, sighing.

CHAPTER 2

The pathway into the quagmire sloped downward. The moist ground became soggier. Puddles of black water pooled around greenish brown grassy clumps. Bubbles rose in the soft mud and popped, releasing pungent gases that irritated their noses and the back of their throats when they inhaled. The bubbling, gooey mud and dark waters resembled a pot of rumbling water about to boil over.

The road they had been traveling was progressively disappearing, being claimed by the swamp. From this point further, they'd have no choice but to rely on landmarks in order to find their way back, which would prove near impossible. All the trees and underbrush practically looked the same. The occasional lampposts had either fallen into the swampy water or the Elfstones from the lanterns had been stolen.

Roble wondered if Lez'minx offered his protection for risking his life to find the altar. He doubted it. Other than voicing his demands through a dead wizard, Lez'minx had since remained silent. Could he see where Roble was? And if Roble had chosen *not* to seek the altar, would Lez'minx even know?

These sudden thoughts made Roble question Bausch's death, but he'd never voice this to Lehrling for fear of possibly offending his new friend. But did Bausch's death occur at the hands of Lez'minx, or had the negativity and fear of not doing so—if Lez'minx had made similar demands to Bausch—been the reason for Bausch's demise?

From what Lehrling had told Roble, Bausch was a seasoned knight, trained by Lehrling, fought in previous skirmishes, and most likely, Bausch should have been capable of disposing three or four Vykings, at least well enough to fend them off, until he and Lehrling could escape. But, he had failed. Had he gotten sloppy? Or had his secret fears sapped his bravery.

A lack of confidence was easily recognized by one's enemies or competitors. Of course, Bausch might have simply sacrificed himself, hoping to save Lehrling's life. Lehrling had already suffered injuries, and perhaps being a man of nobility, Bausch surrendered, thinking that by doing so, Lehrling's life might be spared. But, as Roble had seen firsthand, that was not the case. Had Roble and Shawndirea not come when they had, Lehrling's fate would have been the same, if not worse, and Hoffnung would have lost two Dragon Skull Knights.

"You're quite silent," Lehrling said, scratching his chin. "Are you having doubts about this journey?"

"Not so much about the journey troubles me as finding our way back does," Roble replied.

Lehrling chuckled. "It's not hard to get lost in the swamps."

"I agree."

As a biologist in the Overlands, Roble had done a lot of exploration on the other side of Aetheaon's veil, but never had he trudged through a place without a map or without some foreknowledge of the terrain. The only technological thing he truly missed about the Overlands was the use of GPS. In some ways, without GPS to guide him, he was blind. Adaptation, in the world of science, was the only way for survival, and now, he realized he'd only survive by making similar adjustments.

The rain droplets pelleted harder.

"Rain's setting in," Roble said.

Lehrling nodded. "The wet season's upon us."

Roble cocked a brow and then shook his head. "Perfect timing."

Lehrling laughed softly. "But isn't that always the case?"

Roble smiled and nodded.

"If we hurry, we should be back home before the worst of the rains fill the swamps again," Lehrling said.

Roble questioned the possibility of even returning to Woodnog at all.

Eyeing the darker recesses of the swamps where the large cypress-like trees towered, the sensation of being watched overshadowed Roble. A chill shot down his spine. He tugged on his horse's reins, stopping the horse while he studied the swampy forest.

"What's wrong?" Shawndirea asked.

"Something's hidden in the shadows of those trees," he whispered.

Lehrling glanced in the direction Roble was staring. "Did you see something?"

"No. It's just a ... feeling. What lives in these swamps?" Roble asked.

Shawndirea stood on his shoulder and looked in the direction Roble pointed.

"Lots of things," Lehrling replied.

Roble shook his head. "No, I mean, are there enemies or predators I need to know about?"

"To be honest," Shawndirea said, "few humans or other races ever venture into these swamps."

"That's comforting to know," Roble said softly.

Lehrling nodded. "The swamps have a way of frightening folks from entering more than the old sign's warning. But trust me, the sign causes most to turn back rather than risks the odds."

"I can see that," Roble said, "but that's not an answer to my question. I've encountered numerous creatures ever since I entered your realm. These are too bizarre for me to even try to convince others in the Overlands that they exist. Surely you have some knowledge of what's out here, besides mosquitoes and sprites. Like dangerous races."

"Nothing more than rumors," Lehrling replied.

"What kind of rumors?"

"Giant lizards that walk and talk like humans," Lehrling said with a slight grin. "They wear armor and carry spears and clubs."

Roble's brow narrowed. "By your grin I cannot tell if you're being honest or spinning one of your tales."

"It's true," Shawndirea said. "But they're not mythical. They exist. They're Lizardmen or Saurus. It's just few individuals have ever encountered them and escaped with their lives."

"But some have escaped?" Roble asked.

"Yes," she said. "The few who did were never the same."

"Bards retell these stories in Woodnog taverns and in the southern kingdoms," Lehrling said. "The few men who survived became raving madmen and unable to cope, dying shortly after reaching Woodnog and telling their stories to the medics and healers."

Roble frowned. "Died? From what? Fear? Since my arrival in Aetheaon, I've seen things I never would've believed existed—"

"Poison killed them," Shawndirea said.

"Poison?"

She nodded. "The Saurus' bites contain a poison that no one's ever survived. Well, at least no human. Who's to say how it might affect a different race."

"Which is why few humans make such a bold journey into the swamps," Lehrling said.

"*Bold* isn't quite the word I'd use after learning about this," Roble said.

Lehrling ran a hand through his blonde beard. "Perhaps, the best word is desperate. Generally, thieves or murderers flee into these swamps to escape prison or greedy bounty hunters. It's a gamble, I suppose. The poisoned ones who had survived long enough to reach to a tavern outside the swamps must have been miscreants. Prison would be more preferable than death from their poison."

Roble said, "Why didn't you tell me about this *before* we traveled so far from Hoffnung?"

"Would such knowledge have kept you from seeking Lez'minx?" Lehrling asked.

"No," Roble said, after thinking a few moments.

Lehrling chuckled. "I didn't think so."

"No. I'd have still come."

"See?" Lehrling grinned. "So what's it matter?"

"Mental preparation is all," Roble replied.

"What do you mean?"

"I like to fully evaluate the circumstances before I act. It's good to have a planned escape route in certain situations."

"There's still plenty of time for that," Lehrling said, smiling.

"Not as much," Roble said. "We traveled several days before we reached these swamps. And now, we're venturing into the heart of them? Certainly, you can understand why I'd rather plan ahead. Hell, I'd have even liked to listened to some of the bard's tales."

Lehrling grinned. "Their stories change half the time, depending upon the tavern or how much they're drunk."

"Well, then, at least *part* of their information is true, right?"

"Not always," Shawndirea said.

"How is it that these bards even got the information from the dying victims?" Roble asked.

Lehrling released a hearty laugh and his grin widened. His laughter echoed across the swamp. "These bards are worse than the morticians waiting for the ill to die. Bards who tell haunting tales aren't brave enough to *actually* visit places like this to get their firsthand knowledge. Instead, whenever they hear of someone surviving bizarre incidents, they flock outside where the deathbed is housed, hoping to learn more."

"And this benefits them how?" Roble asked.

"A good story is well rewarded. Gold coins, drinks, food, or perhaps an innkeeper's hospitality for a free night's stay," Lehrling said. "Tale-weavers are simply beggars dressed in fancier clothes."

Celebrities, Roble thought to himself.

"Most bards are little more than parasites," Shawndirea said.

"Unless," Lehrling said, "the bard has faced the danger or accompanied a journeyer in such an episode, which is rare."

"And how can you know if he or she is telling the truth?" Roble asked.

"That's the real mystery," Lehrling said. "You can't ever really discern if it's true or not, as their livelihoods depend upon how well they spin their stories. Some bards actually tell legitimate tales, about the ordeals they've encountered along their travels, or the mishaps of being robbed by highwaymen."

"Are they not highwaymen themselves, if they're lying in order to get free food, lodging, and gold?" Roble asked.

Lehrling shrugged. "I suppose one could look at it that way. The tales don't matter though. Few bards are ever quieted, regardless of the tavern."

"Why is that?"

"Peasants lead uneventful lives," Lehrling replied. "As such, they're looking for something more adventurous, even if it isn't necessarily true. Mead to soften their aching muscles and tired minds, and harder ales to erase the torment of facing the next coming day. That's why the poorer folk listen to the worst tales without squabbling over the minor details. They seldom complain about the taste of their drinks, either, which is why tavern owners are willing to pay a shilling or two of gold or even more, if the bard's tales are highly sought after. As long as the bard can lull the peasants' minds into a place where they're not faced with the depths of depressive misery, they earn their keep traveling town to town."

Roble nodded. The same was true with depressed folk in the Overlands. They were given to their technology, which had progressively worsened over time, snatching away more and more valuable time without people even noticing. Once computer technology dominated his society, he craved to find a place where he could live a simpler life without cellphones, computers, and other time sinks. This proved to be why he had no problem adapting to a realm where these things didn't exist, and where he *hoped*, they never would.

Roble grinned, thinking he didn't possess any adequate descriptions to explain the world he had left for Aetheaon. While he loved the simpler way of life in this realm, he had sacrificed other benefits, which were laws that better protected people from being killed by enforcing severe repercussions to those who murdered others. Unlike Aetheaon. So, he found himself needful of remaining vigilant at all times.

"What are you smiling about?" Lehrling asked.

Roble shook his head. "Nothing. It's not important."

"You're not finding humor in what entertains the poor, are you?" he asked.

"Of course not." Roble's smile faded, and he stared toward the edge of the mired swamp at the line of old trees. His horse snorted and adjusted its front hooves on the ground, possibly agitated at their delay in traveling. Roble patted the side of Bleys' neck, watching the fog or mist that hung between the massive tree trunks. "Have you thought of where we'll camp for the night?"

"Nightfall is hours away," Lehrling said.

"How can you tell?"

"Trust me. You'll know."

"But when dusk settles, and we're in a place like this, where would we camp?" Roble asked. "Nothing remotely hospitable here. And with the steady rain, we need shelter. Those trees are not going to protect us from the weather."

"Rest assured," Lehrling replied. "We won't set up camp in an area like this. Nor would we want to. Far too dangerous."

"My point exactly," Roble said. "Any idea where those folks encountered the Saurus?"

"No," Lehrling said. "But I've a feeling it was much deeper into the swamps than this. Otherwise, Elven scouts and rangers from Woodnog would've reported them as a threat to their kingdom."

"That makes sense," Roble said.

Shawndirea stood on Roble's shoulder. "It's doubtful the Saurus would risk being sighted by anyone."

"Then that means," Roble said, "these men who were bitten had traveled quite a distance into the swamps."

"Indeed," Lehrling said.

"It's simply not possible," Roble said evenly.

Confusion set in Lehrling's eyes. "And why not?"

"Poisoned? And these victims managed to drag themselves back through all this muck and dark water to reach Woodnog? That's impossible. They'd have been delirious long before they found their way out of the swamp."

Shawndirea's mouth twisted as she thought. "Are you implying that the Saurus live closer to Woodnog?"

"No. I've no idea about that," Roble said. "I'm simply saying that if these men were bitten so far from civilization, they'd have never gotten out of the swamp. They'd have most likely died by drowning or gotten eaten by something. I imagine these swamps are filled with other creatures capable of poisoning bites."

"You're probably right," Lehrling said. "However, these men swore it was Saurus that had attacked and captured them."

Roble sighed and then nodded. "No sense arguing over what they saw, as we can't ever know for certain. We've no way to verify it. They might have sworn on it, but if the poison was already affecting their brains … it might only be a hallucination. But consider this … what if some of the Saurus lurk in the deeper pools of water and attack whenever a traveler happens by?"

Lehrling whistled slightly as he considered the question. "That's possible. They'd probably have scouts, too."

Roble eyed the dark trees engulfed by thickening fog for several moments. The wind howled and the raindrops pattered steadily heavier, drumming on the mud and sedge blades. The songs of the insects and birds drowned beneath the pelleting rain, hushing in their retreat.

Lehrling shivered. "The air is suddenly colder, which isn't normal this far south."

"Why do you keep staring at those trees?" Shawndirea asked.

"Because that's the direction we need to go," Roble replied.

"How do you know that?" Lehrling asked.

"I'm not sure how to explain it, but this armor seems drawn in that direction."

"Drawn?" Lehrling said with a half laugh. "Are you saying that your armor is alive?"

"No, but it *is* enchanted," Roble said. "It has the ability to adapt to the weather, keeping me comfortable regardless of the extreme temperatures. Perhaps its seamstress is somewhere beyond those trees."

Lehrling pointed to the path ahead of them. In places where the mud was thinner, rocky cobblestone protruded. A fallen lamppost covered with thick moss rested across the old path. "Looks like an old road."

Roble nodded. "I see it. We should cross to those trees before the water rises."

Roble tapped Bleys' sides, and the horse moved forward. With a howl hidden in the wind, a bright greenish-blue light of a wisp zipped past them and disappeared into the dark trees.

"What was that?" Lehrling asked.

Roble shrugged. "I've a feeling we'll soon find out."

CHAPTER 3

"**W**as that a wisp?" Roble asked. His question was more to himself than the others.

Shawndirea nodded. "I believe so. It *wasn't* a faery."

"Looked like a wisp to me," Lehrling said softly.

"Was it giving us a warning? Or was that an issue for us to follow?" Roble asked.

Shawndirea giggled. "Probably neither. Wisps won't offer warnings to humans. If anything, they'd do the opposite. Only a curious fool would follow a wisp through a dark swamp. Doing so could cause someone to fall into a preset trap. Wisps are a mischievous lot. However, at the rate of speed that one is traveling, it's *fleeing* from something."

"Like what?" Roble asked. The hairs on the back of his neck stiffened.

"Let's not wait around to find out," she replied.

Roble offered a look of concern toward Lehrling, and Lehrling glanced back at the trail and nodded his agreement.

"It's best we hurry," Lehrling said.

Roble nudged Bleys' flank to encourage the horse to pick up its pace. But the horse refused to move any faster than its own stubborn speed. Bleys had never ignored a command before, so its sudden hesitation puzzled him. Looking closer, Roble understood the reason for why the horse was walking so slow. Blending into the mud and old clumps of sedges were tapered tree knee-roots with sharp protruding tips. He winced, realizing the damage those pointy roots could do to the bottom of a horse's hoof. Should a horse stab its hoof with one of those, the horse would have to be put down. Since Bleys was keener to their surroundings than he was, he decided to let it find its through the tree roots.

Roble pointed at the knees. "Careful."

"I see them," Lehrling replied. "Quite common for a lot of the trees, but only where the water usually stays deeper. Once we move to drier ground, there won't be near as many."

Roble nodded, even though it was information he already knew.

"The terrain changes a lot," Lehrling said.

"Looks like wasteland to me," Roble replied.

"For some," Shawndirea said. "But don't be surprised to learn that places humans despise are paradise for other, more devious races."

"Like the Lizardmen?"

"The habitat is far more suitable for Saurus," she said. "But I'm not referring to them."

"Then what exactly?"

She sighed. "We don't know. The quagmire has never been fully explored. So no one knows."

"I see." Roble studied his surroundings, wondering if the wisp might circle back.

These desolate swamps were probably filled with countless skeletons of those who had entered and never found their way back out. The place was already dim from no partial sunlight, so it wasn't possible to base direction from the sun's position. He hated to imagine what this place was like once the night claimed it. He hadn't planned to be here long enough to find out. But, plans often seemed to get disrupted regardless of his intentions, especially in Aetheaon. Harsh environments wrought unexpected obstacles, and these marshlands leading into the swamps *weren't* any exception.

As they rode into the dark cover of the large trees, misty curls of haze meandered around the large brown knots of the tall sparsely leafed trees. The sporadic raindrops increased in tempo and number, drumming against the wide canopy leaves and sluicing into long streams that splashed into widening pools of black water. The deceptive mirrored pools might only be inches deep or could plummet several feet down where the tangles of sphagnum moss could ensnare a person. He worried about quicksand, too, amongst other things, like whether or not they'd encounter predatory animals or thieving highwaymen.

The sky darkened. A flash of lightning flickered from cloud to cloud, shimmering with a spectacular strobe effect. A sudden cool breeze shook the overhead branches, freeing the clinging raindrops from the leaves. The effect was similar to having small buckets of water doused upon them.

Roble pulled the hood of his tunic over his head, and Shawndirea slipped inside the hood next to his left ear. Turning his head slightly, he gave her a slight smile. She was wearing her armor made from the material of his own that he had cut when he had taken it from Bausch's body. The small piece of armor had form-fitted her perfectly, and the place where he had removed the material from his armor had almost instantly repaired itself.

Neither of them could ever deny that the armor was enchanted. He realized that before he was totally ready to accept the power of magic residing in Aetheaon. And now, they were traveling into the heart of the swamps to find Lez'minx, the one who presided over the magic bestowed upon the armor. Or so he wanted them to believe.

Roble was still torn on the acceptance of the *god's* demand and boast, except for a couple of things. One, the armor protected him from the weather regardless of the climate, and even against the rain that seemed repelled from attaching to the material. The second reason was harder to explain because he didn't know how to explain the armor's draw toward a hidden source within the swamps. Though he didn't want to tell Lehrling, it was like the armor was a living entity, longing to be reunited with its maker. The thought worried him, because he wondered if this tugging was somehow inadvertently influencing his decisions without his knowledge.

He marveled at the armor's adaptation to the climate, but for some reason, when he had worn it in the Black Chasm, the poisonous air was still deadly and had almost killed him. But those who had accompanied him into the chasm had died much quicker. He wondered if he had fashioned a mask from the material to cover his nose and mouth, would the poison not have affected him at all? Or was the armor actually living and less susceptible to the poison. He puzzled over the idea on the likelihood of it being alive. During the additional length of time Roble was inside the poisonous atmosphere of the Black Chasm, had the armor been slowly dying as well?

These questions burned inside his mind, but he wasn't in any hurry to ever return to the poisonous chasm to test any hypothesis.

"You're awfully quiet," Lehrling said.

The statement jarred Roble from his thoughts. He rebounded with a slight smile. "I'm simply studying our surroundings."

Lehrling shook his head. "You're a deep thinker, aren't you?"

Roble shrugged.

"I like that," Lehrling replied. He turned his attention back to the path and whistled a soft tune, allowing Roble to remain in thought, which Roble appreciated.

Roble's heart and mind raced at seeing all of Aetheaon's unusual fauna, which were unlike any plants he could identify in the Overlands. If he took these back to his home, most of these plants were unknown in the botany field he understood. Should other botanists learn about them, it would draw the attention of thousands of scientists from around his world. Attention wasn't something he craved. However, he'd be thrilled to share his discoveries with his colleagues, if not for only seeing the awe on their faces. Of course, revealing such unknown plants into the world of science would be met with undying pleas for him to reveal *where* he had found them. He couldn't risk others finding and venturing through a tear in the veil that separated his world from the Realm of Aetheaon.

That had almost happened when Roble had found Shawndirea and his colleague, Deiko, had seen Roble capture her. The encounter was met by Deiko's sudden violence to steal Shawndirea from Roble and Deiko was not incapable of committing murder to obtain her. Deiko actually pulled a gun on Roble with every intent to use it.

Roble realized afterwards that if ever he returned to his home, he must be covert, not allowing anyone to see or learn of his return. He wasn't certain if Deiko had given up his pursuit in finding Roble and Shawndirea. Surely, after all this time he had, but Roble remembered the lust for fame and fortune in his former colleague's crazed eyes.

And should Deiko ever find a way through the veil to Aetheaon, Roble doubted the scientist would survive a day.

Shawndirea scooted closer to Roble and leaned her back against his cheek.

Roble stared at the growing pools of water at the edges of the disappearing pathway. He wondered how many had died in this dismal spot. Dead decaying bodies were most likely sucked deep under the muck. How many had died, trying to find their way out? No doubt that others had been betrayed and murdered in the swamp. The secrets carried by some might have died with them, buried and lost to time. Death would not reveal their secrets and would not give up its dead … Unless? The Plague-bringer.

Roble hunched forward on the saddle and glanced at Lehrling. "Whatever possessed Bausch to come to such a dismal environment for armor?"

Lehrling wiped water from his brow, then shook his head like a dog shakes its wet coat. "Roble, your word choices betray you in our realm. You stand out more than a dragon adorned in lavender feathers would. You know that, don't you?"

Roble frowned. "What do you mean?"

"I've been paying attention to your phrases during our journey, and folks here—even the nobles or any aristocrat for that matter—don't use the words you do to describe our surroundings."

"You expect me to change the way I speak?"

"Not entirely, no," Lehrling replied. "But, pay attention to how the folks around you talk, and in turn, carry on conversation at their level. I've no doubt your apprenticeship in your realm is far higher than our own, but unless you wish to draw suspicion from others about your origin … keep in mind, few in Aetheaon are fond of those from the Overlands."

"So how should I speak?"

Lehrling chuckled. "Just ask the basic question. Did you not mean, 'why did Bausch come to the swamps to get his armor?'"

Roble nodded. "Yes."

"Then simply ask the question without adding upscaled words. It would be rare for us to encounter royalty in our journey to wherever Lez'minx's temple is."

Shawndirea leveled a harsh glare at Lehrling. He blushed. "Present company excepted."

"You realize if I'm a queen that makes Roble a king, right?" she asked.

Lehrling released a long sigh, flashed a forced half smile, and nodded. "I understand, Shawndirea. I'm not questioning that, but does it not make more sense for him to blend in rather than immediately reveal to others that he's different than the rest of us?"

She shrugged. "I care not what others think, least of all the commoners that might cross our paths. So what if he sounds or acts differently? The fact he is different is what had drawn me to him and part of the many reasons I love him."

Lehrling raised his hands in surrender. "Yes, m'lady."

"Don't mock me."

"I'm not. I swear it to the Three Goddesses."

"We're wasting time," Roble said. "What led Bausch into the swamps for this armor?"

Wiping rain from his brow, Lehrling shook his head. "I've no idea. I'm not sure whom he found out here to craft it or how he had ever gained knowledge of such a tailor, especially in the Woodnog Swamps."

Roble sighed. "I'd turn back except I don't think it's in my best interest."

"I agree with you," Lehrling replied. "Sometimes a bit of suffering is better than an agonizing death."

Roble laughed. "No argument here."

"Shh," Shawndirea whispered. "Stop the horses."

Lehrling and Roble exchanged concerned glances, gently tugging back the reins.

"What is it?" Roble and Lehrling said in hushed voices.

"It may be nothing, but with the rain it's difficult to know," she replied. "We've left the sanctity of Woodnog Forests and have entered the swamps. Dark Fae reside here." She slid into the front pocket of his leather vest. "It's best that I'm not seen."

"Why?" Roble asked.

"For the same reason the Ratkin had taken me. But worse, my mother has enemies here; those of the Unseelie Courts."

"But you renounced your claim to the throne," Roble said.

"To them, that doesn't matter. They'd do almost anything to cause her and our kingdom grievance and the fact that I'm married to you—a human—the Unseelie would see us both dead," Shawndirea replied. "Or, they'll kill you and take me prisoner. Either outcome is unacceptable."

"Then it would've been best for you to stay in Faybourne," Lehrling said.

Shawndirea shook her head. "No, Roble is still new to our realm. I cannot bear living without him. I'd never forgive myself if I let him travel to find Lez'minx without me and something horrible happened to him."

Lehrling frowned before giving a half grin. "Do you not think I've enough experience to keep him safe?"

She nodded. "You do, from other humans, Elves, and Dwarves, but dealing with the dark Fae? No, you've never had dealings with their kind before. I assure you."

"It seems to me, young faery," Lehrling said, "that your presence in these swamps draws more attention to us than had you not come at all."

"The fact he's an Overlander captures their attention even more than myself."

"They can tell that?" Roble asked.

"Of course."

"How?"

"Your lack of familiarity with our realm," Shawndirea replied. "Curiosity beams in your eyes, and at your age, that's highly uncommon for any traveler. Your language betrays you, like Lehrling suggested. The Unseelie might kill me and persuade you to join them."

"Why? I'm a human, not Fae. Besides, your mother made it quite clear how much she hates me. I've no doubt that these Fae would agree with her distaste," Roble said.

"To the contrary, my love," Shawndirea said, "they would greet you with open arms and hope to birth offspring from you."

"What?" Roble's brow rose.

"My mother and I are from the Seelie Courts, which takes pride in keeping our bloodlines pure and not tainted with species outside of our own. That's why she hates you for marrying me. Our children won't be pure by the Seelie's standards," Shawndirea said. "The Unseelie have no problem breeding with species outside of their own, and if they discover how much she hates you for marrying me, you'd be a prize for them to capture or enslave to become one of their own."

"*Enslave* me?"

"Yes. They can cast spells to take control of you. It's a bit harder now that you're in our realm. But if they had ever enticed you in the Overlands, you'd remain theirs until they tired of you. You ever hear of a faery ring?"

He nodded. "Yes, actually. A ring of mushrooms where a mythical—"

Shawndirea beamed a half smile while shaking her head slightly. "It's *not* mythical. It's how the Unseelie capture humans from your realm and bring them to ours. The ring under a full moon and during their ritual dance opens a portal into our realm. Should any foolish human step inside the ring ... they are spellbound and delivered to Aetheaon. The Unseelie long for diversity within their courts, which is a direct contrast to our court. Anything to offend our courts is considered triumph."

"Does that mean you bringing me to Aetheaon makes you Unseelie now?" Roble asked.

She gasped. Fury darkened her widened eyes. "How *dare* you!"

"Easy," Roble said, swallowing hard. Her sudden anger unsettled him. The beauty of her eyes was masked by the swelling darkness of her widened pupils. "I'm only asking because I want to know the laws that you abide by. I'm not making an accusation."

Still fuming, she breathed heavily. Slowly the darkness in her eyes faded, but she didn't hide her offense. She spoke through gritted teeth, biting her words with iciness. "I'm not Unseelie, nor will I *ever* be. I hold allegiance to my own, despite what my mother thinks or vows or accuses, and I have not ever faltered. Perhaps I don't choose to view things totally as she insists, but I know you're the one I'm to be with."

"I know that to be true as well," Roble replied. "I've no doubt we are destined to be together."

"And to be fair," Shawndirea said, "it was *you* that brought me into Aetheaon after destroying my wings."

"I know."

"And," she said, scrunching her nose, "*you* made the offer to do so. Not me. The last thing I ever expected was you shredding my wings in your butterfly net. It was painful and not something I'd have sacrificed to *snare* you to come to my realm."

Roble nodded. "I know. Must we rehash this again? I thought this was settled."

"It was, until you said what you said about me becoming Unseelie."

"I didn't say that you are," Roble said. "I only questioned if perhaps that's why your mother—"

"I imagine in her eyes, she'd agree that I've fallen from the Seelie Courts, and she'd be the first to make me an outcast since I've denounced taking the throne. But on principalities, it's simply not true. The whole reason I warned you about the Unseelie and their habits is so you'd be less likely to reveal where you're actually from. But your eyes continue to be filled with wonderment at the least uncommon thing." She feigned by widening her eyes and placing her hands against her cheeks. "Oh, my! That leaf is purple and indented—"

"Okay, dear, you've made your point." Roble cocked a brow and glanced at Lehrling.

Lehrling laughed. "She's right. It's hard for you to mask your surprise at things we take for granted. And in the way you talk, lest you forget."

"I suppose you'll keep reminding me of my speech. But my constant curiosity isn't something I can hide. Nature has always intrigued me and more so now that I'm surrounded by fauna and flora unknown to me." He glanced down at Shawndirea. "And what's common for you is uncommon for me. That makes it difficult to ignore."

"It's those moments that can get you and us killed," Shawndirea said.

"I'm beginning to realize that," Roble replied. "I'll do my best to *hide* my surprise."

"A lot of our plants and animals are dangerous," she said.

"Ours, too."

Shawndirea shook her head. "No, I'm not talking about poisonous. Some have magical abilities that are far worse than poison."

"Magical plants?"

"Yes. Cursed ones."

"Here?" Roble asked.

Shawndirea nodded. "*Especially* here, where some of the Unseelie live. These swampy outlands wall the south of Woodnog to the Misty Sea. The Black Chasm walls Woodnog's western border, which is why the Elves are so protective of their forests. The City of Woodnog is threatened on two sides. These swamps are not only dangerous, but they bury things. Lost cities, temples, crumbled libraries with magical tomes have been swallowed by the mire. More gold is under the quagmire than in most Dwarven vaults, but you'll never see even the greediest Dwarf trying to obtain it."

"Why not?"

"Ghosts and angry spirits are overly protective of the possessions they've lost," she replied. "The Unseelie creatures are even worse."

Roble took a deep breath and glanced around the edge of the trees. "Is this your way of trying to get me to turn back?"

"No. But you should know the odds. You said that you'd like forewarning so you can prepare your mind."

"True, but all of this information you've withheld from me until now? Why wait to tell me?" Roble asked in an even tone.

"I had hoped the need never arose," she replied.

"And it has?"

"Yes," she said softly.

"Why?"

"I don't know why, but I sense the darkness of my rivals, my mother's enemies."

Lehrling shifted in his saddle. His eyes widened slightly. "Perhaps we should head on while there is still light so we can find a suitable place to set camp for the night."

"I agree," Roble said. "We're wasting precious hours of what is considered daylight here."

Lehrling laughed.

Roble frowned. "I wasn't joking."

"Trust me. You'll know when it's night."

"I imagine so, which is why I want to get as far as possible while we can."

A high shriek pierced through the steadily thrumming rain.

"What was that?" Roble asked.

Lehrling shrugged. His eyes narrowed, as he stared into the dark trees.

Shawndirea ducked into Roble's vest. "Unseelie. They've attacked something."

"Let's go," Roble said, tapping his heel to Bleys' flank. Deep inside, the smartest thing would have been to head in the opposite direction. But for Roble, he didn't like the idea of retreating when a painful cry beckoned unknowingly for help. He had to know if he could help. Sometimes, as he would soon discover, saving a victim wasn't in one's best interest.

CHAPTER 4

Frustration rose inside Roble. The horse refused to move at a faster pace, due to the tree knees and other uneven pockets on the path. Even though he recognized the possible danger for the horse, he worried that by the delay, whomever or whatever had been attacked would be dead before he and Lehrling could intervene. He believed he could run faster through waist-deep water than the horse could walk on the path.

A bright greenish flash of light emitted around a narrow bend within the towering, moss-covered trees. The light glowed brighter and the pain-filled scream rose in timbre for several moments before slowly diminishing. The wail weakened until it faded into a whisper.

Roble tugged the reins. Ahead on the path, pinned against a bent dead tree trunk was a wisp. Crooked narrow fingers wrapped around its throat, which upon first glance simply resembled tree roots spindling around the wisp's neck from a deformed clump of mud. Then the mass beside the tree moved.

The grotesque creature stood hunched over, holding the wisp captive. Large hairy moles protruded through the thin layer of oozing mud dripping down its back. Its skin was the same shade of brown as the mud, and had it been dusk, Roble realized he could've walked right past the creature without ever having seen it. Even more alarming was how easily it blended into the soggy earth in the marshier places where it could attack unsuspecting passersby.

A third arm dangled between its shoulder blades, lifeless and useless, the cruelty of deformity, and the arm swayed slightly as the slimy beast raised a sharp blade carved from a crude stone into the air with its left hand. Within a breath of movement, the creature appeared ready to kill the wisp with a swift downward plunge of the blade.

"Stop!" Roble said, sliding off his horse.

"What are you doing?" Shawndirea whispered from his pocket.

Roble ignored her.

Startled, the beast turned and snarled. Its oddly shaped mouth—filled with rolls of broken crooked teeth—curled into a grimace. Slime oozed from the sides of its mouth. Huffing through its narrow mouth, it offered a guttural growl while slowly lowering the blade. Its head wobbled side to side as its narrowing eyes attempted to get a better view of Roble but despite its curiosity, it didn't release the wisp.

The light surrounding the wisp continued to fade, and the creature's hand sparkled, as though the light was being drained from the wisp and the creature was consuming it.

"Blah!" the thing said, widely waving its free hand with the rock dagger at Roble.

It had long thin arms and spindly legs, but an overly exaggerated round body that jiggled and sloshed like gelatin whenever it moved its club-like feet. If this mud creature had a neck, the blubbering, sagging rolls beneath its chin hid it well. The thing looked like a glob of clay haphazardly put together out of proper proportion by a small child, which Roble found almost humorous except for the creature being *alive*.

"Roble," Lehrling said softly, sliding off his horse. "Don't approach it."

"I have no intention of getting any closer," Roble replied. He slid a throwing dagger from a sheath on his belt.

Roble took a step closer to reach a more even piece of ground where he could throw the knife without anything obstructing his aim.

The creature growled fiercely. Its mouth partially closed and twisted. Green spittle sprayed through its teeth. Drool dripped in long sticky streams from the sides of its mouth and wherever the spittle fell, the plants browned and withered.

"That's acid?" Roble said, glancing toward Lehrling.

Lehrling nodded, grabbed the reins of his horse and Roble's, and led them safely outside of the creature's reach. "I see that. Come on, Roble. Mount up. We'll head in another direction."

Roble shook his head. "I cannot do that."

"Don't be a fool," Lehrling said. "We've no quarrel with this creature."

The light from the wisp dimmed. The tightened hand around the wisp's throat radiated a greenish glow that had traveled halfway up the creature's bent arm. Roble guessed the creature was absorbing the wisp's energy or magic.

"What is that thing?" Roble asked.

Lehrling shook his head. "No idea."

Shawndirea peered from the vest pocket. She frowned, studying the creature. "It's a bogshee."

"Is that the Unseelie you sensed?" Roble asked.

"No," she replied, shaking her head. "It's not one at all. It's just a swamp monster."

Roble glanced around. "Then where is what you felt?"

"Nearby. Leave the creature and let's go," she replied.

"It's draining the wisp of its power," Roble said.

The bogshee gnashed its uneven teeth together with a grating sound that sent shivers down Roble's spine. It reared its wobbling head backwards and attempted a roar. All that came from its mouth was a gurgling sound, a loud belch, and a gush of acid phlegm spewed onto the ground, burning and consuming any vegetation it touched.

Splattering raindrops, bit by bit, washed more of the mud from the bogshee's slimy skin.

Roble stared in near disbelief, something he had promised Lehrling and Shawndirea he would not do, but how could he not? The bogshee was an abnormality without any logical explanation for *why* it even existed.

In my world, he reminded himself. He wondered if this thing had pulled itself out of the marshland after the rains began.

"So?" she said. "Is a wisp worth risking your life for?"

"Let it die?" he asked.

"Normally, I'd say that we should rescue it. But if that creature reaches you or Lehrling, it will kill you before you can defend yourself. You saw what its acid spit is capable of doing, right?"

He nodded.

"Understand this," she said. "It reacts differently with human flesh."

"Differently? How?"

"It never stops burning through your flesh. It's a painful death. I've seen the outcome only once, but not on a human. An Elf."

"From one of these?"

She nodded. "Yes. So let's go. Please? I understand your want to help other creatures, but you don't *want* to get near the bogshee."

Roble chuckled, holding his blade between his index finger and thumb. "I've no need to get any closer. And look at it. It can't possible move faster than I can throw."

Shawndirea sighed. "Looks are deceptive, my dear, or haven't you *learned* that yet?"

The trapped wisp emitted a short blast of light, crying softly as the bogshee absorbed its fleeting energy.

In seconds, the wisp would be dead. Its life probably ended whenever its last ray of light was snuffed. Disregarding the warnings, Roble flung the knife, striking the bogshee's thick round gut. Half expecting the blade to bounce off the creature's skin, he was surprised when the knife plunged deep into its flesh.

The bogshee didn't react in pain. Instead, it glanced down at the protruding hilt of the knife with the briefest of curiosity. The massive layers of jiggling blubber congealed around the blade and a greenish ooze leaked from where the skin split open. The stomach muscles quivered, causing the ooze to spill faster. The bogshee stiffened, suddenly acknowledging the foreign object lodged in its flesh as something unwanted. It snarled angrily for a second. Its eyes widened, and a softer whine came from its mouth.

The bogshee dropped its stone dagger on the wet ground.

"Mum-duh!" it said in a dull voice while touching the hilt of Roble's dagger. Foolishly, it grabbed the hilt and tugged the blade free. The greenish goo gushed and spilled onto the ground. The roundness of its stomach shrank as it expelled liquid.

Its eyes glanced at Roble in confusion and almost seemed to be pleading to understand what was happening. The bogshee returned its attention to the liquid spilling from its abdomen. Mumbling sounds came through gasps that held no meaning. It released its hold from around the wisp's neck and then dropped to its knees.

The wisp gleamed only a second longer and slid into a crevice in the tree's bark.

The bogshee sat in its liquid entrails, more confused than in pain or anger. It seemed an unintelligent creature, and other than its odd need to drain the wisp's light, it was rather docile. Even so, Roble remained cautious and drew his sword. Shawndirea's warning rang in his ears, and although the bogshee was injured and perhaps near death, he had been surprised by other creatures before. He wasn't going to risk his life, especially not with Shawndirea inside his pocket, because if he died, she most likely did, too.

Lehrling pulled his sword and stood beside Roble. "You think it's dying?"

Roble shrugged. "I was going to ask you the same."

Lehrling sighed. "I've never seen one of them before."

The bogshee's lips drooped into a sad expression. It placed a hand to its leaking side, cupping a handful of its blood, and stared at it. A few seconds later, life drained from its eyes and it fell forward collapsing onto the ground in a mixture of blood, slime, and mud.

Roble swallowed hard, feeling a slight tinge of remorse, as he didn't truly understand what the creature's motives had been, other than to feed upon the wisp's energy. He knew nothing about the bogshee's nature and whether or not it was hostile toward humans or only pursued wisps. He took a step forward.

"Careful," Shawndirea said softly.

"It's dead, isn't it?" Roble asked.

"I honestly don't know. It could be faking. Maybe it's hoping you'll lower your guard and come close enough for it to attack."

"How could anything live after losing so much … I want to say blood, but …?" Roble grimaced.

"I think it's dead," she said. "But I'd rather not take the chance of being wrong."

"Let's go," Lehrling said, heading back to the horses.

"Not yet," Roble replied.

"Why not?"

Roble tightened his grip on his sword. "I need to see if the wisp is still alive."

"It's most likely dead, don't you think?" Lehrling asked.

"We don't know unless we check."

Lehrling frowned. "That's true of the leaking acid bog beast, too."

"Listen to him," Shawndirea said.

"I am, but if that wisp is still alive—"

"Roble, please," she said, "I understand your want to protect innocent creatures that fall victim to predators, but this world is strange to you. In your world, the same thing occurs, does it not?"

Roble nodded.

She said, "Not everything is clearly good or evil, and since we're in an area where there's more darkness than light, you cannot trust what you see."

"I know," Roble said. "But look."

The wisp flickered tiny rays of blue and green.

Shawndirea sighed. "It's dying. There's nothing we can do."

"Shouldn't we at least try?" Roble asked.

Lehrling glanced at her and rolled his eyes.

"I saw that," Roble said.

Lehrling shrugged and gave a sheepish grin.

Rain sluiced from the trees. Flickering lightning brightened the sky for a moment.

"You're wasting time, Roble, which you keep accusing us of doing," Lehrling said. "Have you changed your mind?Either you're prolonging your encounter with Lez'minx or deep down you realize the best thing we can do is to turn back."

Roble shook his head. "I assure you that neither is the case. But if there's the slightest possibility we can help this little creature, I cannot ignore that by walking away."

"Remember when I said that the wisp was fleeing from something?" Shawndirea asked.

Roble nodded.

"Then our continued delay is allowing its pursuer time to reach us. The bogshee might have been the one to drain the wisp of its light and magic, but it did so only out of opportunity. It wasn't *what* the wisp fled from. The wisp simply chose the wrong place to hide and rest. Quite possibly, she never even saw it before it captured her."

Roble's eyes flicked to the bogshee's corpse. "I would've never noticed it had it not been moving. It blends into the swamp's surroundings quite well."

She offered a slight smile. "Yes, it does."

"Should we expect more of them?" he asked.

"They're rare creatures," she replied. "And with the storms settling in, it was probably taking the opportunity to find a new mud pool to habituate. The dry season has ended and the storms from the seas will continue for several months, which means we'd best hurry while the levels of water in the marshy swamps are low. None of us want to be stuck in Woodnog's swamps for several months."

"I agree," Roble said. "Can I at least check on the wisp?"

She puffed her cheeks and slowly expelled the air in a long exasperated sigh. "I'm surprised you were able to fight in the Battle of Hoffnung without offering aid to the ones the Vykings had flung daggers into."

"War is different," Roble said, frowning. "Vykings were the enemy. This—"

"The wisp could be friend or foe, and in these swamps where the Unseelie reside, most likely she's a foe," Shawndirea said. "For the life of me, dear, I don't know how else to explain this. I love you for your caring heart, but if we stop along the wayside every time a creature is suffering, we'll eventually fall prey to worse things than a bogshee."

"Duly noted," he said.

Roble eased to the side of the path where the bogshee's shrinking body slowly sunk into the wet soil. At the rate of its decomposition, he didn't fear being attacked by it. However, the acid it had spewed was something they still needed to avoid. While the rain might eventually dilute the potency of the acid, who knew how much water that required?

Stepping around the green acid pool, Roble walked off the path and through several small shrubs until he reached the tree where the wisp's light flickered from inside a deep crevice of the bark.

Roble sheathed his sword. He peered closer, trying to see the wisp's body. With his right hand, he reached for what he thought might be one of its feet.

"Don't!" Shawndirea said.

He pulled back his hand. "What? Why?"

"Use a stick or something to free it," she replied. "But don't touch it directly."

"Why not?"

"Do you know for certain that none of the bogshee's acid isn't on it? Besides, even near death, it might have enchanted itself with any sort of spell that could kill a human or bewitch you as a defensive mechanism."

"Never thought about that," he replied.

Shawndirea shook her head. "If I didn't despise the Overlands as much as I do, I'd insist we moved there so you don't kill yourself due to your ignorance of my realm."

Roble laughed. "It takes time to learn and adapt."

"Few ever survive the transition, my dear," she said softly. "Granted, you're fast to learn, but it takes only one blind mistake to get you killed."

"That's true for anyone," he replied.

Roble pulled a broad leaf from one of the shrubs and found a narrow dead twig and snapped it from the side of the tree. Gently, he used the twig to work the wisp free from the crevice and allowed it to fall onto the leaf. Then, he moved the wisp and leaf to a fallen log where he could examine the creature closer.

For what beauty the brilliant glow gifted the wisp to display during flight, its true visage was a hundred times more grotesque. In some ways, the wisp was a more hideous creature than the bogshee.

Roble couldn't help but wonder if the extreme illumination was meant to conceal the ugliness of its features in order to lure others to follow the radiance of its glow. Humans typically were flawed to be attracted to beauty and dispelled by ugliness. What pleased the eyes, most often, were the things humans actively sought, and Shawndirea's advice was most accurate. He had wanted to help the creature because of its adorned brilliance, but deep inside, he understood that he also wanted to help it because of what he had accidentally done to Shawndirea's wings.

He peered down at the gasping wisp. Its eyes parted slightly, and were blacker than obsidian. No color like the radiant light it displayed during flight shown in its eyes. Its hawkbill nose and pointy teeth were not features he had expected to see, either. Warts covered its face and body and its withered skin made a raisin almost look smooth.

"What's wrong?" Shawndirea asked.

"Nothing," he said softly. "Why?"

"You're repulsed. At least your distaste is evident in your facial features."

"I—I expected the wisp to be beautiful like you," he replied.

She blushed. "I imagine she was at one time, but the bogshee drained her light. Without her light, her life and beauty are extracted, too."

"So she was beautiful before it sapped her radiance?"

Shawndirea shrugged. "There's no way to rightly know, my dear. So, what now? You can see it's not going to live. Nothing we can do will restore her powers or her radiance. That's forever gone."

Roble nodded, accepting the fact that nothing could be done. "Should we wait and bury it?"

"No," Shawndirea replied. "Nature takes care of its own."

"Why do you think the bogshee was stealing her light?"

"Not sure. Could be a source of strength as it moves from one mud pool to another."

The wisp gasped. Whispered raspy words escaped its narrow mouth. The words were a phrase and it repeated them a second time. Its body jerked as its last breaths were spent in a sharp laugh. After its final dying breath, the tiny body shriveled into a small pile of dust.

"What did it say?" Roble asked.

Shawndirea swallowed hard and looked into his eyes. "It's a trap!"

CHAPTER 5

*R*oble turned to run to where Lehrling stood with the horses, but before he took a single step, the tree limbs were aglow with hundreds of wisps.

"It *is* a trap!" Shawndirea said, pointing to run back the way they came. "Roble, Lehrling … run!"

"I don't advise it," a voice said from high in the trees. "Unless you wish to die where you flit."

"Dirk?" Shawndirea asked, turning to locate him in the trees. She frowned.

The male faery glided from his perch in the shadowed trees and hovered inches in front of Roble's face. A smirk twisted Dirk's narrow lips. His nose twitched slightly as his eyes stared in a condescending manner.

Shawndirea stood and climbed from Roble's vest pocket. Fury tightened her face and her fingertips glowed fiery green.

"What do you want, cousin?" she asked.

"Your mother's dismissal from the throne," he replied. "I appreciate you denouncing your claim to replace her, which makes it much easier for me to assume her place. But it's time for her to abdicate."

"She won't allow you to rule in her place, nor will I," Shawndirea replied.

Roble's hand slid to his belt within inches of another throwing dagger. He gave a side glance toward Lehrling and discovered a half dozen faery guards hovered around Lehrling's face with their swords drawn. Lehrling's nervous eyes went from guard to guard.

Dirk laughed and flitted upwards, apparently ensuring he was outside of Roble's immediate reach. "You have no say in such matters, former princess."

"I am *still* a Queen," she hissed.

"Not to Elvendale's throne, but to those little precious butterflies you hold

… oh, so, dear." He cupped his hands together and pressed them to the side of his cheek. A moment later, he lowered his hands to his side and fury darkened his eyes. "I, however, aspire for so much more."

"Mother presides over Elvendale," Shawndirea said.

"Istrell is no longer mentally capable to oversee Elvendale, and I have you to thank for that, my beloved cousin. Your decision to pair yourself with this … human from the Overlands has shattered her resolve," he laughed. "You've reduce her to a sniveling sot."

Shawndirea's eyes widened.

"Oh? Did you not know?" Dirk offered an evil grin with an equally degrading laugh. "Yes. You, my dear, have turned her into a wine bibber. So, thank you and congratulations! I've always been aware of the wedge between the two of you. Your rebelliousness over the years has spewed her contempt, but now, oh, her mind cannot function, so she numbs it with the strongest wines Elvendale produces. However, if you ask me, I have the slight suspicion she adds something a tad stronger than the kick of a hearty Dwarven stout."

"I find that difficult to believe," she said.

"Believe it," Dirk said with a short burst of laughter. "After your beloved human survived his venture into the Black Chasm and you married him, she's sunken even deeper. And if you don't believe me, you can always ask Feather."

"Feather? Where is she?" Shawndirea crossed her arms and glanced upward, studying the trees.

Although offended by Dirk's words, Roble kept his silence, studying Dirk and the other faeries with their swords drawn. The other faeries seemed preoccupied with Dirk's heated conversation with Shawndirea. With Dirk's continued bickering, Roble could better find an opportunity to attack.

"Oh, no, you can't ask her *here*," Dirk said. "Feather's practically become the daughter Istrell no longer has. Who are we kidding? The daughter she *never* had. Your mother has placed unmeasurable trust into Feather. Feather displays the perfect etiquette any mother treasures in a daughter. They've bonded quite well, which is a damn shame actually."

"Why's that?" Shawndirea asked.

Roble slid the tip of his dagger from its sheath while Dirk beamed his full attention at Shawndirea. The rain increased its tempo and the rhythm of the droplets seemed to have made it difficult for Shawndirea and her cousin to hear one another. Dirk hovered closer, and Roble hoped the distracting rain allowed an opportunity to develop where he could successfully fling the dagger with enough accuracy to clip one of Dirk's wings.

"Why is it a shame?" Shawndirea asked. "I've known Feather my entire life."

"The shame is that Feather's grown fonder of your bitter old mother, if you can imagine that. Convincing Feather to poison your mother's wine has grown impossible. She outright refuses." Dirk rested his hands on his hips, hovering in the air. "In spite of her being engaged to me, too. Oh, where are my manners? Please accept our invitation to attend the wedding."

"I'm amazed your wings allow you to fly in the midst of this rain," Roble said.

Dirk regarded him for a moment with a cocked brow. With a sneer on his lips, he replied, "Yes, I imagine so. Such minor things keep the simpleminded entertained, don't they?"

"Actually, I'm more inclined to believe that it's your inflated ego that keeps you afloat."

"My, my, he's a testy one, isn't he, Shawndirea?" Dirk said, mocking a yawn. "You know how to pick one, and such a pity he's no match for me in combat."

"If that's a challenge—"

Dirk tilted his nose upward and dismissed Roble with a slight wave of his hand. Several faeries with swords swept from the trees and stood behind Dirk. Their horrid faces were like that of the dying wisp or something often haunting one's nightmares, but some of their facial features were even worse, misshaped, and pocked. "Face it, Overlander, you're outmatched. Perhaps after several years of training, I'll not embarrass you as badly. Whatever she sees in you is beyond any Fae's comprehension. Now, cousin—"

"*Why* are you in the Woodnog Swamps?" Shawndirea asked. "You must reside in Elvendale if you have the slightest hope to ever be crowned and take the throne, even if you are of the proper bloodline. Has my mother exiled you again?"

"Phht!" Dirk said. His eyes narrowed. "She'd never do such a thing."

"She did once before," Shawndirea said.

Anger creased Dirk's brow. "Over a minor misunderstanding. I've gained new favor in her eyes since you've married this filth from the Overlands."

"Is that so?" Shawndirea shook her head. "I highly doubt that since you're seeking to kill my mother in order to assume *her* throne."

He shrugged. "That's only to speed it along. Nothing more."

"Then you ought to be by her side, learning your duties, and not out here in the swamps where the Unseelie reside—" Her eyes widened.

Dirk smiled. "Ahh, I wondered when you'd make the connection, dear cousin. I've joined myself with the Unseelie Court, and I'm building an army that despises Istrell, which has been far easier than I imagined. Volunteers have been flooded from the forests. Your mother has never been a friendly soul, now has she? My alliance with the Unseelie should come as no surprise, being as I see you've decided to do so as well."

"No, I haven't," she said. "Nor would I ever."

"Marrying outside your race, to a human?" he said, wincing. "I'd say that fringes on the border of *becoming* an Unseelie. Ghastly, and frightening."

"You should fear him," she said.

"Fear him? *Roble*? Ha! Why?"

"He could squash you like a slimy slug. And you should do so, Roble," she said with an endearing smile. She clasped her hands together and fluttered her eyelids. "Please? I insist."

"Should he make one sudden move, I'll—" Dirk said.

"What? Kill him?"

"No, I wouldn't do something *that* brutal. I would only command my newfound guards to spear out his eyes. That would crush his spirit and perhaps wither your heart by having a blind husband."

Roble frowned. "As much fun as it'd be to see you attempt such an attack, we must be on our way. I'm tired of standing in the rain, listening to your pompous prattling."

"Oh, you and your human friend can leave," Dirk said, "but Shawndirea is coming with us."

"That's not going to happen," Roble said.

"No?" Dirk snapped his fingers. Dozens of wisps suddenly blared their bright shimmering lights in the trees, revealing more armed faery soldiers that seemed eagerly awaiting for Dirk's signal to attack.

"Don't be a fool," Shawndirea said. "I'm not going anywhere with you. Besides, why should I?"

"It's not a request. I'm taking you as my prisoner. Perhaps when your mother learns you're in my custody, she'll simply hand the crown over to me. With a humble curtesy, mind you, and *not* a commoner's bow."

"She won't."

"You have placed an enormous lot of animosity between the two of you," Dirk said. "However, when she learns your life is in jeopardy and your human husband did nothing to prevent it, she'll intervene. Regardless of her words, her heart aches for you. She'll do whatever's necessary to save you."

Roble flung his dagger, nicking Dirk's shoulder. Dirk winced and emitted a high squeal of a scream that caused Roble to laugh.

The blade continued in a blur and lodged dead center in one of the hovering soldiers behind Dirk. The dagger spun off balance and the hilt struck the tree. Clutching the blade pierced through its chest, the dark faery plummeted to the ground. The weight of the dagger was like an anchor pulling the faery's dead body under the mud.

"Oh, you'll suffer for that," Dirk said with a sneer.

The stones set in Roble's rings glowed, catching Dirk's immediate interest.

The bogshee's deflated corpse suddenly wailed and its thin body moved. Words thundered from its mouth. "It is you who will suffer, if you attempt to harm any of them."

Roble's brow rose in surprise. "It speaks?"

The entire band of faery soldiers turned their attention to the bogshee as it pushed itself slowly to its feet.

A confused expression crossed Dirk's face. He flicked his gaze from the bogshee toward Roble. His eyes revealed his brief moment of fear. "I could have sworn you killed that thing."

Roble shrugged. "As did I. What can I say? I must've missed."

"This—*this* is your doing?" Dirk asked, pointing toward the bogshee. "How?"

"While I'd like to take credit, I'm afraid I've nothing to do with it."

"But your rings," Dirk said.

Roble shrugged. "What about my rings?"

"They—"

"Your only warning," the creature said.

"Or what, pray tell?" Dirk asked with a sly grin. He slashed his sword through the air and faced the bogshee.

"I'll rid Aetheaon of the disease that you are! Roble's under my protection. Don't be a fool. Be on your way."

"I don't take kindly to threats, especially from a … a piece of talking swamp sludge."

"Fool!" The bogshee's eyes glowed yellowish-green.

The dark faeries behind Dirk suddenly dropped their swords and clutched helplessly at their throats. Seconds later, their lifeless bodies dropped to the wet marshy ground. In the trees, the wisps' lights brightened until they could not withstand the sudden surge of energy building inside them. Their tiny bodies exploded, leaving behind splattered glittering gobs that smear the branches, leaves, and tree trunks.

Stunned and overcome by fright, Dirk watched more of his dark faery soldiers fall dead in the mire. The remaining few fled, leaving Dirk hovering in place. His eyes indicated he was unsure of whether he should attack or flee.

"Who are you?" Dirk asked, sheathing his sword.

"Lez'minx."

"Are you Seelie or Unseelie?"

"Neither, but your doom is near at hand."

"What are you?"

"It's best you *don't* know."

Shawndirea smiled. "Do us all a favor and simply end his life like the others on the ground."

The bogshee's strange eyes focused upon her. "That, dear faery, I'll gladly do. That is, if you'll swear your allegiance to me, as your husband has."

"Then, no. Dirk lives, for now," she replied, crossing her arms and frowning.

The bogshee's head wobbled slightly as it returned its attention to Dirk. "Very well. You're spared for today. But should you cross their paths anywhere in these swamps again, I'll know, and you'll die a more horrible death than your former Unseelie allies. Need I explain that to you?"

Dirk swallowed hard and shook his head.

"Now, *go!*" the voice bellowed.

Dirk turned, cast a defeated glance at Shawndirea, and disappeared in a quick dart through the trees.

"Continue on the path you've chosen," Lez'minx said. "You'll find me soon enough."

"By continuing onward to find your temple," Roble said, "I hope you aren't expecting my allegiance to you."

"By taking what I've blessed, I hold your allegiance already," Lez'minx said. "Never forget that. You have my protection, for now. Don't suffer my wrath like those fallen at your feet. Until we meet again."

The bogshee fell face first into the mud and lay silent and still.

Roble held a sword in his right hand and a dagger in his left. He walked toward the bogshee.

"No, Roble, don't," Shawndirea said. "You cannot trust that it's completely dead or that Lez'minx might use it to poison you."

"I know. I'm not going to bother it."

"Then what are you doing?"

Roble sheathed his sword and dagger and then he knelt near one of the dead Shadowfae assassins. He untied a small coin pouch from its belt and placed it on his palm. The pouch grew in size, and the coins rattled when he shook the purse. He poured out several coins, shook his head, and chuckled.

"Gold?" Lehrling asked.

Roble shrugged.

"What is it?" Shawndirea asked.

"Perhaps you should see for yourself," Roble replied.

Shawndirea flew to him and lighted upon his forearm. Lehrling hurried to stand beside Roble and see for himself.

"How dare he!" she said. Anger creased her brow.

"Seems his mind is on overthrowing Istrell. He's already minted coins," Roble said.

Shawndirea seethed. "I should've had Lez'minx kill him. Dirk had best hope our paths never cross again."

Roble held up the largest gold coin. Dirk's side profile was centered with a caption that read, "King of Elvendale."

CHAPTER 6

$\mathcal{R}$oble swung up into the saddle with the coins still in hand.

"Throw them away," Shawndirea ordered in a stately tone.

"Why? We can always melt them down for the gold."

Her eyes narrowed darker. "I'll not have you carry any emblem where he's labeled himself the king of my homeland."

"Perhaps we should keep one to show your mother?" Roble asked.

She shook her head. "No. I don't intend for him to ever gain victory over her. As such, she'll never know. The betrayal might be too much for her. Now, throw them away."

Roble tossed the coins into the muck and watched them sink.

"Thank you."

Roble shrugged but didn't reply. He took several moments to observe the darkening swampy terrain. Lightning flashed. Raindrops pattered atop the leaves, the bent trees, and the several dozen, dead faery soldiers. Thunder echoed, as if it were the closing curtain for the events that had transpired.

He didn't know whether he should be flattered that Lez'minx had intervened before the situation turned into a bloody assault or if Lez'minx's protection demanded Roble's undying loyalty and obligation. But had Lez'minx not acted, Roble realized he, Lehrling, and Shawndirea had been greatly outnumbered. He also knew he wouldn't have hesitated to put his life on the line to save Shawndirea and prevent Dirk from taking her captive.

Even though the soldiers with Dirk were small faeries, their swords were, no doubt, sharp enough to inflict severe injuries, perhaps even fatal ones.

Roble thought about Dirk's threat to blind him, simply as a punishment for marrying Shawndirea. The more Roble thought about this, the angrier he became. Such punishment of losing his sight was far greater than death for

Roble. He'd be forever robbed of seeing Shawndirea's beauty, which was greater than any gem or treasure Roble owned or ever beheld. Dirk's choice for punishment was indeed far crueler than death. Roble held no doubt that he and Dirk's paths would eventually cross again. Whenever that meeting occurred, Roble wouldn't remain gracious as minutes before. Dirk had drawn the magical line, and Roble planned to cross it with pure fury.

Scattered across the tree branches and against higher areas of the tree trunks were glowing splattered globs where each of the enemy wisps had exploded. Roble shook his head. Their remains almost resembled paintballs that had missed their targets, and for a moment he thought about the humor in that, but then he realized, nothing is humorous in war, which was part of Dirk's agenda. With Roble being married to Shawndirea, this was a war he couldn't ignore or dismiss. His obligation was to protect Elvendale by marriage, even if Queen Istrell openly despised him.

Aetheaon offered a lot of things, the chiefest of which seemed to be the constant unrest between opposing forces. He had already fought in one battle, and risked his own life for Queen Istrell by scouting foolishly into the Black Chasm to prove himself to her. In hindsight, he should've refused her challenge, as it profited him no favors or helped any in gaining her approval.

Roble gently tapped Bleys' flank and used the reins to guide the horse back to the narrow path that led deeper into the swamps. With the water steadily rising in the swamps, precious time was fleeting. Nightfall would soon be upon them.

Glancing at a soaked Lehrling, Roble said, "What's your thoughts on Lez'minx now? Is he a demigod or a god? Surely no wizard or mage could perform such a feat."

Shawndirea moved from his pocket and sat upon his shoulder. Before Lehrling offered a reply, she said, "I'm not sure."

Slight fear widened Lehrling's eyes as he looked at the dead faeries. "It's unsettling to say the least."

Roble nodded. He held his reins loosely, allowing the horse to lead at its own cautious pace. "While I don't fully understand the differences between a god and what a demigod is, I must say that he seems to have godlike abilities."

"In what way?" she asked.

Perplexed, he glanced at her. "You saw what he did. He somehow knows exactly where we are, that we were in danger, and he intervened. Doesn't that make him omnipotent or omnipresent?"

"Not necessarily," she replied. "He might have been able to know all of that because of his enchantment upon your armor."

"That's disturbing," Roble said softly.

"Or it could be his rings that you're wearing. Remember I warned you *not* to wear them?"

"Yes, I remember."

"Roble, did you not notice them glow right before Lez'minx made his presence known to all of us?" Lehrling asked.

Roble frowned and looked at the rings on his fingers. He wore the ruby ring on his right hand and the large topaz on his left. After several moments, he glanced at Lehrling. "No, I didn't see that. They really glowed?"

Lehrling nodded. "Quite brightly. Dirk noticed them. I'm surprised you hadn't."

"I was more concerned about how to protect Shawndirea from being taken." He gave her a side-glance. "So if he's not omnipotent, how was he able to kill all those soldiers and wisps, even though he was not physically present?"

Lehrling wiped rain from his brow with the back of his hand. "I have to admit, in spite of everything else, that was mortifyingly impressive."

"I can't argue with that," Roble said. "But anything lesser than a god or demigod … Is a wizard or mage even capable of such a feat?"

Shawndirea pursed her lips. "Magic has no limits, but for one crafting magic from a great distance and actually capable of maintaining control over it, he or she must be seasoned far longer than I've been alive in order to do what he did."

"So he's a god?"

"I cannot absolutely say," she replied. "Based upon what we witnessed, I find that more plausible than not. However, we don't know how far away his temple is, or where it is that he currently resides. If he's closer than we expect, it's less likely he's a god and he's either trying to impress or intimidate you. If nothing else, he wanted our attention."

Lehrling chuckled. "He has mine."

"He asked for your allegiance," Roble said to Shawndirea.

"That's not something he'll ever get, even if Elvendale and my mother would be safer with Dirk dead. The temptation to accept his offer was enticing. If Lez'minx killed Dirk, Dirk's blood would not be on my hands."

"Those faeries Dirk had with him. They don't resemble any of the ones I met in Elvendale," Roble said.

"No, they're dark Fae or more commonly known as Shadowfae from the Unseelie Court."

"So Dirk has chosen darkness over light?" Lehrling asked.

"So it appears," Shawndirea said with disappointment in her voice.

"Why would he do that?" Roble asked.

"Because he knows none of my mother's soldiers would dare oppose her rule. They'd risk their lives for her and our kingdom. Coups are never acceptable or successful within the Fae kingdoms."

"None have ever tried?" Roble asked.

"Tried, yes. But loyalty to the crown and our beloved queens never falters," she replied. "Generally, if any faery is scorned and wishes to cause an uprisal, they're killed almost immediately the moment he or she whispers a hinted plot. Such an execution is never viewed as murder in the Seelie Court. My mother has pardoned several soldiers over the past century."

Roble thought for several moments. He pushed aside a leafy branch as he rode. Beads of water showered from the leaves. In spite of the cold rain, he was dry underneath the armor. Even his beard and hair were not touched by the rain. The same held true for Shawndirea with her tiny armor made from a piece of his armor.

Lehrling, on the other hand, was drenched. His hair was matted and his beard resembled a frayed wet rope from where he had apparently wrung out the water several times. He looked miserable but didn't offer any complaint.

Glancing at Shawndirea, Roble said, "Doesn't your mother worry that other faeries could kill someone they disliked and then proclaim that the faery was guilty of treason?"

"With the exception of Dirk and a few others like him, our honor and valor is prized highly."

"Then what changed for Dirk?" Roble asked.

She shrugged. "He roamed Aetheaon with other humans, rather than ... it hurts me to say ... our own."

"You're saying that humans corrupted him?" Lehrling asked.

"Yes. He allowed greed to consume him."

Lehrling grinned slightly. "I can see that."

"What makes Dirk even think he can obtain the loyalty of Elvendale if he gathers an army and attacks? Even if he succeeded in killing Istrell, he wouldn't gain favor from those who have served her," Roble said.

"You're right," she replied. "He won't."

"Then why pursue it? Why not build his own kingdom?"

"Pride, greed, and his growing bitterness," Shawndirea said.

"Why's he so bitter?"

"Jealousy toward me and that my mother had deemed me to replace her, despite my numerous protests."

"And Dirk knew of this?"

"Of course. It was no secret. Long ago, he and I once were close, like brother and sister. We shared our thoughts, expanded our dreams with one another about our futures, and during one of those conversations, I revealed that I never wanted to assume my mother's place on the throne. Not long afterwards, he grew distant."

"Why?"

Shawndirea bit her lower lip, deep in thought. "I'm not quite certain his reasons. About a year later, mother exiled Dirk."

Lehrling frowned. "What reason did she have to place him into exile?"

"That was never disclosed to me, but around that time was when my mother and her sister came at odds. Perhaps Dirk had shared with her sister,

Aerlene, that I didn't want to the throne. You remember Aerlene at Woodcrest?"

Roble nodded. "Yes."

"Until I found her at Woodcrest, I had thought she was dead, as that was the lie my mother had spread," Shawndirea said. "I think she and Dirk were exiled around the same time."

"Why did she allow Dirk to return?" Roble asked.

"I'm not sure. Mother didn't inform me about a lot of issues after she and I exchanged heated words about my dismissal of being the queen after her passing. I suppose she might have entertained the idea of having him assume the throne or giving him my birthright to the throne. But, I do know that he's the last Fae she'd ever want to see rule over Elvendale now. That much she has confided to me."

The overcast skies became darker, gloomier. The rains showed no sign of letting up. Thunder loomed in the distance.

"What about Feather?" Roble asked. "How does she play into all of this?"

A smile brightened Shawndirea's face. "Feather was like the sister I never had. We spent the majority of our youth playing in the castle. We were the best of friends. That is, until she learned of my ability to heal and rejuvenate butterflies."

"Why? What changed?"

"She did. Jealousy, mostly, as I was capable of something she wished she could do. She resented that butterflies flocked to me and fled from her."

"What are the chances we'll see Dirk before we return to Woodnog?" Roble asked.

"Next to none," she replied.

Lehrling chuckled. "I've never seen anyone go from such arrogance to cowardice in a split second. I'm quite certain he even teared up."

"He is arrogant," Shawndirea said. "He has always been and once he recovers from the shock of what transpired during our confrontation, he'll eventually become so once more. The biggest problem comes after the Unseelie discover all the dead Fae and wisps Lez'minx left behind."

"They'll blame us or Dirk?" Roble asked.

"That depends upon whose story the Unseelie believe. Dirk wasn't the only one to survive. The ones that escaped before he did, had also witnessed what happened."

"Then that should prevent Dirk from recruiting more to follow him," Roble said.

She nodded. "For a while, at least."

A breeze rustled through the trees, shaking blankets of cold raindrops from the leaves.

"Do you know what worries me the most?" Roble asked.

"What's that?" Lehrling asked.

"If Lez'minx knows exactly where we are and when we are in trouble, does that mean that he's able to listen to our conversations?"

Lehrling's brow rose. His mouth gaped slightly. "I never thought about that. Then he'll know all of our conversations."

Panic widened Shawndirea's eyes. "Get rid of those rings. I warned you not to put them on, and you did so anyway. I guess I should have expected that from a human male. Always so stubborn."

Lehrling and Roble chuckled.

"It's *not* funny!"

"We have another problem," Roble said.

"What?"

Roble tugged at the ring on his left hand and then he tried to remove the one on his right. "They're stuck. They won't come off."

"You might need to use some oil," Lehrling said.

"No, I don't think oil would work either."

"Why not?" Shawndirea asked.

"They won't budge at all, like they've become a part of my fingers and fused to the bones. I've used oil or soap to removed tight rings before, but those rings had some give. These don't."

"Why didn't you listen to me?" Shawndirea asked, seated on his shoulder. She pulled her knees to her chest and hugged them. "He has linked himself to you. I warned you."

A chill shot through him. He tried again to pull each ring off. "What can be done? Surely there's a way I can get them off my fingers."

"Let me meditate."

CHAPTER 7

uring the next half hour, they rode in silence. From time to time, Roble attempted to pull the rings off his fingers until they hurt and became swollen. The swamp was darker, and he attributed that to coming nightfall. The darker it became, the more apprehensive he felt. He had hoped they'd find some sort of shelter, but nothing was suitable. The rising swamp waters formed deeper pools and the narrow pathways cutting through strange trees were disappearing. It was an odd sensation to see the land being swallowed by the swamp. They needed to find higher ground before the waters consumed them.

Shawndirea eased to Roble's ear and whispered, "Ride alongside Lehrling and take his hand."

"Wha—"

Before he could finish his thought, she flew into the air and lighted upon Lehrling's shoulder, apparently whispering the same thing to him.

Lehrling exchanged confused glances with Roble, but they did as she requested. When they joined hands, she landed upon them, raised her hands above her head, and mouthed words so softly that only she knew what she was saying.

A bright green orb of light encircled her. The warm and radiance flowed from her and up Roble's arm. When the light subsided, she flew upward and then glided to land on Roble's shoulder again.

"There!" she said with a triumphant grin and a single nod. "That should help."

Roble tried to remove the rings from his sore fingers, but neither budged even the slightest. "It didn't work."

"The spell wasn't to get the rings off."

"Then what?" he asked.

Lehrling rubbed his wrist from beneath the hand that had held Roble's. "My hand and wrist are awfully warm. What did you do?"

"A buffer spell to prevent Lez'minx from hearing our conversations," Shawndirea replied.

"Did it work?" Lehrling asked.

"Of course."

"How can you be certain?" Roble asked.

"Look at your rings."

He did. A greenish sheen coated each of them. Beneath the glow, each stone gleamed, trying to break through her spell. Whatever spell she placed over the stones prevented the stones' light from shining through.

"My magic has encapsulated his. For now, at least. I'm quite certain he'll let us know I've blocked his connection by displaying some sort of an anger fit," she said, smiling. "But, I'm not too worried about that."

"What if it's my armor and not the ring?" Roble asked.

"Not likely."

Lehrling frowned. "Why not?"

"The armor was fashioned specifically for Bausch, but Lez'minx had insisted that Roble take these rings, which was why I warned Roble not to wear them. The rings were meant for you, as possibly magical spy-glasses to keep tabs on you, or us."

"I hope your spell has blocked his ability to listen to us," Roble said. "The rings aren't loosening at all."

"They are fused to you, for now."

"Is there no way to get them removed?"

She nodded.

"How?"

"The easiest way is if Lez'minx will reverse the spell," she said. "The other alternative is to find someone with stronger magical abilities. That might prove more difficult."

"It's doubtful I can persuade Lez'minx to reverse it," Roble said. "He seems to like the idea of having me as his servant."

"Of course he does," she said.

"I still refuse to swear my allegiance to him," Roble said. "Whether I possess the rings and armor or not, I've never submitted myself to him. I've no intention of ever doing so."

"Look ahead," Lehrling said in a near whisper while pointing a nervous finger.

The path narrowed and darkened, getting wetter. Threaded tendrils of fog drifted through the trees, slithering like smokey snakes tightening their grip around the tree branches and trunks. As the fog engulfed the swamp, pairs of red eyes glowed from the canopy and others peered from the holes of hollow trees. Roble wondered if they would've encountered these sinister stares naturally or if these creatures suddenly appearing within the fog were sent by Lez'minx due to Shawndirea's spell.

The rainfall decreased its pattering but the air grew colder. The narrow path between the trees vanished with the fog.

"Nightfall is near," Lehrling said.

Roble glanced toward him and noticed that Lehrling had drawn his sword and lay it across his legs for quicker access. "We have no choice but to keep going. We cannot possibly camp here."

Several thick snakes meandered through bent ferns, slinking and disappearing into the black water.

"No, it's too dangerous to camp near the water and under the thickness of tree branches," Lehrling said.

Looking at Shawndirea, Roble said, "Any suggestions?"

Lehrling said, "We keep moving until we find a place more in the open or some type of ruins or abandoned cottage that we can use for shelter. We need fire, not just to keep warm, but to deter beasts of the night."

"We have a problem," Roble said.

"What is it?" she asked.

"The path has ended."

Shawndirea frowned and stood, peering ahead.

Lehrling rode up beside Roble. "I was afraid we'd encounter something like this."

"Like what?" Roble asked.

"A slow moving creek. So slow in fact, one might mistake it as a flooded part of the swamp, but we must cross it."

"To where exactly?"

Lehrling squinted and then he pointed. "Do you see the bog island?"

After several moments of intense inspection, the mossy bank of a small piece of land materialized. Roble shook his head. "I'd have never guessed."

Lehrling grinned and laughed softly. "Lots of places are hidden in these swamps, as I told you earlier."

"Any idea what's on the island?" Roble asked.

Lehrling shook his head. "Only one way to find out."

"I was afraid you'd say that." Roble sighed, nudged the horse's flank gently with the heel of his boot, and then wondered if Bleys would even step into the water. He'd had a hard enough time convincing the horse to move quickly through the areas where the tree knees jutted upward.

"Be careful," Lehrling said. "I don't think it's too deep, but since we cannot see the bottom, that's no guarantee."

"Tell that to Bleys," Roble said, patting the side of the horse's neck.

Bleys hesitated at the edge of the water. Leaning its head forward, the horse took several deep breaths, sniffing the water's surface. Apparently sensing it was safe enough to cross, the horse stepped slowly into the water. The water sloshed and the peeping frogs at the island's edge ceased their singing.

Several bats flitted through the tree limbs, swooped and arced upward, flying in a near circle before gliding downward again, catching the winged insects skimming the water's surface. By the time the water washed across Roble's knees, the rain had slacked and the clouds parted, revealing the pale yellow moon for only a few moments.

Shawndirea slid from Roble's shoulder into his pocket.

"Everything okay?" Roble asked.

"It will be better once we're away from the hungry bats."

"They don't eat faeries, do they?" Roble asked.

"No, but our wings sometimes confuse bats. Occasionally, they mistakenly attack smaller Fae. Doesn't take much to kill one of us or ... destroy our wings. I don't want to risk it, so I'll stay out of sight for a bit."

Roble nodded. The horse's feet apparently no longer touched the bottom and it swam in the water with its head extended forward. A few seconds passed and its feet touched the soft swampy mud, gained traction, and lunged forward, walking onto the island's bank.

The trees along the edge of the island were thicker, massive oaks and towered higher than the spindly trees and saplings along the swamp trail. The ground was drier, harder. The horse's hooves made odd noises, and instead of walking on compacted soil, the horse walked onto old wooden planks.

"Any idea where we are?" Roble asked.

"No," Lehrling said. His horse stepped from the water onto the shore. "Perhaps long ago a small village resided on this island."

What appeared to be an old cistern was cracked and part of the rock wall had collapsed. Near it was a moss-covered log outline of what might have been a stable. Dry brittle ivy vines held the remaining decayed logs into place.

Roble swung off his horse and led it by the reins. "Looks like there were several huts near what's left of the plank hamlet wall. Doesn't appear to be a temple or place to worship."

Lehrling lowered himself from his horse, stretched his back, and nodded. "No one's lived here during my lifetime."

Shawndirea peered from the pocket and shook her head. "No, you won't find Lez'minx in this rundown place."

"I didn't expect to," Roble said. "But it looks like we've found a place to set up camp for the night."

Lehrling led his horse to a fallen beam and wrapped the reins around it. He opened his saddle bag. "I'll feed the horses, if you gather some dry wood. That is, if you can find *any* wood that's dry."

Roble ran his hand through his beard and then he pointed. "That's building is probably the best place to find scrap lumber. Most of the roof's still together."

Roble broke off pieces of dry ivy vine and then stooped to take several pieces of rotted wood off the ground. Old brown weeds stood in the cracks of the aged, crumbling cobblestone. Even in the fading light, he noticed that none of the foliage was green. He snapped off several dead weeds, which were oddly dry.

Looking around, he frowned. None of the old stones were wet. Not even damp. With all the heavy rain they had ridden through, this abandoned settlement was bone dry.

Lehrling said, "This was most likely a fur trading outpost at one time."

"Wonder why no one's resettled it?" Roble asked.

"My guess is it gets flooded a lot. Or, those Lizardmen might be nearby and prey upon them."

Roble said, "Thanks. Now I can sleep better tonight."

Lehrling chuckled. "Maybe they're a myth."

"Doubtful."

Shawndirea took to flight. "I'll scout the perimeter to make certain we're the only ones on the island."

"No bats to worry about?"

She flung her hands upward. "I'll be okay. I cast a spell to mute the sound of my wings and send my vibrations several feet away from me."

"I'll start a fire in that fallen hut," Roble said, pointing at the small shed-like structure where one corner of the wooden fence had been.

She nodded and took to flight.

CHAPTER 8

*S*hawndirea flew along the edge of the small island's former hamlet wall. She skimmed above the wall and beneath the cover of the tree branches, hoping not to attract the attention of hungry bats or night birds.

Somewhat frustrated by Roble's pursuit to find Lez'minx, she was glad to get a few minutes away from her husband and Lehrling to sort through her thoughts. She loved Roble dearly. Nothing would ever alter her decision to wed him and have him father their children. However, he continued to make rash decisions or failed to follow her advice at times when he should have listened. Of course, he *was* a human and reason sometimes fell on deaf ears. Even she understood this. It didn't matter if he were from the Overlands or had been born in one of Aetheaon's human cities. Humans were bullheaded and needed to experience mistakes—often *repeatedly*—before the knowledge sank through their thick skulls. Sometimes they suffered and endured great consequences because they kept trying the same failed procedure without ever seeing a change in the final result. Thankfully, Roble had better sense than most, and when a trial didn't work, he didn't repeat the same method. He sought a different solution. Yet, his naive actions had been what had placed them in their current circumstances.

"Why did you have to put those rings on?" she said softly while fuming. "I told you. I *warned* you. And look at where we are."

When Lez'minx first made his presence known, he instructed Roble to take two rings off a dead mage's fingers. Shawndirea insisted that Roble not touch the rings, but Roble's logic for taking them was sound. Leaving them meant someone with darker intents might obtain them. She agreed, so he pocketed them. She expected he'd have heeded her warnings not to wear them, but he didn't. Some time later, his curiosity got the better of him and he slipped the rings on his fingers. Nothing noticeably strange occurred, so he never took them off.

Roble's armor taken from Bausch's corpse was enchanted. The magic to protect its wearer from extreme weather conditions wasn't subtle. Both of them noticed the enchantment almost immediately. Whenever they traveled she wore her armor, which he fashioned from a small piece of leather cut from his. When the piece of leather form-fitted around her, she held no doubt it was enchanted. The armor was what saved their lives in the frigid climate of Glacier Ridge.

She sensed the magic, which wasn't essentially a darker magic, but the undertones weren't solely from the Light, either. Her intuition warned her to shed the material. She should have discarded the garment immediately, but due to the harsh weather, she couldn't. She was too cold, suffering with tattered wings and other injuries. She was a matter of minutes from dying due to the bitter cold. Without the armor, she'd be dead. The same was true for Roble. His thin clothing couldn't shield him from the cold.

Even though she sensed its enchantment, she never expected they should pay homage to Lez'minx for wearing it. Bausch must have vowed to do so. And yet, he hadn't. Those details died with him, so she couldn't discern his reasons for why Bausch had sought a magic leather weaver to construct his armor. And then he chose to flee rather than honor his vow. Such theft had cost him his life.

Roble certainly had no clue of such a vow, so she couldn't blame him for taking the armor to allow their survival. At the time, it was necessary. She couldn't deny that. She doubted anyone else suffering through the same conditions would have done any differently.

As far as owing any homage or allegiance to Lez'minx, they owed none. A fact she was prepared to point out whenever they found his temple. Roble never sought the seamstress who pieced the armor together and blessed it, so Lez'minx couldn't demand anything from them concerning the armor. Its discovery was a combined moment of fortune and misfortune.

But the rings …

Shawndirea shook her head and bit her lower lip.

Had Roble not placed them on his fingers, they could've left the rings at the Lez'minx's altar once they found it. To free himself from Lez'minx, Roble needed to remove the rings. Her magic wasn't powerful enough to perform such a ritual. At best, she could only dim the self-proclaimed god's view through the gems. She expected Lez'minx to be angry for her spell. She wouldn't be surprised if he somehow found and scolded her for meddling *before* they reached his temple.

Is he a god?

Shawndirea slowed her pace, glided a bit closer to the broken wall, and then she noticed several broken statues outside an old crumbling rock front of what had been a home long ago. With caution, she hovered at the entrance where stairs descended beneath the floor. A pile of large skulls and bones gleamed white in the moonlight, littering the floor and the stairs.

At first glimpse, the bones appeared old. Gliding closer, she discovered a track of green gooey substance on the stairs. The goo was smeared on the walls. Fresh crimson bloodstains mixed with goo covered some bones.

The cooler air from the cellar wafted toward her, causing her to gag and place her hand over her nose and mouth. The rot of decayed flesh triggered nausea at the back of her throat, preventing her from further investigation into the cellar. Entering the cellar would have been unwise anyway. Something had been killed at the center of the stairs and dragged downward, possibly a few days earlier, which meant the predator lurked below.

Pushing backwards against the air, she flitted upward. They weren't alone on the island. Something lived underground. From the numerous skeletal remains, this being held an aggressive appetite. Whether it was an intelligent creature or an instinctual animal remained to be seen. She hoped they were off the island before they ever encountered it.

She glanced toward the area where she Roble and Lehrling set up camp. In the faint moonlight, she was unable to see them from this distance. If he had started a fire, she could have seen the flames. No fire had been lit yet.

For several seconds, she contemplated returning to Roble and Lehrling. But then she wondered if this creature was in the cellar or was it creeping around on the island? Most likely, based upon her observation of the slimy trail on the steps, it was opportunistic and waited for its prey's curiosity to lead them into the cellar. In the chance that it wasn't in the cellar, she decided to finish searching the perimeter of the falling wall, just in case.

CHAPTER 9

*P*ursing her lips, Shawndirea flew toward the wall behind the building with the cellar. She had only examined one full wall during her flight and part of the one where Roble and Lehrling were setting up camp for the night. With a predator living in the abandoned shack's cellar, she wanted to make certain it was the only place they needed to worry about during the night.

Flying slowly, she kept a keener eye for fallen walls or trees that could house more creatures. She thought it strange the heavier rains weren't falling on this part of the former settlement. The windblown rains were still swirling beyond the tree line and the hamlet wall, as these were visible, but the island remained dry. She took new interest in the strange phenomenon.

Lightning flashed beyond the island's border over the swamps. Heavy thunder followed. During her scouting, she failed to notice that the walls and collapsing thatched roofs were dry. All the vegetation and trees were dead and dried out. After riding for hours in the constant rain, she was thankful for the absence of rain, as it made her search easier, but the air was unseasonably cooler than the surrounding swamp and that troubled her.

An uneasiness settled over her concerning the island, and she came to the conclusion that the island was cursed, which explained why no one resided here.

The creature in the cellar might be the result of the curse, or a guardian placed on the island to ensure the place remained desolate, eliminating future claims or settlements.

Now her curiosity about what lurked in the cellar escalated. Some of the bones were from recent victims, possibly only days before, as the blood stains had not faded. Some of the blood was brighter red and not brown.

Hovering above the hamlet wall, she glanced across its north side and then back toward the building housing the cellar. She flitted to the front of the building where she could see the cellar stairs without fear of getting attacked by what resided below.

She re-examined the scattered bones along the stairs. In the dark shadows, the stairs appeared to take a ninety-degree turn. Without actually descending the stairs, she wasn't certain, but she guessed the stairs turned to the right, descending again.

The goo resembled the shiny ooze slugs left behind on their paths. Almost hidden in a small pile of bones was a sword with holes eaten through the blade. Small portions of chainmail were nearly nonexistent under the bones. Strong acid had killed and dissolved these victims, which unnerved her.

A strange bubbling, gurgling sound echoed below. Shawndirea rose higher but kept her attention on the turn of the stairs. Whatever hid down there seemed to be waiting for its prey to come to it. The ooze was only in the steps. None blotched the floor outside the stairwell. Sensing its approach and worried that it detected her presence, she darted over the building to the wall.

With renewed determination, she set to discover what else might be hiding on the island. Since this creature or creatures didn't seem to leave the protection of the cellar, she wasn't too concerned it would find its way to where Roble and Lehrling were, so there was enough time to inspect the rest of the island wall.

While flying, her mind revisited her concerns.

"Is Lez'minx really a god?" Shawndirea whispered again.

The way Lez'minx had wiped out dozens of Shadowfae renegades without a worry of repercussions meant he wasn't Seelie or Unseelie. Otherwise, he'd have been more sparing or cautious in dropping them. He held no fear of the Fae, and daringly challenged their power. Perhaps he sought a war with them? She'd almost favor such a war provided it didn't involve her. However, he might be successful in masking his ties to either side.

But as to whether he was a god or not, she didn't know and might not know even after they found his temple. He might only be a demigod posing as a god, or a demented wizard wielding magic she'd never known a wizard capable of performing. Of course, Aetheaon possessed an overabundance of demented wizards and mages. Using magic for long periods of time stressed one's mind. The use of magic never came free. It came at a cost, and some-times, at a hefty price. The continued use of magic claimed one's sanity.

Anyone, even Shawndirea, paid a price for the use of magic. She wasn't burdened quite as badly as other practitioners because of her ability to repair butterflies' wings, extending their lives. She was blessed in return for the blessings she bestowed to these fragile beautiful creatures in nature.

Her mind drifted to Dirk and renewed her burning anger toward him. Lez'minx's offer to kill Dirk along with the rest of the Shadowfae who had aligned themselves with her cousin, provided she pledged her devotion to Lez'minx was an overwhelming temptation. She was unable to mask her yearning for Dirk's demise. The removal of the heavy burden Dirk had plagued upon her family and Elvendale would be considered a triumph.

To witness all the evil darkening Dirk's heart and obsessing his mind suddenly erased would enthrall her. She and Elvendale could have been freed of Dirk forever without his death being traced to her. His blood wouldn't be on her hands. Despite the advantage of Dirk's demise, she'd never serve Lez'minx. Dirk could be dealt with in other ways without Lez'minx intervening. She refused to sacrifice her mind and soul to Lez'minx. She valued those more.

Shawndirea was thankful Lez'minx had interceded, as she, Roble, and Lehrling had been greatly outnumbered. While the ending might not have been with their deaths, it seemed likely Dirk held no qualms about rendering permanent injury and deformity to Roble just to spite her. She was proud Roble had not flinched and stood ready to fight, which was surprising, considering he was an Overlander. But still, Roble had not been in Aetheaon long enough to realize that even the smallest races were capable of inflicting pain, maiming, or killing him.

Seeing Dirk flee like a frightened child had been amusing and a reward all its own. His immediate death would not have been nearly as satisfying. His smug demeanor had been crushed by imminent fear. And like Lehrling, she had seen tears in Dirk's eyes.

In hindsight, she should not have allowed Dirk to get away. They should have bound him and taken him prisoner, returning him to Elvendale because he was a threat to their kingdom and her mother. However, had they done so, they'd have needed to keep him restrained at all times during their journey through the swamp. That would've have made their journey longer and more complicated.

While Shawndirea might have her differences with her mother—a vast canyon that divided them—Shawndirea couldn't allow her mother's death. No anger or bitterness toward another deserved death. Eventually, she figured, some sort of truce could be made between she and her mother but not in the immediate future.

Regardless of the current circumstances, she couldn't allow Dirk to take the throne. With the evidence of Dirk's sinister plans, her mother would have executed him in such a way that the entire Fae population in Aetheaon would shutter. His death would become a stern warning to all future Fae children and set them on their best behaviors for life.

Since Dirk's alignment with the Shadowfae and his mission to build an army to overtake her mother's kingdom threatened Elvendale, Shawndirea considered asking Roble to postpone finding Lez'minx to stop Dirk first.

Everything Elvendale held sacred risked forever tarnished should his invasion succeed.

But after what Lez'minx had done in the swamp, she doubted Dirk could rebuild his meager army anytime soon. Lez'minx's patience for Roble to return at a later time was nil.

Besides, Dirk faced pleading his case before the Unseelie Court to explain the reasons for the deaths of the dark faery soldiers that he hired. Dirk might not even survive such a trial, as his recruiting had most likely been secretive. And if he survived, few Shadowfae would be eager to follow him unless he proved he could protect them. If anything, Lez'minx would become better known in the swamps, especially to those who held no knowledge of who he was.

In some ways, Shawndirea wished that she had not renounced her right to Elvendale's throne. Her stubbornness to obtain her independence might plummet Elvendale into utter chaos once her mother became too old or physically unable to rule the kingdom. Since Dirk was an opportunist, he recognized Shawndirea's departure from ruling Elvendale as something he could capitalize on. However, even *his* mother was not likely to dub him as the new ruler.

Elvendale had always been governed by a Queen regnant, as had most other Fae kingdoms. It was unlikely that Dirk's claim would even be accepted by the Elvendale's general population. Not freely at least, which was possibly why he had chosen to gain the backing of the Unseelie to enforce his rule. Even then, her mother's guard would not have allowed it without a battle, and that seemed to be what Dirk hoped for: A war destined to rend the peace Elvendale found as the substance of their foundation.

Now that Shawndirea had wed a human from the Overlands, which was far worse than had she married one from within the Realms of Aetheaon, her right to rule Elvendale had been tarnished, even if she decided to lay claim to the throne. Her mother's indignation stemmed predominately from this issue, more than anything else.

Roble had questioned Shawndirea's allegiance and Dirk had insinuated that Shawndirea had crossed over to the Unseelie Court because she had chosen to marry outside the Seelie Court. The more she thought about those accusations, the more she recognized that perhaps she had unknowingly done so. In order for her to claim back her right to the throne, she must dissolve her marriage to Roble.

Not happening. Her brow furrowed with the thought.

She refused to severe her marriage for any throne. That left only one other option. Roble's death freed her to rule in Elvendale, which might place Roble's life in danger.

While she wouldn't necessarily put it past her mother to attempt to have Roble assassinated, Dirk—on the other hand—would probably do anything within his power to keep Roble *alive* to prevent Shawndirea from reissuing her right. Irony at its best, or at its worst? Although Dirk had openly threatened Roble, it was highly unlikely that he truly wanted Roble dead. It further complicated matters for Dirk's ambition to rule Elvendale, because it immediately ushered Shawndirea to be the next to ascend rule in Elvendale. So regardless of Dirk's attempt to form a coup, he had unwittingly become Roble's ally, further dividing Dirk from Shawndirea's mother.

Shawndirea could plead her case before the Royal Council and hope they'd consider allowing her rule, even though she was married to Roble. It was doubtful she could sway their hearts and minds to side with her, but it was worth trying. Otherwise, she would face the decision of watching everything she loved within Elvendale collapse forever by her staying with Roble, or allowing herself the broken heart of letting him go. Both were tragic fates. Neither were favorable, but her love for Roble outweighed the two. Some would probably consider her choice to be selfish on her part.

Thousands of faeries' lives depended upon Elvendale being ruled fairly and under the structure of Order. Sadly and strangely, she was beginning to understand the reasoning behind her mother's outrageous anger. She realized it wasn't unfounded or outrageous at all.

Had Shawndirea's stubborn streak been too overpowering for her to notice? She frowned and pushed the thoughts to the back of her mind.

CHAPTER 10

Flitting from open door to open door of the crumbling shacks, Shawndirea's mind drifted toward Feather. She and Feather had been friends for nearly their entire lives. She loved Feather as a sister, and the only flaw to Feather's credit was her gullible nature. She was quick to believe what someone told her and trusted others too easily. Shawndirea could not count the number of times she had set Feather straight concerning minor issues.

Dirk must have discovered Feather's vulnerability, too, which was probably why he had chosen her to be his queen. Or, at least, he convinced her of his fake love and promises, luring her to his side. She might have been smitten by his praise and the thought of being a queen made it more appealing because Feather was jealous of Shawndirea's abilities to heal butterflies as one of nature's queens. So, the idea of being the new Queen of Elvendale thrilled Feather.

However, one trait Dirk might not have noticed about Feather was that she held family loyalty to a fault. Since Istrell was like a second mother to Feather, Feather was not about to betray Elvendale's Queen. While her actions to defend her family were admirable, they could prove to become deadly for her. Should Dirk's *love* turn to repugnance, he'd kill Feather without a second thought and in such a way that no one ever placed the blame upon him. Shawndirea couldn't allow that.

A flame lit at the other side of the former hamlet, immediately catching her attention. She paused, looking over her shoulder. Semi-dried kindling and other wooden materials slowly rose in flames. The rising fire revealed the shadows of where Roble and Lehrling stood. She smiled.

While she knew Roble could survive quite easily in the Overlands, she found herself slowly realizing the dangers she harnessed him into his residing in her realm.

He was smart, strong, and devoted; qualities she admired. Naive? No, that wasn't *quite* the word she'd use. But in her world, he faced obstacles he'd never face in his own with creatures he'd never imagined existed. Sometimes his bravery bordered more on facade than actual courage. If she could detect it, others in Aetheaon could as well. Perhaps he was attempting to keep a bold face during his confrontations to assure her he was capable of living in her world and protecting her. The only problem was that he did not possess the understanding or know how to properly react when attacked with magic.

How could he know?

"I must teach him," she reasoned.

Lez'minx was one of those obstacles Roble was not prepared to confront. With Roble's attitude, he might not even survive. She didn't want to say aloud that he needed *her* protection, but in truth, he did. She might not have questioned this had Roble not placed those rings on his fingers after she sternly warned him otherwise. His failure to heed her demand and accept her knowledge wasn't simply because he was human. It was because he was a human *outside* of Aetheaon whose independence was most likely the reason for his defiant petulance. Over time, she reasoned, he'd mature and become more cautious; provided he survived their encounter with Lez'minx.

Given adequate time, he'd figure out these things on his own, but the one thing she didn't want to deal with was bruising or shattering Roble's ego. Not that he possessed any lack of self-confidence or that he'd begrudge her for intervening in situations he was incapable of handling, but men tended to take offense when others fought in their place, as it showed weakness.

Shawndirea admired Roble for his want to confront Lez'minx and reject his offer. Roble indicated his refusal to succumb to Lez'minx's demands or to give his allegiance for the *gifts* blessed by Lez'minx. She believed Roble when he had said that he'd resist steadfast, but she also knew he didn't understand the ramifications of doing so possibly meant his death.

Outright refusal at the temple—if a temple truly existed—would be costly. Roble held no grounds for negotiation since he wore Lez'minx's rings. That troubled her. He had accepted the rings as gifts. Pleading ignorance didn't change that. With them on his fingers, he couldn't deny having worn them, and in her mind, she recognized the binding spell placed upon the rings by Lez'minx. Once worn, they couldn't be removed, except after death or unless Roble was somehow pardoned from the spell's effects.

Such a spell was underhanded because curiosity ate at the mind, especially *human* minds, and a sorcerer thoroughly understood those types of temptations. Bright shining gems and rings enchanted with magic were coveted by all in Aetheaon. Regardless of how much one wanted to ignore their beauty or entertained the thought of what magical power they possessed, the longer

Order, that is. King Erik knighted Geowren and I at the same time. But after Erik's death or perhaps his disappearance since rumors are circling that Erik might still be alive, Geowren disappeared into these swamps."

"For what reason?" Roble asked.

Lehrling shrugged. "The Goddesses only know."

"Hmm." Roble grabbed more dried vines, snapped them, and placed them upon the flames. "Don't you think that a bit odd?"

"In Aetheaon?" Lehrling laughed. "Not if you knew him."

"Is it a coincidence that he'd vanish around the same time as King Erik?"

Lehrling frowned. "Is that an accusation because—"

Roble shook his head. "No, nothing like that. But if someone actually killed Hoffnung's king, isn't it possible that others in the Dragon Skull Order might have been targets, too?"

"I imagine that's possible, but until Waxxon's attack on Queen Taube, our Order never suffered threats for who we are and the king we serve. And since Lady Dawn christened you into the Order, you serve the Crown as well."

"Yes, with my life."

Lehrling approached Roble and clasped a firm hand upon his shoulder. "Aye, I believe you do, which is quite remarkable for an Overlander."

"Why's that?"

"You're not from our realm but yet, you offer your loyalty to defend a kingdom not of your own."

"It is now," Roble said.

Lehrling smiled and offered a slight nod. "Yes! But the point I wish to make is that most from our realm wouldn't have bothered to do half of what you've done for Hoffnung and the Queen."

Roble chuckled. "I'd dare say that the majority of the people in my realm would die trying to find their way back to the Overlands instead."

"No argument there. Most Overlanders aren't strong enough to survive the mental adjustments necessary to comprehend the beasts, races, and magic in Aetheaon. I'll always be indebted to you for saving my life," Lehrling said. "You didn't have to risk your life for me. You could've continued onward. I hope to somehow repay you—"

"Don't burden yourself by wanting to repay me," Roble said. "You've done far more to aid me in understanding and training. I feel like I'm indebted to you."

Lehrling laughed. "I'm afraid an old man's training isn't the best repayment. It comes nowhere close."

"It's far better than what I knew. Plus, I've had the pleasure of gaining a new friend." Roble smiled and crouched at the side of the fire, placing part of a broken wooden plank. "So tell me more about Geowren."

"Why not let a weary ghost rest?"

"So you think he's dead?"

Lehrling's eyes stared blankly for several moments before he acquiesced a nod. "Sadly, I do. Why your interest in knowing more about him? You've only learned about him."

"Like I mentioned, I'd like to know more about these swamps."

"You wish to explore them?" His voice rose with intrigue.

Roble nodded. "I would."

Lehrling winced as he lowered himself to the ground, sat near the fire, and warmed his hands. "If it's a guide you seek, you could always ask Odlon."

"He knows these swamps?"

"Yes. Or you could ask his sister," Lehrling said. "She's an herbalist and quite a skilled alchemist. She concocts incredible magical potions, at a hefty price, mind you. Since rarer herbs abound in swamps, she'd probably know her way around better than he. As to whether she'd allow you to accompany her on one of her harvests, only she can answer that. Odlon could relay her message for you though."

"I shall ask him the next time I see him."

"You mind if I ask you something?" Lehrling said, glancing from the dancing flames to meet Roble's gaze.

"Sure."

"Do you really believe it's best that we continue searching for Lez'minx's temple? Be honest."

"You can turn back, if you want, Lehrling. You're not required to accompany me," Roble said. "Don't feel obligated—"

Lehrling raised a hand and shook his head. "No, I don't mean it like that. It would be foolish for me to depart anyway, as we're safer traveling together. What I ... How comfortable are you about fulfilling the journey to his temple?"

"I'm not *comfortable* about the situation at all. My gut tells me that I'm safer and that *we're* safer, if I confront him. Besides, he proved he can find us, and in part, he's proven to me that he is a being with power I'm unable to defeat."

"And if he commands that you remain his loyal subject?"

Roble scratched his bearded chin. "Still sorting through that. I had thought an outright refusal was the best option, but after seeing him wipe out those faeries without physically being in their presence, I wonder if I should seek an alliance with him instead."

"He's not offering an alliance, Roble."

"I realize that. But would it be a terrible thing if I served him?"

Lehrling's eyes widened. He pulled a pipe and a tobacco pouch from inside his vest. "Surely you jest?"

"Imagine having that kind of power backing you," Roble said.

"Yes, and imagine losing your soul to a ... Well, whatever he may be? You don't what his intentions are."

"Then I should refuse?"

"Compromise, find an alternative that suits you and him. But if you fully yield yourself to him, he might well possess and control your mind to do whatever he wishes. You cannot sacrifice yourself to a power so dark."

"So he's a dark god?"

"Regardless of *what* he is, he must wield dark magics to house his temple in the depths of Woodnog Swamps. Besides, what would Shawndirea think of you submitting yourself to Lez'minx's control? Have you asked her?"

"She's mad enough at me as it is," Roble said softly, glancing over his shoulder and watching the sky, wondering where she was and if she was hiding, listening in on their conversation.

Lehrling chuckled softly. "Angry faeries can be full of mischief."

"Or worse," Roble said.

"You're certain she's mad at you?"

"It's obvious she's been pissed at me since I put the rings on my fingers."

"I didn't want to ask in front of her, but *why* did you put them on?"

Roble winced and shook his head. "Curiosity, I suppose."

"Did you ... feel any power from them?"

"Nothing really. Only fear and dread when I realized I couldn't take them off."

"Ah, yes, afraid of what Lez'minx might do?"

"No, fearful of what Shawndirea would do because I didn't listen to her," Roble said with a smile.

Lehrling grinned. "You see why I chose a bachelor's life, eh?"

Roble laughed. "I once had that."

"Don't be too envious. Do you miss it?"

"No. Although I never sought marriage, I'd never return to being single. My heart aches for Shawndirea whenever she's not near, like now."

"You think she's in trouble?"

"No, but she has been gone longer than I expected, which is why I know she's angry," Roble replied.

"One thing is in your favor, though." Lehrling puffed his pipe.

"Really? And what is that?"

"Lez'minx prevented Dirk from seeking to dethrone Queen Istrell. Shawndirea must appreciate that," Lehrling said.

"I don't how she feels about that. Perhaps that is part of why she wanted some time alone, so she could sort through those thoughts. For now, Dirk's plans are dashed, but I expect that he'll try again."

Lehrling shrugged. "Maybe."

"But even after she learns of what Lez'minx had done to protect us, it's doubtful I'll ever find favor with Shawndirea's mother."

"Isn't that true of any mother-in-law though?" Lehrling asked with a sincere stare.

Roble shrugged. "Perhaps. But the fury and contempt Istrell holds toward me … I doubt such could ever be matched in the Overlands."

Lehrling chuckled. "I agree with you concerning that."

"Istrell was the one who had challenged me to go into the Black Chasm."

"I remember."

"Which is another reason I question why serving Lez'minx might not be such a bad thing."

Lehrling puffed smoke from his pipe and cocked a brow. "What's he have to do with that?"

"Someone pulled me out of the Black Chasm before I died. Someone with powerful magic opened a portal and dragged me through."

"Could've been any wizard or mage," Lehrling said.

"Few people even knew I was there. You were incapacitated at the time."

"I'm no wizard."

Roble chuckled. "I know that. I believe you'd have fought me not to enter."

Lehrling nodded. "It wasn't your best decision, especially since your true goal was to impress Queen Istrell, which I'm guessing *didn't* work?"

"No, it didn't. But I believe this armor is what kept me alive longer than the ragbag army that accompanied me. The others died before my eyes, one by one, along with their mounts. I hate to say it but their deaths were no great loss to wherever they resided, but that's a story for another day."

"The armor has enchantments I've noticed, mostly adapting to whatever climate we're in, so I guess that's possible for it to protect you from the poisonous air in the Black Chasm." Lehrling stared at the fire. "Did you have any other enchantments or blessings bestowed upon you? Protection spells, perhaps?"

"Only a piece of cloth that Shawndirea had given me to breathe through."

"Then that's probably it, more than the armor. Unless Istrell had secretly cast a spell over you."

Roble laughed. "Are you kidding? She sent me there to die, to free Shawndirea from marrying me. That'd be the last thing she'd have ever done."

"True, I suppose," Lehrling said. "The more I learn about Queen Istrell, the more I'm convinced she makes more enemies than allies. But she's not been able to sway Shawndirea to find fault in you."

"She has no need to do so. I'm doing plenty of that on my own."

"I've a feeling it'd take far more than putting magical rings on your fingers to make her desert you. She loves you too much to allow minor mistakes to sway her heart."

"Minor?" Roble tugged hard at each ring for Lehrling to witness. "I'd say this is a *major* error."

"I understand how your curiosity got the best of you, but if you knew you'd anger Shawndirea by putting them on, why did you?"

Roble displayed a sheepish grin. "Because I thought I could slide them back off without her ever knowing."

Lehrling slapped his knee and tried to muffle his sudden laughter. Tears formed at the edges of his eyes.

"It's not funny," Roble said, rising.

"No, it's hilarious."

"In what way?"

"It's Fate's twisted sense of humor. Seems it happens to all of us. We think we can do something without anyone else learning about it, but then irony slips in to ruin the secret."

"Still not funny," Roble said. "Especially not to Shawndirea."

Lehrling wiped tears from his eyes. "I imagine not."

"Oh, you don't need to use imagination to see her anger."

"Sorry. She tries to hide it though."

"Around you, yes. For me, it's entirely a different matter," Roble said.

Lehrling stood and walked to his horse. He opened a saddlebag and pulled out some dried jerky, tossing some to Roble. "While we wait for her to return, we should eat."

Roble caught the strand of jerky, took a bite, and chewed.

"To be honest with you, Roble, I'd have tried on the rings, too."

"Really?"

"Yes."

"Why?"

Lehrling returned to his place by the fire and sat. "Knowing what your armor is capable of doing, if it were me, I'd have wanted to discover what the rings might enable me to do. Any human, Dwarf, or Elf would've done the same."

"They seem to allow Lez'minx to watch us."

Lehrling shrugged. "I believe they do much more than that."

"Like what?"

"We won't know until it's revealed to us, or to you, since you wear them. But they're more than a spyglass."

Shawndirea descended from the sky and hovered near him.

"Well?" Roble asked.

"We're not alone," she replied. "The island is cursed."

CHAPTER 12

"Cursed?" Roble and Lehrling said.

"What makes you believe that?" Roble asked. "Are you certain?"

Shawndirea nodded. "Have you not noticed the abnormalities?"

"Only that there's no evidence of recent rain," Roble replied. "It seems the surrounding storms haven't lessened. But given how badly the rains are on the other side of the river, that's not a bad thing."

"It's not?" she asked. "But if the island never gets rain, isn't that be a curse?"

"Of course. Nothing could survive—" It suddenly dawned upon him. No rain explained why all the trees and vegetation were dead. "But for travelers, finding a completely dry place to lodge for the night is no curse."

"It was for whoever lived here. And recently, it seems, others like ourselves were investigating the island, and now they're all dead. The dryness lures travelers in."

"Couldn't they have moved on? Resettled elsewhere?"

"They might have, but my guess is that they probably didn't. As I said earlier, 'we are not alone.'"

Roble rose from where he sat on the ground. Roble extended his hand to help Lehrling up. With one swift tug, Roble pulled Lehrling to his feet. "Then who else is here?"

"Not a who," she replied. "Some sort of creature lives underground."

Lehrling tapped the burnt tobacco out of his pipe. "What type of creature?"

"A slime creature would be my guess," she said.

Lehrling shook his head. "Not good at all."

Roble frowned, looking from Lehrling to Shawndirea. "Why is a creature made of slime such a threat?"

Lehrling ran a hand through his beard. "They're almost impossible to destroy."

Roble's eyes widened. "Why?"

Shawndirea said, "They have no flesh to pierce and kill them. They're globs of ooze, often composed of strong acid."

"Acid?"

Lehrling nodded. "Yes. Never use a metal weapon you value to try to slice your way through them. They're so corrosive, you'll weapon practically melts in seconds. Metal armor won't protect anyone, either."

"You've encountered them before?" Roble asked.

"No, but I've seen the results from those who have."

"I'd think creatures composed of slime would be common in the swamps, wouldn't they?" Roble asked.

"No," Shawndirea said. "They do not occur naturally. They are creations of wizards or mages and usually the result of their curses."

"If the island is cursed," Roble said, "all of this is the result of an angry wizard?"

"Probably," she replied.

Roble frowned. "What motive would a wizard have?"

"Motive?" Lehrling chuckled. "Some wizards are so pompous because of their own power that whenever they consider a minor insult from others, the offense often gets inflated. To prove his might, the wizard casts a curse to sternly warn others not to trifle with them."

Roble shook his head. "It must be hard to be friends with a wizard."

Lehrling laughed. "Wizards have few friends, which explains their solitary lives and why they're shunned by neighboring villages who want no trouble."

"But on *this* island? This tiny hamlet? What could they have done to prompt such a curse?"

"If this were a trading town for trappers, perhaps the wizard felt mulcted, which is the best possibility," Lehrling replied.

"Or," Shawndirea said, "someone skinned the wizard's familiar and a vendor bought the hide."

"I hadn't thought of that," Lehrling said. "That'd cause severe anger and immediate vengeance would be sought. A wizard's wrath would be never ending."

"Where is this creature? You saw it?" Roble asked.

"I didn't see it," Shawndirea replied, "but there's enough recent evidence on the cellar stairs to indicate its whereabouts."

A worried expression claimed Lehrling's face. "Recent evidence? How recent?"

"Based upon the coloration of the bloodstains, a few days? Not sure what its victim or *victims* might have been."

"Did you see animal bones or human?" Roble said.

She thought for several moments. "Most likely *not* an animal that it killed and ate."

Roble frowned. "Why do you believe that?"

"An animal's instinctive actions are often smarter than the curiosity of humans, Elves, or other races. Dwarves wouldn't hesitate, if gold is below," she replied. "Curiosity outweighs rational thought."

Roble caught the snide comment directed at him, but he pretended not to notice. "Noted. Which building?"

Shawndirea hovered and then pointed. "The building next to the old falling wall."

Roble looked in that direction. "That's only a few buildings away."

"I know."

"Let's check it out," Roble said.

"No," she replied. "Let's *not*."

"We cannot possibly leave the island before morning," Roble said. "I gather doing so is too treacherous and we'd probably not survive."

"You're right," she said, sighing. "We probably wouldn't survive."

"Then we need to know what we're up against."

"*Roble—*"

He drew a dagger and turned to walk to the building.

"Have you not learned anything about your rash decisions?" she asked.

Roble glanced over his shoulder and caught Lehrling's concerned gaze. Lehrling simply shook his head.

"She's right, Roble," Lehrling said. "You even indicated such during our conversation earlier."

Roble sighed. "I don't plan to go to *where* it is."

"That doesn't matter," Shawndirea said. "For all we know, it could be partway up the stairs by now, and if it is, you might not outrun it."

"So these slime creatures are fast?"

"Not usually," she replied. "But that's not something you want to find out afterwards, now is it?"

"No."

Shawndirea nodded. "Good. One thing I sensed about it though."

"What's that?"

"It knows we're here," she replied.

"How could you know that?" Lehrling asked.

"I heard its sloshy movement at the turn of the stairs. It seemed to be hiding, hoping I'd fly downstairs. But it could be partway up them by now."

Roble looked toward the old shack again. "If we cannot leave the island before morning, and you don't want us to investigate the stairs, what do you suggest we do?"

"I could fly over and see if it emerged," she said.

"Isn't that risky?" Roble asked.

"It cannot fly."

Roble said, "Very well."

She turned and flew toward the building.

Roble flicked his attention to Lehrling. "How do we defend ourselves against this thing if we have no means to kill it?"

Lehrling shook his head. "I truly don't know. But she's right. Confrontation isn't in our best interest."

Roble grabbed the end of a large branch and pulled it from the fire. Flames danced on the tip of the branch. "Well, let's go."

"Shouldn't we should wait until she returns?"

"Probably, but if she needs our help, it's better if we're closer to her than not."

Lehrling nodded and took a heavy stick from the fire. "I don't really want to follow you, but I like staying behind even less appealing. Seems to me you're worrying too—"

Shawndirea screamed and a second later, her voice was muffled. Then she was silent.

Roble tore into a sprint.

CHAPTER 13

*R*oble's first thought was that Dirk had followed them to the small island and had either taken Shawndirea captive or he shot and killed her with an arrow. But remembering the fear etched on Dirk's face, it was highly unlikely he'd have returned without a stronger force. Lez'minx had certainly left a memorable impression on Dirk.

After Shawndirea screamed, Roble considered the idea that since Dirk probably wasn't responsible, Lez'minx had somehow found them. Shawndirea's spell-blocking Lez'minx's vision through the rings had angered him, and somehow he had located them and sought revenge for her interference.

Silently, he berated himself for allowing her to travel into the swamps with him. She shouldn't suffer for his foolish mistakes. His learn-as-you-go attitude was too risky to practice in Aetheaon, and not only were his actions placing his life in danger, but those he loved as well.

This journey to find Lez'minx was one he wished he could've taken alone. But Lehrling had insisted he travel with Roble, not because Lehrling knew the swamps and could guide him to wherever this supposed *temple* was, but because Roble did not adequately understand the creatures and races in this realm. And when Shawndirea had discovered the two were headed into the swamps, she refused to remain behind.

Her magic, she insisted, could help aid and protect them. Instead, her magic might have wrought the wrath of a god, a demigod, or a crazed mage or wizard. They had no way of knowing exactly what Lez'minx was until they found his temple and met him face-to-face, provided he was actually a physical entity.

"Shawndirea!" Roble shouted. He slowed his sprint to a sudden stop near the opening of the shack. He waved the flaming torch all around to light up places where her body might be. Having spent the majority of his lifetime in the Overlands as an entomologist, his keen eyes looked for the tiniest of creatures in the most unusual places. In the flickering light, his eyes searched every crack and crevice at the open doorway before he turned his attention to the decayed outer walls. "Shawndirea!"

His chest ached from the harsh beating of his fear-stricken heart. He gulped several deep breaths and then exhaled slowly, trying to calm himself. He realized his foolishness for shouting, as doing so brought immediate attention to his location, but he didn't care. He'd gladly sacrifice his life to save hers, if necessary.

She didn't reply, and he couldn't find her. He feared the worst, looking for her body along the edges of the wall and broken blocks. His knees weakened, his heart hammered in his chest, and he became lightheaded. With his vision darkening, he was seconds from collapsing. He fought the urge and reached to place his hand against anything to maintain his balance.

"Lehrling," Roble gasped. "Do you see her anywhere?"

Halfway stumbling to stop his thundering feet, Lehrling used his torch to wash more light in the darkened areas. With sadness in his voice, he replied, "No."

Both torches illuminated the stricken look of panic on Lehrling's face. His worry to find Shawndirea was evident. Like Roble, he'd sacrifice his life to protect the faery's. Having such a devoted friend warmed Roble's heart, and he believed it was more than fate that Roble and Shawndirea had come upon Bausch's hanging body. The armor Roble now possessed was the key that linked them all together, and part of the reason they were exploring in the swamps.

"She has to be here, somewhere," Roble said, frantically searching the outside of the building.

Lehrling's hand sternly gripped Roble's forearm. He yanked Roble back. "Watch out!"

At the entrance of the stairwell the acid-filled beast sloshed forward, making strange gurgling noises as it moved. Without legs, it moved like a sluggish fat snail, pulling itself forward with the base of its body.

Mesmerized, Roble stepped backwards, studying its appearance. He was unable to look away, much like one watching the destruction of a coming tornado. But part of his fascination came from trying to identify this creature's anatomy rather than comprehending how it was even alive. After several moments of analyzing the creature, he found what he assumed was its face. The face was contained *inside* the green creature. It didn't have an actual head or arms or legs. It moved like a slug but its form wasn't elongated. Instead, it was more like a carpet of moving sludge, sloshing side to side but maintaining a partially standing appearance as it crawled up the stairs.

Roble instinctively walked back until he stood alongside Lehrling.

"Do you think … it ate her?" Roble asked.

Lehrling swallowed hard. He opened his mouth but no words ever came.

"Mmm-fff-mmph!"

Lehrling pointed. "There she is!"

Roble turned. Shawndirea's body was partially enclosed inside a spider's web between a large rock and the fallen beam of another building. A glob of ooze dripped from the rock, inches from the web. Since no slimy trail linked the ooze to the stairwell, he assumed the goo was the creature's spit. The acid components in the ooze ate holes into the bubbling rock. He imagined what damage the spit could do to human or a faery's flesh. He swallowed hard; relieved Shawndirea escaped its attack.

"Damn," he whispered.

Roble rushed to Shawndirea and set his flickering torch on the cobblestone. With his forefinger, he thumped the hairy spider still trying to spindle more webbing around her. The spider dislodged from the web and sailed a short distance through the air before landing in a pile of dead ivy. He carefully released Shawndirea's fragile wings from the sticky web. He pulled the thicker webbing from her mouth.

"Are you okay?" he asked.

She nodded, wiping stickiness from the outside of her mouth. She frowned, trying to locate where the spider had landed. He recognized her vindictive expression. He pitied the spider should she locate it.

"I'm fine, other than the gummy webbing on my face and wings," she said. "But be careful. That creature can shoot its acid drool even farther than I anticipated. I dodged but didn't see the spider's web."

Roble helped her peel away the web from her wings. When most of it was removed, he reached for his torch. The dissolving rock stopped bubbling, absorbing the acid, but only after half the stone had liquefied.

"Roble," Lehrling said. The panic in his voice matched the fear in his eyes. "Let's get away from here while we can!"

Lehrling hurled his flaming torch at the ooze creature. The torch was extinguished, being sucked into its gelatin body. The flame had caused no damage.

"Run!" Roble said, knowing Lehrling couldn't move as quickly as he.

Lehrling ran.

Half mumbling, Roble said, "There must be a way to destroy it."

"No one has ever succeeded in doing so," she said, sliding into his pocket.

"*Yet.*"

"It's highly unlikely we will," she said.

"Can't you use a spell to rip it apart or something?"

"As I've told you, my magic is for healing or self-preservation."

"And what about those mosquitoes?" Roble asked.

"Don't taunt me."

"Well?"

Shawndirea huffed. "Okay, so I've never tried. After what just happened with the spider, I'm even less inclined to try."

"Fair enough. I've never seen a monstrosity like that," he said.

"Give it time, Roble. You'll see far worse in my realm."

Roble ran behind Lehrling, offering the light of his torch to guide their steps without worrying about obstructions along the pathway. Periodically, Roble glanced over his shoulder to check the ooze creature's pursuit. Best he could tell, it wasn't following them, but since he held the only light source, he couldn't be certain.

"The weirdest thing is that it does have a face with a mouth," Roble said. "If it's capable of eating larger prey, I'm fairly certain it doesn't need the mouth to do so."

Shawndirea nodded. "You're right. The acid partially dissolves flesh as its slime encapsulates the victim. Then the acid consumes everything else."

"If you saw a pile of bones, why didn't it dissolve those?"

"It probably sucks out the marrow," she said. "The rest of the bone it discards."

"It looked like a partially dissolved shield was inside its body. Several arrows protruded from its outer membrane."

Shawndirea nodded. "Some magic enchantments resist acid."

When they reached the campfire, Lehrling leaned over with his hands on his knees and panted. "Perhaps this island wasn't our best choice for staying through the night."

"It doesn't look like it's leaving the safety of those stairs," Roble said.

"I wish I could take comfort in that," Lehrling said, rising and wiping sweat from his brow with a old piece of cloth. "None of us know *what* it will do. There's no guarantee it won't make its way to us during the night or eat our horses while we sleep. One of us needs to stay awake until morning. We could take turns."

"I'll take first watch," Roble said. "It'll give me time to figure out a way we can destroy it."

Lehrling's eyes widened in disbelief. "You can't be serious."

Shawndirea crossed her arms, sighed, and rolled her eyes. "He is."

Roble chuckled, seeing her reaction. Indeed, she knew how his mind worked, even though most of the time she rejected his proposals and tried to sway him differently.

Roble smiled. "I am."

"We don't even know how to kill it," Shawndirea said. "Your weapons and my magic cannot not hurt it. It's best we keep our distance until morning and depart. If we don't attack it, we're more likely to all survive with our lives and without injuries."

"We cannot allow it to live," Roble replied.

"Oh, we *can*," she said with a firm brow.

"If we don't kill it, we allow it to continue devouring others who explore this island. I don't want that on my conscience. Do you?"

Shawndirea bit her lower lip and shook her head. Her eyes finally met his. "What do you propose?"

He shrugged. "That's why I need to remain awake, so I can figure out a way to kill it."

CHAPTER 14

eep in thought, Roble and Lehrling sat on the crude remnants of a large hexagon stone once used for the base of a support wall. The stone was smooth across its top and wide enough to allow Roble and Lehrling adequate room to sit back to back comfortably. Two wooden support beams that had been atop the stone had separated, fallen, and stretched across the floor.

Lehrling placed several thick branches upon the dying fire. Rising embers floated into the calm night air. Though the night felt pleasant, the thundering storm continued raging outside the island's perimeter. Lightning flashed like flickering nets overhead, and yet no rain blessed the barren island.

Roble stared into the fire, almost oblivious to his surroundings. Lehrling tossed another branch onto the fire and gave Roble a sharp glance. "If you plan to keep watch first, you *must* feed the fire. You lose the light of the flames, and we become vulnerable."

"Sorry," Roble replied.

Lehrling grinned. "You're lost in your thoughts?"

"Most of the time."

"Have you come up with any ideas for how we could kill it?"

"A few. Whether or not they'd work, I can't predict any success."

"We could gamble that it won't leave the stairwell," Lehrling said with a hopeful smile. "Rather than gamble our lives trying to kill it."

"I know," Roble said. "But, as you mentioned, we've no idea of what its intention is."

Lehrling nodded. "Where's Shawndirea?"

Roble pointed to his pocket. "Asleep."

"I tried to sleep, but it's hard to rest when something like that is nearby."

"Don't trust I'd stay awake?"

"Not so much that but I was getting cold and afraid the fire would die."

"I'll keep better watch on the fire," Roble said, adjusting himself on the stone block. He looked at his glove and frowned.

"What is it?"

"My glove is white."

Lehrling stepped closer. "So it is."

Roble grinned.

Lehrling cocked a brow. "I recognize that look. What are you thinking?"

"I think I know the creature's vulnerability," Roble replied.

"From *that*? How?"

"There's a reason it doesn't leave those stairs. I should have seen that earlier." Roble stood.

Lehrling frowned. "I don't understand."

"Can you get me the axe from the saddlebag?"

"Sure. Why?"

Roble grinned. "We're going to make a weapon to destroy that beast."

"With a stone?" Lehrling asked, glancing over his shoulder.

"A sharp, piercing stone."

"What are you talking about?" Shawndirea said, rising from his pocket and stretching. She took to flight and hovered above them. Lehrling returned with the axe.

"He says he can make a weapon from this stone that will kill the ooze creature," Lehrling said, wiping sweat from his brow.

"Don't be absurd, Roble," she said. "The best swords, daggers, arrows, and axes have failed to stop it, and you think you can destroy it with a rock?"

"Why not? Has anyone else ever tried it?" Roble asked.

"No one would entertain such a foolish attack," she whispered. Although she reply was curt, her eyes beamed with interest, wanting to see what he planned to do.

Roble took the sharp edge of the axe and scraped a line across the stone's flat surface. By his guess, if he hit the stone hard enough and luck enabled the strike to properly cut through the stone, a third of it might break free. At that angle, he could sharpen the stone's edges enough with the axe to pierce the flesh of any animal or beast.

Roble looked at Lehrling and said, "Step back and shield your eyes."

"You know that's the *only* axe we have," he said, getting out of the way. "Axes are for chopping *wood*, not rock."

Roble grinned, swung the axe over his head, and closed his eyes on the downward swing. The blade struck the stone with a quick singing of the metal. The metal tore through and busted the stone. He opened his eyes. At least a third of the stone dropped to the floor, but instead of one clean heavier slab, the larger section broke into two, near equal portions.

Roble shook his head and grimaced.

"Something wrong?" Lehrling asked.

"I hoped to only have two pieces, not three. This will have to do."

"At least the axe is intact."

"There's that."

Shawndirea hovered lower, inspecting the white stone. "I don't understand how this will make a weapon capable of killing that thing."

"It might not," Roble replied. "But, it's the best weapon to kill it. It's the best option we have."

"Why?"

"I'll explain later, if it works."

"And if it doesn't?"

He shrugged. "Then it won't matter."

"Roble," she said, "there's no need to pursue or attack it. The only time we should engage is if *it* attacks us."

"I realize that, but I know why it won't leave the stairwell," Roble replied.

"Why?" Lehrling asked.

"Because of *these* stones."

Lehrling and Shawndirea exchanged glances and frowned.

"When I was freeing you from the spider's web, something occurred to me," Roble said.

"What?" she asked.

"The creature wasn't put on this island to kill the inhabitants. It was placed in the stairwell to protect something hidden down below."

"How do you know that?" she asked.

Roble shrugged. "Call it a premonition or a hunch, but a thought came to me. The more I've thought about it, the more I believe that's the reason the creature exists. It's guarding something. The only reason the townsfolk died was because they tried to find a way to get around it."

Shawndirea shook her head. "If you don't think it'll leave the stairwell, why do you want to kill it?"

Roble grinned. "I want to know what's so valuable in the cellar."

Shawndirea rolled her eyes. "Of course, you do! Typical human, but I wonder if you're not a *Dwarf*. It's best we let guard whatever it is, if what you say is true. It's not worth the risk."

Lehrling howled with laughter. "A Dwarf? Hilarious!"

Roble frowned. "But what if it's something valuable to us?"

"It's not, Roble," Lehrling said, wiping tears from his eyes. "Don't let greed dictate your actions."

"It has nothing to do with greed," Roble said evenly. "Riches aren't what I seek. Sure, my curiosity lures me, but overall, my motive is to prevent this creature from killing future explorers."

Lehrling regarded Roble's words and nodded. "Fair enough."

"Dear," Shawndirea said, "you need a better weapon. I'm sorry, but *this* is a fool's weapon."

"If you don't want me to use this to kill it, fine. Then simply remove the spell upon these rings and I'll consult Lez'minx directly about the best way to kill it. Who knows? Perhaps he'll intervene and kill it for us. I imagine this would be a less challenge than killing three dozen Shadowfae mercenaries."

Her brow narrowed and her jaw tightened. "And all this time you keep swearing you won't serve him? Secretly, you crave his power."

"No, I don't," Roble said. "And I don't plan to serve him in any capacity."

"You just said—"

"I know what I said, but I said it to get your attention. You need to stop treating me like a child," Roble said. "Have *some* faith in me. I've knowledge from my realm that you've never been exposed to. Just like I don't understand things in Aetheaon, your world has no understanding of mine."

"This isn't one of them," she replied.

"I'm willing to bet my life on it."

Shawndirea placed her hands on her hips. Her face contorted through anger, confusion, surprise, sadness, and desperation. "I'd rather you didn't wage such high stakes. Lehrling, speak to him!"

Lehrling chuckled and then quickly coughed. "What makes you think he'll listen to me more than you? He's in *love* with you. I assure you that he and I have no such pact."

"Reason with him," she huffed.

"I offer my sword to aid you since I already know you'll refuse any advice from either of us," Lehrling said.

"That's *not* reasoning!" Shawndirea glared at Lehrling.

"No, it isn't, but if you want him to remain alive, we'd best do something to help him. Arguing is ludicrous at this point."

She darted in the air and circled around so she hovered directly in front of Roble. When his eyes met hers, she said, "So you're determined to do this?"

"Only because I believe it will work."

She tilted her nose upward and scrunched it. "Fine. What do you need us to do?"

"Right now," Roble replied, "I could use some twine and a sturdy straight stick."

With a frown, she said, "You plan to spear it?"

"Something like that."

"I'll get some rope from the saddle pack," Lehrling said.

After Lehrling was out of earshot, she said, "Why must you be as stubborn as my mother?"

"No more than you are."

She gasped and placed her right hand over her heart. "You think I'm—"

"Yep. You're every bit as stubborn as she," Roble said. He used the sharp axe blade to shave away the sides of the white stone. Slivers and bits of white powder cascaded onto the worn floor of the old shack.

Instead of spewing angry words, she thought for several long moments. "Perhaps that's what drove the wedge deeper between she and I."

"Probably."

"I don't want that to happen to us," she said softly.

She wiped a tear from her cheek.

"It won't," he assured her.

"How can you be sure?"

"Love stands the test of time," he replied. "I'm sure you're aware of that?"

"It's what every female hopes to secure."

Without stopping his work with the axe, he said, "Every man holds the same hope, too. Shawndirea, there'll never be a day when my heart stops loving or yearning for you. I wish you trusted my decisions."

"I've tried, but then you have moments when your actions are quite fool- ish. Like the rings—"

"I know. You don't need to keep reminding me. You're a faery, *not* a harpy."

Her eyes narrowed for a moment. She noticed his slight grin and burst into laughter.

After several minutes, Roble set the first broken piece of the stone atop the remainder of the support stone. He had shaped it into a long pointed triangle. About fifteen minutes later, he set the second one beside it, which was almost identical in size and shape.

"What now?" Lehrling asked, handing Roble long strands of twine.

Roble smiled, placed the axe head on the ground, and set his right boot an inch or so above the head. "We're going to need a new axe."

Pushing his boot against the axe, he pulled the axe handle toward himself, snapping the handle free.

Lehrling's mouth dropped open. "Why? Why'd you do that?"

"You'll see."

CHAPTER 15

After several minutes of strategically positioning the two sharp-pointed slabs of stone on each side of the axe handle, Roble finally managed to tie the twine tightly around them, producing a double-bladed short spear. The blades were sharp enough to pierce through any skin or leather, which held a great advantage; however, the weight of the weapon was far greater than he expected. With a short handle and the heavy rock blades, the only way it could effectively kill the ooze beast was by getting close enough to thrust the spear into it.

Another problem how fragile the stone was. Should he miss, the stone could shatter against a harder surface. The creature's thin skin or membrane didn't appear impenetrable, which benefited the creature in its ability to spread around and swallow a victim. Piercing its membrane wasn't the problem. But once the blade passed through, the real danger was the gushing acid that would spill out.

"What more do you need?" Lehrling asked.

"I need the two of you to distract the creature," he replied.

Lehrling's eyes widened. "Wh-what?"

"Why?" Shawndirea asked.

"I need to plunge this into its body without it noticing my approach. If it sees me before I successfully stab it, I'm dead because it will spit its acid on me."

"Wait," she said. "I thought you were going to throw this at it."

Roble nodded and then gave a slight shrug. "That had been the plan but the blade's too heavy and I won't have the accuracy I need if I throw it."

"See?" Shawndirea said. "I'm warning you not to do this."

"I can do this if you will help."

"It can spew its acid quite a distance," she said. "At such a close distance, it won't miss."

"I know. That's why you two need to distract it."

"And what if there are more than one?"

"We'll deal with that when the time comes," Roble said. "With as little prey as it happens upon, there shouldn't be more than one, so we should be okay."

"Roble," Lehrling said, "I can't run fast, nor am I as agile as I once was."

Roble gritted his teeth and strained as he picked up the heavy weapon and carefully propped it upon his shoulder. With his shoulder sagging beneath the spear's weight, he questioned whether he should attack the ooze monster or not. He was strong enough to swing the weapon, but would he be fast enough? Most likely, he wouldn't get a second chance should he miss the first time.

Taking a burning torch from the fire, Roble handed it to Lehrling and then pointed toward the stairwell.

Roble said, "I realize you can't see it in the darkness from where we stand, but there are several pillars made out of this stone. Those are good places to hide. If it spits acid at you, step behind one of the pillars. These stones absorb the acid."

Uncertainty creased Lehrling's brow. "Is that true?"

"Yes," Roble said, nodding. "Shawndirea, allow it to see you, but don't get too close."

"I truly hope you know what you're doing," she said softly.

"We're going to find out in a few minutes," Roble replied, walking away from the campfire and toward the building.

Thunder rumbled in the distance. Faint lightning flickered from the surrounding storms and offered the briefest amount of light to illuminate the building and the two pillars for several seconds.

Roble pointed. "Lehrling, there are the pillars."

Lehrling swallowed hard enough to be heard. "Will the creature even be able to see me from that point?"

"Throw small rocks in its direction or speak loud enough to draw its attention, but not before I get into a better position."

"How will I know when to throw rocks?"

"I'll make three short whistling sounds," Roble replied.

Lehrling met Roble's gaze. "Three?"

"Yes. You won't mistake them. It won't mimic a bird at all."

Lehrling nodded and turned to head to the pillars. "Good luck, Roble, and Goddesses' speed."

"And to you. Don't make yourself an easy target. Stay close to the pillars."

Shawndirea flittered near Roble. "I wonder if your purpose lately is to make me an early widow."

"Believe me, I have every intention and interest of living a long life."

"You have odd ways of showing it. Since this creature hasn't pursued us, you have no reason to attack it. It's almost like you've declared war."

"It's not a war, but I suppose I'm drawing it into battle," Roble replied. "But tell me, should more innocent people die?"

"We don't know that any who died were innocent. Most likely, they were thieves and murderers trying to enter the cellar."

"All who travel to this island cannot be those of ill repute. We aren't."

Shawndirea beamed a smile. "We're the exceptions."

Faint cloud lightning flickered, casting a strobe light effect over the building for several seconds.

"Damn," Roble said.

"What is it?"

"I don't see the creature. There's not enough light."

"Well, it is the middle of the night."

"I should've brought a torch."

"No, dear, not if you plan to sneak up behind it. A flame will draw its immediate attention," she said. "I assume you wish to lure it in Lehrling's direction?"

"Yes. If it leaves the entrance of the stairwell, I can stab it from behind."

"I never took you to be a backstabber," she said with humor in her tone. "You seem above that."

"Normally, I'd agree, but this isn't a fight with a human or another race." Roble sighed, took another step toward the opening of the building and squinted. "I still can't see the creature."

"I hope you're right about it not ever venturing away from the cellar," she said.

"Me, too."

"I'll fly closer and see if it's in the stairwell."

"Be careful."

"Always," she replied. "I may need to use magic to get its attention. Once I locate it, I will cast an illumination spell to allow you to see it."

"I appreciate that."

Shawndirea took flight. Another brief flicker of lightning revealed the opening of the building. She entered through what had been the doorway and after the last bit of lightning vanished, she was no longer visible. Fear crept into his mind, but he shunted it away.

With his recent streak of luck, he half expected to turn around and find the ooze beast right behind him. He gave a nervous glance over his shoulder, but with limited vision in the darkness, he relied more on trying to hear the creature instead of seeing it. After a few seconds, he ascertained the thing was still in or near the stairs.

Shawndirea zipped upwards through the open ceiling of the building, her body radiating a greenish sheen. In seconds, she returned to Roble. "It's in the stairwell. I'm not certain how far down the stairs go, but it seems to patrol them. It's on its way up."

"Good. Thanks."

Lightning flashed and blasted trees in the forests across the water from the island. Thunder echoed and shook the ground. Roble took those few moments to focus on the fallen wall to the right of the stairwell.

Nervousness creased Shawndirea's brow. "Do you wish for me to capture its attention and get it to leave the stairs sooner?"

"Wait for my signal first."

"What are you planning to do?"

He pointed. "I think I can climb to the top of the broken wall near the stairs. If so, that gives me a better vantage point. Maybe I won't need to stab it at close range. Once I'm up there, I'll whistle."

She hovered closer and kissed his cheek. "Don't get killed or maimed or—"

Roble nodded. "I don't plan to."

"Few ever *plan* to suffer an agonizing death. Being dissolved by acid is almost equal to burning to death. Perhaps even worse."

"I'd best hurry if I want to scale the wall before it reaches the top of the stairs," he said.

"I'll be nearby overhead. When I see it, I'll make certain it keeps its attention on me and not you."

"Just be careful."

Roble crouched and walked slowly toward the edge of the building. Even though the wall had partially fallen, he still needed to enter through the fallen doorway to climb the wall, which meant he might meet the creature at the top of the stairs. While he hoped the ooze monster moved slower than a slug, he had no knowledge of how fast it could carry itself up the stairs.

He hesitated at the entrance, almost fearful to step through. His heartbeat thudded in his ears. He was more nervous than he wanted to be. It was good to be cautious, but with all the objections Lehrling and Shawndirea had given him, he suddenly doubted his actions.

He readily defended himself against Lehrling's insinuation about Roble wanting to kill the creature dead so he could get the hidden wealth below. Roble had not lied. His first motive was to ensure that no others were killed by the ooze creature. And if indeed it were created by magic to guard the cellar, something extraordinary must be below this forsaken hamlet. By killing the creature, he earned, at the very least, the right to see what the creature was protecting.

Listening, no sounds of a sluggish, sloshing creature echoed from the stairwell, which was about five feet from the doorway. Roble slipped through the door, lowered the stone weapons at his side, and pressed his back partway against the tilted wall.

Shawndirea hovered above Roble. With a faint greenish glow outlining her, she nodded and motioned for him to climb.

Roble placed one hand into a gap where two missing planks had once formed part of the wall and pulled himself upward. He planted one foot into a groove, pushed, and before rising, he gripped the double-tipped spear tightly. The stone head was almost too heavy to heft along with his own weight, especially since he was climbing with only one hand.

He used his feet for leverage, but each time he lifted one foot to climb higher, he lost his balance for several seconds. And during this climb, each passing second was more valuable than the last. His hand, wrist, and biceps ached from the strain of holding the spear. But without the spear, there was no need to reach the tilted top of the wall.

Shawndirea appeared beside him and whispered, "Hurry. It's almost to the top of the stairs."

Roble grunted and offered a slight nod. He heaved the spear upward and pressed the handle against the bent section of the wall. The slope allowed him enough surface area to set it down, but the steepness prevented him from totally releasing the handle. With less weight working against him, he raised his right foot and found a place to step higher. Attempting his best balance, he used both hands to grip the spear's handle and slide the weapon into a narrow groove where it wouldn't fall.

Once he secured the weapon, he pulled himself onto the slanted wall and sat down. His right arm burned with pain. He massaged his wrist, forearm, and his biceps for a few moments. He doubted an hour's worth of rest was enough recovery time for how he planned to attack the creature. He hoped his weakened arm didn't hinder his accuracy. Should he miss, he wasn't getting another chance.

Shawndirea waved her hands together to the left of the stairwell, close to where the two pillars set with Lehrling hidden behind one of them. A bright orb of green glowed with enough vigor to brighten the floor and the entrance of the stairwell.

Roble took a sharp breath when the glob of churning acid slopped from the top step onto the old floor. He couldn't tell if it saw her light or not. He wondered if it sensed his presence. Shaking his tingling hand to ward off its numbness, he whistled and then he grabbed the spear handle with both hands, lifting it over his head.

CHAPTER 16

In spite of his aching arm, Roble waited for Shawndirea to lure the ooze creature from the stairwell. He attempted to hide his worry and hoped the darkness shadowed it enough that Lehrling and Shawndirea didn't notice. Although the weapon should kill the acid beast, he hated putting their lives into danger by using them as bait so he could attack unnoticed. The best-set plans always appeared better in one's mind than they did when the action was actually playing out.

Shawndirea twirled swiftly in the air and fired a green bolt of energy at the creature. Although the bolt did no harm, it captured the creature's interest. It spat a wad of acid at her.

Shawndirea spun, flew upward, and then descended close to the creature. Bolts of green shot from her hands, but the monster absorbed them. Incredibly it picked up its pace and spat again, narrowly missing her. She dodged but lost her balance and spiraled downward, catching herself on the rough floor.

A sharp pain stabbed Roble's stomach. He wanted to run to her and help, but even if he hurried, he wasn't faster than the creature's ability to cover her with acid.

Tendrils stretched from the acid beast's sides and elongated like a mass of octopuses legs reaching for her.

Shawndirea lay on all fours, shaking her head, trying to regain her composure.

Lehrling growled, stepped into the open, and threw several small stones, striking the creature with remarkable accuracy. "Are you okay, Shawndirea?"

"I'm fine." Her voice resounded with a tinge of anger.

"Look out!" Lehrling said.

84

A large wad of spit soared in her direction. She rose and shot into the air. The acid splattered on the spot where she had lain.

Roble breathed a sigh of relief as she glided through the air. He cursed under his breath for having put her into the situation.

The glob of ooze moved from the stairwell and was almost outside of Roble's range. Holding the spear overhead, he pushed off the wall with his feet and jumped. If he missed and the stone-blade's points shattered, he was dead. Lehrling and Shawndirea could escape with their lives, but he'd be absorbed by the creature. Death in an instant.

Roble descended and Shawndirea screamed, apparently noticing his leap. He stretched his arms outward and extended the weapon as far as possible. The sharp tips of the spear gouged and split through the outer membrane of the creature. A gushing pool of acid and goo flooded out from the creature. The heavy stone blades frothed and foamed, pulling the acid into them.

With Roble's momentum, he was going to fall face first into acid. His right arm and shoulder burned with pain, but adrenaline surged through him. He tightened his hold on the spear handle enough to push himself upward like a pole vaulter. He spun into the air and crashed on his back several feet from the spreading acid pool.

Shawndirea swooped and hovered above him. "Are you okay?"

Pain radiated down his spine and jagged pangs shot through his arms and legs, riveting a torrent of agony throughout his body. His knees and back throbbed from the impact.

"You did it!" Lehrling shouted.

Roble gave a side-glance toward what was left of the creature and partway smiled.

"I should've never doubted you," Shawndirea said, wiping a tear from her cheek.

"I shouldn't have put you and Lehrling into danger. You almost were hit by the acid."

She smiled. "Almost doesn't count, does it?"

Thudding footsteps approached. Lehrling knelt beside him and placed a hand on Roble's shoulder. "Roble, are you okay, son?"

Roble groaned but half smiled at Lehrling's words. "Never better."

Lehrling frowned. "Somehow I don't believe that."

Roble chuckled. "Minus the pain. The best thing besides killing it, is that I missed the pool of acid."

"In that regard, I suppose you're right," Lehrling said, offering his hand to pull Roble to his feet.

"Give me a few minutes," Roble said.

Lehrling nodded. "Sure."

Shawndirea's eyes flashed green and she pointed a stern finger at Roble.

"You said that you made a spear to throw at it. You never told me you'd jump and ram it into the beast."

"Yes." Roble acquiesced a nod. "That had been my intention. But my arm was too sore to throw accurately."

"Foolish!" Her eyes darkened.

Roble stared at her, somewhat bewildered. Moments earlier, her demeanor had been loving and relieved. Now, she was consumed by sudden anger.

"Perhaps," Roble said, taking Lehrling's hand and getting pulled to his feet. "But effective."

Lehrling nodded. "You have to credit him for that. It worked, but how?"

Shawndirea turned her angered gaze from Roble and looked at the vanishing acid pool. Her anger subsided to curiosity and she glided closer. A frown tightened her brow. "What magic is this?"

"It's not magic," Roble replied. "It's science."

She flicked her gaze toward him. "What do you mean?"

Lehrling walked to the edge of the acid. "Yes, please explain."

Roble arched his back and then rolled his shoulders, gripping his aching arm. "In short, the reason this creature didn't leave the stairwell was due to the outside stones' composition. They're limestone, which counteracts the strong acid inside the beast, basically neutralizing and making it ineffective. The creature's outer membrane was probably thick enough to prevent damage whenever it crawled across the stone, but not if any of its skin was cut deep enough for the stone to touch the acid."

"So you knew the spear could kill it?" she asked.

"I was fairly certain."

She frowned. "But not absolute?"

Before he could offer reply, the ground shook. A forceful gust of stagnant air rushed up the stairwell and bellowed. Shrieks followed and dark bats rushed out of the stairwell and into the night.

"What is that?" Roble asked, steadying himself on the shaking ground.

Lehrling's footing wobbled, and he fought to remain on his feet. Roble gripped his arm and prevented his fall.

"I'm not certain," Shawndirea said softly. "But my guess is that since you killed the creature, you've broken the spell, opening whatever is sealed below."

"Then let's go see what's down there," Roble said.

"That's not advisable," she replied. "You might have unlocked a magical door and released a creature worse than the acid beast."

"My gut tells me otherwise." He turned and ran toward their campfire.

"What are you doing?" she asked.

"Getting another torch."

CHAPTER 17

*R*oble led the way down the crude stairwell, despite Shawndirea's livid protests. The flames of his torch singed and melted away cobwebs, roasting the plump spiders that had constructed them. Using the light as his guide, he tried to avoid the occasional broken step they happened upon.

He offered for Shawndirea to sit on his shoulder or in his pocket but her only reply was a sharp intense glare that meant he should say nothing else to her for a while.

Severe moodiness was a rarity for her, mostly nonexistent since he had proven he was a man of his word by risking his life to bring her back to her homeland.

But ever since they had entered the swamp, her temperament grew more fiery than she'd ever displayed in the past, even toward her mother. He found this dilemma strange and disturbing.

On this journey, she seemed easily riled and tended to lash out, holding less compassion toward him, which was also unlike her. Their relationship had always been respectful, caring, and loving. Was she unknowingly directing her bitterness toward Dirk at him? Had Lez'minx somehow cast a spell on her or perhaps one of the dark Fae had done so before it died?

Something troubled her deeply. Although he wanted to discuss her inner turmoil to get to the root of the problem, the current timing wasn't appropriate. Besides, he knew her well enough that she wouldn't hold such a conversation openly in Lehrling's presence. Personal situations she and he sorted through together in the privacy of their home.

Thinking about Lehrling's edgy reaction to Shawndirea's heated anger every time she scolded Roble for his impulsive actions without evaluating the

"

risks, it almost seemed Lehrling was the one on the receiving end of her tirades. At least he was acting like it, so Roble wasn't about to address Shawndirea's sudden anger issues, even though he truly wanted everything smoothed over. He wanted her to be lighthearted and fun-loving again.

The farther down the stairs they went, the sweatier the walls became. Water trickled and dripped down the cold walls. Small puddles gathered between some of the sunken rocky stairs. The dank air reeked with the slightly soured aroma of mold and mildew.

The thought occurred to him that perhaps the acid beast wasn't a necessary element to protect the depths under the hamlet at all. Who in their right mind would continue downward when nothing but treacherous traps could lie ahead? He chuckled, realizing that it meant he *wasn't* in his right mind at all.

Shawndirea's wings fluttered softly behind his head. He could nearly picture the scowl on her face during her silent protest during their descent into the cellar.

Although Lehrling had eagerly agreed to explore the cellar with him, he was unable to hide his nervousness in the glow of the torch each time Roble glanced back to make certain Lehrling was still following.

Lehrling held his short sword in hand so Roble slid a dagger into his left hand. For some reason, Roble didn't expect any other creatures at the bottom of the stairs.

The stairs turned back on themselves four times before ending at the opening to a large room. No creatures were visible. No hungry growls or glowing eyes welcomed them. He was thankful that the sensation of being watched didn't overshadow him. At least they were safe, but what none of them expected was the vast amount of knowledge they were about to uncover.

The tip of the torch Roble held, offered less and less light and produced more and more smoke. Soon, all they'd see were the reddish embers glowing in the darkness of the cellar before they were enveloped inside total blackness. Before the final flames died, he scanned the opening and found a stone pot of pitch with two soaking torches. He grabbed one and quickly touched the flame to it. The pitch on the torch roared to light, revealing the contents of the room.

"My word," Lehrling gasped.

Several crude tables were covered with dusty cobwebs. Piles of rolled scrolls and books were scattered atop the tables. A quill with a long black raven feather rested in a ink pot. On one table, a map of Aetheaon was spread out. Heavy glass orbs weighted down each corner. A dozen or more unlit candles had long ago melted into their holders. Dried wax that resemble icicles were frozen and covered with dust.

Shawndirea flew past Roble and used her magic to zap green fire blasts at each candle's stiffened wick. Slowly the room was aglow.

With sudden apprehension, she whispered, "A wizard once lived here."

"Are you sure, faery?" Lehrling asked.

With bewildered eyes, she glanced around the room before she lighted upon the closest table and ran her hand along the spines of ancient books. "These are magic volumes, scrolls, and extensive notes. Rare books most likely stolen from another alchemist wizard."

Lehrling eased closer to view the items. His eyes widened.

"What is it?" Roble asked.

"It can't be," Lehrling replied.

"What?"

Lehrling picked up an unrolled scroll with a dried red wax seal beside the signature.

"The stamp is from a Dragon Skull pendant," Lehrling said in a near whisper. He held up the scroll, studying it.

"That's odd," Roble said."

Lehrling took a sharp breath and he stared in disbelief as he looked from the seal to Roble. "It belonged to Geowren."

"How do you know that?" Roble asked.

"His signature is beside the seal." Lehrling pointed. "And that's his dagger on the table. I'd recognize the hilt anywhere. See? His name is engraved on the blade."

Roble picked up the blade and examined it. The dagger was weighted properly, but to Roble's disappointment, this wasn't a throwing knife, but impressive in its own right. The hilt was designed with silver and gold. More than a dozen rubies were inset and stunning as the stones captured the light of the torches. This was a prize for anyone who carried it.

"Why would he leave it?" Roble asked.

Lehrling shook his head. "He wouldn't deliberately."

"Perhaps he was trapped down here and became a victim of the ooze creature?"

"No," Shawndirea replied. "I think the creature was his."

Roble frowned. "Did he control magic, Lehrling?"

Lehrling flicked his gaze from Roble and stared at her questionably. "Not to my knowledge, no. Why did you say that, Shawndirea? He was a common knight like myself."

"If this is his writing, there wasn't anything *common* about him. He was a wizard or at the least, an apprentice of one." She stood atop a drawing of the ooze creature and the details for how to summon it from a certain combination of different ingredients were written beneath it, along with the written incantation.

"If the creature belonged to him, where has he gone?" Roble asked while studying the information of the ooze beast on the aged parchment. "And why was he down here?"

Lehrling thumbed through a stack of loose parchments much like the one with the wax seal, only the others were different. "These are entries, like a journal. The other—" He held the signed one closer to a candle's flame to read the words. "This is a letter."

"To whom?" Roble asked.

Lehrling's brow rose. "Queen Taube."

CHAPTER 18

"Queen Taube?" Roble asked, looking over Lehrling's shoulder.

Lehrling nodded and moved the parchment closer to the candle-light. "Yes."

"What does it say?" Shawndirea asked.

Lehrling squinted and read the letter aloud:

"My Dearest Queen Taube,

May the blessings of the Three Goddesses be upon you.

I recently discovered that King Erik was never killed in the war against the Dredgemen and that he was taken prisoner and is most likely still alive. As your, and his, devoted knight, I've taken it upon myself to find where he's being held prisoner. Once I locate his exact whereabouts, I shall arrive at Hoffnung's Courts and gather my Dragon Skull brethren together, so we can bring him home safely. And to those who betrayed the throne, justice will find them by my sword. They will pay dearly for these atrocities. Their crimes will not be ignored or forgotten.

Forever in your service,

Geowren

"King Erik lives?" Shawndirea asked with a growing smile of hope.

Lehrling wiped a tear from his cheek, his face flushed red, and he was too choked up to speak. Twice he attempted to say something, but his voice crackled too badly. He simply shook his head and held up a hand, mouthing, "Sorry."

"Why didn't he ever send this letter?" Roble asked.

Lehrling placed the letter on the rickety table. Taking a deep breath, he braced his hands against the tabletop, trying to regain his composure.

"Perhaps his journals have those details," Shawndirea said.

Lehrling's body shook. He reared back his head, released a trembling laugh, and shook his hands in triumph. "Oh, by the Goddesses above! King Erik lives! Greater news could not befall us!" He clasped Roble's shoulder with fierce strength. "You were right to kill the ooze creature!"

Ambition overtook him, fresh tears streamed down his round cheeks into his blonde beard, and he thumbed through the parchments. He chuckled and then released a long sigh. "We must find Geowren so we can aid in the return of our King."

"Easy, Lehrling," Roble said, placing a comforting hand on Lehrling's shoulder. "All in good time."

"Good time?" Lehrling shook his head. His eager smile didn't fade. "For so long we've wondered about the welfare of our King. Was he dead? If so, where had the body been buried? If alive, where is he? Now, we have this news—"

Roble nodded. "Great news that it is, but when exactly did he write the letter?"

Lehrling placed his finger to the bottom of the letter. His smile retreated slightly, but the brightness in his eyes didn't lessen. He sighed. "About a year ago, but that's more recent than I would've imagined."

"That's not too long ago, I suppose," Roble said. "But, we need to know where Geowren traveled from here, track his steps, and hopefully find him. That might be as hard as finding King Erik. A person can travel quite a distance and to a lot of places within a year's time."

"Yes. Yes, you're right," Lehrling said, taking a couple of deep breaths to calm himself. Still, his smile beamed. "I mustn't get ahead of myself. But Goddesses, what a glorious day! And we've got you to thank, Roble! Indeed, it's no accident that you found me."

"I can't take the credit for all of this," Roble said.

"Your stubbornness to kill the ooze beast allowed us to get to these chambers," Lehrling said.

"Don't forget," Shawndirea said, "that his stubbornness is what nearly killed us all. And had that occurred, all of this remained lost and buried."

Roble ignored her bitter jab. "The best information we can gather is in his journal. You said that he was not a practitioner of magic?"

"No. I've never seen him wear a blessed trinket or a magical charm, other than his Dragon Skull pendant."

"Then how'd he learn magic?"

From across the room, Shawndirea said, "This might interest you."

Roble turned in her direction. She fluttered above an iron box cage. "Isn't that a torture cage?"

"They can be modified for such," she replied, "but this specific cage was designed with the purpose of imprisoning a wizard and prevent him from using his magic. See the runes welded at the top? I wouldn't dare fly into this cage for fear it'd drain all my power."

Roble nodded. "So Geowren was keeping a wizard prisoner? Why?"

Shawndirea shrugged. "With the right enchantments, Geowren could have been transferring a wizard's power to use for his own spells until he developed better use for his own. It's rare for someone without natural magical abilities to succeed, as one's magic tends to be loyal to its caster. The risks are often greater than any reward."

"Then why risk it?" Roble asked, gripping the iron bars of the cage doors.

"To learn spells?" Shawndirea said. "He certainly wrote out a lot of scrolls."

"Why would a wizard offer his spells, even if he was being held prisoner?" Roble asked.

"That you'd need to ask Geowren, or the wizard if the wizard's still alive. Geowren might have tortured the wizard to divulge his or her secrets."

"Unlikely," Lehrling said. "It was not in Geowren's nature to torture another living being."

"Perhaps not when you traveled with him during the time of peace," Shawndirea said. "But if he learned this particular wizard had knowledge of who had taken King Erik prisoner, don't you think that's enough motive to do everything possible to obtain that information?"

"It would be for me," Roble said without giving his comment a second thought. It dawned upon him that he held undying devoted loyalty to Hoffnung, even though he was not from this realm.

Holding the bars of the cage, Roble pictured a trapped angry wizard set with vindictive urges that if ever freed he'd torment Geowren, cast severe pestilence upon the Dragon Knight, and enjoy every moment of suffering he could bestow upon Geowren. Looking toward the crude tables with the numerous scrolls, Roble visualized Geowren busily dipping the quill into the ink well and vigorously writing down various spell methods onto the yellow parchments as dictated by his prisoner.

Collecting dust on a nearby table was an odd crystal ball, far different in shape and color. The ball resembled an eyeball of a large creature, and perhaps it was, knowing the strangeness of Aetheaon and some of the most unusual vices he had already witnessed. He wondered what parts of his compassion he was sacrificing by residing in a realm far different than his own homeland. Aetheaon had less governing laws and a kill-or-be-killed mentality that was in its own right, the law for one's survival. Justice here was not the same.

Lehrling nodded. "For that? If the wizard knew where Erik was? Yes, most any of the Order would go to almost any length to find the truth, especially after learning Erik is alive. Our oath is to the King and Queen of Hoffnung and we'd die to defend the throne."

"But how do you capture a wizard?" Roble asked with a slight grin.

"Not easily," she said. "But it can be done. Generally by surprise or a quick thwack to the back of the head. An unconscious wizard is generally a powerless one. But it's nearly impossible to sneak up behind one. It can only be done if one is capable of getting past a wizard's circle of protection. Or, drug his wine and wait for the effects to occur."

"Some of these entries are interesting," Lehrling said.

"Like what?"

"Apparently the wizard controlled the island at one point and was a tyrant. Let me read this:

The townsfolk on this modest island—Polderholm, it is called—were most welcoming, but not the overseer, Mad Vyssisk, a dark wizard. He ordered me taken prisoner when he saw my Dragon Skull pendant. He would have had my head removed and feasted upon my heart and liver had not the protection of the Three Goddesses overshadowed me.

At least, it is they I give the honor and glory to, for they allowed me to turn the tables on this crazed wizard, who is not human, but some sort of reptilian man. His scaly skin and long tail with sharp plated tips that ran down his spine were weapons in their own right. Confining him without injury to myself was quite the feat.

To my surprise, Vyssisk has been quite insightful in his instruction and I've learned magic in ways I've never fathomed. Keeping him alive, for the time being, is in both our best interests.

However, time is not a luxury in his cellar. Other reptilian men dressed in leather armor, carrying flimsy shields and iron weapons, have attempted to make their way down the stairwell. But the magical doorway I created has tricked them thus far. Needless to say, I chanced a view of the surface and found that these creatures had killed all the humans inhabiting the Isle of Polderholm, leaving the town deserted.

With time fleeting my hope, I gathered poisonous leaves, clumps of peat moss, and several buckets of acrid swamp water, brought them to the cellar and resealed the magical doorway. I placed these ingredients into a small pit and cast an incantation I read aloud from one of Vyssisk's spellbooks, not even certain it would work. It did. Gryme was spawned.

I suppose a little luck came with the magic, as the slime creature could have killed me upon its maturation, but instead, he—it—has been as loyal as a dog is to its master. Instead of using the magic door, which had been slowly draining my own strength, Gryme patrols the stairs. Strangely, I've developed a fondness for Gryme since he dissolved and ate three thieves who arrived on the island late one evening and descended the stairs with the intent of robbing and killing me. It was then I learned Gryme could spit harsh acid. Of course, the three thieves were unfortunate during that discovery.

Roble shook his head. "Great, I killed his pet."

"You had no knowledge of that," Lehrling said with a deep chuckle. "None of us did. To it, we were enemies, trespassers."

"When we find Geowren, let's not mention that to him," Roble said.

Lehrling cocked a brow and chuckled. "It'll be our secret."

"How did he capture Vyssisk?" Shawndirea said.

"He doesn't say, and the rest written here is brief. This might have been the last entry he wrote before he left the island. Gryme remained behind to protect this cellar." Lehrling paused for a moment and frowned. "Yet, it makes no sense why he left his prized dagger on the table."

"Perhaps he left in a hurry?" Roble asked.

"He must have," Lehrling said. "But if Gryme was guarding the stairwell, *what* did Geowren flee from? How did he escape the island so quickly?"

A blue flash brightened the far end of the cellar.

They turned in the direction of the light.

"What was that?" Roble asked, sliding daggers from the hidden sheaths in his belt.

The light faded.

Roble crept along the edge of the wall toward the spot. The light shown again.

Lehrling pulled his sword. "Be wary, Roble."

"Yes," Shawndirea said. "Don't forget this was a wizard's lair. Old spells might still be hanging. The last thing you want to do is trigger one of them."

"I understand," Roble replied. "But the source of the light is perhaps an answer to a lot of our questions."

CHAPTER 19

*R*oble slipped alongside the wall holding his daggers to his sides. His silent footsteps would have impressed Aetheaon's greatest thief, Crukas. Only a ghost walked more quietly.

The light flickered dull blue but revealed something Roble would've never noticed without its illumination.

The wall he walked along didn't actually meet the other wall. Instead, a gap used as a doorway stood in-between. The unusual construction was an optical illusion. Looking dead on, the eye projected the two walls meeting, but physically, the corner didn't exist. For all they knew, the wizard or Geowren might have been watching them without their knowledge.

The light shown from the short adjoining narrow hallway, which happened to be a dead end.

Roble eased closer and then moved cautiously to the other wall so he could look into the hidden passageway. A magical blue oval, every bit Roble's height, shimmered and rippled like a vivid wall of water. But this wasn't water. It was a magical doorway, a portal. And the wave sensations swirling within the oval were mesmerizing.

"What is this?" Roble asked, amid his guess that it was a gateway.

"A magic portal," Shawndirea said. "It's capable of teleporting you to another place or city."

Lehrling sheathed his sword. He approached the portal with eagerness. "Geowren must have escaped through here."

"Perhaps," she said.

Roble grinned. "Then let's see where he went."

"No," Shawndirea said, shaking her head. "That's not a safe thing to do. We've no idea what's on the other side or where it will take us."

"But if Geowren took it—" Lehrling said.

"What if *he* didn't," she said. "What if the wizard he held prisoner somehow got free and took Geowren prisoner? This portal could lead to a hostile city where we'd be taken prisoner or worse, killed."

Roble sighed. He ached to know where the portal led. But rather than press the argument to enter in order to satisfy his curiosity about what was on the other side, he chose not to argue the matter. Shawndirea was already angry enough with his recent rash decisions, and her anger had somewhat subsided since her intrigue was captured by the magic tomes and scrolls. To go against her warning of the portal's possible dangers would be a dozen steps back. No sense ruining a bit of progress for being able to destroy the ooze beast.

Clasping a hand on Lehrling's shoulder, Roble said, "She's right, Lehrling. I want to know where this leads as much as you, but what if it's a one-way passage? Our horses are tethered above. We cannot leave them to starve."

Lehrling ran his hands through his hair and groaned. "I agree, but oh, we've learned so much this day. We're so close to finding King Erik. We can't dismiss this opportunity entirely."

"We're not," Roble said. "But view all this information as hope revitalized. Hope renewed. Who knows? Lez'minx might have answers to some of our questions."

"I wouldn't put faith into that," Shawndirea said with a narrowed brow.

"It's not faith," Roble said. "Perhaps I can barter."

"What more can you offer? He already holds his gifts over your head," she said.

"Everyone wants something," Roble said. "Meanwhile, let's gather together some of these wares, scrolls, and old spell books. I see a woodcutting axe in the corner, which looks better than the one I had to snap to make the spear handle. Geowren's not in any hurry to use them, if he ever bothers to return at all. Do you see anything useful, Shawndirea?"

She nodded and grinned. "Much."

AFTER SEVERAL HOURS of sorting through the scrolls, books, and bottled potions Geowren had left on the table, Roble and Lehrling gathered up armsful of the items to store in their saddlebags. Since most were useful for magic, and Shawndirea expressed a direct need for some items, they needed to protect the parchments from the heavy rains after they departed Polderholm.

Shawndirea found a cloak that had been flung over a chair. She sensed an enchantment upon it, but the true nature of the protective spell she couldn't discern. But the cloak's composition of meshed green leaves was waxy and after pouring water over it, the material proved to be waterproof.

They wrapped the paper scrolls and books inside the cloak and tucked them inside Roble's saddlebag. Roble tied the woodcutting axe between his saddle and the bags. Lehrling placed Geowren's dagger into his belt sheath with a sense of pride.

After Roble and Lehrling climbed onto their saddles, Roble said, "We didn't get any rest, but it's best we leave this island before the chance something might come through the portal."

Lehrling nodded in agreement.

CHAPTER 20

*A*fter two days of endlessly riding the faint remnants of a road covered by shallow water and thickening muck, they had not found any towns, hamlets, or ruins. They encountered only one fork in the road almost a day earlier. Roble took the path to the right because his armor tugged that direction, indicating they should follow the path. Although making such a decision based upon that drawing impulse was odd, Roble trusted the sensation, believing their journey would be somehow fulfilled on that pathway. And even now, the enchantment surrounding his armor encouraged him to continue down the path before them.

With the scenery seldom changing, Roble wondered at times if they were simply lost and traveling in a circle. And if not, they were exploring deep inside Woodnog's Swamps. The only prolonged certainty in the journey was the constant rain, drab fog, and the eerie feeling of being watched from the shadowy trees. Whether those eyes belonged to wild beasts, Shadowfae, or ghosts doomed to wander the swamps, none of them knew. Pressing forward remained their only option until they found a town or reached a seaport where they could set sail to Hoffnung or Oculoth. Traveling back through the swamps to Woodnog was too dangerous.

No fresh hooves or boot prints disturbed the trail. Given how the terrain worsened the deeper into the swamps they rode, Roble was not surprised.

Shawndirea's mood switched between being pleasant but without any forewarning, she seethed suddenly into fearful, heated anger. He figured her rage came because he was the reason for their journey. He didn't blame her for the outbursts because silently he berated himself for not having turned back days earlier.

The cold rain dripped from the leaves and fir needles that meshed together to form a natural leaking ceiling. Cascading raindrops pelleted the rising dark waters. Brilliantly colored snakes, unlike any Roble recognized in the Overlands, slithered away from the path. Whether poisonous or not was left to be determined, but he didn't intend to find out.

The howling wind shook long flowing curtains of wet moss that resembled Spanish Moss, as the darkness of another approaching night slowly greeted them.

How much more misery must we endure? Roble thought.

Roble cast a side-glance at Lehrling. His poor companion was drenched, and even with a blanket pulled over his head, Lehrling was unable to escape the rain. Chilled, and perhaps achingly cold, Lehrling's lower lip trembled and occasionally he hugged himself, shaking. His body involuntarily fought to warm itself without much success.

The sun had not blessed them with its presence since they entered the swamp and with nightfall, the dangerous cold weather would bite Lehrling more viciously.

Wearing Bausch's enchanted armor, Roble and Shawndirea were dry and unaffected by the weather. Unless they found a shelter from the rain where they could light a fire, Roble feared Lehrling might soon suffer hypothermia or succumb to pneumonia and die. Despite the weather, Lehrling had not complained. Surprisingly, he remained awake and had not fallen from his horse due to lack of sleep and the exposure of the unforgiving climate. Even highwaymen were not so foolish as to expect travelers here.

"How are you faring?" Roble shouted over the loud drumming, heavy rain striking the broadleaved branches overhead.

"I—I'm o—ka—y," Lehrling said, forcing a smile. His head bobbled. His jaw quivered and his fatigued eyes pleaded for sleep.

"No need to lie, Lehrling," Roble said. "I keep hoping we'll find shelter."

"As do I," Lehrling said, holding the soaked blanket tightened beneath his chin. "Now, do you under ... st—stand why folks who enter these swamps seldom return?"

"You couldn't have painted me a clearer picture, my friend!"

Lehrling pointed ahead at a thicker set of trees. The grove was the beginning of a forest that might offer shelter, but where the rains still plummeted. "We press on through there!"

Roble steered his horse closer to Lehrling. "Regardless of what's in those trees—dangers or monsters or predators—we're stopping for the night. We have to get you out of this rain."

"We can't stop," Lehrling said wearily. His eyes grew more tired and his face paled. "Not here. We're easy targets."

"We've ridden constant through two and a half days of rain. It's not going to let up," Roble said. "We stop at the first rise of ground where water isn't pooling. You cannot keep going through this down-pouring rain without sleep."

Anger stirred in Lehrling's eyes. The paleness of his face reddened and spittle flew from his lips. "Damn the rains! I'm not helpless!"

"No, you're not," Roble said, shaking his head. "You're one of the strongest men I've been blessed to call my friend. But we all need a fire for warmth, some food, and lots of sleep."

"Good luck lighting a fire in this blasted rain!" Lehrling glared at the forest canopy. "Nothing's dry enough to start a fire."

"We'll find a way," Roble said. "Perhaps Shawndirea could use her magic—"

"I'm envious of her," he replied. "All warm and dry, curled inside your pocket. Must be nice not facing the wrath of these cursed elements."

Roble simply nodded. He ached inside because of Lehrling's suffering. "We'll find some way to light a fire. I promise. We must sleep. Otherwise, our minds become our enemies, making us delusional by seeing things that aren't there. We've enough danger without adding more of our own."

"Agreed! But tell me, Overlander, do you still desire to explore these wonderful swamplands? Perhaps you could buy a parcel of land to settle?"

Roble grinned and shook his head. "No thanks. As for further exploration, I've no particular want to see more. I've had a drastic change of heart."

"Then you've grown wiser than you appear," Lehrling said with a quick wink. "Of course, looks cannot be trusted in the absence of light."

Roble laughed. *Good. Keep him talking. He jokes, so he's trying to keep his mind off their current situation.*

"My apologies for my temper," Lehrling said after several moments. "I've—"

"You've no reason to apologize," Roble said.

Lightning flashed, exposing the watery floor beneath the slick dark trees. Pools of water broke apart, forming meandering streams that flowed around fallen trees, mossy rocks, and wicked shrubs that looked like hunched creatures ready to charge and pounce. Another bolt of lightning zagged above the canopy. Heavy thunder rumbled its unforgiving wrath.

In the flash of brightness of the heated light, Roble studied the shrubs. He was more than certain one of them was a creature and not a plant. The horses blew air through their nostrils and stamped their front feet, fearful of moving ahead. Roble patted the side of his horse's neck and coaxed the horse forward.

"Easy, Bleys," he said. "What's troubling you?"

Shawndirea stood inside Roble's pocket and stretched, releasing a long yawn.

"At least *one* of us is getting some sleep," Lehrling said with a tinge of bitterness. "You've slumbered in warmth for hours now."

She frowned and glanced at Roble. "Is this true? Have I slept that long?"

"It's been awhile," he replied.

"My apologies," she said.

"None needed," Roble said.

Lehrling grumbled beneath his breath.

Roble said to Shawndirea, "It just means that you'll keep first watch when we set up camp."

"Here?"

Roble sighed. "No other places have been suitable."

"You call this *suitable?*" she said.

He shrugged. "At least the trees are thicker."

"So we've still not found a town? Not even an abandoned settlement?"

"We'd have stopped if we'd found such a place," Roble said. "But no sign of humans, Elves, Dwarves, or any other races. No fresh tracks in the mud, either."

Shawndirea sighed. "I know you would've stopped. I simply find it ... odd ... that no settlements are here."

More lightning flickered, illuminating the forest. The outline of an old shack became visible, but only for that moment. Under the next brief flicker of lightning, the shack was no longer there.

Roble rubbed his tired eyes. "I could've sworn—"

"I saw the old hut, too," Lehrling said. "I swear I did."

"Yes, it was there," Shawndirea whispered.

What remained of the dusk-like light was gone, replaced by a deep, thick blackness. Glowing eyes blinked around various fallen trees, crevices, and on low-lying branches. Enchanted was the last word he'd use to describe the forest that snared his mind with horror unlike anything Roble had witnessed since he entered the Black Chasm. Death floated through the trees and he hoped their paths didn't cross."

Wind rustled through the strange trees. The smell of death and decaying leaves wrought an acrid bite when they inhaled.

"I hate to tell you this," Shawndirea said. "But we cannot stop in these woods for the night. Not if we expect to live until morning."

"The same thought has occurred to me, too, but we're too exhausted to continue," Roble whispered. "Lehrling cannot travel much farther or he'll collapse. We're already seeing things that aren't there."

"No," Shawndirea said. "We'd not all three have the same exact delusion. That's not possible."

"Then where's the old shack?"

"It's still there."

Lightning flashed.

She pointed. "See?"

Roble's armor tightened around him, squeezing like the greeting hug of a friend not seen in years. "We tie the horses and stay inside the shack for the night.

"That's not a good idea," she said.

"You have a better one? Because riding throughout the night is *not* an option."

Roble tapped his horse's flanks gently and directed it to the shack. He slid from the saddle and tied the horse to a post near the front porch. He hurried and helped Lehrling down from his saddle before tying his horse beside Bleys.

Roble took bold steps onto the porch. The boards creaked beneath his weight. No light shone through the cracks around the worn door or the boarded windows. At first, he didn't think anyone lived inside. Those doubts subsided when he raised his hand to knock and the door opened on its own. The hinges creaked.

"Welcome, guests," a frail voice said from inside. "Come in and rest yourselves from your travels. I've been waiting for you."

CHAPTER 21

*R*oble hesitated outside the door, contemplating whether to enter or not. None of them had touched the door. He hadn't *even* knocked. And yet, the door swung open without anyone standing inside the threshold. As best he could tell, no one stood behind or had *physically* pulled the door open.

"I'm afraid that I'm getting delusional, Lehrling," Roble said in a whisper.

"If you are, I'm already there," he replied.

Several oil lanterns hanging on the beams over the porch flickered to light, their wicks burned softly and then rose to sharp-tipped flames, casting white beams across them. Two large moths fluttered from the rafters and circled a lantern. The sudden light revealed a half dozen snakes coiled around the porch supports that they had walked under without ever noticing due to the darkness.

Wind rattled the hanging chimes that were fashioned from what might have been made from the finger bones of a human, Elf, or Dwarf. Perhaps these slender hollow bones were a combination of all three. This macabre decoration was another reason Roble agreed with Shawndirea's concern about entering this home. Going inside was probably not in their best interests but neither was traveling further in the cold rain. He was almost ready to turn around, but his armor nudged him closer to the door.

For the first time during his journey into the swamps, chills swept through his body, but not from the weather. His curiosity to look inside the old shack equaled his desire to turn and run. Nothing about the verbal greeting seemed threatening, but one could never read intention from a voice or even detect the possible deception in a gentle smile.

Stunned, Roble glanced toward Lehrling, expecting to see increased fear in the old man's eyes. Instead, Lehrling shook from the cold. Water dripped off his clothing and puddled around his boots. The soaked blanket on his shoulders slipped from his hold and dropped to the porch with a heavy splat. His longing for warmth crushed any fear he might have about entering the shack.

Roble knew Lehrling couldn't travel any longer. Not tonight. None of them could. Death might await them inside this rundown shack, but it most certainly did should they attempt to ride another night without sleep. He glanced at the side of the shack beyond the porch and pictured the lingering figure of Death smiling with his scythe in hand. Perhaps it was due to his lack of sleep, but he held no doubt that the mental illusion was no illusion at all. Death's silhouette was cloaked in the shadows.

Heat rushed through the open door and enveloped them with nurturing seductive comfort. The light of a fire flickered across the threshold as though a thick curtain had been cast aside, allowing the comfort of warmth and light to repel the uneasiness of the cold, empty darkness. Logs in the fireplace crackled. The rich aroma of fresh meaty stew made his mouth water. Roble's stomach growled.

His mind attempted to warn him of how prey becomes blinded to the lures of intelligent predators. However, hunger and exhaustion blocked any rationality. Even Shawndirea had not whispered a word since the door opened.

"Don't you know an invitation when you hear it?" the woman's crackling voice said. "Either come in or shut the door. You're letting precious heat out."

"Apologies," Lehrling said, without further hesitation. He stepped inside the door and waited for Roble to follow. "May I sit at your fire?"

"Ah, help yourself," she replied, waving her feeble hand in a sweeping gesture. "And if you drip water across my floor, clean it up."

Lehrling smiled eagerly and nodded.

The light of the fire only offered to reveal a faint outline of the woman's seated form near the center of the room.

"You?" she said, pointing a shaky finger at Roble. "My magic enchants your armor, but you're *not* the man who requested me to make it."

"No, I'm not," Roble replied. He leaned down, trying to see the woman's face, which was recessed into the shadows of her hood.

"Why do you wear his armor?"

"It's a long story."

She struck a match and touched it to a candle on the small table beside her rocking chair. As the candle's flame rose, she peeled back her hood. Her white blinded eyes peered at him, a ghastly sight, and he worried that staring too long might imprison his soul. Her eyes were horrifying to look at, and yet, he found it difficult to look away. It seemed by her actions—though she was blind—that she could still see. "Child, I've all the time in the world. Care to explain why you wear the armor I tailored and enchanted?"

Lehrling sat on the hearth as close to the flames as was possible. His body shook involuntarily. "You knew Bausch?"

The woman's neck craned slightly, and her attention turned to him. "Yes, he sought me to tailor this leather armor. I could've blessed it with almost any enchantment, but he suffered from a fever he contracted after traveling for days in the swamps searching for me. Like you, he was near freezing, near death, which is why he begged for armor that adapted to the climate."

"Who are you?" Lehrling asked.

"Moorsis." She turned her attention back to Roble. "I assume Bausch is dead? Otherwise, he'd still be wearing this?"

"Yes."

Moorsis shook her head slightly and cackled. "I told him to pay homage to Lez'minx for allowing me to bestow the enchantment upon the armor. I suppose he chose not to. As I had told him, magic comes at a price. It's never free. Fool that he was, he didn't believe me, and the price he paid was his life."

Lehrling removed his gloves and placed his cold shriveled hands closer to the fire. His skin was almost blue. "He never told me about any of this, about you, or how he had gotten the armor, though I had asked."

"And yet," she said, "you're all here?"

"Yes."

Moorsis smiled. "I sense other magic in the room. Fae magic? Yes, a faery. Am I right?"

Shawndirea cleared her throat. "Yes."

A sneer tightened the old woman's wrinkled lips. "Odd that you've paired yourself with a human mate. An Overlander, too."

Shawndirea's eyes widened. She gave Roble an uncomfortable glance.

Moorsis smiled. "Yes, I see far more than my physical eyes could have ever gifted me with vision."

Roble's stomach growled.

"Young man," Moorsis said, "stew boils over the fire. You and yours help yourself. Indeed the night will be long, and you need a place to rest. The storms will not pass for weeks yet."

"What is the cost?" Roble asked.

A wicked smile crooked across her face. "You have a great deal of wisdom at such a young age."

Roble wasn't sure about how to take the compliment. It wasn't about wisdom but more about politeness in how he was raised. One should never assume hospitality, as accepting someone's offer—like the rings he now wore —indebted a person, and he'd already made that mistake. He didn't want to oblige himself further to anyone else. "I don't know about young, but—"

"The stew is free. You owe no debt to me. Since Bausch never paid homage for that armor, the duty now falls upon you. I'm sure you're aware of that. Otherwise, you'd not have journeyed so deep into these grim swamps. Lez'minx has made certain you'd seek him out since you wear his rings."

Roble grabbed a crude wooden bowl. Dipping the ladle into the stew, he filled the bowl and handed it to Lehrling, who nodded with eager appreciation. Roble filled another bowl for he and Shawndirea to share.

"Yes," Roble said. "I was foolish to wear them, as now I cannot pull them off."

Moorsis howled with laughter that sounded painful as it crawled up her throat and exited her feeble lips. "Often, it's the subtle things that snare the innocent. But no matter, you must pay homage for the armor."

"I never requested the armor to be made," Roble said. "I never asked for your enchantment upon it, either, so I don't understand how—"

"Doesn't matter," she replied. "You wear it. Your ignorance of the enchantment doesn't excuse the cost. It shouldn't have taken long to discover its unique attributes. Learning that, you still have chosen *not* to discard it, which means you have accepted it as your own, does it not?"

Roble sighed. "It does."

"And for the blessing, you must pay the price."

Roble cupped the hot bowl in his hands and sipped the rich broth from the side of it. "What's the price exactly? Does accepting the rings and the armor constitute me to be his servant?"

She leaned back in the rocking chair. Her brow narrowed. "That, my child, is between you and Lez'minx. I only fashioned the armor, as is my skill. The armor itself, is not Lez'minx's, but the enchantment *is*. He has blessed it in favor of the one who wears it."

"So if I abandon the armor, I'm free from this obligation?"

Moorsis shook his head. "No, not now. You've worn it for too long. You've imprinted yourself to it, and it has molded to you. In its own way, the armor understands you. It must bind to you to constantly maintain your comfort no matter the climate. Do you understand this?"

"Yes," Roble said. "I followed its impulses to find you. But I thought it was leading us to Lez'minx's temple."

She smiled. "You're only a day or more's journey from him. Getting there is easy, but leaving … that's yet to be determined. But I must warn the faery, the spell she used to tarnish the rings, to block Lez'minx's magic and his sight, has angered him. I suggest she remove it before you depart in the morning. Or your meeting with Lez'minx will not end well."

"He's no right to invade our privacy," Shawndirea said.

"He has every right," Moorsis replied. "Since the rings are his and his magic is on them, he can view their surroundings to know their whereabouts and retrieve them whenever he chooses. They do not belong to your husband.

The bearer has granted Lez'minx access to every conversation and every action after the time they're worn."

A look of horror and contempt washed across Shawndirea's face. "What? How dare Lez'minx partake such a vile abomination with his magic!"

Moorsis stiffened in her chair at the venom spewing in Shawndirea's voice.

Fury set in Shawndirea's eyes. "Regardless of Roble wearing these rings, Lez'minx has forever violated my trust. Nothing he ever says could lessen my disdain toward him."

"Careful, faery," Moorsis said softly. "Be careful of the insults you lash toward him."

"Why?" she asked. "How do *you* perceive his pretentiousness? Or are you merely an envious pawn mesmerized by his power?"

The elderly woman took a sharp breath. Anger stirred in her strange white eyes. Her bony hands clenched the arms of her rocker tightly and her mouth narrowed.

Lehrling sat stunned. He lowered his empty bowl onto his lap. His eyes flicked from Shawndirea to Moorsis before he finally glanced at Roble.

Silence filled the room. A greenish tint encircled Shawndirea and Roble realized she was moments from casting a harsh spell of her own. He had witnessed her full fury a few times, and the outcomes had been devastating. But he understood her anger and it was his own doing. The rings had given Lez'minx direct access to spy on their activities, which was the last thing Roble would've considered.

Roble's grandfather spent his life as a trapper in the Overlands. Because of his pastime, Roble always pictured snares in the physical sense. But now, he must factor in the unseen things, such as magic, ghosts, and deities.

He stared uneasily at Shawndirea and then watched Moorsis. The old woman had not moved. He doubted she'd even taken a single breath. Was she mortified by Shawndirea's confrontation or was her silence buying her time? He became more uncomfortable. Did she possess direct access to communicate with Lez'minx and was awaiting his directives?

Before Moorsis answered or reacted, Shawndirea said, "Is he a god, as he wishes us to believe?"

"Silence!" Moorsis said, bolting forward and pushing herself to her feet. She staggered to gain her balance. Spittle frothed at the sides of her mouth. It was difficult to tell if lunacy had taken hold of her or if she was possessed by Lez'minx. The tone was no longer that of a generous elderly woman who politely welcomed them upon their arrival.

Anger flared in Shawndirea's eyes. Green orbs of energy encircled her hands. Her eyes narrowed and she readied her hands to release the magical bolts at Moorsis. "Don't try to silence *me*! I've bitten my tongue throughout this entire journey, but learning that Lez'minx has spied on us for the past several weeks has awakened an inner rage like I've never felt before. Now, answer me! Is he a god?"

"Don't threaten me," Moorsis said, tilting her head back and raising her hands above her head.

"You're an enchanter," Shawndirea said. "I'm not. I was *born* with my magic. You were not. You're nothing more than a vessel Lez'minx tinkers with. My magic is far more powerful than yours, a hundred times greater, so unless you're ready to experience it firsthand and become a bag of powered bones, my advice is for you to sit down and answer me."

Roble took several steps backwards, unaware that he had even moved. He had never seen Shawndirea enraged to this degree. She was never one to boast of her power and openly threaten to kill with her magic. The thought shocked him, as she always insisted her magic only worked to heal. Was she bluffing? The narrowness of her eyes and her furrowed brow indicated she wasn't making an idle threat.

He understood her anger, the feeling of betrayal by Lez'minx's visual spying and eavesdropping, because the same emotions and anger flowed through him. His mind had been backtracking the things he might have freely said about Lez'minx when he was unaware of Lez'minx's spying. During this time, Roble and Shawndirea had discussed their future, been intimate frequently, and unknown to them, Lez'minx was been an unseen presence in their company.

Moorsis reached inside her robe and formed a fist. She held something tightly.

"Sit!" Shawndirea said.

Perplexed, Moorsis plopped down in her rocker. Her mouth hung open but she offered no words. With an old piece of cloth, she wiped spittle from the sides of her mouth. Her complexion paled and she appeared ill. In short, she looked defeated. With a weak voice, she said, "You're right. It was foolish of me to challenge an Unseelie."

"I'm not Unseelie," Shawndirea seethed.

"Have you deceived yourself, faery? You're every bit Unseelie. Darkened rage controls you. You're married to an Overlander human. Those attributes make you an Unseelie."

Shawndirea lighted upon the floor, looking at the flickering green orbs of energy glowing on her hands. When she realized the degree of her anger and the power surging through her, the orbs shrank and vanished. She gathered her composure, looked at Roble and Lez'minx, and said, "Lez'minx is not a god, and I can tell you why."

CHAPTER 22

*R*oble watched Shawndirea with genuine concern. She looked confused minutes after he expected her to assault or kill Moorsis. Shawndirea seemed to become more unhinged the further they traveled into the swamps. He wanted to help her, but he didn't know how.

"Do you wish to know why he *isn't* a god?" Shawndirea asked.

Moorsis turned in the direction of Shawndirea's voice. "You know not what you speak, faery."

"I should have recognized it much earlier," Shawndirea said, "but he's not a god, Moorsis. Otherwise, he'd have no need to spy upon us through those rings. He'd know our actions and our location without the use magic-eye portals through inanimate objects. He's a deceiver, projecting magic to heighten the *illusion* of his power. Deep inside, you know this to be true."

Moorsis lowered her head. Tears leaked down the cheeks.

Shawndirea softened her voice. "I perceive you worship him because of your physical blindness. He's made a pact with you, hasn't he?"

Moorsis sat in silence for several moments before offering a slight nod. Her shoulders slumped.

"In return for your adoration, he gifts divination to you. But he requires you to beguile and proselyte others, deceptively forcing them to venture to Lez'minx's temple to offer their homage. Whatever enchantments they receive are not free."

"Magic is never free," Moorsis mumbled. Her body drew into itself even more, as if she wished to vanish.

"No, it isn't. But the price comes to those who choose to channel and wield it. What you don't tell those who have sought you is that if ever they change their minds—"

"No, that's not true," Moorsis said with a narrow brow. She leaned back in her chair, formed a bridge with her slender hands, and rested her chin upon them. Tears rolled freely down her cheeks. Sadness filled her voice. "I sternly warned Bausch about the repercussions. I've warned others, too, but with Bausch, I was more particular."

"Why more for him than the others?" Lehrling said, setting his bowl down and rising from the hearth.

Moorsis leaned forward and lowered her head. Roble couldn't tell if it were from shame or if she was sorting through the proper words to explain. She clasped her hands together, around an object, which made him even more wary. He slid a hand onto the hilt of a throwing knife.

"Bausch was like a son to me," Lehrling said. "Tell me."

Moorsis sighed and wrung her wrinkled, veiny hands together while clinging to the object. "He had a gentleness I've never seen from the others who came with their selfish requests. An honesty. He offered to help with things around my cottage while I busied myself tailoring his armor. Understand, that when I finished the armor and he took it, I wanted to give it to him without requiring him to pay homage. His soul contained a pureness, and I—I was the one who blemished it."

Lehrling wiped tears from his eyes.

Shawndirea cocked her head to the side. "While I believe most of that to be the truth, Moorsis, you're not telling us everything. Reveal it now and redeem a bit of your soul."

"What else?" Lehrling asked.

Moorsis' hands shook. "Lez'minx wanted Bausch in particular because he was a Dragon Skull Knight loyally serving Queen Taube. Lez'minx had cast the fever upon Bausch, making him so ill that he craved healing and became even more desperate to find me. When he arrived at my cottage, I looked into his soul and saw his pure innocence. I didn't want to make the armor, knowing the price he'd suffer. I wanted to shoo him away, scare him into running, but doing so would've sealed his death anyway, due to his fever. Lez'minx insisted I tailor the armor. I did, but not because he commanded it. I was overcome with compassion for Bausch due to his constant chills. He was hours from death when he arrived. Much like you tonight, knight."

Roble frowned. "Why was it important that Bausch was a Dragon Skull Knight and what did it have to do with this?"

"Lez'minx has many vessels he works through in Aetheaon."

"Like you," Shawndirea said.

"Yes, faery," Moorsis replied. She tightened her hands in a prayer-like fashion near her heart. "*Like me*. He has spies under his control in every major city. Some are princes that have sought great wealth and power and vie to obtain their father's or mother's throne, even if it requires overthrowing their own flesh and blood. Lez'minx wanted Dragon Skull Knights subjected to him because he hoped to eventually find where the great dragons were hidden. That's his true ambition. To control a dragon to do his bidding. Since Dragon Skull Knights are in allegiance with the dragons, he must make at least one subservient to him."

Roble exchanged a worried glance with Lehrling.

"So this guise was intended for that purpose?" Lehrling asked, placing his hand upon the hilt of his sword. "For Lez'minx to infiltrate our order to take the reins of a dragon?"

"Yes," Moorsis said, sadly shaking her head. "Kill me if you must, knight, as I have betrayed your Order and Hoffnung's throne."

Lehrling drew his sword. His eyes narrowed. He sensed something not right, apparently, so Roble slid a dagger from his belt.

"You don't get pardoned so easily," Shawndirea said. "You must atone for your atrocities."

Moorsis sighed. She unclasped her hands, which revealed the pendant she had been holding. Thunder rumbled outside. The winds rattled the rafters, and the room grew colder. The candles flickered but never extinguished. A rush of air expelled from the fireplace. The old woman smiled. "That seems fair. What do you require of me?"

"Some answers."

"Such as?"

Shawndirea glided into the air, closer to Moorsis, and whispered, "Is Lez'minx able to hear and see us right now?"

"Get away from her, Shawndirea!" Roble said.

Moorsis grinned madly and nodded. "He's been here the entire time, my dear."

Shawndirea glanced nervously around the room. "Where is he? Through what has he been watching?"

The old woman gripped the object she'd been hiding in her hands and revealed the emerald pendant she wore on a silver necklace. "Through this."

Roble frowned. "He's been listening to us the entire time?"

"Fools!" Moorsis shouted, rising with deep laughter and rabid madness. Energy flowed around her and shot from her fingers.

Her face glowed with boldness and her voice was not her own. Roble recognized the voice from when Lez'minx had demanded Roble find his temple and offered the magical rings to him.

The whites of Moorsis' eyes became blacker than ink. "You think you have more power than I? Meet your deaths this night!"

CHAPTER 23

*R*oble scrambled and rolled on the floor before the wave of energy that rushed from the old woman's hand knocked him against the closed door. Shawndirea swooped and landed inside Moorsis' hood that hung down the old woman's back. Lehrling flung over the sewing table, drew his short sword, and dropped behind the table. With wide eyes, he tried to peek around the edge.

The room shook fiercely as though the walls buckled and the roof was collapsing. The destructive force was not from the storm. The unleashed power was not hers. Lez'minx was working through her. Roble wasn't sure why he understood this, except that Moorsis seemed helpless as she visibly resisted his control.

Her contorted body was outstretched like an X, and she levitated several inches off the floor. The magnitude of Lez'minx's power flowing through her caused the veins in her face to swell. Her blind eyes were like black saucers that led to an eternal abyss. She was helpless, groaning, and her bones crackled. Roble found himself having pity for her. Gurgling sounds rumbled in her throat. He doubted she had any control left over what was happening. If her body was strained any further, Roble feared she'd be torn apart.

"Where are you, faery?" the voice boomed deeply from Moorsis' mouth like channeled from a chief demon in Hell. "Test your magic against mine now if you think me less than a god, faery. I will turn *you* to dust."

Moorsis jerked and her fingers spread wide. Though she couldn't physically see and because of his control over her, she was unable to voice her pain. Sadly, Roble realized that death was better for her than this unnecessary torture and he hated to be the one to give her such mercy. He readied his dagger.

"I've given you my protection, Roble, and this faery of yours only hinders what you can become. Follow the swamp path northeast of this cottage, and in the better part of two days, you will reach my temple. I offer truce and compassion for when you find me, and I will spare the faery, if you vow to—"

Roble rose to his feet and flicked a dagger directly for Moorsis' heart, but instead the blade shattered the glowing emerald held by the prongs of the pendant. The blade deflected, missing its true mark. Shards of the emerald ricocheted off the floor, the ceiling, and the walls.

Moorsis wailed, dropped face first to the floor, and clenched the necklace tightly in her wrinkled fingers. She yanked it from her neck, tossing it across the room. Gasping for air, her blackened eyes gradually returned to their milky white, as what Lez'minx's power over her vanished. Profuse sweat beaded her face. Involuntary groans came with each labored breath she took. She writhed on the floor.

Shawndirea flew from the woman's hood and rose with green flames covering her hands, ready to end the old woman's life. Roble waved his hand to catch Shawndirea's attention and then he shook his head. With the emerald destroyed, her link to Lez'minx was gone. Moorsis aged quickly and was more feeble than before, devoid of her spirit and soul. She resembled one of the undead. A breathing corpse.

"You ... freed me," Moorsis said weakly. "I bid you ... my thanks."

Even though Roble was ashamed for attempting a deathblow with his dagger, he readied a second dagger, not fully certain Lez'minx had fully released her or that other possessed vessels might burst through the door to attack.

"In return for freeing me, ask ... what you will ... but," she said, "ask now. My body grows weaker. Without his pendant, my life ends soon."

Shawndirea cautiously circled Moorsis so she could see her face. "Is Lez'minx immortal or not?"

Moorsis' hands pressed the floor, allowing her to look up, as if trying to see Shawndirea through her blind eyes. Her voice was weak. "Honestly, faery, I don't know. For many years, he led me to believe he was a god. The blessings he bestowed to me convinced me in part. The abilities he granted me, thrilled me. He found me after I had crawled into the Kryptas Cemetery. I was dying, perhaps breathing my last. I sought to die where my husband rested."

"Did you see Lez'minx or were you already blind?" Shawndirea asked.

"The disease I suffered, which was the same as my late husband's, had blinded me by the time I reached his grave." She coughed harshly. Her body spasmed for several moments before she continued. "No, I never saw him. But he helped me to my feet after expelling the disease from my body."

Blood leaked from her mouth. She lowered her head against the floor and took ragged breaths.

"So you don't know if he's a demigod, or merely a mage or wizard who flatters himself unwittingly to think others should bow before him like meager peasants?" Shawndirea asked. "Tell us, please. We've been trying to sort this out for weeks now."

"How could I possibly know? I've told you the events for how he entered my life," she said softly. Her breathing rasped. She balled her hands into loose fists. If she lived much longer, it'd be a miracle.

"Has he visited you in person since the cemetery?" Roble asked.

"No. Not since he gave me the amulet you destroyed."

"That's how he kept communication with you?" Shawndirea asked.

"Yes. As long as I wore it, he promised I'd never die."

Roble approached her, still holding his dagger. "Does he have any weaknesses?"

"I do not know," Moorsis replied softly. "I'm sorry I cannot be of more help."

"It's okay," Roble said.

Shawndirea nodded. "What little you've told us is helpful."

"My biggest regret for accepting Lez'minx's gift of a longer life is that I didn't die to be buried beside my husband." With those words, Moorsis took her last breath.

Roble knelt beside her, checked for a pulse, and shook his head. "She's dead."

Lehrling sheathed his sword. "Now what?"

"We get some sleep," Roble said, slowly standing.

"After all of this? Surely you jest. How can any of us possibly sleep?" Lehrling said.

Roble gave a quick smile. Color had returned to Lehrling's face and his chills had subsided. The fire and hot stew helped, but his tired eyes and fatigue were still evident.

Lehrling returned the smile, shook his head, and placed more dry wood upon the fire.

"I'll place a protective barrier around the cottage, and I'll keep watch while the two of you sleep," Shawndirea said.

CHAPTER 24

*R*oble awakened the following morning feeling more rested than he had in days. Shawndirea sat atop his stomach with her knees hugged against her chest as she watched the door. Her intense focus indicated her thoughts about other matters were more pressing than any fear of what might attempt to break through her magical barrier.

Lehrling snored loudly, closer to the fire, and Roble wondered how he had slept through the grizzly bear raucous Lehrling displayed. Despite Lehrling's opposition to sleep after Lez'minx's confrontation and Moorsis' death, he was the first to fall asleep.

"What's troubling you?" Roble said.

Shawndirea stiffened at his whisper. Without turning, she said, "You're awake?"

"Or this is an odd dream."

She turned with a half grin and shook her head. "Nothing that's occurred since we entered the swamp has been a dream."

"I know, but something's bothering you. You've a lot on your mind that you've kept bottled up inside. Do you mind telling me?"

"Later," she said. "There's much to be done today."

"I agree, but if these things on your mind are a hindrance, we're about to enter unknown territory where distractions can get us killed. So, please?"

Her lips twisted in an usual way, which he found incredibly beautiful. "The things I need to discuss you have no knowledge of, so telling you doesn't remove my anxiety."

"Doesn't hurt to ask, now does it?" Roble grinned.

"Thrice, I've been accused of being Unseelie," she replied.

"Which is hurtful to you?" Roble clasped his hands together behind his head.

She nodded. "It's horrifying."

"Why?"

Shawndirea pursed her lips. "It means I've abandoned the traditions of my family. I'm no longer fit to abide in my mother's kingdom. I fear whenever we have children of what they might be or become."

"I don't understand."

"See?" she said. "That's why I need to consult other Fae who can properly discern whether it's true or not."

"I understand that, but what do you mean about our children in the future?"

"They will be Unseelie, regardless, as they are not pure Fae. They will not be welcome in Elvendale."

"Your mother is—"

Shawndirea shook her head. "This has nothing to do with her. This is outside of her control, even if she chose to lovingly accept our children. In a sense I've been exiled, but my mother has never openly suggested or commanded it. There are two courts. The Seelie and Unseelie. The path I've chosen has altered my future greatly."

Roble didn't like the idea that their children would be considered outcasts by Shawndirea's immediate family. They'd be descendants of Elvendale's monarchy but held no future right to the throne. No one likes to be shunned. He wondered how that might affect them as they matured.

He sighed. "Because of me your life has grown worse? So, now you regret ... *us?*"

"No!" she whispered harshly, shaking her head. "I treasure what we have. I love and need you always. Your determination to ensure I got back to Elvendale from the Overlands proved you'd risk everything to protect me. Had your friend been the one that had captured me ... I'd be dead."

"Deiko wasn't my friend."

"That's beside the point. You revealed to me your heart, your love, and your devotion, which made me want to spend my life with you. However, I also understand the reason for my mother's fury over my decisions, and it's not simply because of you. It's due to the Courts, and while the Seelie Court won't tolerate my decision and will exile me, the Unseelie Court will embrace and cherish the thought at welcoming me into theirs."

"Why would your exile from Elvendale please the Unseelie?"

Shawndirea sighed. "Because I'm royalty who has chosen to break my allegiance to the Seelie. It sickens me to know they relish my mother's misery. The fact that Dirk has sought their help is all the more reason for why I don't want to associate with them. It's a bitter realization."

"You despise the Unseelie?"

"No, I don't despise them," she replied softly. "I just don't want to be identified as one of them, because I will never partake in their type of magic."

"If others consider you Unseelie, that doesn't mean that you're evil, does it?"

"It's how I'll be judged. For those who've known me since birth in Elvendale, yes. It pains me to say it, but their shunning of me will always cause me pain. You witnessed how my mother reacted that I had chosen you and rejected my claim to the throne."

"Yes. No need to remind me. And doing so has become a disadvantage."

"No, never."

Roble looked into her eyes. Reading her love for him melted his heart. But the last thing he wanted was for her to lose her nobility and the respect of Elvendale. Those were priceless. "Mind if I ask you something?"

"Sure."

"I've noticed a vast change in you since we began our journey to the temple. You've been a lot angrier and more vindictive. Do you mind explaining why? I mean, does it have to do with what you've explained?"

"Some of it does."

"But there's more?"

She nodded. "Things I don't wish to discuss yet."

"And what about Dirk?"

Her eyes narrowed and darkened. "What about him?"

"Is he the reason for your bitterness?"

"No more than usual."

"Do you regret that Lez'minx didn't kill him?" Roble asked.

"I considered it. I really did."

"I know."

"Really?"

Roble nodded. "I saw the hatred in your eyes as you stared at Dirk. I could tell you were struggling with the decision."

"That's why I didn't hastily reply," she said, "because Dirk would be dead, and I'd be indebted to Lez'minx. There are better ways to deal with Dirk."

"Such as?"

Shawndirea smiled. "My mother."

Roble chuckled and then winced, imagining the Istrell's wrath when she learned of the planned coup.

"It's not a laughing matter," she said.

"For what happens to Dirk, it is."

Shawndirea shook her head. "But it won't be for Feather. She'll be tried as a co-conspirator, which means her death, too. I love her like a sister, so I cannot allow that."

"Your mother would have her executed?"

"Yes. Poor Feather. She's not violent at all. Naive? Yes. But not violent. If she fully understood Dirk, she'd tell my mother."

"But why doesn't she tell Istrell now? What Dirk's plan is?" Roble asked.

"Feather probably doesn't believe he'd really attempt a coup. She tries to see the good in others, even when it doesn't exist. She's a blind, trusting soul to those who are evil and corrupt, believing they'll eventually change," Shawndirea replied. "If Feather's not protected, Dirk will likely kill her, too."

"What can you do?"

"I need to get her out of Elvendale. And since I've not officially been banished, I can find and tell her before it's too late, provided I'm able to do so."

"I'll gladly go with you."

She shook her head. "No, that might cause even more problems. With mother and all."

"I understand." Roble sighed. "Of all we've seen yesterday, I regret that we cannot move Moorsis to Kryptas Cemetery."

Shawndirea smiled. "That won't be a problem."

"What do you mean?"

"Look for yourself."

Roble glanced across the room to where Moorsis had died the night before. Her body was gone.

"What—"

She sighed. "The life Lez'minx had restored to her was not one of luxury. She was a tortured woman held under Lez'minx's control. There's no way to tell how long he kept her alive to do his bidding."

"Her body vanished?"

Shawndirea shook her head. "No. It crumbled to dust. She must have been a couple of centuries old. Once his spell was broken, her body suffered rapid decomposition. Her dust is in that jar on the table. The hardest part for us, provided you want to bury her remains near his, is finding the cemetery."

"She was a victim all these years?"

"She was."

Roble nodded. "I could tell she was reluctant in obeying Lez'minx during our battle last night, but she was too weak to fight him. I believe what she said about not wanting to make the armor for Bausch."

"I do, too."

Lehrling's snoring resounded with an extremely loud gurgling, causing him to cough harshly and awaken. He blinked and rolled to his side, coughing up phlegm. After clearing his throat, he smiled. "Good morning. I see we survived the night."

Shawndirea rose from Roble's chest and hovered while Roble eased up into a seated position. He rubbed his eyes and then pushed himself to his feet.

"We did," Roble said. "Now, let's see if we can survive the day."

CHAPTER 25

*A*fter they ate their fill of the bubbling stew over the fire, Roble extinguished the flames. He wanted to do more, like scrub out the pot for Moorsis, but since she was finally freed of Lez'minx's hold and found eternal rest—he hoped—he didn't see a need to tidy up.

Several candles flickered, casting an ominous array of shadows across the walls. He grabbed the bottle containing Moorsis' ashes off the table and walked to where Shawndirea hovered.

Shawndirea studied the spines of the dozen or so magic books tucked into a tiny bookshelf. She cocked her head to the side and puckered her lips while her mind raced.

"Find anything you wish to take?" he asked.

She grinned. "All of them."

Roble's brow rose.

Lehrling frowned with evident protest.

"Don't worry," she said with a giggle. "I know we don't have much room, but these books and scrolls are invaluable and rare. There's only a dozen of them. If they fall into the wrong hands—"

"We could set the cottage on fire," Roble said.

"What?" she asked, perplexed. "And attract more attention to ourselves?"

Roble shrugged. "We won't be here afterwards."

"It's possible the fire might not be enough to destroy them. Some spellbooks are protected by incantations of the owners."

"Whichever of these books you desire the most, I'm sure we can take those," Roble said. "We'd have room, wouldn't we, Lehrling?"

Lehrling huffed. "Not much, unless you wish to consider discarding what little food left in our packs. We gathered a great number of books and scrolls at Polderholm. Are you planning to become a wizard, faery?"

She leveled a frown at him. "Not at all. Anyone who practices magic has the potential to learn new spells, rituals, and potions. Sometimes the knowledge we learn from others' magic allows us to enhance our own spells to make them stronger and grant greater outcomes. Any information I glean is beneficial to us all."

"Some of these books favor dark magic," Lehrling noted. "Not for those who practice in the light."

"I know," she replied. "I was hoping to find something to remove Lez'minx's rings, and perhaps find a spell to protect us when we face Lez'minx."

"You believe she was that good at writing spells?" Lehrling asked.

Shawndirea shook her head. "These aren't her spells, but spells Lez'minx worked through her."

Lehrling pulled one book from the shelf and thumbed through it. "The writing is horrendously jumbled and overwritten in places."

She flicked a quick gaze at him and shook her head. "She was blind. What do you expect? She didn't write these down to read. She wrote them, most likely, as a means to record the actions she was required to undertake by Lez'minx's orders."

"Hmm." Lehrling tucked the book under his arm. "So, you don't think Lez'minx has any knowledge of these books?"

"That'd be my guess," she replied. "Lez'minx didn't dictate them. I think she wrote them from memory for others to find after her eventual death. Besides, he never healed her blindness, so he probably never suspected she kept notes of his incantations through her. Remember, she was a vessel he crafted his magic through."

"You think these books might teach you how to reverse his spells in some of these texts?" Roble asked.

Shawndirea nodded. "It's possible. Written spells reveal patterns a sorcerer follows for enchantments. Patterns are never one-way. One can discover ways to reverse a spell. Sometimes."

Lehrling grabbed two books. "We'll make them fit in our packs. But if we're only a day or so from his temple, you won't have time to read all these."

She grinned. "I read fast."

Roble shut the door behind them and stood on the creaky porch. Mold and assorted lichens formed odd patterns along the woodgrain and with the constant moisture, the boards were slick and treacherous. Oddly enough, the creaking of the boards when walked across didn't indicate their weakness. They simply yielded to the stress like a tree did to an extremely harsh wind. Bending allowed longevity.

Much like with humans, he thought. Adaptation and the willingness to bend to rough conditions had allowed Roble to survive crossing the veil from the Overlands into the Realms of Aetheaon. His open mind enabled him to formulate an understanding that everything seen on the surface wasn't necessarily the facts or the truth. Often, in Aetheaon, the underlying aspects came from things not visible, like magic.

Few scientists in his world could be swayed to accept things not provable by straightforward *physical* methods. What separated Roble from his colleagues was his undying curiosity. His innate ability to question *everything* rather than take a blind opposition to things that defied logic allowed his survival.

According to Lehrling and Shawndirea, the majority of humans from the Overlands lost their minds and died soon after crossing the rift. Their demise shouldn't be a small wonder. In a place where nightmares were real, their minds simply couldn't accept the facts, and rendered them incapable of adjusting. When minds couldn't cope ... death was the best solution rather than living in an alternate reality. A mind without hope caused one's body to die.

For some reason, Roble thought about Deiko. When Deiko tried to take

Shawndirea from him at gunpoint in the Overlands, his obsessed colleague was willing to kill him so he could reveal to the world his discovery of a faery. The man was a danger to himself and others. Now that Deiko knew the Fae existed, Roble wondered if the deranged scientist would continue his pursuit until he found a way past the veil into Aetheaon. Should he successfully do so, was Deiko able to survive such knowledge or would it destroy his already unstable mind?

"Are you ready to leave, Roble?" Lehrling asked.

The question jolted Roble, pulling him from his thoughts. "Yes, sorry."

The storms from the day before had subsided. The rain was replaced with a light mist that hung strangely in the air. The cool breeze brought with it the stagnant acrid smell from the gathered pools of swamp water. No longer did the threat of Death's presence await at the side of the shack like Roble had sensed the night before.

Crickets and frogs sang a constant melody that, in spite of the creepy element of the swamp, was quite pleasant. If only the chorus was all one had to go by, no one would fear the hidden dangers within the shadows. But he knew the deceptive true nature of the swamps.

Fog hovered like a yellowish-white veil, which obscured the surrounding trees, vines, and shrubs even more. Were they being watched? The fog made it impossible to see *what* might be watching them.

"We aren't alone," Shawndirea whispered, gliding from the porch and flying to the tied horses.

"I sensed that as well," Roble said.

Lehrling gave a nervous glance toward the fog-shadowed trees and rested his hand upon the hilt of his short sword.

"How long did we sleep?" Roble asked, untethering his horse.

"A long time," Lehrling said with a refreshed grin. His eyes were brighter than they had been in days. His complexion had regained their healthier tone. "It must have been. I've not felt this rested in months."

"But is it early morning or is night approaching? I can't tell," Roble said, scanning the trees.

"Does it matter?" Lehrling asked.

Roble shrugged.

Lehrling nodded and swung up on his saddle. "From what others have told me, the time of day is always a mystery in these swamps. Of course, nightfall itself is never a question. My guess is that it's midmorning. Not quite noon or the temperature would be much warmer."

"One aspect neither of you are taking into consideration is *where* we are," Shawndirea said. "It's not just the swamps that we've entered, but the deeper we go, the darker the forests and swamps become until we've reached the Unseelie territory."

"I take it that's bad?" Roble asked.

"Being as I'm from Elvendale? Yes, it's very bad, especially since I don't have an invitation."

"You need an invitation?" Lehrling asked.

"It's not *required*, but to remain on their good side, it's advisable," she replied.

"How do you know when you've crossed into Unseelie territory?" Roble pulled himself onto his saddle.

"Woodnog resides upon the last pure territory of the Seelie Courts as one travels south. The Elves of Woodnog are of the light and worship the day. Where we are now, at least from what I'm sensing, is the in-between. The tension between light and dark struggles. Magic from both sides languishes slightly, but that doesn't mean the magic from either side isn't any less deadly."

"Then what does it mean?" Roble asked. He tapped Bleys' flank, and the horse walked onto a narrow muddy path that cut through the trees. Roble looked over his shoulder to view the cottage one last time. It had vanished.

"Basically," Shawndirea said, "it's the enclave where the two Courts draw the line, a truce, so to speak. It's mutual ground where leaders from both sides can convene for whenever certain trespasses have occurred or skirmishes between the two Courts have arisen. As such, it prevents one party from entering the other's territory to seek retribution without fear of assassination."

Roble said, "Isn't that still risky? One ruler could send an assassin instead."

"Both sides generally send diplomatic envoys that attempt to settle the problem. You'd be surprised how well it actually works most of the time," she said. "The enclave is also a place for recruitment."

Lehrling frowned. "Recruitment?"

Shawndirea nodded. "Yes. The Shadowfae soldiers with Dirk were possibly from an assassin's guild, which resides in the Unseelie territories."

"And yet, Lez'minx had no trouble killing them," Roble said. "Shouldn't he worry about that?"

"Not necessarily," she replied. "His temple is probably in the dimmer areas of the swamps where neither light nor darkness rule, perhaps a recess within the enclave. He's in the astral realm that divides Order and Chaos. He might draw his magical energy from either side or both, ever how he chooses."

"That still doesn't give him the right to kill dark Fae," Lehrling said.

"No, it doesn't," Shawndirea said. "However, the Shadowfae crossed from their territory into the Seelie's. Lez'minx could justify his actions since they were trespassing. The best thing the Unseelie Court could do is deny all knowledge of the assassins and assume innocence."

"How certain are you that Lez'minx's temple is in this enclave?" Roble asked.

"It's highly doubtful he'd have requested your presence if he lived within the Unseelie territory, as all of us would be killed immediately," she replied.

Lehrling scratched his beard. His eyes revealed his curiosity. "What's to say that won't happen in the enclave?"

She grimaced. "Blood must not be shed in the in-between, otherwise the consequences usher pestilence upon the entire family of the one that spilled the blood. Such a curse is far worse than death because the entire family is then permanently exiled from their city and the Court. It's something never to be taken lightly."

"You know this to have happened?" Lehrling asked.

Shawndirea nodded. "Yes. Once. Trust me, no one in Elvendale would even wish what transpired in the aftermath of that incident upon their worst enemy."

"So we're safe while we're inside the enclave?" Roble asked.

"So to speak," she said. "But once you leave, regardless of which side you enter, there's always the chance of being attacked by Fae who have the ability to travel through shadow dimensions. Often those killed by them never saw their killers. These Fae travel through shadow doors swifter than an eye can blink. They are masters of stealth and highly skilled assassins. Some probably watch us right now."

Nervousness returned to Lehrling's eyes, and he searched the trees.

"So Unseelie can be recruited in the enclave?" Roble said.

"Or Seelie. Typically, if someone travels to the enclave, it's most likely to hire Unseelie. While I don't actually know, I'd wager Dirk hired those Shadowfae to fight under his command."

"Why there?" Lehrling asked.

"Two reasons," she replied. "One, it prevented Dirk from risking his life by crossing into Unseelie territory to hire his recruits. And two, those assembled with Dirk and set out to attack us were arrogant *young* Fae with high hopes of rising in the Courts. They are skilled fighters, but instead of thinking rationally, they're more eager to shed blood with their weapons. Older Fae weigh out the situations instead. When you enter the enclave, you might not see a single potential recruit, but hidden in the veil of shadows a dozen might await the first sign of earning gold for a bounty."

After leaving Moorsis' shack, Roble wasn't certain the path they followed was the correct one. Even Lehrling seemed confused. Roble's armor triggered no impulse, like it had for them to find the shack. He assumed it was only drawn to her, not Lez'minx. After several minutes of discussion, they finally agreed to continue down the partially visible path that led deeper into the swamps.

The drab yellow fog acted like a stained filter against the bent trees weighted by dripping moss strands and curled vines. The fog prevented the true vivid colors from being displayed.

One of the most eerie aspects for Roble—other than the strange creatures, poisonous plants, and magical elements—was the blindness by which they traveled. No maps existed for the Woodnog Swamps, and now Roble understood why. No one could discern which direction he or she was headed. Marking landmarks in a terrain that vastly looked similar at every bend offered no true benefit.

Roble couldn't shake the sensation of being lost inside a swampy maze. It was no wonder why people entered these swamps, only to never leave. The deeper they traveled into the swamp, the more he feared they might end up being amongst its victims as well.

"How the hell did Bausch find his way through these swamps?" Roble asked. "For him to travel to Moorsis' shack and return to Woodnog quickly—"

Lehrling shook his head. "I honestly don't know. He was a better tracker than I."

"I wish I had a compass," Roble said.

Lehrling laughed.

"Why's that funny?"

"I have one. I looked at it hours ago. According to the pointer, there's no north or south, east or west. The needle spins erratically."

"What are the chances we ever find our way back?" Roble asked.

"First we must find the place we're searching for."

"True." Roble laughed.

Lehrling grinned. "Don't say I didn't warn you about these swamps."

"If all goes wrong, I have myself to blame."

As Lehrling and Roble rode slowly along the trail, the animals and insects hushed, leaving only the soft sound of hooves pressing into the muck. Pools of water hid beneath leafy colonies of duckweed. The denseness of the water-covering plants was deceptively dangerous, especially within the shadowed areas. Some water pools appeared solid while others offered unique places for poisonous creatures to hide.

Shawndirea sat on Roble's saddle pack where Moorsis' books had been tucked inside. Without heavy rain, it was unlikely the hard covers and spines on the books suffered much damage. She held a small oval-shaped glass over one of the book spines and sat with her eyes closed.

Lehrling glanced at her. "Are you taking a nap?"

Without opening her eyes, a frown creased her brow at his interruption. "No, I'm *trying* to read."

Lehrling cocked a brow, shook his head, and shrugged at Roble with a slight grin. "With your eyes *closed*?"

Roble peered over his shoulder. "Shouldn't you *open* the book to read it? That looks like a magnifying glass to me."

She huffed and opened her eyes. "It's a sacred scryer stone given to me by the Elven priestess, Daena Bellas. It enables me to scan books to remember relevant information concerning spells and magic without reading every page individually."

"Where can I get one of those?" Roble asked. "Talk about a timesaver. Having something like that during my studies would've been priceless."

She rolled her eyes and sighed. "They are rare, for obvious reasons."

"What reasons in particular?" Lehrling asked.

"To limit a wizard's or mage's knowledge. Imagine if someone like Lez'minx possessed this stone. With the proper teleport spell, he could enter any wizard's private library and obtain all his or her knowledge in a matter of hours. Expanded knowledge of that magnitude would greatly increase his power. Any wizard would become unmatched. Such a wizard could kill wizards and mages one by one."

"So knowing this and that we're searching for Lez'minx's temple," Roble said, "why would you bring the stone?"

She grinned. "I tuck this into a magical invisible pocket in Shadow whenever I'm not using it. No one except me can retrieve it."

"How did this … Daena obtain such a stone?" Roble asked.

"She made it."

"I see. Why'd she give it to you?"

"She was too tempted by its abilities that she no longer trusted herself."

Lehrling took out his pipe and filled it with dried herbs from a pouch. "Wouldn't it have been better for her to have destroyed it?"

"Are you suggesting I cannot be trusted?" Shawndirea asked, crossing her arms and giving him a shrewd stare.

"No, not at all, but if such a stone, like you mentioned, got into the wrong hands … it just seems that destroying the chance of that ever happening would have been better," Lehrling took his pipe and extended it toward her. "If you could be so kind as to doing me a favor? You mind lighting this?"

She waved her hand, brought a green flame to her fingertips, and tossed the small flame on the pipe. Lehrling puffed the pipe to prime the smoldering herbs before the flame died. He smiled.

"Thanks."

"It's good she has control over the height of the flame. Otherwise, your beard would be gone," Roble said with a grin.

Lehrling's eyes widened for a moment, and then he grinned. "I trust she's used magic long enough to be accurate. I'll keep better watch on ensuring I don't anger her before asking her to light my pipe."

"Another safety reason for *why* I don't smoke," Roble said, chuckling. "I suggest not making a request for a light whenever she's mad though."

Lehrling laughed.

"If I may get back to reading?" Shawndirea said.

"Of course," Roble said. "You should have plenty of time. For all I know, we might be riding in circles."

Lehrling shook his head. "If that were true, we'd be back at the cottage."

"The cottage vanished," Roble said.

"It did?"

"You didn't notice?"

"I never looked back. Perhaps I should've," Lehrling said. "Such a shame Bausch never told me of his venture to visit Moorsis. I've no idea from whom he had discovered her abilities. We traveled together all the time."

Roble said, "At some point, the two of you must have parted for several days. There's no way he came this far and returned in a day or two."

Lehrling puffed his pipe. His eyes went distant in thought. "Now that I think about it, we journeyed to Woodnog for a spell. He mentioned something about seeing the smith to have his weapons sharpened and his armor patched. That must've been where he learned about Moorsis."

"He never told you he was leaving Woodnog?"

"No," Lehrling said softly. "I was … attending to other … more personal matters."

"How long was Bausch gone?"

Lehrling chewed on the pipe's stem, shook his head, and grinned. "To tell the truth, my memory escapes me."

"Told you that you're getting old."

"My lapse of memory has *nothing* to do with my age." He gave a side-glance toward Shawndirea and then whispered, "Woodnog has … places where some of the most beautiful Elven maidens serve the pleasantest wines —strong wines, mind you—and … uh … entertainment, so to speak."

"I see."

"I might be missing a week of my life. My mind draws a blank from when I entered the erm, *tavern* and when Bausch returned. Probably took several days for me to sober up."

"Just because I'm reading," Shawndirea said, "don't think I cannot *hear* you or that I'm unaware of these *taverns* you speak of in Woodnog."

Roble chuckled and Lehrling blushed dark red.

"And Roble," Shawndirea said, "if ever Lehrling invites you to one of these taverns, you will politely and hastily decline such an offer. Agreed?"

"Noted," Roble said.

"No, do you agree?" she said with an icy tone.

"Of course. Yes."

"Not to offend, faery," Lehrling said, "but Roble has no *need* of such a place."

"Nonetheless," she said before going silent.

Roble glanced at Lehrling who held a sheepish grin. "You still miss Bausch. That much is evident."

"Every single day," Lehrling said. He took a sharp breath and held it. When he finally exhaled, curls of smoke exited his nose.

"I'm confused as to why upon our first meeting," Roble said, "you mistook me for Bausch and swore I was his ghost."

"It was he I saw," Lehrling said. His misty eyes stared into Roble's. "I swear, even now, that it was him and not you. I don't understand why my eyes played such tricks on me. Perhaps it was from the shock of watching him die and I had been helpless to stop it. Remorse, maybe?"

"Recall what Moorsis told Roble," Shawndirea said. "The armor Roble wears has imprinted with Roble. At the time Roble rescued you from the Vykings, the armor still identified Bausch as its true wearer. And no doubt, Bausch's rage toward these Vykings for having killed him lingered. Bausch's spirit was certain they were going to kill you so he sought immediate revenge. As I recall, Roble wasn't in control of his actions. He never responded to my shouts for him to take cover. Bausch somehow controlled Roble through the armor."

Chills ran down Roble's spine. "I vaguely remember my actions that day. I'm good at throwing knives. It was something I started practicing when I was a teenager. My targets were wooden. In some ways, I'm guessing, the armor sensed my abilities and connected with my skills. Only once in the Overlands did I ever considered throwing a knife at a person, but that was because he had pulled a weapon on me while threatening to take Shawndirea. Other than that, I've never entertained the thought of using a knife to kill an enemy."

"And yet, you did to save me," Lehrling said.

"In part. Again, my actions weren't entirely my own. They couldn't have been. I didn't know Vykings were a separate race from ordinary humans, and at least one of those was a demon."

"Part demon," Lehrling said. "They also saw Bausch approaching the campfire. Not you. They swore you were his ghost."

"True. But despite their race, it takes a firm commitment to throw a knife at a living person. Much more to throw with the accuracy to kill without hesitation, which, had I full control of my faculties, I'd have not done. I'd have weighed the consequences thoroughly. In my world, what I had done was murder, even in self-defense. But I didn't have a moment to consider that. I didn't hesitate."

Shawndirea said, "Bausch's hatred toward them was powerful enough that he replaced your visage with his, Roble. He wanted them to suffer intense fear before their deaths. He wanted them to know they weren't the victors. Bausch sought vengeance and through you, he achieved it."

"How do you know this?" Roble asked.

"Because I wear a piece of the armor and sense its awareness," she replied. "Something else you might try to retrieve is how the imprints of Bausch's sword skills also remain, so if you concentrated properly, you might link to that knowledge and benefit your ability to fight with a sword."

"Part of Bausch then lives on," Roble said softly.

Lehrling's expressions showed his discomfort, so he changed the subject. "So faery, have you learned much in your reading?"

She sighed. "Not as much as I had hoped. That volume explained how Lez'minx extended her life to become his slave, which she hated from the beginning."

"Really?" Lehrling asked. "I'd think anyone would want a longer life."

"She loved her husband dearly, and for months she grieved her loss. She wrote that if she could undo her pact with Lez'minx, she'd have chosen death instead. She hated the absence of her husband and her mind never recovered. The longer she lived, the more she resented Lez'minx."

"If that's true," Roble said, "why didn't she rebel against his hold earlier."

"In a way, she was. Writing down all these accounts as evidence was her greatest rebellion."

"Have you found anything about these rings?" Roble asked.

"Unfortunately, no. I still have two other books to read. She was a tailor and not a jeweler. She probably wasn't the one who enchanted the rings.

Since you took the rings from a dead mage, Lez'minx probably has other enchanters under his control. We may never know who enchanted them."

Ahead on the shadowed path, a worn wooden and bent sign post stood where the trail forked. One pointed toward Kryptos Cemetery; the other toward Purity Lake.

"Purity Lake?" Roble asked with laughter in his voice. "I cannot imagine naming anything *purity* in these putrid swamps. Since we're at the cemetery, let's find Moorsis' husband's grave."

CHAPTER 28

*R*oble studied his armor while the horse walked the pathway toward the cemetery. A bit of uneasiness passed through him as he considered the possibility of the armor being a living entity. He liked that the enchantment protected him from the elements of nature, but what disturbed him was how it had enabled his abilities to fight and kill the Vykings.

This meant the armor held the partial ability to read his thoughts and perhaps his memories, imprinting those into its self for resourcefulness. Exactly the level of access to his mind the armor possessed, he didn't know.

The trail toward the cemetery altered from the wet swampy muck that they had grown accustomed to seeing. The soil became black and compacted. Gradually, the flora changed from thick clumps of floating sphagnum and sedges into a bright green carpet of fine moss with dots of yellow and blue flowers, which was a welcoming sight.

No puddles of water stood in the lower recesses. The groves of trees diminished. Pitcher plants and fern fronds increased. Soon, they found themselves in a place where no trees shadowed the path. But the sun still didn't bless them with its presence over this glade, either. The thick gray clouds remained dismal and dim like a shadowy veil.

Thorny ivy with crimson flowers larger than a man's hand curled and held fast to the wooden remnants of old cottages and structures forgotten in time.

"This was a town?" Roble said more to himself than as a direct question to Lehrling and Shawndirea.

Lehrling nodded. "I believe so."

"Perhaps Moorsis had lived here," Shawndirea said.

Lehrling rode ahead of Roble toward an ivy-covered sign. He pulled back the vines to reveal the town's name: Tangled Grove. An X was carved through the words. Beneath it was a smaller sign with the new name: Glades of Sorrow.

Shawndirea took her scryer stone, chanted whispered words in another language, and extended her hand forward. Her hand and the stone vanished, as though she had slipped them into an invisible pocket. Roble realized this was what she meant by placing the stone into shadow.

Afterwards, she stretched and took to flight, gliding to the sign. She peered across the buildings buried in lush green ivy and other types of vines.

Roble sighed and swung off the saddle. "The sign at the fork indicated Kryptos Cemetery was ahead. Nothing about these two towns though."

She lighted upon the sign. "The cemetery is probably here. The town has been deserted for quite some time. The heavy growth of plants and the decaying, fallen structures hints that no one has tended the area for years."

"By the looks of the town, Moorsis must've been under Lez'minx's control for decades?" Lehrling said.

Shawndirea nodded.

Roble took Bleys' reins and held them so the horse could graze. "I wonder if anyone's capable of living in these swamps. First a barren island, and now a ghost town. Neither place was burdened by the constant rains, either, which are ideal places for people to live. It's odd no one lives here."

"I agree," Lehrling said. "I'd have never thought any land in these swamps would be like this. This place probably thrived long ago."

"Perhaps," Shawndirea said.

"I wonder what happened to those who lived here?" Lehrling asked.

Tall bamboo-like poles lined several rows of what once was a garden. A furry creature scurried between the leafy plants and squealed as it ran away. Several birds darted from their hiding places and flitted into other shrubs to hide.

Shawndirea shrugged. "Moorsis indicated they were afflicted with a disease."

"No survivors?" Roble asked.

"She never said in her writings. They weren't fortified with walls and from the looks of their houses, they lived modestly off the land. Probably a peaceful settlement."

"If they were, this wasn't the safest place for them to reside," Roble said, pointing. Across the former hamlet, dark trees lined the far edge of the opposite border. "I've a feeling this glade is in the center of the swamp."

She nodded. "I agree. Perhaps after the disease, they fled?"

"Where would they go?" Lehrling asked. "They're surrounded by the swamp at least on this side."

"And the other side," Roble said.

"Who knows?" Shawndirea said. "The Saurus might have ransacked the place."

"For what purpose?"

"Slaves? Food?" she said.

"Then where is the cemetery?" Roble asked.

"We can look for it," Shawndirea said. "Or you could bury her remains here."

Roble shook his head. "No, she had expended her last energy getting to her husband's grave before Lez'minx found her. She deserves to be buried beside him."

"We don't owe her anything," Shawndirea said.

"This isn't in return for a debt, but to allow her to rest beside her husband. No one else would do this," Roble said.

She smiled but offered no reply.

Lehrling cleared his throat. "The disease might've killed a few of them, but worse things befell them."

"Like what?" Roble asked.

Lehrling used his boot to brush aside a blanket of ivy. A dead body. Not human. Dried leathery skin clung to the skeleton, which had a long curled tail. "By this evidence, it's safe to assume the Lizardmen exist and at the very least attempted an open attack."

"Let's find the cemetery, so we can get out of here," Roble said.

CHAPTER 29

*R*oble and Lehrling used their swords to slice a path through the tall grasses and thick vines. By the overgrowth, Roble guessed that no one had entered this small hamlet in the better part of a year. At least, not from the direction they had entered.

Nothing was notable about the simple architecture of the cottages. All of them were identical. No larger structures towered nearby, so they didn't seem to have had a governing body presiding over them.

After fifteen minutes of flying and examining the buildings, Shawndirea returned and pointed. "The cemetery is on the other side of those two cottages."

Roble and Lehrling hacked their way between the cottages to find a circular patch of land with crude rocks for gravestones. Names were chiseled into the rocks, and they read them one by one.

"Did she ever mention her husband's name?" Roble asked.

"No," she replied.

"What are ya lookin' for?" a voice said from behind a tall wall of grass. "Haven't the dead suffered enough? Be gone, ya grave robbers, or I'll be burying the lot of ya in the ground beside them."

They turned, trying to find who had spoken.

"Go on, now!" The tip of an arrow was visible through the wall of thick grass. Slowly, the tip emerged farther, revealing the small crossbow. "I don't want to kill you, but—"

Roble took a step toward the hidden archer; provided he was an archer. "We've simply come to bury someone who should've been buried here long ago."

"And who might that be?" The tiny voice crackled as he spoke.

"Moorsis," Roble replied.

"Moorsis?" The crossbow lowered slightly. "You—you have her body? That's not possible. Cause she had to have died years ago."

"We have her remains."

"How'd you come upon them?"

"It's a long story, but it's the only reason we've entered this glade," Roble said. "She made known that she wanted buried beside her husband."

Timidly, the gruff halfling lowered the crossbow and stepped from the wall of grasses and vines. His clothes were woven from leaves and grass, as was his hat, which allowed him to stand unseen. A long green cloth cape flowed down his back. His face was smooth except for the muffs of his thick blonde sideburns. His brown eyes were large for his short stature. He stood a little over three feet in height.

"Come," he said. "I'll show you her husband's grave. Me name's Dolan."

They followed him, giving their names as he hobbled around the circular graveyard. Unlike the grounds surrounding the abandoned buildings, these plots were tended and neat with flowered wreaths adorning the crude stones.

"Here's where her husband be buried," Dolan said, pointing.

Roble held the jar of Moorsis' remains. He wasn't certain whether to bury the jar or to spread her dust over her husband's grave. To prevent the wind from scattering her dust, he decided they should bury the jar.

Dolan stepped closer. With a frown, he said, "How long have you been carrying those?"

"Since this morning."

"And how do you know that's her?"

Shawndirea explained their encounter with Moorsis and the spell Lez'minx had placed upon her. She then asked if Dolan knew where to find Lez'minx's temple.

Dolan scratched the side of his head. "No. I've never heard of him. She said that he came here and found her dying?"

Roble nodded. "Yes."

"Hmm. I suppose it's possible or perhaps he spoke to her through the ethereal and took her without anyone seeing," Dolan said. "That's possible, too."

"She told us a disease spread through your hamlet," Shawndirea said. "And that she contracted it."

"That was over fifty years ago. I'm surprised she was still alive. The disease was short-lived. Only a handful of the town died because of it."

"We saw the remains of a Lizardman near the sign of the town. Are they what killed the others?" Roble asked.

Dolan shook his head. "No. The *Saurians* raided and nearly took the entire town hostage, but their efforts were met with strong resistance."

Lehrling ran a hand through his beard. "You fought them?"

"Oh, no, we weren't the resistance. The Saurians were met by a different race altogether. They defeated the Saurians within an hour and freed those taken captive."

Lehrling frowned. "What race came to your defense?"

Dolan's brow rose and he shrugged. "All I was told was that they looked like frog people. They were fast, agile, and quite skilled at taking the Saurians' weapons. A human warrior with them."

"A human?" Lehrling said.

"Yes." Dolan studied Lehrling and Roble for several moments. "What are those pendants fastened to your armor?"

"These are worn by Dragon Skull Knights of Hoffnung. Was he wearing one?" Lehrling asked.

"Perhaps. I cannot really say."

"Why not?"

Dolan laughed. "I wasn't even born. These are legends I learned during my childhood. My elders mentioned something about a Dragon Skull Knight."

"Geowren?" Lehrling said in a near whisper.

"Vaguely sounds familiar," Dolan said, scratching his chin.

"So you're the last of the townsfolk that lived here?" Roble asked.

"No. Others were with me earlier, but they fled when they heard you chopping through the tall grasses," Dolan replied. "They're skittish. Me, I wanted to know who our trespassers were."

"Trespassers?" Lehrling said. "No one lives here."

"You're right no one lives here." Dolan winked. "Me and me brothers and sisters tend the graves once a week. We scout through the streets to check for squatters. It's still our land."

"Moorsis wasn't a halfling," Shawndirea said.

"No, she wasn't."

Shawndirea said, "Then who originally settled the Glades of Sorrow?"

Dolan smiled. "Humans mostly. My family was a group of refugees slogging our way through the swamps to the south. We happened upon this settlement during its prime, and rather than send us on our way, they invited us to join them."

"Where are the former settlers now?" Roble asked.

"They moved to the east through a narrow swamp at Dagger's Tears."

"Dagger's Tears?" Lehrling looked at Roble with an odd expression.

"You've heard of it?" Roble asked.

"No," Lehrling replied. "It's such an odd name."

"The town's named after the lake, which is shaped like a slender curved dagger. At one time, the lake had been a large sharp bend in the major river running through the swamps. It has no current or connection to the river now," Dolan said.

"An oxbow lake," Roble said.

Lehrling cocked a brow. "I assume a term from the Overlands?"

"Yes."

Dolan said, "It's a lake. A small one. Our new town resides upon the inner bank. The main river flows alongside it. Other than a sliver of land between the lake and the river, we're almost an island, which gives us better protection."

Dolan smiled and reached for Moorsis' remains. "If you'll allow me, I can bury her remains. Afterwards, I'd be happy to escort you to Dagger's Tears."

Roble gave the bottle to Dolan. Dolan reached behind his back and removed a small hand scoop from his belt. He dug a hole deep and wide enough to tuck the jar into the earth. He covered the jar and gently tapped down the soil and smoothed it with his hand, making it almost impossible to see where the jar was buried.

"Come," Dolan said with a slight grin. "It's been a while since we've had visitors. It proves to be a most glorious day."

CHAPTER 30

*R*oble and Lehrling retrieved their horses, saddled up, and followed Dolan through a narrow path where the tall grasses bent slightly. This was the obvious route Dolan and his brethren used to come or leave the Glades of Sorrow.

Although Dolan hobbled, he walked with his shoulders squared and his head held high with a sense of haughtiness. Unlike some folks Roble had met in the past, those who somehow felt inferior because of their shorter stature, Dolan possessed high self-confidence. He didn't seem to fear confronting people twice his size, and had proven so at the cemetery.

"Have the Saurians attacked your village since you moved to Dagger's Tears?" Roble asked.

Dolan shook his head. "No. They fear the deep river and the lake."

"I'd think they could swim," Roble said.

"They can, but not successfully while wearing armor. But lately, a group of them have made their presence known."

"What do you mean?" Lehrling asked.

"They stand across the small lake each night. I suppose it's meant to threaten us, but they cannot pass that direction."

"What about those frog-like creatures?" Roble asked. "Do they live in the lake or river?"

Dolan continued walking without glancing over his shoulder. "I've never seen them. I suppose it's possible, but they are of legends we were told long ago. It's doubtful others in Dagger's Tears have seen them since."

"Doesn't mean they're not keeping watch over your town," Roble said.

"Speculation on my part won't help you," Dolan said. "I can introduce you to folks who might better answer your questions."

"What about the Dragon Knight?" Lehrling asked. "Can anyone can give me information of his whereabouts?"

Dolan shrugged. "I honestly don't know."

Lehrling sighed. Disappointment sagged his facial features. His fingers tightened around the reins.

Roble offered Lehrling a comforting smile, but the additional toll of this journey also weighed upon Lehrling. Losses were difficult to shake, especially when a stubborn mind refused to stop analyzing the absences of loved ones. Some people grieved themselves to death.

Moorsis' conversations were painful reminders of Bausch's unfortunate fate. Any healing scars Lehrling held for getting past Bausch's murder were ripped afresh. Now, Lehrling sought further clues for whether Geowren was alive or dead. Roble didn't blame him.

Although Roble didn't know many members of the Dragon Skull Knights, except the recent ones Lady Dawn had dubbed into the Order, he understood the heaviness of loss when a member of the Order died or disappeared. They were brethren and sisters loyal to King Erik and the dragons of Aetheaon.

If the death of a loved one was known, it was easier dealing with the loss. But when no evidence was available to determine if someone was dead or alive, the mind and heart kept hope alive. Lehrling's sentiments to gather his brethren together was great and honorable, and because of Lehrling's convictions, Roble felt obligated to offer his assistance in such a mission.

Shawndirea had returned to Roble's pocket and kept silent. She wasn't brooding over any issues, but she showed fatigue. She needed rest more than usual.

Dolan walked ahead with his crossbow balanced between his hands. After they left the Glades of Sorrow, Dolan was less apprehensive but said little. At least he was honest in expressing his lack of knowledge concerning their questions, unlike the Dwarves. Dwarves spun tales, and if confronted about information they didn't have, some were quick to loft fictional tales as possible reasons.

The grassy patches diminished and their path returned to the bland mire with thick sedge clumps and foul pools of dark water. The stagnant air hung thick and the overcast sky seldom offered no rain.

A strange cry echoed from the wall of reeds and cattails ahead. Dolan stopped and raised a hand. With the sudden change of flora, Roble expected they were close to the river. Dolan whistled in reply.

Three male halflings emerged from their hiding places in the reeds with spears in hand. Two female halflings appeared from behind with their bows ready to fire. Like Dolan, their clothing was made from weaved plant material. They were masters of camouflage.

"All is well," Dolan said. "I'm taking them to meet Lady Versis."

"Why?" a halfling with greenish-brown hair asked. His sideburns and eyes were jet black.

"They have questions, Rufus."

"Questions? How are you sure they mean us no harm?" Rufus asked.

"They are Dragon Skull Knights, like the one who rescued us many moons ago," Dolan said.

Rufus' frown raised in surprise. "They are?"

Lehrling nodded. "Yes, we are."

Dolan frowned. "And ye all would know this had you not *fled* from the cemetery."

"Fled?" the other male halfling said, puffing his cheeks and huffing his feigned anger.

"Yes, Hob, you fled," Dolan said. "Scrambled through the weeds like wee frightened kittens, the whole lot of ya."

Shawndirea stood inside Roble's pocket, stretched, and flew upward and lighted upon his shoulder.

"Look, Merla," one female halfling said. Her sky blue eyes radiated her immediate astonishment. "'Tis a faery!"

"Don't believe me eyes, Cora," Merla said, beaming a smile. "But it is. Never thought to see a faery here. Oh, except those *dark* faeries. Those I don't like. They frighten me."

"Frightening sights, they are!" Cora said, coming closer. "And what be your name?"

"Shawndirea."

Cora and Merla smiled.

"Lovely name," Cora said. "As is your beauty."

Shawndirea blushed, in spite maintaining a guarded appearance.

"Oh, yes," Merla said. "And your wings, more beautiful than any butterfly."

Dolan ignored Cora's and Merla's fascination and made the introductions. "Now, if we can continue? I'd like to get our guests to Dagger's Tears before the night settles. I'm surprised you aren't already there, the way you scurried."

Rufus gave Hob an embarrassed smile and a quick shrug. "We were actually returning to the Glades of Sorrow to make certain you were still alive."

"Really?" Dolan said. "I'd have been long dead or eaten had Roble and Lehrling been Saurians. Not a scrap of me left to take back to Dagger's Tears. What excuse would ya have given then?"

"Our apologies," Hob said. "Truly."

"Pfft!" Dolan marched past them. "What we lack in height, we *usually* make up for in spirit! It's what allowed our survival when we were exiled from Willowbend. And look at ya now. No wonder our protests went unheard by Willowbend's council."

Rufus sighed. "We'll do better next time, Dolan."

"The next time?" Dolan said. "Next time of what? Getting *exiled* from Dagger's Tears?"

"No," Hob said. "The next time strangers approach."

"For me, there might not've been a next time." Dolan glanced over his shoulder and waved Roble and Lehrling to follow. "Come on. Dagger's Tears is not much farther."

CHAPTER 31

*P*erhaps the distance to Dagger's Tears wasn't a great distance from the Glades of Sorrow, but reaching the settlement wasn't without perilous difficulty and cautious maneuvering slowed their progress significantly.

Grasses and slick mosses splotched the exposed path. Rotten planks of a former road were sunken, creating jutting sharp stakes that caused even more problems. The visible ones indicated that other pointed tips were covered by mud. Beneath these planks, adhesive muck fastened around the horses' hooves like a thick glue. Strange sucking sounds popped when the horses pulled a hoof free.

The horses backed their ears and their eyes widened, as if recognizing the dangers hidden under the mud. A sharp fragment could stab into the soft frog of a horse's hoof or the animal might break one of its legs. Such crippling injuries meant the animal would have to be put down, which was not an outcome Roble wanted.

Roble swung off Bleys, sunk up to his calves in mud. He figured without his added weight, the horse could walk better. He took a broken plank for leverage and worked his feet into shallower mud. Lehrling climbed from his horse more carefully and followed suit.

Roble and Lehrling didn't need to encourage the horses to keep moving. The horses understood that if they stopped, the mire would suck them down. Roble doubted they could free them if that happened. Without the weight of riders, the horses moved somewhat easier. The closer they traveled toward the river, the more solid the ground became.

Dolan and his party of halflings practically glided across the plants and mire without so much as leaving a single footprint. Roble figured this was due to the halflings' light weight, which made tracking them through the swamps impossible. It made perfect sense for them to travel from Dagger's Tears to the Glades of Sorrow to tend the graves and inspect their former town, as they could do so without a trace. Between their lack of footprints and their camouflaged clothing, the halflings also made the perfect spies.

With this in mind, Roble wondered whether the halflings' motives were truthful or not. Dolan had asserted more than a few times of how they had been exiled from their homestead in Willowbend. That was enough for Roble to take more caution. *Why* had they been exiled? Usually, exile occurred as a form of punishment, either for crimes or rumors of possible upheaval.

Roble hoped Dolan was telling the truth for how he and his group had become residents in the Glades of Sorrow, but then, the original name of the town was carved out with a new name in its place. Again, he found himself not wanting to think the worst of someone, but his skeptical mind always called into question the possible hidden motives.

To almost all of their questions, Dolan was devoid of any direct answers, lacking complete knowledge, if not fully evading with vague responses. Of course, Dolan might not actually know since he was insistent that he and his party had not been a part of the township during the time the referenced events occurred.

A gentle breeze brought with it the stench of the river and dead rotting fish. From his vantage point on the high river bank, Roble saw the swollen brown river in the distance. For a wide river, the water didn't have a steady flow. The only movement was the dancing rippling effect caused by the sudden wind gusts.

They were less than twenty yards from the river's edge. Dolan led, with Rufus and Hob a bit behind, and they walked to the sides of Roble and Lehrling. The wind ruffled their capes. Cora and Merla closed off the rear. The halflings didn't seem to be an aggressive race, but they were protective. They seemed more suited for farming or using their crafting skills but overall, they were not especially suited for war.

As they neared the water, the mucky ground hardened. Layers of stone and flat rocks were firmly stacked to provide a stable platform for loading and unloading wares from boats or small rafts.

Roble wondered how they moved goods to or from the weathered stone dock. Perhaps this dock was built before the former town was abandoned? Whatever the case, the horses were relieved to leave the mire and get on firmer ground.

No bridge crossed this massive river. Beneath the gray clouds, the river appeared darker. The deep river was probably filled with fish and reptiles capable of swallowing a halfling in a moment's notice.

Across the river were large cottages and buildings constructed upon high stilts. Fires burned in braziers at the turns of the stairs and along the upper balconies. Strangely, one's eyes were directed toward the flames with the same passion as a moth traveled toward light. The dismal swamp held little radiance, so it was natural the fires were seen from afar. And yet, according to Dolan, the Saurians had not attacked their settlement between the river and the crossbow lake.

Dolan raised his hand and faced Roble and Lehrling.

"I'm certain you have a way to cross," Roble said, "without us leaving our horses on this side of the river."

"Of course," Dolan said.

"Then we swim?" Lehrling asked.

Rufus and Hob laughed.

"Only a fool would attempt such a feat," Dolan said.

Insulted by their laughter, Lehrling frowned. "Then how?"

Dolan placed his fingers against his mouth and whistled a shrill note. Then he reached into his vest pockets and took out two Elven glow-stones. Turning to face the swollen river, he tapped and held the stones together. A beacon of yellow light shot across the water's surface and struck a bent piece of glass on the other side. The light bent at an odd angle and careened off another mirrored glass nearby.

From the tall reeds and cattails, several halflings appeared on the opposite bank. They reached into the water's edge and heaved two heavy ropes and pulled. In between these ropes, two more halflings approached the river, holding huge pieces of meat on the end of long thick poles.

The water across the river swashed and rippled with loud splashes. Slowly the top of a large shell emerged. The giant turtle dug its thick claws into the river's bend and stretched its huge head toward the clumps of meat. A hungry groan echoed. The size of the turtle captivated Roble. It could easily eat him or Lehrling. The massive jaws could snap and slice through an arm or leg of a Vyking without much effort. He supposed the turtle could do the same to a Saurian as well.

The two halflings holding the meat backed from the turtle's reach, causing the turtle to pull itself out of the water. The dozen halflings tugging the ropes wrapped them around a harness attached to the rear of the giant turtle's shell. The tension of the ropes increased as the turtle kept following the meat.

"By the goddesses," Lehrling whispered.

The higher up the bank the turtle walked, the tighter the rope's tension became. Within several minutes, the ropes rose from the river, pulling a heavy object to the surface. Water dripped from the ropes and then the ferry platform appeared at the edge of the bank where Dolan stood holding the Elven glow-stones.

Rufus and Hob ran onto the platform, wiped away mud from two metal bars that were flush with the wooden boards of the raft, and pushed the bars upright to lock them into place. Once the bars were secured, Rufus took one coiled muddy rope and pulled it through a metal eye at the top of one bar while Hob did the same on the opposite side. They threaded the rope through the steel eye and then fastened the attached latches to steel anchors barely visible on the stone dock.

Dolan smiled with great satisfaction. "Almost ready."

Roble stood in disbelief for several moments. He shook his head and glanced at Lehrling before bursting into laughter. "I'd never believed it if I didn't witness it firsthand. Is this why the Saurians don't attack Dagger's Tears?"

Dolan lowered the Elven glow-stones and separated them. Their strong light slowly dimmed before he slid them into his pockets. "There are worse things than these monstrous turtles under the water."

"Worse?" Lehrling said, coughing and shaking his head.

Rufus nodded. "Yes. Several dozen of these muck turtles lurk in the river's mud, but Tinker is the largest and most loyal."

Tinker?

Perplexed, Lehrling gave Roble a shrewd stare. "What could be worse?"

"Sometimes," Roble said, "it's not best to know."

"It's better to know what to fear so I'm better prepared should I ever encounter it," Lehrling replied. "Especially, if I fell into this dingy river."

Roble chuckled. "*Don't* fall in."

"Hurry," Dolan said. "Get the horses on the platform. Just because Saurians won't swim across the river doesn't mean they won't ambush us here."

Lehrling and Roble led their horses onto the raft, which was fastened with large steel eye-rings to a lower set of ropes beneath the water to prevent the raft from being towed away by the river's current.

After everyone and the horses were on the raft, Cora approached Roble. "Where's the faery?"

"Asleep," he said.

"We'd like to talk to her," Merla said with broad smile.

Roble peeked inside his pocket. Shawndirea was curled, hugging her knees to her chest in a fetal position and shivering. Sweat beaded her pale face.

"Are you okay?" he whispered.

She didn't reply with words. Her desperate, pleading eyes glanced weakly at him. She gently shook her head. She had fallen deathly ill.

CHAPTER 32

Shock coursed through Roble. Since Shawndirea wore the armor, she wasn't shaking because she was cold. Something else was taking its toll, causing her to suffer violent chills.

Had she contracted a disease when they were inside Moorsis' shack or when they entered the Glades of Sorrow? Due to her size, he doubted she'd been bitten by a mosquito, as she'd have seen and defended herself against it.

Lez'minx had threatened her before he lost contact with them inside Moorsis' cottage. Lez'minx was bent on killing her for meddling by blocking his eavesdropping enchant on the rings. Had Lez'minx cursed her? And if so, how could Roble break the curse?

Dolan appointed positions where each of them should stand on the raft to effectively tug the thick ropes and pull the raft across the river.

"Since you and your horses are extra weight," Dolan said to Roble but his eyes were on Lehrling, "the two of you need to help."

Roble nodded. "Sure."

Merla read the worry in his eyes. "Is all okay?"

"Do you have a healer at Dagger's Tears?" Roble asked.

"Yes," Cora said. "Why?"

"Shawndirea is sick."

Merla placed her hands to her cheeks and she gaped. "I hope it's nothing serious."

Roble fought tears and tried to swallow the lump in his throat. "I hope not, either."

Lehrling approached Roble. "What's wrong?"

Roble shrugged. "I've no idea. Shawndirea has broken out in a sweat and is shivering."

Lehrling's brow creased with concern. "She has a fever?"

"Perhaps. The quicker we get this raft across the water, the sooner we find out," Roble said.

Lehrling nodded and cracked his knuckles. "I'm not as strong as I used to be, but I'll give it my all."

"That's the most any of us can do," Roble replied. He stood beside Dolan, grabbed the rope, and said, "Don't you ever worry that enemies might figure out how to find your raft and use it?"

"No. It's not possible," Dolan said. "The raft can only surface when the turtle has pulled the underwater ropes to full tension. The raft is useless otherwise."

Roble grabbed the rope and pulled until his muscles strained. Lehrling stood at the front and pulled the other rope. They strained for several minutes, but the raft didn't budge.

"That's it!" Dolan said. "Put your backs into it!"

Lehrling dug the heels of his boots against the raft boards and tugged harder, leaning back until he nearly sat down. "It's ... not ... moving."

Dolan stepped in front of Lehrling and pulled the rope. "Keep pulling! The raft must break free of the muddy river bank. Once it does, it'll be easier."

Gentle raindrops plinked on the river.

Roble's brow furrowed. His biceps and shoulders burned. He tugged with such force that his heartbeat thudded in his ears. Leaning forward, he grabbed the rope and yanked again, falling backwards but remained steady. Heat reddened his face from his exertion. He held his breath, straining every muscle fiber in his arms, legs, and back. He kept pulling until he neared unconsciousness. Finally, the raft broke free of the mud with fierce buoyancy. The river's current swept the raft away from the shore.

Roble fell on the raft and expelled all the air from his lungs and then gasped heavily for deeper breaths. Pain equivalent to a million needles being stabbed into his arms, back, and legs forced him to hug himself.

He opened his eyes to near blackness, as the invitation to collapse from fatigue overwhelmed him. Lehrling looked to be experiencing worse pain due to his age and lack of endurance.

Roble used the rope to pull himself up. His fingers clung to the rope, and he used it for a guide wire to steady his numb legs. He wanted to help Lehrling stand, but Roble didn't have the strength to walk. Releasing the rope could prove fatal as he might fall into the muddy river. He'd drown if he did. His arms and legs were spent. No way he could swim and pull himself back onto the raft. He disliked the idea of becoming chum for whatever river monsters waited below.

After a few minutes, he regained partial balance and against his aching muscles' disdain, he pulled the rope again. Rufus, Hob, and Dolan worked together to match the strength of his tow.

When Roble released, the raft moved swifter across the river.

Dolan released the rope, and rested his hands on his knees. He gulped air for less than a minute. "They'll pick up the slack now."

"Who?" Roble asked.

"On the other side of the river," he said, pointing. "They're pulling the central rope that's attached to the raft's underside. The worst part was breaking the raft free of the mud, which is why no one can steal the raft."

Roble panted and wiped sweat from his brow.

"Go on," Dolan said. "Take a seat and rest. You've earned it."

Normally, Roble would protest such an invitation and continue to prove his strength by toiling with the others, but not today. He lowered himself and sat against one of the metal bars. He opened his pocket and glanced at Shawndirea. Her body trembled.

Carefully, he placed his index finger beside her. She rose to her feet and hugged his finger. He lifted her and let her lie on his left hand. Her pale face was haunting. Even when her wings had been shredded, she'd never shown fear like she did now.

Lehrling rolled over onto his hands and knees and huffed. "How's she doing?"

"Not good," Roble said, softly.

Merla and Cora seated themselves near Roble. Cora opened a small weaved basket. "We've no medicine or herbs, but we have honey, if she's able to eat some."

Weakly, Shawndirea said, "Please."

Merla tore a piece of bread off a loaf and Cora pulled the dipper out of the bottle. A golden yellow strand of honey oozed off the dipper and coated the bread.

"If I may?" Merla said, extending the bread to Shawndirea.

Shawndirea offered a weak smile and stuck her entire hand into the honey. Closing her eyes, she licked the stickiness off her fingers.

"Portia is our healer," Cora said. "She'll know what to do."

"I hope so," Roble said.

"She will," Merla said.

Cora offered a compassionate smile. "You love her, don't you?"

"She's my wife," he replied.

Cora and Merla exchanged perplexed glances.

"You're married to a faery?" Cora said.

Roble nodded.

"Then she's Unseelie?" Merla asked.

Shawndirea frowned but was too weak to protest.

"No," Roble said. "She's of the Seelie Courts."

"She cannot be," Cora said.

"It's true," Roble said.

"What Cora meant is that she shouldn't be here."

Concern furrowed Lehrling's brow. "Why not?"

"She's passed through the in-between and entered the Unseelie territory," Cora said. "You must get her back to the in-between unless she's been granted permission to explore this region."

"Why would that cause her sickness?" Roble asked.

"It could, especially if she has enemies in the Unseelie Courts," Merla said.

"Does she?" Cora asked.

Roble shrugged. "I don't know."

"I don't," Shawndirea said in a faint voice. "But my mother has a *lot* of them."

"Who's her mother?" Merla asked.

"Queen Istrell."

Merla and Cora scooted away from Roble.

"You know her?" Roble asked.

"We know *of* her," Cora said, swallowing hard.

Roble grinned. "I'm not fond of her either."

Merla took a deep breath but her expressions reflected no recognition of any humor in his statement. With a firm gaze, she said, "It's best you *not* mention her mother's name while you're in the Unseelie territory. Unless you find comfort in immediate death."

"Her reputation is *that* bad?"

Cora's brow narrowed. Anger tainted her soft voice. "I've never thought that all humans are fools, but as lightheartedly as you're acting, you're warming me up to the notion. You've no idea the hatred this faery's mother has stirred within this region."

"Believe me, yes, I do. I wasn't trying to belittle the danger. Istre—"

Cora pointed a stern finger. "*Don't* say her name."

"Sorry. She tried to have me killed, so I know the levels she'd go to cause disruptions. Her cousin isn't much better."

"Her cousin?" Merla asked.

"Dirk."

Merla and Cora took sharp breaths.

"We know of him, too," Cora said. "He's part of the reason for why we were exiled from Willowbend."

"Steady yourselves!" Dolan said, grabbing the rope firmly. "We're about to hit bank!"

CHAPTER 33

*R*oble braced his back against the metal pole seconds before the front of the raft struck the river bank. The collision wasn't as bad as he had expected, so he only leaned to the side for a few moments.

A dozen halflings descended the side of the embankment, grabbed the ropes that secured the raft, and pulled it off the water to prevent it from rocking while the horses were led off to the mired ground.

Dolan was met by others and before he could speak, he was greeted by numerous questions about why he'd brought humans across the river. He profusely explained his reasons.

Cora and Merla helped Roble stand.

"Come with us," Merla said. "We'll take you to Portia. Once you explain the situation to her, she can formulate the proper treatment for Shawndirea. At best, maybe all you need to do is get her to the in-between so her symptoms will subside. At worst, someone has placed a curse upon her."

"Merla!" Cora frowned and shook her head.

"Well, it's possible," Merla said in a hushed tone.

"Concentrating on the negative doesn't help anyone. Focus on bettering the situation. Maybe we've some herbal teas or tonic—"

"Not to be impolite," Roble said, "but could we skip the unknown prognosis and see what Portia *might* know?"

Cora nodded. "Sorry."

Roble stepped off the raft, still holding Shawndirea in his hand. She looked at him, but her eyes were distant. He didn't know if she even saw him.

"I'll get the horses," Lehrling said, "and catch up to you as soon as I can."

"Thanks." Roble lifted Shawndirea closer to his face and whispered, "Don't leave me. Let's hope Portia can heal you."

Roble's boots sank in the mud, and he struggled to reposition his feet without falling. The path at the top of the bank was covered with flat rocks that began a road toward the stilted shacks.

CHAPTER 34

The world surrounding Shawndirea crashed around her like a black sea sucking her into an abyss. Though the cold dark waves didn't actually exist, her hampered breathing was equivalent to inhaling viscous liquid.

Roble's voice echoed through the depths that seemed to span through continuous caverns of darkness. Light fled from her vision. The inky gray gel enclosing her turned to blackness where neither sound nor vision prevailed.

She found herself helpless, lost, and fleeting from the Realm of Aetheaon and the man she loved. In desperation, she attempted to thwart the sinking sensation pulling her further away, but nothing she tried slowed her descent. Her strength was fleeting and nausea turned her stomach.

Shawndirea only accompanied Roble into the swamps because she wanted to protect him, but now she was the one who needed rescued. But where she was, he doubted he'd ever find her. Irony was cruel and unforgiving.

The deeper into the Woodnog Swamps they traveled, the harsher the strain she suffered. Forces unrecognized were slowly sapping her, draining her magic, and now it seemed, her life's energy.

Strange as it was, she couldn't pinpoint the source. Her first reaction to these attacks resulted in her lashing anger and unfortunately, Roble suffered the most from the building fury inside of her.

She wasn't bewitched, nor did the power of a cast spell surround her. What puzzled her was that she should've detected the exact moment they left the in-between and entered Unseelie territory, but nothing alerted her. Not the slightest tinge or even a tingle pricked her mind.

Since she had denounced her right to the throne of Elvendale years earlier, the Unseelie should have welcomed her with open arms, as her recantation inadvertently resigned her place in the Seelie Court. Shawndirea never considered those repercussions when rejecting her mother's request to ascend the throne.

For one court to gain royalty members from the opposing court was rare and would be considered a monumental victory.

Could Dirk have somehow gained favor in Siofra's—the Unseelie Queen— eyes. It was possible, as he was quite deceptively persuàsive at times, which meant the Queen might have sent the assassins with Dirk to kill Shawndirea's mother. After Lez'minx intervened by killing the faery assassins in one sweeping instant, Siofra might believe Shawndirea had ties with this supposed god, which made her a direct enemy of the Unseelie Court.

While Dirk possessed unique charms, she doubted Siofra could be beguiled by him. But if by chance she believed Dirk, Shawndirea was no longer welcomed in either court.

Solitary Fae existed, but few ever chose that path. Alliances were necessary in order to survive against others that wielded magic. Enemies abounded on both sides of the in-between, and collecting bounties on rebellious faeries held rewards prized greater than monetary value. Some assassins enjoyed the thrill of the hunt and the challenge involved, especially when the prey has the magical ability to fight back. Then the challenge was to determine whose use of magic and cunning were stronger. If Shawndirea chose to become solitary, she became a target from both sides, as would Roble.

The only advantage of being solitary was that she could draw magic from either court, which didn't necessarily mean she'd become more powerful. Being despised by both courts held no advantage. The benefits weren't worth the risk of being hunted. Solitary faeries never lived in peace, except in the neutral in-between, and that was a narrow terrain. She was almost better off to return to the Overlands with Roble.

Some Fae in Elvendale might continue protecting her, rather than pursuing. She was favored highly above her mother, and she understood why.

Queen Istrell ruled harshly. Her bitter attitude soured even the most loyal subjects into near revolt at times. She believed the Fae in Elvendale were more disappointed in Shawndirea's denouncement than was her mother. She imagined the celebration Elvendale would display should Shawndirea ever wear the crown.

Shawndirea's greatest enemies were some of her direct family, particularly Dirk. Although he wanted the throne for his own selfish purposes, she understood he'd never be the direct heir. He couldn't survive the trials necessary to assume the throne. Only female Fae survived the series of trials with the exception of one: Oberon.

Oberon was the revered Emperor of the Fae across multiple shadow realms. At least, that was whom Istrell held her allegiance to and insisted Shawndirea do as well. Shawndirea possessed no knowledge of whether

Oberon had ever graced Aetheaon, but surely he was the one who presided over her mother's trials to be worthy of being crowned Elvendale's Queen a century earlier.

If he issued the trials, none had ever spoken of his visit. Shawndirea suspected Oberon never announced his presence upon his arrival and might've taken a different form altogether. What better way to discover the darker secrets others held in confidence or to learn the names of those slandering your name?

To her knowledge no Kings had ever presided over the Fae in Aetheaon. That wasn't to say all realms conformed to this ideology. The rulers of Fae in Aetheaon were strictly matriarchs, and probably always would be.

She suddenly realized why Dirk had chosen Feather to be his queen. She could withstand the requirements necessary to survive the trials. With her as the Elvendale's new Queen, he was betrothed as the residing King, giving him the authority to indirectly rule the throne through her. As subservient as she was, she'd never deny his requests with the exception of not killing Istrell. Dirk could devise no scheme worthy of convincing Feather to kill Elvendale's Queen, as Feather viewed Istrell as a motherly figure.

As King, Dirk could mandate edicts and pressure others to comply insisting that *the Queen orders so*. While Dirk was cunningly persuasive, he was unable to hide the violent repercussions he'd inflict should someone take a stand against him. Few would ever dare question his demands, and those that did would serve as examples for others in the future.

Without Feather or another female to wed Dirk, he remained a strong prince in the Seelie Courts, could even preside over his own kingdom should he so choose, but a prince was the highest level of hierarchy Dirk could ever possess absent his marriage to a queen.

"Why have you forsaken your own?" a male voice within this blackened void asked. His soft voice carried authority and his demand cascaded like riveting thunder quaking through this abyssal pool.

She saw nothing. Blackness and cold blanketed her.

"I have not," she replied.

"But you have. Marrying a human has altered your path for greatness."

"I've no desire … for greatness. I'm content as the Butterfly Queen."

"That's a *minor* title."

"Nothing's minor when I use my blessing to restore the longevity of nature's most beautiful fragile creatures."

"Don't be a fool, child. The Seelie has great need for you, for your wisdom, and for your undying compassion. Don't tarnish your calling. You cannot balance between both sides. Death comes for you, even as you hear my words. Never forget that you've been forewarned. Your future is not with the human. Accept your fate to rule and abandon the silliness of your selfish desires."

"Who are you?" Shawndirea asked in a curious angered tone.

No reply came. Just emptiness, coldness, and the sensation of plummeting deeper into this bottomless dimensional pool. No more could she hear Roble's voice. No blessing of light gave her vision.

Darkness. Constant thick darkness.

Drifting, falling, light as a feather carried by the softest child's breath.

She felt like she was at the veil that divided deep sleep and eternal rest. If she failed to find her way back, she was certain Death's icy, boney fingers extended toward her, calling her away from her life, and claiming her soul and spirit … Forever.

CHAPTER 35

*A*t the hamlet's central building, Roble followed Merla and Cora up the long wooden ramp that led to the wraparound balcony. The crude buildings stood on tall stilts and were constructed from roughly hewn boards as a precaution for possible floods. These buildings could withstand heavy rains and flooding. The thatched roofs were made of dried sedges, mud, and thick moss.

Shawndirea's breathing remained shallow. Her eyelids had not fluttered since they had left the raft. Her radiance was fading and her complexion grayed.

His focus on her blinded him to his surroundings. Before he realized it, he stood outside Portia's door. The balcony was several stories above the ground, giving a perfect view of the dagger-shaped oxbow lake. Around the lake, fishermen stood on docks watching bobbers float on the dingy water. Other fishermen worked feverishly on small flatboats, bringing up their traps in the light of large glowing lanterns.

Merla knocked on Portia's door. A light breeze rattled the wind chimes made from long hollow bamboo stalks.

"Enter," a soft voice said from the other side of the door.

Merla eased the door open. Light flickered beyond the threshold. "I hope this isn't a bad time to interrupt."

"Is there ever a proper time for interruptions?" Portia asked in a light, amused tone.

Merla smiled. "I suppose not."

"What do you need?"

"Dolan met a party in the Glades of Sorrow—"

"Enemies?"

"No," Cora said, stepping through the doorway. "Allies."

"Allies? You've come to such a conclusion in so little time?"

"Not without reason," Merla said.

"And what reason is that?" Portia asked.

"Roble has a faerie that's deathly ill." She hesitated for a moment. "Not a dark faery."

"I see. And why does he possess a faery to begin with?"

Roble frowned. "I don't possess her."

Cora said, "He does not own her. He's married to her."

"Married?" Portia said.

Portia appeared at the door. With a stern gaze she met and searched his eyes. Her odd-shaped eyes reflected a disturbing, bizarre sheen. Roble forced himself *not* to look away. He couldn't afford any action to be considered rude. She was the host and a healer, and he desperately needed her help.

The halflings insisted the residents from the Glades of Sorrows were human, but it was obvious she was not. Her eyes were similar to those of a fish. The sheen seemed to be a second eyelid to further protect from injury, or perhaps, he reasoned, to allow her vision outside of water.

After several moments of peering into his eyes, her rigid attitude lessened and she relaxed. She smiled and looked at Shawndirea in his hands.

"Please," Portia said, "bring her inside. Cora, set a kettle over the fire. Merla, light some dried jasmine and sage. Smudge the rooms. We cannot allow any negativity to enter my home."

"Yes, Portia."

Roble walked with Portia to a table near the center of the room. Her long brown hair flowed down her back.

She grabbed a thick pillow of moss and set it on the table. "Lie her here."

Roble placed Shawndirea on the soft moss. Except for the slightest rise and fall of her chest, he'd have thought her dead.

"How long has she been like this?" Portia asked.

"A few hours."

"Good that you got here."

"You know what to do to help her?" Roble asked.

With a worried expression, Portia shook her head. "No, but there are things I could try, with your permission, of course."

Roble hesitated.

She rested her webbed hands on the table. He almost expected to see scales on her skin, but her skin was coated with a thin layer of dark green moss. As best he could tell in the dim light, this was her hair and not moss somehow adhered to her flesh.

Portia smiled. "To ease your worry, I'm a healer who prides herself in protecting and healing those who enter my home with whatever ails them.

And for a faery, I'd go even further to ensure her a longer life. I assure you I'd never harm her."

Roble sighed. "I appreciate that."

"Her wings are magnificent," she said. "I've never seen such a beautiful faery in these parts. From her beauty, I'd say she's from the Seelie Courts?"

"Yes," Roble said, nodding. "She's the Butterfly Queen."

"This is Shawndirea?"

Roble nodded. "You know of her?"

Portia laughed softly. "All Fae know of her. I've heard of her, but her beauty far surpasses the description told in tales. She's far from the safety of her kingdom. How'd you convince her to marry you?"

"I didn't convince her. She found and chose me."

Her narrow lips formed a sly grin. "I see. Has she any symptoms other than a fever?"

"None to my knowledge. She has been fatigued, as this has been a stressful journey."

"Destination?" she asked.

"That's something we're unsure of."

"I see. Rambling aimlessly through a horrid series of swamps and marshes that spares few. Hardly a task for a human and a faery. Only fools wander through this region of Aetheaon. Certainly you have a reason."

"We're trying to find a temple," Roble said.

Her eyes flicked to his with uneasiness. "A temple? To which god or goddess?"

"Lez'minx."

She pursed her lips and her odd eyelids blinked. "I know of no such god. We know of many, but none by that name. Why do you seek him?"

"It's a long story."

Portia nodded. "In Shawndirea's condition, she's not going anywhere soon. We've got time."

CHAPTER 36

*L*ehrling led the horses to the edge of the oxbow lake to let them drink. The muddy water was calm but the smell of decaying fish and stagnant water made him gag. While the horses drank, he watched the lake activities.

Several children carried small baskets of dark crayfish and red fish on their heads from the docks where two men finished tying a small flatboat to a post. One man stood on the boat and handed heavy traps to the other.

None of these workers were halflings. They all were human.

"Geowren, how long's it been since you were here? Are you still alive?" Lehrling whispered.

These unanswered questions pained his mind. Perhaps he had grown too sentimental as he aged. He longed for the days of his youth when adventuring didn't take such a horrible toll on his mind and body. He wished he could turn back time, not for himself, but to somehow rescue Bausch and prevent his death.

Lehrling had never recovered from the loss, and he doubted he ever would. Roble's friendship helped ease the pain, but it wasn't the same. Bausch was like the son Lehrling never had. That wasn't a loss that passed easily.

He wiped hot tears from his eyes with the back of his hand. Now that he knew Geowren had visited the Glades of Sorrow, his hope rekindled that he might discover the Dragon Skull Knight's whereabouts.

When the dragon sisters reemerged from hiding, Lehrling expected Geowren to return and help claim back Hoffnung from Lord Waxxon. But Geowren didn't, leading Lehrling to believe Geowren was dead.

Geowren was loyal to a fault when it came to his duties as one of the

Order. He was the one knight who had not given up on finding King Erik alive.

"I feel it in my bones," Geowren had said, when they were seated at the Bent Oak Tavern in Woodcrest. "Our King lives, Lehrling. He *is* alive."

"As much as I want to believe that," Lehrling said, "we've no evidence he's alive."

Geowren wiped beer foam from his black beard. His coal-dark eyes peered into Lehrling's but not with anger. Geowren's eyes beamed with eternal hope. "He lives, Lehrling, as surely as you and I do."

"There's been no declaration for ransom."

"This has nothing to do with gold."

"Then what?"

"Power. Revenge."

"By whom?"

Geowren stood and placed several gold coins on the table. "That's what I aim to figure out."

"Hoffnung's crown has no enemies."

"*Any* kingdom has its enemies," Geowren said. "The worst enemies are those who never reveal their open hatred for you. So will you travel with me?"

"Where are you headed?"

"To the Woodnog Swamps."

"There? Why? King Erik vanished far north of Hoffnung at the opposite end of the continent."

Geowren grinned. "I know. That's why the swamps would be the last place someone would search."

"That makes no sense."

"It makes perfect sense."

"Then explain it to me."

Geowren sighed. "Ride with me and I will."

"Not without Bausch."

"Where is he?"

Lehrling took a gulp of his mead and set the tankard on the table. "He's at Pig-sty Tavern. He fancies a barmaid there. I've told him he's wasting his time, but—"

"Let him have his fun." Geowren chuckled. "He's too old for you to be hover over him like a protective father. Don't spoil his fun. Remember how it was during our youth? Nah, we didn't want chaperones. Ride south with me."

Lehrling hesitated and thought about the perils of being a young man infatuated with a beautiful maiden. Hell, being an adult fearful of courting a lady held perils of its own and why he never settled down. "If you can wait—"

"Waiting puts us farther away from finding him."

"What reasoning can you offer that we'd not be wasting our time by riding south?"

"The Black Chasm. The City of Mortel. That's *two* reasons. If you need a third? Tyrann."

"Tyrann? You think he's responsible? He's never ventured outside of the chasm. It's his stronghold."

"He plays an integral part in King Erik's abduction."

"How would that benefit Tyrann?"

"I travel to discover the true reasons. The Black Chasm neighbors the swamps. Barrier Pass has prevented the chasm from expanding east, but if ever the Fae and Elven magic fails along that barrier, Woodnog will be consumed by Tyrann. If Woodnog falls, Tyrann's power increases to a level that I don't even want to imagine."

"You cannot enter the Black Chasm," Lehrling said. "None have survived."

"You're not listening, friend. I've no intention of entering the chasm." He placed his hand on Lehrling's shoulder and squeezed. "You stick around for Bausch, if that's your decision. Eventually, you'll let him mature into his manhood. Maybe. Once I find the evidence I expect to uncover, I'll send word to Queen Taube so she can gather you and the rest of our Order together. King Erik isn't dead. It's more than a gut feeling. Ever since he knighted me, I've felt a bond with him and the great dragons."

"No one's seen a dragon in ages," Lehrling said.

Geowren's black eyes narrowed. "Maybe not, but they're not dead, either."

"Then where are they?"

"I've no idea, but my guess is that they're still trying to locate Erik. Their bond is with him, and we're bonded to Erik through our Order and the rituals we were sworn to partake. Do you not feel King Erik's spirit."

Lehrling swallowed hard. His mind wanted to believe Erik was alive. All of Aetheaon wanted to believe it, but Lehrling didn't feel this *bond* Geowren talked about. "I wish I did."

"Find a place of solitude, fast, and meditate," Geowren said. "Then you'll recognize the truth. Visions will come to you more clearly than I stand before you. I sense King Erik lives but he's hidden and hidden well."

"If you could wait until morning—"

"No time. Do as I say. Fast and meditate. Seek the truth."

"But—"

Geowren chuckled and ran a hand through his black beard. "Bausch *is* a man, Lehrling. Send word by a raven where we're heading. He'll can find us. Let him practice his tracking skills."

Lehrling sighed.

Geowren's boots thudded across the dusty hardwood floor, he opened the door, and gave Lehrling a hearty laugh before closing the door behind him.

That was the last time he saw Geowren.

Lehrling watched several lads toting baskets of fish from another dock.

"I should've gone with you, Geowren," Lehrling whispered. Tears heated his eyes, but he withheld allowing their release.

In retrospect, had he gone with Geowren, Bausch might still be alive. Bausch might've successfully romanced Sarey. So many things would be different. But, he'd have altered so many other predestined necessary events. Roble and Shawndirea would've died in the harsh cold instead.

Of course, Lehrling might have died for traveling into the swamps with Geowren. Lehrling didn't fully know whether Geowren was alive or not. Fate was not for humans to control. Even after harsh losses, what was the point in questioning or continuing to relive it over and over in one's mind?

Lehrling shook his head and berated himself. He was where he was supposed to be with Roble and Shawndirea. He hated that Bausch was dead and gone, but for whatever reasons the Three Goddesses destined it. Roble and Shawndirea could have emerged anywhere, but they exited at the right place and time that benefited them and Lehrling. He continued to openly express these thoughts to Roble, perhaps to reaffirm for his own benefit instead of Roble's; and yet, Lehrling ignored the obvious truth even though he spoke it.

No more.

Lehrling could no longer live in the past. He needed to push forward and never look back.

A smile spread across his face. He glanced at the muddy surface of the lake and for several moments, the image of Bausch's face materialized as he remembered his apprentice.

"Son," Lehrling said, choking back tears. "I must let go of my hurt. Your spirit and my fond memories shall linger with me until my death. One day, though I cannot guarantee this will occur, we'll meet again in another realm or on a different plane, so we can reminisce. Until then, my destiny awaits."

CHAPTER 37

*T*wo boys carrying heavy baskets of mussels stopped to admire the two horses with Lehrling at the lake's edge. Their curious fearful eyes indicated they'd never seen a horse.

"Where can I stable these two horses?" Lehrling asked the boys.

Sheepishly, they looked away, turned, and picked up their pace without answering. With the heavy baskets, the boys' steps turned into a slow run.

Lehrling cocked his head to the side and ran his hand through his beard. Perhaps they had heard him talking to himself and thought he was deranged? He chuckled. Sometimes he questioned it himself.

"You can tether them anywhere," a woman said from the dock with a gentle smile. Beside her was a long string of gutted fish stretched across a table. "Or you can let them roam. They're surrounded by water, so they won't wander away. No one will bother them. Folks here are afraid of horses."

Lehrling regarded her with a kind smile. The woman was, by his guess, in her late thirties, but her rugged appearance made her look older. She was dressed in modest clothes with a thick leather apron tied around her waist. Fish scales, guts, and blood stains coated the apron. Her hair had fallen from its bun and loose. Dry fish scales clung to strands of her hair. A few scales stuck to her soiled face, which she tried to wipe away. She tucked her skinning knife behind the apron string, left the dock, and headed toward him at the water's edge.

Her dimpled cheeks were prominent as she smiled. He marveled at her sapphire blue eyes. Captivated by her eyes, he kept his silence for too long.

"Is ... is everything okay?" she asked, cupping her hands together while cautiously approaching him. "You ... seem out of sorts. Were you *talking* to yourself?"

Lehrling blushed and nodded. "I'm fine. Just sorting through things."

"Out loud?"

"Yes."

"You are?" she asked, leaning forward in keen interest.

He frowned with confusion.

"Your name?" she said. "What is your name?"

"Forgive me for my rudeness. My apologies, dear lady," he said, beaming even redder and slightly bowing, extending his hand. "Sir Lehrling of Hoffnung and a Dragon Skull Knight. And what is your name, if I may ask?"

She extended her calloused hand, even though it was grimy with blood stains and fish scales. He ignored the mess, her chipped stained nails, and gently kissed the back of her dirty hand.

"Collette," she said, taking by surprise with his kiss.

"A lovely name. A pleasure to make your acquaintance."

She shook her head, blushing. "You're too kind. You and your friend are already the gossip of our town."

"We've only just arrived."

She shrugged. "No matter. Word travels fast through our hamlet. We seldom get visitors and worry often of invasions. Even if we possessed fighting weapons, our numbers are not great enough to defend against a small invasion. It's good to have kind knights arrive. It's been a while. A bit over twelve full moons, I'd say."

"Has another knight like us visited here?" Lehrling asked.

"Not for some time. Do you know him?"

"He's a dear friend of mine. Can you describe him?"

Collette walked to the edge of the lake, squatted and dipped her hands in the water, and scrubbed them. When she finished, she stood and wiped hands on the underside of her apron. "His hair and beard were blacker than the night. At first, the mystery surrounding him frightened us. His smile indicated he knew more than what he'd ever reveal. His laughter was delightful, if not sometimes haunting. But like you, he demeanor was polite. Is that the man you knew?"

Lehrling nodded. His heart raced with excitement. "That's Geowren."

She smiled at the mention of the name. "Yes, I believe that's the name he gave."

"How long did he stay?"

"Three days, if memory serves me."

"Did he say to where he was traveling?"

"Southeast to Spellhaven," Collette replied.

"Spellhaven?" Lehrling rubbed his bearded chin. His mind searched. Then, thinking aloud, he whispered, "Morgana's Cove is a port near there. What would he be seeking there?"

Puzzled, she said, "I've no idea. He never said."

"Sorry," Lehrling said, shaking his head. "Me thinking aloud again."

She frowned. "You talk to yourself a *lot*."

"I'm afraid so." He tried to suppress his embarrassed smile. "Are you sure the horses will be okay out in the open near the lake?"

Collette nodded. "Yes. No one will bother them."

"Because those turtles near the ferry—"

"Oh, there's nothing like that in the lake."

"Good to know."

"If there were, we'd starve. I cannot imagine how much those giant turtles must eat."

Lehrling grinned. "I'm certain they had their eyes on these horses. I heard their stomachs rumble."

Her brief burst of laughter was soothing to his ears. She smiled.

"Why are people afraid of these horses?" Lehrling asked.

"They're such magnificent beasts," she replied, "but so large and terrifying at the same time."

"Are you afraid of them?"

"Yes, actually."

"Here," Lehrling said, gently taking her hand and walking her to the side of his horse. He placed her hand to the side of his horse's neck. With his hand over hers, he glided her hand to rub the horse's coat. "See? He won't hurt you."

"Not with you beside me."

Lehrling laughed. "I've never seen this ol' horse attempt to hurt anyone."

"What's his name?"

"Patch, because of the large white spot on his flank." Lehrling ran her hand up the horse's neck and then to the side of its nose.

"He's beautiful."

"I think he likes you," Lehrling said, slowly pulling his hand from hers.

She looked into Lehrling's eyes with a flattered smile on her unwashed face. Even with her rugged appearance, he was enthralled by her radiant inner beauty, which overshadowed any amount of grime. Realizing by her widened smile that he had stared into her eyes for too long, his face reddened. For once during the entire journey he was glad the heavily overcast sky was growing darker, so she couldn't see his heated face.

"Well, thanks to you," she said, "I'm less frightened by him. I'd have never stepped close to it without your invitation."

Collette turned to Patch, rubbed its nose, and sweet-talked the horse.

"I'm surprised you don't have horses here," he said.

Amusement flowed softly in her voice. "We're river folk. We live off the river and this lake. Ever since those reptilian beasts invaded the Glades of Sorrows, we've been forced to resettle here. As you can see, our land is limited. We've no need for horses."

Lehrling nodded. "That's true."

Without looking away from the horse, she said, "What brought you to Dagger's Tears?"

"My friend was told that Portia is a healer."

"She is," Collette said. "Is your friend ill?"

"No, but his wife is."

"His wife?" she asked with a frown. "I only saw the two of you."

"She's a faery."

Collette pondered for several moments. "A faery?"

He nodded.

"How is that possible? I mean … well—"

"Marriage between races and species isn't unknown," Lehrling said.

"I know *that*," she replied. "I meant … consummation."

"Oh!" Lehrling's face blushed even hotter. "Ah, well, due to her magical abilities, she can perform a ritual to where she becomes the size of a human."

Collette smiled and lowered her gaze. "So can she stay that height?"

Lehrling shrugged. "I suppose she *could*, but that would be something you'd have to ask her. Provided she recovers."

"Have hope. Portia's been a blessing to us." She lowered her voice and looked around cautiously. "She's not like us."

Lehrling frowned. "What do you mean?"

"She's different. She looks human but she's not."

"What *is* she?"

"We don't rightly know. Once we were forced from our former village, we found her gathering herbs, mosses, and other items she needed for her incantations."

"She already lived on this island?"

"No, but she helped us establish our new settlement. She has great magical abilities."

"In what way?"

Collette smiled. Her eyes brightened as she remembered the details. "She somehow walled up the river so that the ropes to make the raft bridge could be tied from one side to the other. It taxed her a great deal, but she held the wall of water for two full days, giving our men enough time to construct the anchored posts on both sides."

Lehrling shook his head in disbelief. "I'm surprised the men didn't sink to their waists in thick mud."

"The riverbed was bone dry. She has powerful magic."

"Amazing," Lehrling said.

Collette nodded. "She's sworn to protect us in return for food and a place to live." Collette ran her hand down Patch's neck to his back, and then looked at the saddlebag. One of the scrolls Lehrling had taken from Polderholm stuck out. She stared at it with keen curiosity. "What is this?"

"Something we came across at an island."

She yanked it from the bag. "May I?"

She didn't wait for a reply and unrolled the thick parchment. Her eyes studied the writing but displayed her confusion. "This is a spell scroll. Are you a sorcerer?"

He chuckled. "No. Far from it."

"And yet, you carry this?"

"It was something we discovered."

Collette frowned. "If you can't use magic, why keep it?"

"It might come of use later."

"Can you read it? I don't recognize the language."

"Nor do I. But there are translators."

"Fool's folly," she said.

"There's a tavern by that name," Lehrling said with a grin. "I've visited it several times."

She didn't smile. Instead, she waved the scroll in the air and repeated the words.

Confused by her reaction, he opened his mouth to speak but a sudden disruption captured his attention.

From the docks around the oxbow lake, bells clanged in rapid succession.

"What's that?"

"Time for us to leave the lake for the night. Hurry!"

CHAPTER 38

*A*lthough Collette insisted it was safe to leave the horses out in the open, the cacophonous rattling alarm bells caused Lehrling to instinctively grab the horses' halters and lead them away from the lake. Before he turned, a dark cloud spread across the gray horizon, much more different than the normal overcast sky.

This moving cloud was alive and approached at a rapid rate. Sharp shrills pierced the air. A heavy sound carried in the wind. A flapping with increasing rhythm the closer the cloud came.

Three passing children that carried baskets of fish, crayfish, and mussels dropped their heavy loads and rushed toward the houses to seek shelter from the ominous cloud.

"What's going on?" Lehrling said, hurried with the horses while trying to catch Collette.

"Nightfall comes," she said. "And with it come the creatures of the night."

"That's the reason for the alarm?"

She nodded.

"What's coming?"

"Bats," she replied without looking over her shoulder. "You should hurry."

"They are a danger?"

"On occasion."

"You said the horses would be okay left to themselves?"

"Yes," she said. "They'll be fine."

"Then why is everyone fleeing because of the bats? Do these bats attack people?"

"No. They only eat insects."

"Then why is everyone running?"

Collette paused and faced him. She offered a patient smile while she explained. "During their feeding frenzies to capture insects, the swooping bats have hit folks in the head or caused other near fatal injuries. The last one injured was a young boy fishing on the dock. The bat struck and knocked him into the lake. He almost drown. The bats are quite large. While they don't pose a significant threat, we cannot risk such accidents."

"Okay, I understand."

"Since most insects favor the water, that's where the bats readily feed," Collette said. "They're earlier than normal. But we don't regard the bats as our enemies. They're beneficial to us."

Lehrling lowered his head slightly as the bats circled from the water and groomed the air along the lake's banks. The bats' glowing red eyes were fierce, narrow slits like glowing embers. With them came the stench of brimstone, which made him wonder where these bats hid during the day. These bats were huge. Their graceful acrobatic dives and circles were neat to watch, but he realized the danger of being within the feeding swarm.

"Should we pick up the baskets of fish?" he asked. "No need leaving them here to rot."

Two men running from the docks stooped and grabbed the baskets and then ran toward the line of stilted houses.

"They have them," she said. "Now hurry."

The chirps and fluttering wings increased in a maddening whirl of action. The sky darkened under the blanket of bats, and an odd odor filled the air.

Lehrling sighed. "I cannot get used to constant dusk."

She frowned. "Is there any other?"

"Surely you've seen the sun?"

"No, I have not. Travelers have mentioned it."

Lehrling gaped and his eyes widened. "You've never seen sunlight? I—I cannot imagine."

"I hope one day to venture outside the swamps to witness it myself."

"Perhaps you will," he said. Then he pointed to the scroll held tightly in her hand. "May I?'

"Oh, sorry. I didn't realize I was still holding it. Here."

He smiled and took the scroll. "Would you mind showing me which building Portia is in? I should check on Roble and Shawndirea."

Collette pointed to the largest building near the center of the other buildings. It was also the one set on the highest stilts with a balcony that overlooked the rest of the small town. "She's in that one."

Lehrling studied the building for a moment and then the surrounding terrain. Only buildings towered above the soggy marshy ground. No large trees or thin saplings graced the hamlet.

The folks rushed up various ramps to the balconies of the homes. Lehrling didn't want to get lost in a wave of people he didn't know. And even though he'd only met Collette, he felt safer in her company and uncertain how others in the hamlet might treat him.

"I'd be honored if you'd accompany me," Lehrling said with a smile.

She forced a smile. "I'd love to, Lehrling, but I'm not presentable to be in Portia's presence. I must clean all these fish entrails, blood, and scales from myself and find cleaner clothes."

His heart sank. He enjoyed talking to her and feared if he lost sight of her that he might never see her again. He sighed. "Ah, yes, I suppose if I were covered in all of that, I'd want to get cleaned up as well."

"Oh," she said, pointing to a longer building with heavy smoke coming from its chimney. "Attend your business with your friends at Portia's home, and meet me at the lodge in an hour? Everyone will be there. Cooks prepare our supper from what we've caught in the lake."

The wind carried a delicious aroma. His mouth watered.

"They've already begun cooking," she said. "I'd best hurry. You don't want to arrive late. The best fish are served first, as they cannot be dried or preserved with salt."

"I'll look for you," he said, leading the horses toward the hamlet.

Collette smiled and quickly turned away. He watched her rush along the worn trail atop old timber planks to avoid the mire. Though he hardly knew her, her absence already made him ache. He wanted to talk more. He wanted to invite her to travel with him, Roble, and Shawndirea—once Shawndirea recovered from whatever ailed her. Nothing would please him more than to see the look on her face when she witnessed a sunrise or sunset for the first time. His heart quickened as he imagined her stunned smile.

What a drab life to be enclosed in a place where the sun never graced the sky. He wondered how he could best offer an invitation to her. What could he say to convince her to journey with him?

"You're an old fool," he whispered to himself. "She'd take no interest in traveling with a man twice her age. And here I am again, talking to myself. Perhaps it's because I know the depth of my own conversations to sort through my problems are always greater by myself."

Lehrling rolled his eyes and slapped his palm against his forehead. He glanced around to see if Collette was watching him talk to himself. But she was gone, lost in the small crowd of children and folks hurrying to get inside.

You've got to stop talking to yourself.

He laughed and led the horses to Portia's residence.

After leaving the horses near the long building's support timbers, Lehrling was met by Merla and Cora, descending the long wooden ramp.

"How is Shawndirea?" Lehrling asked.

"No better," Cora said.

Lehrling winced. "Any idea what's wrong?"

Merla shrugged and offered a hopeful smile. "Portia's attempting to find out. If anyone can detect what the faery's symptoms indicate, it's Portia."

Lehrling glanced up the ramp. "Is it okay for me to check in on them?"

Cora smiled. "Sure. We can walk you up."

"I appreciate that."

CHAPTER 39

*W*hen Lehrling entered Portia's home, he was greeted by a heavy wall of smoke flavored by various incenses, herbs, and sage. His eyes burned and he coughed.

Candles flickered on different shelves and tables around the room. A large candle burned on the center table. Roble leaned and rested on his elbows on the tabletop, staring at Shawndirea's near lifeless form on a soft pillow of moss.

Roble's fingers intertwined like he was in prayer, but he wasn't praying. His attention was attuned so much on her that he didn't notice Lehrling's approach. Worry chiseled furrows into his brow. His eyes were plagued by despair.

Lehrling placed a hand on Roble's shoulder and squeezed, jarring Roble from his near trancelike state. "Any word?"

The lost expression in Roble's eyes didn't have reason for a reply. He simply shook his head.

Lehrling patted Roble's back and stood in silence beside his friend. He glanced at Shawndirea. She repositioned herself slightly on the pillow but her eyes remained closed.

Roble's eyes brightened with hope at her sudden movement but after several more seconds, that brief glimmer of hope drained because she remained still. Apparently this must've been the first time she had moved since Roble arrived.

Rather than commenting or luring Roble into conversation, Lehrling remained silent and offered his support by taking a stool beside Roble. Only if Roble chose to talk would Lehrling speak, which Lehrling had learned during his years of growing wisdom. Silence was more comforting than words.

Roble's worry weighted like a heavy anchor. It was obvious that his thoughts were concerned only Shawndirea's well-being and her recovery. Lehrling questioned why Shawndirea's health had suddenly plummeted before they reached Dagger's Tears.

She had not been outside of Roble's pocket from the Glades of Sorrows to Dagger's Tears, so she shouldn't have been exposed to anything capable of causing such an ailment. Yet, she suffered. Roble's concern became Lehrling's.

With Shawndirea in such a condition, near death it seemed, Roble was in no frame of mind to confront Lez'minx in the god's temple. Roble's resolve was shattered. He was worried more about her life than his or anything else. Seeing Roble's turmoil made Lehrling question even pursuing a relationship with Collette. Albeit the current thought was premature at best, seeing Roble's heartache cutting to his core was an ache Lehrling didn't need, not after having lost so much already.

Shawndirea groaned, rolled to her side, and yet her eyes didn't open.

"She seems to be getting better," Portia said, gracefully walking to the table. Her movement was more gliding than walking.

Lehrling was taken back by her odd eyes, but he did his best not to reveal it. Collette was right. Portia was not like them. She wasn't human, not that it mattered, but he wondered what race she was. Her unusual features were not familiar to him.

"But what's wrong with her?" Roble asked.

Portia shrugged. "That's a mystery I've yet to solve. Nothing that I can find presents itself. Perhaps she's simply fatigued from journeying into the Unseelie territory? But as for any identifiable sickness? Nothing's out of the ordinary. My advice is for you and your friend to join the others at the lodge and eat a hearty meal."

Roble frowned. "No. I cannot leave her in this condition."

"You do her or yourself no favors by staying. You're tired, wearied from your travels, and without food and sustenance, you'll soon find your own health diminishing. Would she approve of such behavior?"

Roble sighed. "No, she wouldn't, but I don't feel right leaving her."

"She's safe here," Portia said. "That much I guarantee. Her ailment isn't getting worse."

"Why would her being in Unseelie territory cause her to get sick in the first place?" Lehrling asked.

"Typically, it shouldn't. But, crossing from one side to the other can bring fatigue," Portia said. "Now, although rare, magics from both Courts might be fighting to possess her."

"That could happen?" Roble asked.

"It's rare," Portia replied. "But not impossible within the Fae population. They attribute allegiance to one court, refute both courts, but for one to hold allegiance to both? I've not known any to take that path."

"She swears to uphold only the Seelie Court," Roble said. "She abhors the Unseelie Court, especially when others insinuate that she's Unseelie."

"Odd."

"What *exactly* is odd?" Lehrling asked.

"That others sense her Unseelie ties instead of her Seelie."

"It's more than obvious to assume she's Unseelie since she married me," Roble said. "Being as the Seelie will reject her since I'm not Fae."

Portia smiled. "Based upon principles, that might be considered true, but others sense that she taps her magic from the Unseelie. However, I sensed automatically the magic of the Seelie upon her. It might surprise you and her that those who verbally reject their opposite court are also the ones who are secretly appealed by it."

"It all confuses me," Lehrling said.

"For most humans, that's the case. But if she's somehow tapping magic from both Courts, no one rightly knows what the effects are. Since she's past the in-between, or the Fae's common ground, she might be overwhelmed by its saturation."

"So what's she suffering right now is not due to a curse or disease?" Roble asked.

"I don't believe so," Portia said. "Her body's simply reacting to being attuned to magic not totally familiar to her."

"We should go eat. I'm famished and I know you must be, too," Lehrling said. "From the aroma outside, this'll be the best meal we've had in weeks."

Roble flicked his gaze from Shawndirea to Portia.

"She'll be fine," Portia said. "In fact, you might return to find her awake and hungry as well."

Shawndirea curled into a fetal position. Nothing indicated she suffered pain of any sort. She looked to be deep in sleep. Almost peaceful. Color had returned to her face and her breathing was more pronounced.

Roble glanced at Lehrling. "What do you think?"

Lehrling's stomach growled. He rubbed his stomach and grinned. "That interruption speaks volumes, don't you think?"

"Never let your stomach lead your mind," Roble said.

Lehrling frowned, offended. "I'm not. But I agree with Portia. You'll renew your strength after eating, and your outlook will be better as well."

Roble sighed and pushed himself away from the table.

"If her condition worsens," Portia said, "and I don't believe it will, I'll send for you immediately."

Roble nodded.

Portia offered a warm smile, in her attempt to settle his nerves. "I understand your worries. You don't know me well enough to fully set aside your distrust, but my reputation rests high with the kind folks of Dagger's Tears. My life's been dedicated to healing, and I'd sacrifice my own life to protect any of those who live in our hamlet. I'd even do so for the two of you, if required. So please, go enjoy a hearty cooked meal, meet the wonderful folks that call this place home, and when you return, you spirits should be better than before."

"Come," Lehrling said, patting Roble's shoulder.

"Merla, Cora," Portia said. "Escort our new friends to the lodge so they can dine."

The two halflings offered slight bows and motioned Lehrling and Roble to the doorway.

At the threshold, Lehrling paused as Roble turned one last time to look at Shawndirea.

"She'll be fine, Dragon Knight," Portia said. "I can never understand why those from the Overlands worry and stress more than those in our realm."

CHAPTER 40

*R*oble stepped behind Lehrling onto the crude ramp. Merla pulled the door closed and they headed downward.

The evening breeze lofted with a delicious aroma, causing the intense hunger Roble had been ignoring to ignite. Despite his ravenous appetite, his heart and mind remained focused on Shawndirea. It was difficult and somewhat selfish, he thought, to separate himself from her and enjoy a good meal. Due to this, he doubted he'd *enjoy* the food.

Like Portia mentioned, Roble didn't know Portia well enough to suspend his distrust. He truly wished he could believe she could be trusted. She didn't seem to poise any threat, but through his ordeals to protect Shawndirea—and nearly failing a couple of times—being worried and on edge was a normal reaction.

Lez'minx had been the most recent threat. He still wondered if Lez'minx was the true reason for Shawndirea's sickness. If that were the case, her illness was his fault. His curiosity with the enchanted rings was the only reason for them to face Lez'minx.

Roble's mouth watered from the drifting aroma of the food. Before Roble realized it, they were already walked halfway to the lodge where two large chimneys rolled gray smoke.

"Smells great, huh?" Lehrling asked.

The question pulled Roble from his intense thought. He nodded. "It does."

"You never answered my earlier question," Lehrling said.

Question? Roble frowned.

Apparently Lehrling never stopped talking since they descended the ramp. Roble was so concerned with Shawndirea that he missed everything Lehrling had said.

"I'm sorry," Roble said. "What did you ask?"

"Were you able to find out anything about Lez'minx from Portia?"

"No. To be honest, I never discussed anything other than what could be done to help Shawndirea. As for Lez'minx, she says she's never heard his name."

"And if she said it," Merla said evenly, "she meant it."

"I didn't mean for that to sound disrespectful," Roble said.

Merla shrugged. "You'll find no other more honest and forthright than she. She's a healer and the last of her tribe. It's impossible for her to cast any negative spell or to lie or to cause harm to anyone."

"Impossible?" Lehrling asked, cocking a brow. "And you believe that?"

"Yes. Whatever she does is magnified tenfold back toward her," Cora said. "She's more than two centuries old. She's lived that long because of the healing she's given to others. To do evil, even in the slightest, is her automatic death. And due to her age, most likely, she'd probably die before she spoke the first word of an evil incantation. Shawndirea's probably far safer with Portia than anyone else."

"Then what could she do if someone tried to kill or abduct Shawndirea?" Roble asked. "If she cannot inflict harm—"

"That wasn't what I said," Cora replied. "She cannot cast evil spells to harm others. That has nothing to do with protection spells against those who wish to do her or others harm. It's not evil to defend your life or the lives of others whenever threatened."

"So what she's saying is this," Merla interrupted. "You needn't worry about Portia doing any harm to Shawndirea. Nor will she allow any harm to come to her."

Roble nodded, feeling a bit more relieved but he'd never fully stop worrying about Shawndirea until Lez'minx was dealt with. Lez'minx wasn't one to simply throw out a threat without intention. So Roble needed to take precaution at all times concerning Lez'minx. His threat on Shawndirea's life still hung and burned Roble's ears.

Roble scanned the edge of the lake. "Where'd everyone go?"

Lehrling explained about the giant swarm of bats. "These were the largest fanged beasts with wings I've ever seen."

"This isn't like that time you *almost* caught a dragonkin larger than a pony?" Roble asked with a wink and sly grin. "Even Boldair doesn't tell tales that tall."

Lehrling's brow rose in question before he grinned and laughed. "Oh, no, *that* was fictional. Because Boldair was in our company that day was exactly *why* I exaggerated. He wouldn't do any less."

"That's true. I have to agree with you on that," Roble replied.

"But I'm not exaggerating about these bats—"

Lehrling and Roble ducked at the same time. A second later, they'd have been struck in the face by a trio of huge bats. Their *swooshing* wings rang in their ears.

"*Now* do you believe me!" Lehrling asked.

"Absolutely," Roble replied. "Impossible to deny."

"Those bats are pesky at times," Cora said. "But for the amount of pests they kill, I'd gladly yield an early hour per night to a curfew. Less labor for us to endure anyways."

Merla laughed with a high-pitched, gleeful sound. "Some of the fish are larger than us. If the townsfolk grow desperate, they could use us as bait."

Roble almost laughed aloud, but thought it better not to, as strangely the idea had crossed his mind as a joke. "What did you mean about Portia being the last of her kind?"

"Again, not what I had said. She's the last of her *tribe*."

"What race is she?" Lehrling asked.

"I'm not sure," Merla replied. "All I know is that her tribe was south on the river near where the river splits near Spellhaven."

"And they're dead?" Roble asked.

Cora shrugged. "It's possible. She doesn't rightly know. A great flood washed away her village when she was a child. She never found other survivors and somehow survived on her own for many years in the hidden depths of the swamps."

"By herself?" Lehrling frowned with curiosity.

"She's never said, but eventually she moved upriver. We first encountered her when we were forced to leave the Glades of Sorrow," Merla said.

"Interesting," Roble said softly.

Cora stopped at the foot of the steps at the longest stilted building. "This is our lodge. The dinner bell hasn't rang yet, but due to the bats arriving earlier than normal, it's okay for us to head up and find ourselves a seat."

Roble nodded. He glanced toward the other houses and buildings. Other folks with fearful expressions on their faces peered through the slight cracks of their open doors. He guessed they were looking for the bats because after a few seconds, they emerged and started down the ramps of their buildings.

"After the two of you," Roble said, extending his hand.

"You're our guests," Cora said. "It's only fitting that the two of you proceed ahead of us."

Lehrling offered a broad grin. "As knights and gentlemen, we cannot impose rudeness by walking ahead of you young ladies. Besides, it's best since you're familiar with the seating arrangements so you can show us where to sit. I'd hate to find myself in a magistrate's chair."

"As would I," Roble said.

"You've no need to worry of that here," Merla said. "We're all commoners who share the labors equally. No one presides over us. Whatever situations arise are generally handled in a large group meeting where we discuss and decide what's the best for everyone."

"And that actually works?" Roble asked.

"You seem surprised by that," Cora said with a curious frown. "Why?"

Roble chuckled. "Because in my world, problems never get settled like that. It quickly turns to hostility and dangerous fighting."

"It works perfectly fine for us," she replied.

"Then you live in quite a pleasant place," Roble said.

"We've no council like larger towns or cities. No ruler, which is what we prefer. Why should one or a few select individuals make all the major decisions for the entire hamlet?" Cora asked. "Such power often turns into greed, giving the overseers the opportunity to make laws more beneficial to themselves by ignoring those who have greater needs."

"It's a far from perfect system," Roble said. "But that's also the problem with vast amounts of diversity and needs. It's impossible to achieve equality. Where I once lived, total chaos explodes because everyone holds their views and needs higher than everyone else's. Common courtesies are rare. Folks don't discuss communal needs and goals. They simply try to yell over those they disagree with. I wish your system worked in my land. I'd have had a more difficult time leaving it behind."

"You're more than welcome to stay with us," Cora said.

Roble shook his head. "While I appreciate the offer, I must decline. I've too many obligations elsewhere."

"As do I," Lehrling said.

Cora opened the door. Merla stepped across the threshold, peered around the room, and then motioned Roble and Lehrling to enter. Within a few seconds of coming inside, Dolan marched to Cora and Merla with a stern frown. The fierce anger in his eyes almost magnified his stature, and if properly measured, Dolan would have been a giant.

"Where have you two been?" he demanded. "You've been holding me up."

Merla met his glare with one of her own. "Portia requested that we aid her a bit *longer*. If you've a problem with that, take it up with her."

The frown disappeared from Dolan's face, and he paled slightly. "Places, please."

Cora said, "As soon as we show them where the plates and utensils are, and where they're welcome to sit, we'll join you."

"You best hope your instruments are tuned," Dolan whispered. "Without time to rehearse, I don't want embarrassed like the last time."

"It will be fine," Merla said.

Dolan huffed and walked away.

"Come," Cora said. She led them to the line to get wooden plates, bowls, and utensils.

"It seems rude for us to be served first," Roble said.

"Nonsense," Merla said. "You're our guests. Guests are always served first. Now, if you'll excuse us, we need to get on stage before Dolan's head explodes."

She and Cora hurried away.

Roble exchanged curious glances with Lehrling. "Stage?"

Lehrling shrugged. "Let them do what they need. I'm too famished not to help myself, rude or not."

"The smell's inviting enough," Roble said. He took a bowl and followed Lehrling to the line where clay plates of hot food simmered.

The door opened and the townsfolk bustled inside.

Lehrling took portions of cooked fish, mussels, and a huge bowl of soup. Roble followed him and took the same.

"Let's eat," Roble said, walking toward one of the tables.

CHAPTER 41

*A*fter they had taken their seats, Roble noticed Lehrling kept his attention on the door. Roble devoured all the fish and mussels on his plate but Lehrling had not yet touched his.

"What happened to your being *famished*?" Roble asked. "After eating jerky and dried fruit for days, I'd think you'd welcome freshly cooked food. This is the best food we've had in weeks, but you've not eaten a bite."

Lehrling glanced at his plate and poked at the food. "It looks great."

"Are you waiting for someone?" Roble asked.

Lehrling blushed. "In a way I guess I am."

"Who?"

Lehrling's face reddened. He took a bite of fish. Chewing, he said, "You're right. The food is wonderful."

"You scoundrel," Roble said with a broad grin. He playfully thrusted an elbow into Lehrling's side. "I guess you need a chaperone at all times, eh?"

"No-o-o," Lehrling said with a frown, shaking his head. He huffed and wiped his mouth. "That's not necessary. It's nothing like that. But I did meet a woman at the docks while tending to the horses. She's who informed me about the bats before they descended like a mad storm."

"She must be someone special to keep you watching the door so intently," Roble said.

He shrugged. "I enjoyed the few minutes we shared talking. She's someone I'd love to talk with a lot longer. A *lifetime* longer."

Roble chuckled. "That's quite serious insight toward a woman you've only met."

"Don't mock me," Lehrling said, taking another bite. After several more chews, he said, "This is the best thing I've eaten in years. Better than anything the chefs at the palaces make."

"I'm not mocking you," Roble said, softly.

Lehrling took another bite and savored it, closing his eyes. "Food's almost magical."

"I agree. It's the most flavorful meal I've had since I've entered Aetheaon."

Lehrling swallowed and sighed with delight. Waving his fork above his plate, he said, "Roble, have you ever met someone and during the first few minutes of talking, something about the person connected to you? I know she's a stranger, but I feel like we've met in—" He paused and chuckled. "I feel like I've met her in a different life. Sounds preposterous, I know. Only one life—"

Roble shook his head. "No, it's not preposterous. It's a deep connection. I've felt it at times, when I was much younger and before I met Shawndirea and left the Overlands. It's an infatuation that opens the door between the two of you to spend more time to get to know one another."

"Kind of like you and Shawndirea?"

"No, not at first," Roble replied. "She held great fury toward me because I had caught her in a butterfly net and destroyed her wings."

Lehrling nodded. "Ah, yeah, that's right. She had every right to be furious."

"I agree. But maybe this woman—"

"Collette," Lehrling said, wiping his mouth with a cloth napkin. "Her name is Collette."

Roble tried to hide his sly grin. He didn't wish to fluster Lehrling further by teasing him, so he averted the temptation. "Maybe Collette's the one for you?"

"Oh, no, she's too young." Uneasy, Lehrling shook his head fiercely. His chubby cheeks wiggled beneath his blonde beard.

"What's age got to do with it? As far as that goes, what does race or species have to do with love at all?" Roble asked. "Until I met Shawndirea, never in a million years would I have ever thought a human could marry a faery, simply because our height differences are a factor. Yet, due to her magical abilities, she's able to transform to the height of a human. Age, my friend, is the least obstacle."

"I know I've overthought that issue. But still, she intrigues me. She told me that she's never seen the sun during her lifetime. Can you imagine that?"

Roble frowned and thought of such a possibility. "Actually, no. However, these past few days I've wondered if we'll *ever* see the sun again. But never seeing the sun during my lifetime? That's something I've always taken for granted, I suppose."

"Exactly! You see, I'm the same way. And if she were the one for me ... I'd love to see her eyes the first moment the brightness shines on her face."

Watching Lehrling's beaming smile, Roble smiled. "That would indeed be a moment."

Several instruments strummed from a small stage across the room. Dolan sat on a stool with a dulcimer set across his lap. Cora held a bass much taller than he expected a halfling capable to hold. Merla held a lute. After checking their tuning by playing a few chords for adequate harmony, Dolan nodded and they strummed a soft melody.

The tables around the one where Roble and Lehrling sat began filling with the townsfolk. Bustling and soft conversation chatter soon drowned out the music. Roble tried not to feel uncomfortable, but all eyes were upon him and Lehrling. Curious questions whispered amongst the crowd. Roble understood they were intrigued by their visitors.

A young lady that Roble estimated to be in her late teens approached them with a tall pitcher. She set two clay flasks on the table before them.

Offering a slight smile, she said, "Bitter beer?"

"Please," Lehrling said, returning the smile. "Thank you."

Roble nodded and slid the flask over to where she could pour easier. "Thanks."

Lehrling took a swig and his face creased like a prune. "Ghastly."

"Bitter, I take it?" Roble said, laughing.

He cleared his throat. "Horse piss would be kinder."

"Where's your lady friend?" Roble asked. "Did she indicate *when* she'd meet you?"

Lehrling shrugged. "All she said was that she'd meet me for supper. I expected her arrival already because she told me the best food was served first. She was right about that."

"I guess she didn't warn you about the beer?"

Lehrling rubbed his throat. "Nope. Guess the potential romance is gone now."

Roble chuckled. "That bad?"

"You try it."

"Think I'll pass."

"Quite wise for an Overlander," Lehrling said with a wink. He gasped and his eyes widened slightly.

"What is it?"

Lehrling lowered his head and looked at his plate. "That's Collette. She just entered through the door."

CHAPTER 42

$\mathcal{R}$oble studied Collette when she stepped inside the lodge door and looked around. She appeared excited and a little nervous as her eyes searched the tables. She wore a plain gown and worn boots. Her brown hair was combed neatly and hung around her shoulders. In comparison to the other women in the room, Collette had invested time in making herself more presentable.

"That's her?" Roble asked, nodding at the door.

Lehrling's eyes widened. He looked down and whispered, "Yes. What should I do?"

"First, greet her with a smile," Roble said. "Don't act like a child. You're a man. Be bold and brave. No sense being nervous. Your introductions have already been made. Ignoring her entrance will make her feel like you aren't interested in her."

"It's not that."

"Then what?"

"She's more stunning than I ever imagined," Lehrling said, braving himself to cast a glance and smile in her direction to which she smiled and nodded modestly. He waved and his grin widened.

Roble said, "She's beautiful. Are you saying you didn't notice before?"

"You'd have had to see her before. She was covered with fish guts and scales and blood, and even then, her beauty shone through."

"Don't worry about the age difference then," Roble said.

"Why's that?"

"If she went to the trouble of making herself more presentable in such a little amount of time, she must have some interest in you."

"I could only hope."

"Don't sell yourself short. I might tease you about your age from time to time, but you've still got *some* life in you."

Lehrling rolled his eyes. "Gee, thanks."

"You know I'm only kidding."

Lehrling chuckled. "I know. Would she really try to impress me like that?"

"If you like a woman, wouldn't you attempt to make yourself more attractive when you met her again?"

"Don't I look presentable enough?" he asked, suddenly plucking bits of food from his beard and trying to comb back his hair with his fingers.

"You look fine," Roble asked. "I simply gave that as an example. You'd want to look your best, right?"

"Sure." He looked to see where Collette was. "Are you sure I look okay?"

"As presentable as any traveling knight is expected to be."

Lehrling raised his right arm slightly and sniffed at his underarm. "Gad! The bitter beer tastes better than I smell."

"Calm down."

Lehrling sighed. "I'll try. I just don't understand why she'd go to the extra trouble to make herself more attractive when I was *already* attracted to her."

"You told her?"

"Well, no, not in *direct* words." Lehrling chewed his lower lip. "I hinted, and I'm certain I blushed several full sunsets of red while talking to her. Generally, that's the biggest hint. Isn't it?"

Roble nodded. "Being as she's never seen the sun—"

Lehrling frowned. "I'm being serious."

"I know. Forgive me," Roble said. "Blushing is a definite sign from some. But be yourself. Nothing more than how you acted when you first spoke to her. Don't act cocky, unless you want to send her running the other direction."

Lehrling shook his head and chuckled. "I can't believe I'm your elder and getting advice from you about women. Not that that's a bad thing. Obviously, I misread Sarey's interest in Bausch and ruined that opportunity for him, so I should take advice rather than give it."

"Just keep your composure and compliment her. Here she comes."

Collette approached from the opposite side of the table and smiled at Lehrling. "Would you mind if I sit across from you?"

Lehrling stood. "Not at all."

Roble stood as well.

Due to how the tables were arranged, Lehrling was unable to make his way around the table to help seat her. He motioned his hand instead. "Please."

With a slight blush, she sat and replied, "Thanks."

"Collette," Lehrling said, still standing. "I'd like you to meet my fellow knight and my closest friend, Roble. Roble, this is Collette."

"A pleasure," Roble said with a slight bow.

"Likewise," she said.

After they seated themselves, Roble picked at the remaining bits of food on his plate, trying not to start the conversation for Lehrling. Lehrling was obviously nervous. Too nervous for words, so Roble gently tapped Lehrling's foot with his boot.

Lehrling cleared his throat. "You look … lovely this evening."

"Thanks," Collette said, blushing.

"And you were right," he said.

"About what?"

"How great the food is."

"Visitors find it delightful, but for us, eating this every day gets tiresome."

"I imagine so," Roble said.

Collette turned her attention to Roble. "May I ask? How is your … the faery recuperating?"

Roble said, "She's not fully recovered. But Portia believes Shawndirea had gotten past the worst."

"Good news then?" Collette asked.

"In a manner of speaking," Roble replied.

"Portia knows what she's talking about and is very knowledgeable."

"That's what I keep hearing," Roble said.

"None have ever said a bad word about her," Collette said.

"Some seem to fear her."

"Reverence is not fear," Collette said.

Reverence? Roble frowned. "According to the halflings, no one rules over Dagger's Tears. Is that true?"

"It's true."

"But Portia seems to hold some control over everyone," Roble said. "What you call reverence … well, let me say … comes across as fear in the eyes of those who might question her authority."

Collette's eyes shifted nervously from Roble's and then to Lehrling's. "She holds no authority. She is equal to the rest of us."

"I simply was trying to understand her position," Roble said. "So forgive me if I asked more than I should."

She ignored Roble's statement and kept her gaze on Lehrling. "When do you plan to leave Dagger's Tears?"

Lehrling thought for a moment before glancing at Roble. "Once Portia says Shawndirea is well enough to travel?"

Roble nodded. "Yes, once she's safe to travel, we're moving on."

"Where will you go?" she asked, looking at Lehrling with disappointment.

"That's something we don't know exactly," Lehrling replied.

"Why wander from the safety of Dagger's Tears when you don't know your destination?"

Lehrling opened his mouth to reply, but hesitated and glanced at Roble.

"Actually," Roble said, "we hoped Portia might have known the where-abouts of a temple we seek."

"She doesn't?"

Roble shook his head. "No."

"If she doesn't," Collette said, "it's doubtful I can help you, either."

Roble smiled. "So far, no one has had any information to help us in our search."

Lehrling said, "Yes, we keep traveling deeper into the swamps without any clue of where we are or what direction to take."

"Dagger's Tears and the Glades of Sorrow are the only places I know," she said. Her eyes suddenly beamed hope and her voice became cheerier. "Like I expressed earlier, I want to travel outside these swamps one day to see the things you've seen."

"And dear lady," Lehrling said, "I'd be honored to take you from here and show you those places."

Roble's brow rose at the quickness of Lehrling's offer. While he wasn't totally surprised by Lehrling's eagerness to fulfill Collette's dreams, Roble didn't want her to get her hopes up too soon. Their quest to find Lez'minx and for Roble to break his ties to the god or demigod or whatever he was, was nowhere near over. The trip ahead proved to become even more dangerous.

"You would?" she asked.

Lehrling's eyes were lost in hers. His infatuation overtook him. Nothing Roble said at the moment could sway Lehrling from the promise issued to Collette. Roble recognized that lost smitten look on other people's faces. Such a person never accepted logical advice, even from those with the best intentions. Whether given by friends, family, or counselors, such advice fell on deaf ears.

"Over my dead body!" a rugged voice bellowed several tables away.

Immediately, Roble and Lehrling looked in the direction of the man's voice. Seated at the table was an older man, perhaps ten years Lehrling's senior, but a man whose voice thundered in spite of his small stature. The man wore a thick patch over his left eye with a deep scar that traveled from his upper lip, across his missing eye, and gullied a nasty trail across the man's bald head. The anger in his gaze and the tightness of his jaw were evidence of his furious objection.

"Father!" Collette said.

The man adjusted himself in his chair and leaned forward, which took a great deal of his energy, as he was missing his left leg from the knee down. How he lived after suffering such injuries was a mystery to Roble.

Collette's father propped upon the stub of his left arm and firmly pointed his right index finger at Lehrling. "You dare enter Dagger's Tears and attempt to fill my daughter's mind with your lofty tales, trying to take her from us?

She belongs here, with her family, and not wandering through the godforsaken swamps—"

Collette stood with tears in her eyes. Her face reddened. "I've no hope here, father! None. There's no life for me in a world of shadows, constant rain, and sheer misery. I always reek of fish! This place is nothing but a prison for me."

"Silence, Collette!" he said. "You've no need for a suitor outside of Dagger's Tears when several hardy men have already asked for your hand in marriage."

"None I'd have myself to be with," she replied, promptly crossing her arms.

Two of the younger filthy fishermen looked hurt and disappointed by her statement and lowered their gazes.

Dolan, Merla, and Cora stopped playing their instruments and exchanged stunned glances.

Lehrling turned his chair around, smiled graciously, and said, "Sir, I meant no offense to you or your family. I find your beautiful daughter to be one of the finest ladies I've ever had the pleasure of meeting."

"In the matter of a half hour you've come to such a conclusion?" he snarled.

"The brevity might seem hasty," Lehrling said. "But how can one not see that? She is indeed a—"

In a gravelly tone, he said, "Knight, hold your tongue. You're not amongst friends at the moment."

Roble's hand instinctively slid over one of his hidden daggers. He turned in his seat.

Lehrling noticed Roble's fingers tense and apparently recognized the intense glare in Roble's eyes. He shook his head and whispered, "No, Roble."

"That cannot be accepted as less than a threat," Roble replied.

"I'd have you two knights depart in the morning, *without* my daughter."

"*Father*—" Collette whispered. She wiped tears from her eyes and glanced toward the lady seated beside her father. "Mother?"

Her mother glanced at Collette's father with a bit of fright and stammered, "You're being unfair, Jaux."

Jaux leveled a quick frown at her. She turned and looked down, suddenly silent. Jaux returned his hardened gaze at Lehrling. "Knight, I'm sure you tell that to all the young lasses from town to town as you and your brotherly knights travel, seeking the fairest maidens to add notches to your belts."

"That's the furtherest thing from the truth, sir," Lehrling said, his voice shaking with anger. "I've no notches on my belt, nor do I ever seek such shallowness in relations. The Dragon Skull Order holds a prestigious reputation with all cities, towns, and hamlets throughout Aetheaon. As a Dragon Skull Knight, I've devoted myself to Hoffnung, my King and Queen, having denied myself many things, one of which is marrying and having a home."

"Bit old for that now, don't you think?" Jaux said.

Lehrling fought to suppress his anger, giving Roble a side-glance. "It's true that I'm not as spry as I once was, but—"

"But *nothing*! I'll not have you ride into our hamlet, filling my daughter's head with all sorts of delusional dreams that might well lead to her death." Spittle flew from his crooked, near-toothless, mouth. He paused to wipe his lips with the back of his hand. "She has her home *here*. Not with you and *not* elsewhere."

Collette fumed as her fading fear of her father turned to anger. "He never filled my mind with delusions. Every day I stare at the river and I wonder what's to the north and what's to the south. Curiosity eats at me. I want more than this life. Forgive me for dreaming about more than *this*. If I choose to leave Dagger's Tears, that's my decision, father. Not yours," Collette said.

"Mind your tongue," Jaux said. "We cannot afford the loss of our people migrating to lands unknown. You see my physical condition. *This* happened with my helping to establish Dagger's Tears."

Lehrling stood. "I've not so much as even *hinted* at marriage. I've not offered a proposal. I simply said that I'd be honored to show her these places she desires to see. That much is true. Why does that draw outrageous hostility from you?"

"You're trying to lure her away from us," Jaux said.

"Preposterous!" Lehrling said. His face reddened.

"Father, he's not offered any proposal, nor have I sought that," Collette said. "But I want to see what's outside these swamps. I'm tired of this meager life and toiling away from morning to dusk with no pleasure in sight."

"What do you expect to find outside the swamps? That you can shake trees and have gold coins rain to the ground?"

"No," she said. Fiercer anger burned in her eyes. "My desire is not for monetary treasure. I hope to bless my senses with the rarer beauties my eyes and ears have never beheld."

"Our lives are dangerous enough living *inside* our hamlet," Jaux said. "Far worse lies outside of Dagger's Tears. On the fringes of our borders unnatural creatures constantly seek to destroy us. Why else do you think we fled the Glades of Sorrow? You're no different than the rest of our community. You're not a knight or warrior capable of defending yourself. You've no magical wards to keep you safe. You're a commoner, as we all are."

Roble stood. His hands rested on his belt.

Lehrling reached a frantic hand to grab Roble's forearm, but Roble stepped outside of his reach.

Roble's eyes searched the faces of the others seated at their tables. Finally, his gaze rested on Jaux. "If I may, I'd like to address the room."

Although tired and weary, the other townsfolk lowered their forks and nodded slowly, giving him permission to speak.

CHAPTER 43

"I'll try to make this brief," Roble said.

"You'd do us all a favor by doing so," Jaux said. His one eye narrowed and his mouth twisted with his angered disgust.

Roble's jaw tightened. He glared at Jaux. "If you're one for bluntness and insults, I can offer that, too. But be forewarned, if your threats escalate, you'd best be ready to back your hostile words with a blade."

Jaux's face softened slightly, but more in response to the angered stares that the others seated in the room displayed toward him. Several of the men shook their heads at Jaux.

Roble wondered how little the others favored Jaux. The old man's soured demeanor had probably already rubbed the majority of the hamlet's attitude toward him raw.

Roble took the moment as an opportunity to make a point and hopefully sway the support of the townsfolk. "As I understand it, no one in Dagger's Tears presides over everyone else. Isn't that a fact? Or is it you, Jaux, who somehow believes, due to your physical condition, that your word is law over all the rest? Do you govern these people?"

Jaux paled and swallowed hard. He adjusted himself slightly.

"He does not!" a grimy man seated at a table behind Jaux exclaimed. His fury brought spittle to the sides of his mouth, and he appeared ready to bolt at Jaux.

Others grumbled their agreement.

Jaux tried to make himself smaller in response to the tension building around him. He sighed and his pale face grew slack, as did his jaw.

"Lehrling and I are, as he mentioned, Dragon Skull Knights. We never prey upon those we visit, and we pay for any goods and services we need. We do not submit ourselves to charity, nor do we ransack any village. The oath we've sworn demands we uphold our behavior above all others or we'd be held accountable before our Queen and the Order. Lehrling's a man of honor, respects everyone he meets, and he'd give his own life to defend the crown or any of his friends. Even those he has just met. His heart is far larger and worth far more than all the treasure hidden inside the dragons' lairs.

"That being said, I'll add that I share the same attributes, with one exception. I never take threats directed toward me or any of our knights lightly. I react to defend those within the Order with swift judgment. Often with a blade if the threat becomes physical. Understand that we're simply passing through, and we greatly appreciate your hospitality. But as for Jaux dismissing our arrival and demanding we leave in the morning, is that a decision he so rightly has?"

Almost all of the older men and women shook their heads.

"Because," Roble said, "my wife is ill and she's with Portia. I refuse to leave Dagger's Tears until she's able to travel. If any oppose our stay, voice your opposition now."

A man with greasy hair and a matted beard sat upright. "Jaux hasn't the authority to dismiss you and Sir Lehrling. We're a community that has always made precedent as a body through a group proposal. I, for one, vote that you stay until you're able to travel."

"As do I," another said.

"Me, too," an elderly man stated. And the sentiment echoed throughout the room.

The women in the room nodded their agreement.

"We appreciate this," Roble said. "Now, what is your statute concerning one of your residents that wishes to leave your hamlet?"

"None have ever left," another man said.

"Ever?" Roble couldn't hide his surprise. "So none of you have been outside the swamps?"

He shook his head. "Of course, *some* have been. Just none of our original settlement have ever left to explore what lies beyond the swamps. Over the years, we've gained new residents who got lost in the swamps and entered our hamlet, seeking shelter. Since they feared moving onward, we offered them refuge. But none born in our settlement have left. We know the outside dangers and how foolish it'd be to leave the safety of our haven."

"Do you oppose Collette's decision to leave?" Roble asked.

Their gazes returned to Jaux. If Roble had ever seen a more sour expression on a man's face, he couldn't recall it. The bitterness contained within Collette's father came from a deep place. Roble didn't believe the man was intentionally hostile. A great deal of his vileness stemmed from his injuries. Jaux didn't have any prosthetics to aid him and was apparently suffering each passing day without the ability to leave his chair.

"Folks of Dagger's Tears," an elderly man seated several chairs away from Jaux said, "how many favor allowing Collette to journey with these two honorable knights? Give a show of hands."

Only three refused to raise their hands: Jaux and two of the younger men that Roble assumed must have been Collette's hopeful suitors in spite of her open rejections.

Jaux gazed around the room at those with their hands raised. He was disheartened, and then dismayed when he noticed his wife's hand raised along with all the others to allow Collette to leave. He grumbled in silence, shaking his head.

Tears glistened in Collette's eyes. She wiped them away and smiled. "Thanks be to all of you."

"Well, what now?" Jaux asked.

Collette ignored his question and directed her attention to the townsfolk. "Please, back to eating. Blessings to you."

When Lehrling faced her, she said, "I need to get some food before it's gone."

After she walked away, Lehrling lowered himself into his chair, as did Roble. Lehrling shook his head and sighed. "That was interesting. You have a way with a crowd."

Roble chuckled. "Thanks."

"Of course, the threat of using weapons to those who opposed was quite the majestic touch."

Roble whispered, "Jaux doesn't seem to have many friends amongst his own hamlet, which isn't surprising, given his radiant charm."

Lehrling coughed to cover his laughter.

"I've the feeling that any weapons drawn by those in Dagger's Tears tonight would've been aimed at him and not us," Roble said.

"A victory, all the same," Lehrling said.

"Is it?"

Lehrling frowned. "What do you mean?"

"We cannot take Collette with us."

"Beg pardon?"

"She's not safe once we find Lez'minx's temple and confront him."

"We cannot leave her here after all of this," Lehrling said. "You had them call for a vote. They voted in her favor. Imagine her heartbreak and humiliation. Look at her now."

Roble watched her at the cook's line, filling her plate. Her face glowed with renewed vigor.

"You dash her dreams now," Lehrling said, softly. "You extinguish her light forever."

"Be honest, Lehrling. Do you think we can possibly protect her against Lez'minx?"

Lehrling took a bite of his food and thought while chewing slowly. His eyes went distant for several long moments. He swallowed. "At the success we've had in finding his temple thus far, Roble, it's highly likely that we're *not* going to find him."

"No? And what if he finds us?"

Lehrling took a sharp breath and held it, considering the possibility.

Roble nodded. "He's found us once, and given that Shawndirea's health faded soon afterwards, who knows if her spell that overshadows his view through these rings has vanished? Besides, he vowed harm to Shawndirea because he knows her importance to me. That's what villains do. They attack your loved ones to make you bend to their will or to punish you. Lez'minx would attack Collette to weaken you. Is that what you want for her?"

Lehrling sighed and wiped his mouth. Sweat beaded his brow. "No, it's not."

"Neither do I."

"So you think Shawndirea's sickness was caused by Lez'minx?"

"Portia seems to believe it's not, but I cannot shake the possibility that he's the one responsible." Roble took a whiff of the bitter beer and pushed it away.

"My suspicions match yours," Lehrling said. He leaned closer to Roble and whispered. "Collette's coming. Can we *not* mention leaving her here until tomorrow? I'll try to find a way to break the news to her softly, alone. But tonight, I can't bear seeing her—"

Roble nodded and stood. "Understood. No need to upset her. Look, I'm going to leave you two alone so I can see if Shawndirea has gotten better."

Collette beamed a smile at Roble.

"Collette," Roble said. "It's been a pleasure meeting you. I need to excuse myself."

Her eyes glistened. "I hope all is well for your faery."

"She's my wife, not a possession."

"Yes. My apologies," she said, nodding. "Thank you for addressing everyone in my defense."

He glanced at Lehrling. "You know where to find me."

Lehrling nodded. "May the Three Goddesses bless Shawndirea and may good news await you."

CHAPTER 44

*A*s Roble made his way back to Portia's home, his horse and Lehrling's were grazing at sprigs of swamp grass under a neighboring stilted building. Bleys raised his head and nuzzled his nose against Roble's hand.

Roble unfastened his saddlebag, slung it over his shoulder, and then he took Lehrling's saddlebag and carried them to Portia's home.

Night insects voiced a harsh chorus from the tall grasses, sedges, the river bank, and the few thorny shrubs scattered between the houses. He ascended the ramp to Portia's home and paused at the top balcony. He leaned against the railing and studied the area.

The ominous night didn't offer the slightest hint of moonlight. The mystery of the constant cloud cover and fog disturbed him. Nothing in science of the Overlands explained the phenomenon. The swamps were indeed cursed to remain in shadow.

The heavy fluttering of wings overhead indicated the swarming bats were still hunting insects. Unlike most people, he found bats intriguing and held no fear of them, regardless of their size or numbers.

Torches blazed in braziers at each corner of every building, offering a slight dot-to-dot outline of the village. Several watchmen patrolled the river's edge. Their lanterns bobbed side to side as they walked the bank. Several men stood in the glow of a large fire near the ferry where he, Lehrling, and Shawndirea had crossed earlier.

The folks of Dagger's Tears were fishermen and lived off the land. They were peaceful, modest people. What weapons did they have to defend themselves from invaders? They deserted the Glades of Sorrow without much resistance. The buildings and homes left behind remained habitable.

Were the giant turtles in the muddy river enough to prevent the Saurians

195

from crossing and attacking. After seeing the massive turtle tow the ferry and knowing more of these abnormal giants lurked in the water, Roble would never swim in the river. The jaws of those turtles could rip a man in half with little effort.

The narrow land area between the oxbow lake and the river was outlined by fiery braziers. He imagined, if viewed from the sky, this outline resembled a large burning eye.

The echoes of the patrols alerting one another that all was clear caught his attention. After their cries, the men at the large fire continued their quiet, murmuring conversations.

A moving row of torches caught his attention. Beyond the oxbow lake, a trail of flickering fire serpentined in an odd fashion until it formed a curved line along the outer edge of the lake. None of the guards noticed. Perhaps at ground level they were unable to see their approach. Were these Saurians or a different band of potential invaders?

From the center of the line, one torch intensified. The flame was not fiery orange like the others. The fire held an icy blue with a purplish outer glow. The fiery orb increased its intensity. Its odd steady incandesce indicated it was not normal fire. This light was the product of magic; possibly from a sorcerer or something far worse.

Roble glanced at his rings in the faint flickering of a glowing lantern on Portia's balcony. The rings' stones were still tarnished like burnt lightbulbs, and offered no pristine glow. Shawndirea's spell held. Lez'minx was unable to track them through the rings. However, that didn't mean he was unaware of their location at Dagger's Tears. The torchbearers might have arrived on his behalf.

Either way, the torchbearers were potential enemies. Since the only one capable of using magic inside Dagger's Tears was Portia, she needed to be alerted about the group on the other side of the oxbow lake.

Roble hurried along the edge of the balcony and around the corner until he came to Portia's door. He raised his hand to rap upon the door and hesitated. Various worries and dreads about Shawndirea's welfare shot through his mind. He imagined the worst of all possibilities for her fate had occurred.

His worst fear was that Shawndirea had died from the strange sickness. A lump grew in his throat, making *not* entering a somewhat better option than discovering the truth. Stepping inside, he'd know one way or the other. Was he ready to accept and cope with the possible loss?

Another fear was that Portia had taken Shawndirea and fled, as some races considered Fae blood a priceless ingredient in their rituals and spells.

"Come inside," Portia said in an annoyed tone. "Your delay entering is not necessary."

Her statement caught Roble off guard. He pushed open the door. Incense greeted him. Candles and lanterns brightened the room. His gaze immediately sought the table where he left Shawndirea. To his surprise, she sat and drank from a tiny cup.

His face brightened and he rushed to the table. He sighed heavily and whispered, "Ah, thank goodness, you're alive!"

A curious smile spread across her face. "Of course, I'm alive. I was only in a deep sleep. You thought I was dying?"

Roble frowned. "I wasn't certain what you were suffering from, especially since Lez'minx had threatened your life. I feared he might have somehow placed a curse on you."

She took another sip from the cup. "No, he has done no such thing."

"You've experienced this type of deep sleep before?"

She shook her head. "No."

"Any idea why this happened?"

"Portia and I have been discussing this," Shawndirea replied.

Roble flicked his gaze toward Portia. "How long has she been awake?"

"Soon after you left to eat," Portia replied.

"Sorry I didn't stay," Roble said, looking at Shawndirea.

"Quite all right. You mustn't grow weaker worrying over me."

"Why did you slip into this sleep?"

"Portia and I believe it occurred because I passed through the in-between into the heart of the Unseelie territory. My body, mind, and spirit needed time to adjust. Of course, someone within the Unseelie might've cast resistance spells against me, hoping I'd leave."

"They'd seek to harm you?"

She shrugged. "Their goal might only be to discourage me from going further into their magical flux. But something else might be responsible."

"Like what?" Roble asked.

"Those spellbooks we kept. The ones I read at such a rapid pace."

"How would that affect you?"

"Devouring too many darker spells at a quick rate? I can't be certain, but I grew weaker not long after I tethered them into my memories."

"Wouldn't that *increase* your strength?" he asked.

"It could, depending upon the magical ties. Since a lot of those spells are contrary to the type of magic I wield, it's possible I suffered an internal struggle as my mind attempted to balance the knowledge."

"Tell him what you learned from entering the dream realm," Portia said.

Roble stared at Shawndirea with genuine curiosity.

"I'm still sorting through all of the meaning," Shawndirea said. "I'm can't properly discern everything yet. But it seems the Seelie awaits my return. I was told *not* to cast aside my ties to the Seelie for the Unseelie."

"By whom?" Roble asked.

Shawndirea's brow furrowed. She pursed her lips. "That part remains a mystery. He, or she, never revealed a name. Although, I did ask."

"More information might come in her future dreams," Portia said.

"Yes, this is true," Shawndirea replied.

Roble leaned his face lower. She stood, rubbed his bearded cheek, and gently kissed him. "I feared losing you."

"You've not yet, love," she said softly.

"I've learned to expect the unexpected."

Shawndirea smiled. "Anyone should, regardless of what realm they live in."

Roble glanced at Portia. "Thanks for watching over her."

"Any time. May I ask how you enjoyed your meal?" Portia asked him.

"It was amazing."

"And the hospitality?"

Roble chuckled. "I'm sure you'll learn more of that tomorrow."

"Oh? Something I should concern myself with?"

"You behaved yourself, didn't you?" Shawndirea asked with a sly smile.

"As best I could, given the circumstances. But a larger concern awaits beyond the oxbow lake."

Portia's brow rose. "Like what?"

Roble described the line of torches.

Portia smiled. "Oh ... They come every evening and stand throughout the night. They've done this for several months now."

"You don't view them as a threat?"

"They are a potential threat, but they cannot get past my magical barrier. They've tried and never succeeded."

He told of the odd light from an orb.

Portia stiffened and concern overshadowed her face. "That's never been witnessed before. Come, show me."

CHAPTER 45

Roble stepped beside Portia onto the balcony with Shawndirea seated on his left shoulder. He walked around the side balcony and was greeted by a harsh sticky breeze that hinted of coming rain. The humidity made breathing difficult by magnifying the acrid odor of the surrounding stagnant water pools.

Roble pointed at the line of flickering torches. At the center was the icy blue glow. "There."

Portia placed her hands upon the railing and studied the orb. Her eyes widened with fear. But once she regained her composure, her eyes narrowed. "The one with that orb hasn't been here before."

"How can you be sure?" he asked.

"I'd have sense it."

"But you didn't sense this before I brought it to your attention," Roble said.

"I sensed something. I assumed it was Shawndirea's magic after she awakened."

"I sensed the sorcery, too," Shawndirea said. "But it's not Lez'minx."

"That's good, I suppose."

"In a way," Shawndirea said. "But it means we don't know who we're facing."

"How can you be certain it's *not* him?" Roble asked.

"Lez'minx's magic is much darker."

"Will your magical barrier hold?" Roble asked Portia.

Portia clucked her tongue and exhaled what sounded more like a slight hiss. "We can hope. Like Shawndirea said, 'we don't know who we're facing'. Regardless, whomever stands across the oxbow understands Dagger's Tears' greatest weakness."

"And what's that?" Roble asked.

"The oxbow doesn't have any massive turtles to defend that front. Should the torchbearers break through the magical barrier, they can swim across the lake unharmed."

"What weapons do you have to defend yourself?"

She said, "A few archers, but no trained swordsmen. My magic, of course. Nothing else. Dagger's Tears is filled with docile people."

"What about your people?" Roble asked. "Merla said that you're the last of your tribe."

Portia took a deep breath. After several moments, she replied, "I am."

"I didn't mean to dredge up bad memories."

"Decades of time have eased the pain but not the loss."

"Does that mean you're the last of your people?" Roble asked.

"I do not know. But, since I never plan to travel outside of Dagger's Tears, I might as well be."

"What race was your people?"

Portia smiled slightly. "We are half-breeds, the offspring of forest sprites and dryads. Because our characteristics were far different than those of our parents, we chose to occupy one of the less miserable marshlands north of here, nearer to Woodnog. Our land flourished where we beheld the sunshine, unlike the rest of the swamps."

"What happened?" Shawndirea asked.

Portia shrugged. Tears formed in her eyes. "I choose not to dwell on it. Otherwise, my bitterness will turn to malice and destroy me."

"I understood a massive flood—"

Portia nodded and politely held up her hand to silence him. "Yes. That flood was unlike anything that ever occurred in these swamps. Nothing like it has ever happened since."

A hot blast of lightning zigzagged over the river and ripped a narrow trench through the muddy bank. Thunder shook the sky and the ground. The patrols near the river's edge sprinted for cover under the closest building. The torchbearers across the lake didn't waver. They held fast.

Shawndirea stood on Roble's shoulder and made her way down his arm until she reached the railing. "You believe someone used magic to cause the flood, don't you?"

"I do."

"Why?" Roble asked.

"The Shadowfae are darker than most understand. They're the worst of the Unseelie, full of spite and viler than an angered demon."

"Why was your village be their direct target?" Roble asked.

"Because we are healers. Not only do we heal folks of various races, we also heal the land. The radiance of our land was reversing the darkness of the swamp. The sunlight blessed our efforts. The more sunlight that shone through the veiled sky, the quicker the land was healing. The Shadowfae sternly forbade our efforts, but our elders refused to yield to the their demands."

Lightning flickered from cloud to cloud. Drizzling rain spilled steadily. Roble hoped the rain doused the torches and sent away the line of potential enemies. They held their places, not even shifting their weight. Strangely, the rain didn't dim their torches.

The bluish orb glowed harsher, causing Roble, Portia, and Shawndirea to shield their eyes. They braced themselves. After the intense light faded, they realized the one with the orb had cast a protective dome over his troops, preventing the rain from extinguishing their torches.

"Do you think those are Saurians?" Roble asked.

"That'd be my guess," Portia replied. "But from this distance, I don't know. They could be Shadowfae."

"If I were fully recovered and stronger," Shawndirea said, "I'd fly over to examine them."

"No," Roble said, shaking his head. "Don't even consider it. Especially not in this weather."

Shawndirea offered a tired smile. "I barely have the energy to *flutter* right now, so you needn't worry about me flying. But I'd like to know exactly what is taunting Dagger's Tears."

"As do I," Portia said.

"Why haven't the warning bells sounded?" Roble asked.

"If these invaders get past the barrier, the alarms will be sounded. Trust me, our watchmen see them. Watching in silence allows us a better opportunity to study their intentions, which so far has been to intimidate us."

The blue orb flashed, sending a blue streak of fire at the oxbow lake. When the magical flame struck the invisible magical barrier, the light turned green and was quashed, fading quickly.

"Your barrier seems strong enough," Roble said.

"That was a test to check its vulnerabilities."

"If the watchmen are studying them, why can't they discern if these are Saurians or not?"

"They stand exactly far enough away to prevent a human eye from clearly seeing their forms. And a thin layer of mist and fog rises off the lake after the night temperature falls further obscuring sight."

Another blue bolt of fire hurled at the magical barrier. The clash of magic fire striking the barrier produced a low thunderous tone. The fire faded.

"That … was a bit stronger," Portia said.

"What seems to be their motivation?" Roble asked. "If they've done this for months and not crossed the barrier and the oxbow, why do they continue to return night after night?"

"Intimidation."

"I get that, but what do they gain or what is it that they want?"

"If they're Saurians, they will ransack the town and take our children as slaves. The elders they'd eat. If they're Shadowfae, they know I'm here and want me because of *who* I am," Portia said softly. "Come, let's return indoors."

CHAPTER 46

"Why do the Shadowfae want you?" Roble asked, closing the door.

Portia crossed the room and stood near a trio of tall burning candles. "Because they were unsuccessful in killing off our entire population."

"I thought you were the last—" Roble said.

"To my knowledge, I am," she replied.

"You'd think they'd do that?" Shawndirea asked. "Even if a dozen of you survived the massive flood, you're separated, which weakens your power. Why would they still pursue hunting you down? The Shadowfae are Unseelie. They generally welcome anyone with a drop of Fae blood into their courts."

Portia shrugged. "My kind are Unseelie but our magic stems from a deeper well, so to speak."

Roble frowned. "What exactly does that mean?"

"Your wife could explain it better and more in-depth. Essentially, our power is greater than theirs. The Shadowfae are the darkest of the dark Unseelie. They use vile tactics to magnify their magic. Had they directly challenged our encampment with their magic, rather than use nature to produce a rampaging flood in the dead of night while we slept, we'd have easily beaten them. Perhaps, we'd have even wiped out the majority of them." Portia's jaw tightened, and she turned away. "I'm sorry. I cannot discuss this further at the moment."

Sensing the growing hostility in Portia's voice, he remembered what Merla had told him. Portia's longevity lasted as long as she never sought to unleash her magic into a wrathful rage. Causing her to reflect on the loss of her people was rubbing a raw wound. Any further discussion might rip the scar wide open. It would for Roble, if he were in her situation. His wrath would know no end.

Portia noticed the two saddlebags. "What is in those? Something magical?"

"Spell books and magic scrolls," Shawndirea said.

"From where?"

"A lot of these we found in Polderholm," Roble replied. "Others came from Moorsis' cottage."

"Moorsis?" Portia's eyes widened. She untethered one saddlebag and flipped the flap over. "I've heard of her."

"A swamp witch," Roble said.

"Yes. Her husband's buried in the Glades of Sorrow. But no one knew of her body's whereabouts."

Roble explained how Lez'minx had resurrected her to do his bidding and that they returned her remains to the Glades of Sorrow to be buried.

"This is the same Lez'minx whose temple you seek?"

Roble nodded.

"Why do you seek him?"

"To be released from these rings," Roble said, holding up his hands. "He cast a spell on them and now I cannot take them off."

"I see." Portia's brow furrowed as she silently evaluated the situation. "He kept Moorsis his prisoner for all those years? Making her do evil things by enslaving those who sought her magical enchantments?"

Shawndirea smiled. "That's putting it politely."

"As I said before, I do not know him, but now, you've piqued my interest," Portia said. "I must meditate about the situation. Could I read through these magical scrolls and books?"

Roble cast his glance toward Shawndirea, as questioning whether it should be permissible or not. Shawndirea nodded.

"I need solitude. I have an extra bedroom on the other side of my home. You're welcome to it tonight. I shall do my best to find the whereabouts of his temple by the time morning comes."

CHAPTER 47

*A*fter Lehrling and Collette finished eating, they left the bustling lodge where the others continued carrying on conversations. He stood near the balcony beside her under the glow of an oil lantern. Several drab moths circled the flame.

They stood in silence for several minutes. Leaning against the rail, he made several side-glances at her, but she never turned to meet his gaze. Even without the light of the burning wick, Lehrling believed the glowing excitement on Collette's face would allow him to see her features in the pitch darkness. Her broad grin tugged the deep dimples in her cheeks. She seemed a whole new person than when he had met her at the lake.

Nervous, and uncertain how to start a fresh conversation, he said, "You were right about the meal. I've eaten at royal banquets and I must confess the food here is more savory and delightful than anywhere I've been. In fact, I might have eaten far more than my fair share."

Immediately, he regretted those words, patting his swollen stomach. He feared she might think him a glutton. But his words didn't register with her. They drew less attention than whistling wind through densely leafed branches. She almost seemed in her own little realm. Perhaps her mind carried her to such a place. Her intense gaze was like a child playing a new game. Enriched delight danced inside her.

Her smile radiated and her voice became giddy. "I'm glad you enjoyed the meal. Oh, I *must* thank Roble for taking a stand against my father and coming to my defense like he did. I—I'm so excited. I don't know what I should do next."

Lehrling smiled, but silently he berated himself for not being the one to have challenged her father. Roble had proven his backbone once more, which was something Lehrling seldom found himself capable of displaying. He wasn't a coward but he hated the idea of public confrontations. His voice stammered in the rare instances when his anger escalated. However, the more Lehrling thought about the situation, the less he liked the idea of being harsh toward her father, in spite of her father's bullying attitude over her and his lashing anger directed at Lehrling and Roble.

Roble could be viewed as a hero for abruptly scolding the old man in front of the hamlet, but Lehrling—had he been the one to confront her father— might later have been viewed in a much lesser light, especially if things between he and Collette soured. She might turn her anger toward him and blame him for whatever tragedies they might suffer.

"What should I pack? What should I leave behind?" Collette asked more to herself than to Lehrling. Her voice was softer, almost childlike. Suddenly, he viewed their age difference much broader than before. She had been isolated for so long that perhaps her mind was not fully matured for independence or what it meant for her to leave her family and Dagger's Tears behind.

He was slightly amused by her happiness, wanting to join in her celebration, but the sudden idea of leaving the hamlet was causing her to regress and sound more like a child than the solemn lady he had first met.

She paused and grew silent. Her brow furrowed and she wrung her hands together.

"What's wrong?"

"How will I journey with you?" Collette asked. "You only have *two* horses. From what I noticed earlier, you've no extra room for me or *my* belongings. Of course, I don't possess much. I live modestly, as it is. All of us do. I've a couple of work pants and tunics. They won't take much room. I suppose I could walk—"

"No lady can walk through these swamps. It's far too dangerous," Lehrling said. "I'd not hear of it."

"Certainly there's no room on your horse for the two of us," she said.

"I'm not *that* big," Lehrling protested with a forced smile, trying not to show his actual offense. He was still a good fifty pounds lighter than when Roble had rescued him a year earlier. He was quite proud that he'd not gained it back.

"I wasn't implying that," she said. "But the mire and quicksand and the streams you need to cross. The more weight your beast bears, I imagine the less surefootedness he'd have. Or am I wrong?"

"While that's true, Collette, he's a young strong stallion and capable of bearing our weight."

"See?" She sighed, rested her elbows on the balcony railing, and clasped her hands together.

Lehrling stared at her side profile. Her sad eyes looked across the darkened hamlet. He wanted to pull her into his arms to comfort and tell her they'd find a way. He realized that doing so built up false hope and that wasn't fair. Not to mention, he didn't know her well enough to be so bold or how she'd react since she kept herself at a safe distance from him, which was suitably fine. If she fawned over him or constantly fluttered her eyelids when looking at him, he'd think less of her.

She was a lady. Everything about her indicated such. She wasn't giving any mixed signals, but he found himself standing on the bridge between the hope of them becoming more than friends or her seeing him as a doting old fool she viewed as an uncle or a replacement father figure.

Besides this raging emotional conflict struggling inside his mind, he needed to break the news to Collette that she couldn't travel with them until after the situation with Lez'minx was resolved. Seeing her near broken spirit because they didn't have room for her, he dreaded how much worse her reaction might become when he gave her worse news.

"I'll simply have to walk," she said with a firm nod. The excitement and boldness in her eyes renewed. She stood upright, faced him, and placed her hand on his forearm. "I can walk alongside you."

"No, Collette, walking would be a foolish dangerous thing to do. Snakes, poisonous plants—"

"I deal with those things every day, Lehrling. I've snatched poisonous snakes from fishnets and cut off their heads with my skinning knife. I recognize most of the poisonous plants, as many grow within our hamlet. I'm more than capable of taking care of myself. If anything worse encounters us, I expect that you and Roble will offer me protection, right?" she asked. "After all, you're both knights."

Lehrling sighed and patted her hand.

"Oh, don't tell me that I cannot travel with you after Roble's remarkable display? Almost the entire hamlet voted in favor of me leaving. Do you realize how embarrassed I'd be if left behind?"

"Yes, I understand. Collette—"

She jerked her hand away.

Lehrling stepped closer and in a pleading tone, he said, "I've not said anything either way, now have I?"

"Your actions speak loud enough. You said that you'd be honored to show me the things my heart desires."

"You've no idea how overjoyed I'd be to witness you beholding the beauty of the sun and new lands." Lehrling offered a caring smile. "Collette, please calm down. Your emotions are running everywhere."

She clenched her hands around the material of her dress, took a deep breath, and exhaled slowly. "I'm sorry. You're right. There's just so many ideas rushing through my head right now." She laughed. "I must sound like a brainless fool to you."

"No-o-o—" he said.

"I hope you don't mind my endless prattling."

"I love listening to you talk."

"From the time I rise in the morning until late in the evening, all I've ever known is cleaning and gutting fish, hanging them on lines to dry, and helping women wash garments in that dingy lake. It's constant toil. Nothing exciting. No future outlook. It's a … dismal life."

Lehrling nodded, not offering no words. He could never survive her living conditions.

"For all the years of dreaming and imagining what's outside our community and knowing that now, thanks to Roble and you, my dreams can be finally fulfilled. But I still struggle with my fear of it being snatched away. It's not real until Dagger's Tears is out of my view. Being denied after it's within my grasp would totally devastate me. Understand, I never act like this. I honestly don't."

"I understand."

"No, you don't. Even I *don't* understand my behavior. So many pent up emotions and thoughts are bursting through my mind. It's difficult to reel them in. Thank you. I need to thank Roble, too, because what you've done and are going to do makes me happier than I ever imagined I could become. I'd rather die, if this opportunity disappears." Collette wiped away fresh tears. "I can't survive the pain of such a broken heart."

Lehrling was a loss for words. He couldn't tell or deny her the opportunity to travel with them. Roble could protest, and he would, but since Roble had a sturdier spine than Lehrling, Roble needed to break the sorrowful news to Collette. Lehrling couldn't. He couldn't break anyone's heart like that.

A bright blue fire danced across the sky. In that moment, Lehrling noticed the line of torchbearers across the lake. The blue fiery orb exploded and vanished.

"What was that?" Lehrling asked.

Collette looked and shook her head. "I don't know."

"Who are the men with the torches?"

"We don't know, but they stand along the lake border every night."

"For what purpose?"

"We don't know."

A second blue bolt sped through the air and struck an invisible barrier, vanishing upon impact.

"Those blasts aren't something we've seen before," Collette said.

Lehrling grabbed her hand and squeezed. "Well, so much for me asking you to walk along the edge of the lake, huh?"

Curiosity creased her brow at his suggestion. She smiled and looked into his eyes, studying him, and then she lowered her gaze, blushing. "I suppose so."

A blast of harsh blue light exploded against the magical barrier and shook the ground. The impact shushed the insects and night birds. Cries of alarm echoed from the night watchmen. The alarm bell clattered with extreme urgency.

"Let's find Roble," Lehrling said. "He's at Portia's, but I don't know which direction to go."

"Follow me and I'll take you."

efore Roble carried Shawndirea to the other side of Portia's home, the building's foundation shook. Seconds later, the alarm bell at the docks clattered. In spite of his fatigue, he stopped and turned.

Roble glanced at Portia with curiosity. "That was pretty severe."

Portia balanced against the table to prevent falling. "Indeed. If they didn't break through the barrier with that, it won't be much longer before they do."

Roble placed Shawndirea on the table. "I'll be right back."

"You're *not* leaving me behind," Shawndirea said, frowning.

"You're too weak to—"

She fumed. "That's for me to decide."

Roble opened his mouth, but she pointed a firm finger and narrowed her eyes a bit more.

She said, "I need to see what's happened. Even from a distance, I can at least advise. Trust me, I'm not going to fly into battle. I'm not foolish. But I can still help Portia."

"She's right," Portia said. "At this point, I could use any magical knowledge available since we don't know who we're dealing with. Besides, we cannot waste valuable time arguing about it. We need to know if they've broken through the barrier."

Shawndirea took a step back and attempted a short sprint into flight, but her wings didn't lift her off the table. Roble caught her on the palm of his hand. Rather than saying anything, he placed her on his shoulder and headed to the door.

Inside, he grinned that she was as stubborn as he, making them the perfect match.

Around the corner on the balcony, the yellow line of flickering torches had not moved. They stood their ground. The light of the blue orb intensified again.

"The barrier withstood that last attack," Portia said. "But I don't expect it to for much longer."

"Can you reinforce it?" Shawndirea asked.

Portia stood in silence. Her eyes saw what Roble's could not. At least from his perspective, he believed she actually saw the magical line of the protective barrier to secure the hamlet's perimeter. "I can try, for what little it'll probably do."

"Why's that?" Roble asked.

"It took days of meditation for me to properly align the barrier and connect it to the terrain."

Shawndirea lowered herself onto the balcony rail.

The watchmen of Dagger's Tears rushed with torches to the inside bank of the oxbow. If the barrier fell, the enemy still needed to swim across the narrow lake. Swimming should make the intruders more vulnerable than being on foot.

Townsfolk spilled from the lodge and stood along the balconies in the glow of torchlights. Their frightened voices chattered with cacophonic intensity.

The sorcerer's orb glowed like a small blue star. The intense light was too much to view directly. The sorcerer held fast, but didn't hurl the bolt.

"What's he doing?" Roble whispered.

Shawndirea's nervous eyes peered into his. "He's funneling more magic. Brace yourself. The next bolt might be worse than an earthquake."

"So the barrier won't hold?"

Shawndirea shook her head. "I doubt any building in Dagger's Tears will be standing after his next explosive attack. This sorcerer desires to be as destructive as possible."

"Silence, please," Portia said in a whisper.

Portia arched her back and raised her hands toward the sky. Her eyes rolled back. The light from the nearby lanterns dimmed as she pulled their energy to her. The wooden balcony planks buckled and creaked.

Roble stepped back and stared in awe. Thick roots formed around her feet and curled up her legs, across the balcony, and spindled down to the wet ground. The mossy hair on her arms stretched into tendrils of ivy and weaved across the balcony rail and down the thick corner supports holding the building.

Shawndirea drew her magic from the earth and its flora, but Roble had never witnessed anything as incredible as what Portia was doing. She was truly becoming one with nature. Her face and skin hardened like thick tree bark.

"Roble!" Lehrling shouted from below.

Roble peered over the balcony and placed his finger to his lips.

Lehrling nodded. The ground quaked from the sorcerer's attack on the magical barrier. Lehrling looked down, and almost fell backwards, shuffling his steps. Coiled at his feet were ivy vines and roots connecting Portia to the earth. They rustled and writhed like large snakes ready to strike.

The intensity of the blue shimmering orb sent out humming vibrations. The hairs on the back of Roble's neck stiffened, as though they were standing in an electrical field of magic. With Portia having little time to prepare was she able to ward off the next powerful strike.

The collision of her magic against the sorcerer's could cause an explosion that might kill them all. Roble took Shawndirea into his hands and held her close to his chest. She pressed her cheek against him, but her bewildered eyes couldn't be drawn away from what might happen next.

The warm humid air strangely cooled like the moment before black clouds released heavy rain. The forewarning wasn't due to a natural storm. The brewing storm was far worse. So much so that the drizzling rain ceased. Fog crept across the river, hiding the river banks like giant tethered ghosts.

More than a dozen yellow streaks of lightning cut the sky. All the strands of lightning connected into a fierce single blast, which struck the ground at the edge of the oxbow. The rumbling thunder quaked and shook the area with severe force. The blue orb dimmed.

Had the sorcerer missed? With the swollen fiery magical, blue light, Roble expected the abrupt impact to send shock waves hurtling their direction.

Between the curved tip of the oxbow and the river, a net of energy zipped across the wet ground like a glowing spider's web or a fisherman's flung net. The radiating sparks crackled, zigzagging toward the line of torchbearers. The ground lightning was a frightening display of power scorching every-thing in its path.

One by one the torches were snuffed, followed by the hideous terrorized screams of creatures not human. The silence of death quickly followed. Only the invading sorcerer remained standing. The blue orb atop his staff dimmed and went black.

The strange electrical waves of jagged energy crept across the dead bodies and encircled the sorcerer, slowly wrapping around his legs and encasing him like a fiery blue cocoon. The sorcerer emitted a harsh rasping sound, as he struggled to get outside the electrical-fiery web. He reared back his head and held up his magical staff. Shouting in his strange language, he was trying to either break free or summon his source of magic into the orb. But whatever netted around him doused his magic and robbed him of whatever strength he possessed. After a few minutes of helpless resistance, he dropped facedown into the mud. His long serpent-like tail rose and stiffened for a moment. As the last of its life faded, its reptilian tail grew limp and dropped to his side.

"You did it!" Roble said. "They're all dead, even the sorcerer."

Portia opened her bewildered eyes. Stiff like a tree, she stared across Dagger's Tears at the fading chain lightning. Unable to move, she said, "I didn't do that. That wasn't me."

Perplexed, Shawndirea said, "That wasn't you?"

"No. I'm still trying to draw more magic from the earth, but little is available. What happened? What did you see?"

Roble told her about the netted chains of lightning and how it killed all of the invaders.

"You didn't cast the waves of chain lightning?" Shawndirea asked.

"No." Portia closed her eyes. Her roots and tendrils regressed.

"Then who did?" Roble asked.

Portia didn't speak for several minutes. Her appendages recoiled and reshaped. When she returned to her normal appearance, she staggered and fell against the balcony rail. She was too weak to hold herself up.

Roble rushed to her side and looped his arm beneath hers, keeping her steady and preventing her from plummeting headfirst over the rail. "Let's get you inside."

Portia panted. She braced herself against him. Sweat meandered from her damp hair and down her face. "Thank you."

Before Roble walked her to the door, Shawndirea climbed on his shoulder. Lehrling and Collette ascended the wooden ramp and were standing on the balcony. Lehrling hurried and opened the door for them.

"What happened out there?" Lehrling asked.

"We're still trying to figure that out," Roble replied. He led Portia to a cushioned chair where she plopped down. "They were Saurians, and now they're all dead."

"Saurians? How could you tell from this distance?" Collette asked.

Portia's head lulled to the side. The slits of her eyes revealed that she was partially awake. Her transformation had drained her energy and was taking its toll, weakening her by the second.

Roble offered Portia a wineskin. She accepted it with a weak hand.

"I saw the sorcerer's long reptilian tail in the light of the magical lightning," Roble said.

Portia nodded. "Nothing else in these swamps would've challenged us with such an attack."

"Not even the Shadowfae?" Roble asked.

"The Shadowfae have no need enter from that direction. They can cross the river by flying."

Collette squatted at the side of Portia's chair. "Killing them sapped all of your energy."

"I didn't kill them," she replied.

Shawndirea sat on the edge of the table near Portia. She remained extremely weak, too.

Collette shook her head. "They weren't killed by their own race or their own magic."

"I agree," Portia said. She gulped down the contents of the wineskin.

"It wasn't me," Shawndirea said.

Portia's door home flung open and harshly struck the wall. An outlined shadow stood outside, but not enough light revealed who or what the visitor was.

"It was I. I killed them all."

CHAPTER 49

*R*oble turned toward the doorway with his hands resting on his belt. With a causal movement of his fingers, he grasped the hilts of his concealed throwing knives without drawing attention to his movement.

"Might I ask your name?" Roble asked.

"Why should I reveal it to *you*?" the female replied. "You're not the host of this house, nor are you her servant. You're a stranger to her, but I am not."

"I'm sorry but I don't recognize your voice," Portia said, leaning her head against the back of her chair while barely able to focus her tired eyes on the door. "Who are you?"

The woman stepped across the threshold. She was dressed in leather armor. With both hands, she held a long staff with a shimmering emerald orb flickering at the top. Her eyes were like Portia's, only a darker green. Her long braided hair was moss green and hung down her back like curled ivy. She smiled, revealing her pointy teeth. "Do you not recognize your own sister?"

Portia studied the woman's face. Her eyes widened with sudden recognition and she gasped. "Daphne?"

"Yes."

Thick tears like beads of oil etched slow meandering paths down Portia's cheeks. "I never figured you survived the flood. I thought I was the only one who had."

Daphne's face almost glowed. She rushed to Portia and embraced her. "Quite a few of us survived. The flood scattered us to different areas of the swamp. It took me years to find others. I suspect the more I hunt, the more of us I shall find. We're not *that* easy to kill. But our magic's weaker when we're apart from one another. That's why I'm gathering our tribe back together."

"Where are those you've already found?" Portia asked with great interest.

Daphne's uneasy gaze passed from each of those in the room. She hesitated giving an answer.

"It's okay. They can be trusted," Portia said.

Her eyes remained uncertain, untrusting. She studied Roble's eyes for a long while. Her eyes narrowed when she gazed at his rings and then scoffed. "Perhaps. But it isn't something I'll risk. I'd rather not reveal that unless it's in private."

"I understand, sister, but I'm too weak to be left alone. Did you travel here with a party?"

"Aqese and Ki'wese are examining the dead Saurians and await for my return. They expect you to return with me."

Portia frowned. "I'm in no condition to leave. They are more than welcome to come here."

Daphne smiled. "I'll inform them."

"How'd you find me?" Portia asked.

"I sensed your aura as we headed upriver. You seemed troubled, stressed. After seeing the invaders I understand why. What has placed you into such a weakened state?"

"I attempted to summon a petrification spell to bind them to the earth and have the mire suck them under," Portia replied.

Daphne pursed her lips and cocked a brow. "A spell so simple depleted your energy?"

Portia nodded. "Yes."

"My dear sister, have you been out of practice for so long that a minor spell depletes you?"

"I had no time to prep beforehand."

"Still—"

"I know," Portia said with a tired smile.

"You must journey with us to rebuild your strength," Daphne said.

"To where?"

"Linden-hold."

"Surely the flood destroyed it ages ago," Portia said.

"It's our home. If enough of us return, we can heal the scarred land and return it to the prominence we once knew and where we thrived. And should the Shadowfae attack us again, we'll be prepared."

"Dagger's Tears needs me."

Daphne shook her head. "They simply use you."

"That's not true," Collette said. Lehrling placed a gentle hand on her shoulder.

"Isn't it?" Daphne said harshly. "What does she contribute to your hamlet other than her magic? Bit by bit her strength has been taken from her because of your greed."

"Don't blame them," Portia said. "This was my choice. I was tired of living alone. I want to heal those who are afflicted, regardless of the cost to me. It comforts me."

"The cost is more than you should suffer. What have they given you in return?"

"A home. Protection."

"*You* protect *them*," Daphne said.

"In a sense, yes. But, they've welcomed me as part of their extended family. They supply my food and gather whatever herbs and ingredients I request for my magic."

"*We* are your family. Our kind. Never forget that."

Portia sighed. "Until now, I thought *I* was the last of our tribe."

"You should've been able to locate us, like I located you."

"I tried."

"Recently?"

Portia looked away. "No. It has been many years. But I've accepted this as my home."

Daphne waved her hands in the air and spiraled. "Home? This?"

Shawndirea crossed her arms. "This doesn't seem to be the most friendly of reunions for two sisters who've not seen one another for decades."

Daphne frowned. Her eyes shimmered like silvery dew in harsh sunlight.

"Why scold her," Shawndirea said, "when you could mend her with your own magic and strength?"

"Well, faery, she'd not be in this weakened state had she not chosen to live where others continuously sap her power." She faced Portia. "Do you not understand why you're so weak in Dagger's Tears?"

Portia shook her head. "I've not given it much thought, but I've never experienced this level of feebleness until today. I've always held my strength, even to heal others, even when I helped heal this faery."

Shawndirea and Roble looked at her with sudden curiosity.

"You healed me?" Shawndirea asked.

"Of course. Somewhat, anyway. Enough to awaken you. Perhaps rejuvenation is a better term. You seemed a bit askew."

Roble frowned. "Then why didn't you tell me that you could awaken her?"

Portia ignored the question and returned her attention to Daphne. "I've done what I know to do. To heal those who come to me and not harbor wrath toward those who do us wrong. Had I sought vengeance, my life would've already ended."

"But this is *not* your home," Daphne said. "This town is the very reason you nearly died tonight while trying to perform a simple spell. Your magic isn't what it should be. You've not regenerated your aura. Your mantle's razor thin. And do you know why?"

"I'm sure you'll tell her," Shawndirea said.

Daphne's jaw tightened. "Sister, as half-dryads, we draw our greatest strength from the forests, from the trees. Dagger's Tears is barren and stagnant. Your hut is surrounded by water, *not* trees. Not the magical life source we need and desire to maintain our strength. Sunlight is also essential, which isn't found in the depths of these cursed swamps.

"You probably would've died, had we not arrived and destroyed the Saurians. Your tendrils were deep in the stagnant mire, searching for aid from our kindred trees, but the nearest tree is far beyond your grasp. Instead of drawing magic from nature, nature was sapping you. Your death would've ended the magical barrier and allowed the Saurians to cross easily."

Portia took a deep breath, closed her eyes, and shook her head.

"The Saurian sorcerer was drawing his power from your magical barrier. He fed off of you. His next bolt would have shattered the barrier."

Shawndirea's anger lessened and she uncrossed her arms. "That's a valid interpretation."

Daphne gave her a shrewd side-glance, rolled her eyes, and shook her head. "Without trees, you've not been able to renew your magic for years. Each time you healed someone, your energy lessened."

"If dryads' magic is drawn from trees," Roble said, "what prevented her from taking magic from the land? Swamp soil is composed of layers of rich sphagnum mosses, which enriches trees and plants' growth outside the swamp."

"Even you, Overlander, should know that you cannot draw life from the dead. Since these swamps are cursed, the dead matter was stealing her magic and draining her life without her realizing it. The land is cursed. The only reason we survived in Linden-hold was because our combined energy birthed new life into the earth. Our magic was slowly dissipating the curse, causing the Shadowfae despise us all the more."

Portia nodded. "How do we know Linden-hold still exists? Can you find it?"

"We've have mapped most of the southern Woodnog Swamp region. Linden-hold remains to the north, based on my memory of familiar landmarks. However, decades have passed and some places no longer exist. As to the structure of our former settlement? Most likely it's in ruins. But with the bond of our regathered tribe, we can rebuild it. Once it's reestablished, sunlight will bless our tribe again."

Collette gave Lehrling a bright smile.

"You've mapped the southern swamps?" Roble asked.

"Yes."

"I'd like to study those maps, if you don't mind."

Daphne gave him a curious stare. "Daring enough to venture deeper into places where even holy deities dare not tread?"

"Actually," Portia said, "he and his party are looking for a temple."

"A temple?" Daphne asked with curiosity.

Roble nodded.

"Whose temple would that be?"

Portia adjusted in her seat. Her tired eyes looked at Daphne. "The name I'm unfamiliar with, but he has insisted Roble venture to it. His name is Lez'minx."

"Lez'minx?" Daphne's eyes widened.

"You know him?" Portia asked.

"You know him, too," she replied.

Portia shook her head. "I do not."

"Ah, but you do, sister. Only you know him by a *different* name. He's one of us."

"What's his true name?"

"Runefel," Daphne replied.

"Our brother?"

"The same." She glanced at Roble. "I noticed your rings. Has he bewitched you with them?"

"Yes. I cannot remove them," Roble replied.

Daphne chewed her lower lip and shook her head. "Humans are so gullible."

A slight grin stretched on Portia's lips.

Roble frowned as Shawndirea suppressed a grin.

"What did you hope to gain by wearing them?" Daphne asked.

"I wanted to see what they were capable of doing."

"He never told you?"

"No."

"Why be such a fool?" She didn't await an answer. "*Did* you learn anything about the rings?"

Roble cleared his throat. "He was using them to spy on us."

"Our brother," Daphne said, looking at Portia with a sly grin. "Still up to his old tricks."

"Indeed," Portia said.

"You remember what he did to us the last time we saw him before the flood?"

Portia nodded. "I shall never forget. I swore he'd regret that, but after the flood, my hope of repaying his ill deed was washed away."

"We should lower our voices, lest he hear us," Daphne said softly, glancing at the rings.

"Shawndirea cast a spell to prevent him from using the stones as looking glasses," Roble said.

A wild grin spread on Daphne's face and the points of her sharp teeth made the smile more sinister. "Good. That allows us to catch him off guard when we confront him."

Lehrling said, "You'll help us?"

"Oh, what we have in mind has nothing to do with the solution to your problem. I sense Roble is more indebted to Lez'minx than what he's yet revealed." She came closer and slid her hand along his leather chest piece. "His magic flows through your armor, too, does it not?"

Roble nodded.

"Instead of diving an inch, you dove a mile."

"Can you remove these rings?" Roble held his hands out.

Daphne shook her head. "I cannot. Only he can. The true question should be, 'Will he?'"

"You don't think he will?" Roble asked.

Daphne shrugged. "It depends on what he wishes to con out of you."

Lehrling sighed with relief when he looked at Roble. "At least now we know that we're not going up against a god or a demigod."

Daphne chuckled. "A god or demigod would have more mercy on you than Lez'minx. He's incapable of such. What is it that he demands in return for these … gifts? Let me guess. Devoted loyalty? Reverence?"

"He never told me what he wants, but he threatened Shawndirea's life. For that, I will find him," Roble said sternly. "It won't be a meeting he'll enjoy once we find his temple."

Daphne was humored by his statement. "He doesn't have a temple. He lives in a cave beneath a massive swamp oak, much like a worm burrows in filthy mud to hide."

"He also killed a few dozen Shadowfae mercenaries," Shawndirea said.

Daphne's face withered. "He has always been good at making enemies, but this time he might have gone too far."

Portia nodded. "I agree. Since we have a common enemy with Roble and his party, it's time we take action and join his cause, sister."

"My dear Portia, I believe you're right. It's long overdue."

CHAPTER 50

The following morning Roble awoke with renewed energy. With heightened senses, he was more alert than he'd been during their entire excursion into Woodnog's swamps.

Still asleep, Shawndirea's face glowed with brighter radiance. He gently nudged her, hating to awaken her from her peaceful sleep.

Her eyelids fluttered open. Seeing him, she smiled.

"How do you feel?" he asked.

She stretched her arms and yawned. Her brilliant eyes searched the room. "Oddly, I feel so much better."

"So do I."

"I feel spritely," she replied with a sly smile. She stood, moved her wings, and hovered above the pillow. She zipped across the room and back. "My strength has returned, and I'm bursting with liveliness I haven't possessed for days. It's almost … magical. Wait—"

"What?"

She placed her index finger to her lips and motioned toward the door. Her odd frown heightened his curiosity.

Roble walked to the door with her flying beside him. Before he touched the door handle, a humming sensation filled the air. The hairs on his neck rose and his skin tingled beneath the armor. The humming sound was similar to fluorescent lights in the Overlands, but the prickling along his skin indicated something more hung in the air.

He grabbed the door handle and turned.

"Careful," Shawndirea whispered, fluttering upward.

Roble nodded and pulled the door inward. The humming grew louder. The pulsation radiated pleasurable warmth. A giddy feeling overcame him.

Portia and Daphne stood at the table. In the center of the table a large luminous, yellow Elfstone pulsed a steady glow of light.

Portia beamed. No signs of her weariness from the night before tugged at her eyes. She no longer appeared wilted. Her face glowed. Her skin tone was far different than when he met her. Portia's features resembled the transformation of a drought-sickened plant being regenerated with new growth after a summer rain. Her hope was renewed.

Daphne was correct about the swampland draining Portia' aura. Portia's new vigor revealed to Roble how close to death she was when they had met. He'd poorly assumed her odd gray skin was normal.

"Good morning," Portia said, glancing at Roble and Shawndirea.

"It's a far better morning," Shawndirea replied.

Daphne smiled. She unrolled a large parchment across the table while Portia placed heavy objects on the map's corners. "While you slept, I sketched a map of the swamp to the north where Linden-hold once thrived. Of course, this is from my memories before the massive flood, so some of the landmarks might not remain."

Roble studied the map. "Where do you think Lez'minx is?"

Daphne placed a finger to the northeast of Dagger's Tears on a thickly wooded area. "Here."

"The Ruins of Saggy-nook?"

She nodded.

"What's there, besides the ruins, of course?" Roble asked. His eyes studied her crude map.

Portia smiled. "About a century and a half ago, as children, before we were shunned and set off to establish Linden-hold, we spent a vast amount of time playing in those ruins. These ruins were once occupied by Orcs. A few artifacts we found support that theory."

"Orcs?" Roble asked.

She and Daphne nodded.

Daphne said, "Other artifacts indicated humans were there, too. One was enslaved to the other, as neither race ever co-exists peacefully together. We've always believed the Orcs held greater power, though it cannot be proven."

"What caused this town's demise?" Roble asked.

"It wasn't a town. Saggy-nook—a name we gave it as children—had been an incredible city. Its real name was in a language unknown to us and carved above the grand entrance ways. Most of the city has sunken beneath the swamp's mire over time."

Shawndirea frowned. "Why would Lez'minx reside there?"

Daphne shrugged. "The massive swamp oak was near the center of the city. Beneath its giant roots are catacombs where we loved to explore. Even as children, we sensed the well of unending magical power connected to the tree. We fed off its source to increase our own. Even if the lower levels of the city are sunken, the oak is far too tall to ever be engulfed."

"Wouldn't the saturated ground cause the roots to rot?" Roble asked.

Daphne smiled. "For an ordinary tree, Overlander, that most likely would occur. But magic protects the tree."

"Then it's safe to say," Shawndirea said, "that Lez'minx wields the tree's magic for his own benefit?"

Portia glanced at Daphne with grave concern. They nodded.

Daphne said, "Yes, he must be."

"Then we've a greater problem than we thought." A worried expression claimed Shawndirea's features.

Lehrling frowned. "How do you mean?"

"Daphne and Portia draw the strength of their magic from the trees." Shawndirea clicked her tongue against the roof of her mouth and crossed her arms. Her eyes revealed the depth of her thoughts, which were suddenly over-shadowed with equal concern as that of the two sisters. "Such a tree, already empowered by powerful magic, could wreak total devastation toward cities if someone properly siphoned the magic for his or her own use. If that's his magic source, he'll be worse to confront than a demigod or demon."

Lehrling's brow rose. He swallowed hard. "W-w-worse?"

Shawndirea said, "He killed two dozen Shadowfae assassins in an instant. With this power, he's able to do far worse." She looked at Daphne. "Has he always been capable of murder?"

Daphne took a sharp breath and after a few moments of thought, she shook her head. "No. He's prone to his mischievous pranks, but never harmed anyone. But, understand, neither of us have seen him since the flood. I wasn't certain he was alive."

Portia nodded. "He's hidden himself well."

"Why haven't either of you sought to return to Saggy-nook?" Shawndirea asked.

"It was a fondness of our youth," Daphne said, "but not a place to set up residence."

"Why not?" Roble asked.

"Ghosts," Portia said. "Strange magic-feeding creatures are attracted to the magical tree. These creatures are dangerous for others who wield magic to encounter."

"Why?" Roble asked.

"They drain magic from anything. If ever they capture someone or some-thing with magical abilities, they feast until the individual's life source is drained," Daphne said.

Roble remembered the Bogshee draining the wisp's life.

Lehrling frowned. "Why attack and steal magic from others for their magic, when they could feast on the tree instead?"

Daphne said, "Being near the tree is so pleasurably overwhelming that their minds become frenzied. They're intoxicated by the flow. Crazed by the sudden flux, they seek to eliminate any competition. We witnessed bloody battles. No triumph came in the victory because those who fed directly on the tree didn't live long. Instead, the rush of power caused many to explode like old wineskins filled with new wine."

"This never affected you?" Shawndirea asked.

Portia folded her hands, resting them upon her stomach. "We were new to our abilities, so our spells were basic. Our desires were modest. We had no reason to gorge ourselves from the excessive magic flow and we didn't understand the driven need of these creatures and wizards. We watched from the boughs, hidden behind the leaves. We questioned and learned through observation. However, the longer we watched, the more uneasy we became in viewing the tree as a sanctuary. We witnessed more death than those fighting at the front lines of battle. We couldn't live in peace, even inside the tree, because eventually, the madness would overtake us. As children, these bloody battles between overzealous feeders, mages, and wizards frightened us. We almost became the victims caught between two dueling wizards, so we vowed to never return. As an adult, I realize the dangers of returning because I understand magic more than I had then. Our arrival might be taken as a challenge to others tapping into the tree's source."

"If Lez'minx lives with access to this wealth of magic, why is he interested in me?" Roble asked. "I'm hardly someone—"

"It's not necessarily you that interests him," Portia said. "It's his ability to work *through* you and others that lessens the toll upon himself."

"In what way?" Roble asked, frowning.

Shawndirea smiled. "Magic, my dear, always comes at a price. How many times must I make this point?"

"She's right," Daphne said. "Some wizards and mages imprison slaves and sacrifice them to use the darkest sorceries and lessen the cost to themselves."

Lehrling's brow rose. "Dear me. I never fathomed such a thought."

"There are far worse sorcerers," Portia said. "Imagine what Tyrann does to maintain the darkness shrouding the City of Mortel?"

Lehrling shuddered but didn't reply.

"Roble, this is why Moorsis did whatever Lez'minx demanded, and perhaps why he enticed you with the burden of the rings," Portia said.

"He's never demanded me to do anything except to find him," Roble replied.

"Therein lies the danger," Daphne said.

"Why?" Roble asked.

Shawndirea's brow narrowed. "Yes, why?"

"If he's indeed at the tree, he might be luring you and Shawndirea so he can sacrifice you to funnel greater quantities of magic from the tree without suffering direct repercussions to himself."

"Dear Goddesses!" Lehrling gasped. "Roble, we mustn't go."

"Oh, but we must," Daphne said.

"Are you mad?" Lehrling said, angrily.

"No, but to save our brother from himself, there's no better place to confront him," Daphne replied.

"You are mad," Lehrling said. "It's his territory and his power outweighs yours, Portia's, and Shawndirea's combined! We cannot survive this."

"The only ones capable of talking sense into him are his kin," Daphne said.

Portia nodded. "Most likely, he thinks us dead. And if so, his anger to afflict others with pain might only be his retaliation for Linden-hold's destruction."

"That's no justification," Roble said.

"Perhaps in your world," Daphne said.

"No. In any world, nothing grants one the obsessive need to become an executioner."

Daphne eyed him fiercely. "I'm certain your faery has informed you of how things work in our realm? Has she not?"

"She has but—"

"No, you need to fully understand what it's like in a world where magic reigns supreme. You don't. You haven't a clue," Daphne said. "It shows in your actions. You appreciate magic for as long as it benefits *you*, but for whatever reason, your ignorance blinds you. When one is harmed by magic, or loved ones are killed by it, one capable of using magic has every right to retaliate."

Roble's eyes narrowed. "That makes the one seeking vengeance as bad as the one he casts against."

Daphne stared at him in silence, never flinching or looking away. After reflecting on his words, she said, "No, it doesn't. It's justice. There's no equal ground when magic's the weapon. It's more about outmaneuvering the other to gain the upper hand, and take advantage of the enemy's vulnerability."

"Doesn't that violate an ethical code of some sort? Magic should be respected," Roble said. "Shouldn't it be used to benefit and not harm others?"

"To some degree," she replied. "But like men who carry swords or any weapon, shouldn't those be used only to protect the weak?"

"Yes."

"And yet, kings and queens invade other cities or small townships whenever the mood strikes them, ransacking and taking whatever wealth the weaker hold. Whom does that benefit?"

"No one," Roble replied. "But magic should be viewed in a more sacred right and respected. Its essence requires tribute in order to properly wield it, but that's ignored in so many regards, at little thought to the possible repercussions. Were you ever an apprentice?"

Daphne's jaw tightened. Her strange eyes almost glowed. "We're half dryad. We're attuned to magic. We've no need to be apprentices."

Roble shook his head in disbelief. "Anyone who can tap into the magical resources should be properly trained. Without proper guidance, magic becomes misused. Not everyone's pure in mind and spirit. Very few ever are. If one cannot control his or her emotions, the havoc one could cause by unleashing spells is immeasurable. Not all of the Shadowfae faeries Lez'minx killed are guilty of the flood."

"How dare you!" she spat. "You come from a world where magic has long faded and you're telling us how *we* should behave?"

"Faded?" Roble glanced at Shawndirea with confusion. "Meaning magic was once a force in the Overlands?"

Shawndirea nodded.

"Yes, you fool. Those in your world that are still capable of using magic have hidden themselves or wisely found breaches in the veil and passed through to our realm or into other realms where magic flourishes."

"You ever stop to think that perhaps magic is less accessible in my realm because of the abusive practices sorcerers conducted centuries ago?" Roble asked. "Who's to say such cannot occur here?"

The question caused Daphne's anger to lessen. She broke eye contact with him, sighed, and reflected on his words. She nodded. "You may be right, Overlander."

Shawndirea said, "We're all on the same side here. We've no reason to hash out such a bitter debate about formalities. Although, at another time, it might be critical for us who use magic to reflect on its true usage in our lives. Roble and I need to find Lez'minx for our purpose, and apparently, that's your desire as well."

"You're right, faery," Daphne said softly. "And though it pains my pride to admit it, your husband's chastisement is not without merit. I, along with so many others, have taken the use of magic for granted. But, I must add, there's no confronting our brother without using magic to defend ourselves. I'm guessing you're not opposed to that?"

Roble held his hands out, palm-side down. "All I want is to be released from his rings and any commitment he desires me to behold. I'm not going to witness his death. Nor do I wish to see him harmed. I wanted freed from his bonds. Whatever you find necessary when you find him, I'll leave that at your discretion."

Daphne smiled. "Fair enough."

CHAPTER 51

*R*oble stood at the table and studied the swamp map. He traced his finger along the river and said, "Why are there so many ruins in the swamps?"

Daphne said, "Kingdoms, over time, fall. Fertile prosperous places alter over time. Climate changes. Rains cease in some regions and increase in others. The wind's direction switches. These are beyond our control. The living either adapt, move on, or perish. Magic doesn't dispel what nature intends. However, a lot of the ruins in the Woodnog Swamps came *after* the raging flood."

"If you'll forgive me for being so blunt," Roble said.

Daphne, Portia, and Shawndirea glanced intently at him.

"I mean no ill-will or criticism by what I'm about to ask. It's merely my curiosity—"

Daphne's eyes narrowed. "A cat holds less curiosity than an Overlander."

Portia chuckled. "Please, sister, let him ask his questions. As with anything, receiving answers to our questions is how we learn."

Daphne sighed. "Very well. Go ahead."

Roble took several seconds to carefully reflect on his words before speaking, as he didn't want to cause any further resentment from Daphne. She held a bitter taste toward Overlanders. "Based upon your earlier statement, what makes you believe the Shadowfae are responsible for the massive flood? What proof do you have?"

No anger surfaced on Daphne's features. "What occurred … is forever etched in my mind and scarred my heart. The flood came like a sudden tidal wave and wasn't the product of continuous excessive rains. On the air that night traveled a dark force with a heavy presence. Evil saturated the night breeze. Portia, Runefel, and myself stood outside on a balcony watching the first moon rise when that eerie breeze cut through the trees. The flood was not nature's doing."

Portia nodded. "I agree. I felt it, too. The three of us attempted to form a shield of protection around ourselves, but we didn't have enough time. We clung to one another as the large wave of water crashed around our village. I stood between Daphne and Runeful, desperately holding their hands as they held mine. The volume of water and its immense pressure drove us deep underwater. The current yanked us apart. The dark water prevented me from seeing where they went. Then, my world went black."

"As did mine," Daphne said, wiping away tears.

"I'm sorry," Roble said with genuine regret. "I understand your anger. My anger would be as furiously heated as yours. But, how do you know the Shadowfae were behind it? Could it not have been a dark mage or wizard? Or from another?"

"Time's wasting," Daphne said, rolling up the map. "It's best we head upriver while the day is early."

Portia looked at Collette. "You need to stay in Dagger's Tears."

Collette's eyes moistened with tears. A hurt expression overtook her facial expressions. She shook her head. "No. Lehrling promised to take me with them."

"It is not safe for any of us," Daphne said. "It'll be difficult enough for Portia and I to protect our party. Lehrling and Roble have faced battle and are trained for combat. You put all of us at risk."

"Roble?" Collette said, glancing toward him with desperate eyes.

"I have to agree," Roble said. "I had told Lehrling the same thing at the lodge."

Her eyes narrowed at Roble. "Was that before or *after* you had them vote in my favor? I thought you were standing up for me. Otherwise, why the vote?"

Roble sighed. "Look, I didn't address them for that reason, but the matter came up. I needed to know what authority your father held, which turned out to be none. They granted you freedom to travel. But moments later, I realized the danger you'd be in if you left now."

Hurt overshadowed her. She turned toward Lehrling. "Why did you let me believe I could still leave this mudhole? I assumed I couldn't go and you swore you'd find a way."

"Collette," Lehrling said with a soft tone. "I didn't know how to tell you without breaking your heart. Honestly, I didn't. I was still hopeful that if I talked to Roble—"

"You must find a place for me to depart with you," Collette said. "I refuse to stay here. Not when you promise me I could leave."

"Hastily," Roble said with a slightly hardened stare toward Lehrling. "We'll return for you once this is taken care of."

"No," Collette said, wiping away tears. "That simply will not do. I must go."

"Roble," Lehrling said, sheepishly. "Is there not a way that we can take her?"

"We only have two horses," Roble said.

"She can ride with me," Lehrling insisted. "Or I can walk alongside her."

Daphne frowned. "You walking will only impede the journey. That cannot be allowed. For us to be successful, Lez'minx … Runefel must be taken by surprise. Any advanced notice of our arrival and we'll all be dead."

"*Please*," Collette said.

"I'll stay behind," Lehrling said sternly. "Travel on without me."

Shawndirea gasped. "*Lehrling!*"

Roble's eyes narrowed. "You'd forsake helping a friend who saved your life on more than one occasion?"

"I'm no match for him. I can't fight against magic."

Roble's tone became sour and bitter. "King Erik didn't directly knight me, but Lady Dawn did, which makes me part of the Order. If this be your decision, so be it."

"You've given me little choice," Lehrling replied.

"Love can be so blind," Roble whispered.

"Coming from a man who risked his life and the world he knew to bring a faery into a realm to where he's a stranger?"

"Careful," Shawndirea said. Her eyes darkened.

Daphne cleared her throat. "Before this escalates into swords being drawn—"

"That'd never happen," Roble said. "I'd never attack a friend. No matter how much I disagree with his ideology or his extreme lack of common sense. Besides, he'd be no match for me and he knows it."

Lehrling lowered his gaze to the floor, and regret made Roble's heart ache for the sting of his insult.

Daphne sighed. "I have a proposal."

Lehrling and Collette turned their attention toward her and asked, "What?"

Daphne looked at Portia. "I may regret this."

Portia shrugged.

Daphne rolled her eyes. "*This* is why dryads tend not to seek communion with humans and this maddened thing called *love*. We've room on one of our rafts for Collette, but once we reach Saggy-nook, our protection over you ceases until our affairs with Runefel have ended. Is that clear?"

"Yes," Collette said. "Bless you."

"Save the blessings for yourself," Daphne said. "You're going to need them. As for Lehrling, since you've allowed your reason to be swayed by uncertain passion, she's your responsibility once we confront Runefel. So whatever should happen to her, she'll have you to thank or curse for it. None of the blame falls on the rest of us. Can you live with that?"

Lehrling swallowed hard and remained silent for several moments. His eyes searched the floor. He didn't glance at Collette or Roble for support in his decision. Finally, he nodded. "I will."

Collette rushed to Lehrling and wrapped her arms around his neck, squeezing tightly. He placed his arms around her.

"Then, let's get ready to depart. We mustn't be exposed during the night. At all times, remain alert to whatever might follow us during our journey," Daphne said. "Within the shadows, our enemies await."

<h1 style="text-align:center">CHAPTER 52</h1>

*R*oble stood on the river's bank beside Daphne. The rest of her party paddled the rafts against the bank, so everyone could board. Collette and Lehrling stood a fair distance away. Collette embraced her friends and her mother. She held a small bag with what few possessions she wished to take.

Shawndirea and Portia conversed, but outside of Roble's range of hearing.

While Aqese and Ki'wese helped Collette onto a raft, Roble admired the rafts' architecture. The raft bottoms were shaped like large flattened canoes but the stems of the rafts were coiled tendrils fashioned from thick ivy vines. Near the center of the gunwales, small masts with narrow sails that shimmered like meshed spider webs stood ten feet in height. The olive-colored wood camouflaged with the water, making the rafts hardly noticeable, especially from a distance. In areas where the trees darkened the water, the rafts were probably invisible.

Both of Daphne's companions wore hooded cloaks, almost the exact color of the rafts' wood. Their faces were grained like polished lumber, which he found incredibly odd. Their complexions benefited and allowed them to blend into the trees.

A few times they glanced his direction and glared at him. Roble realized he'd been rudely staring at their features for far too long. But not in a bad way. He loved the diversity and unusualness of the different races in Aetheaon and the intrigue was more than his curious mind could handle.

Daphne's skin radiated as she overlooked the river. A cool breeze flowed past them. The mossy tendrils on her arms rose and swayed like minuscule blades of grass.

"You never answered my question earlier," Roble said. "So I must assume you cannot actually prove the Shadowfae are responsible for the flood."

"Assumptions can get you killed," Daphne replied, under her breath, without the slightest glance in his direction. Her tone indicated she was tired of his repeated questions.

"Is that a threat?"

"Not so much a threat than it is advice. Advice that might aid your survival this time tomorrow."

Tomorrow? That soon? He attempted to quash his rising apprehension. After all this time, he'd finally confront Lez'minx, but he wondered what he gained by doing so; and worse, he feared what he might lose.

As much as he admired Portia and Daphne for their abilities and what they were capable of achieving, their ambitions for confronting their brother were far different than his own, especially Daphne's reasons. She was not as effective at hiding her inner anger and rage as Portia. Her meeting with Lez'minx or Runefel—as he was actually known—was not going to be affable in any way.

Something Runefel had done in the past had soured her affection toward him, and her need to get vengeance outweighed any former cordial familial ties. Daphne wasn't the same as Portia. Daphne was capable of inflicting pain and suffering on anyone who crossed her without a second thought, which made Roble wonder why Portia didn't believe she could do the same.

Daphne's strange eyes stared across the river. Her gaze indicated she was brooding, perhaps planning what she planned to do to their brother. Although he'd rather not meet Runefel, he had no other choice if he wanted the rings removed. However, he feared Daphne might kill Runefel before the rings got removed.

Roble wasn't certain what happened to bound magic once the wielder died. He wanted to believe the death ended the magical ties to whatever the sorcerer had cast during his lifetime. That seemed the most reasonable outcome, but nothing in the Realm of Aetheaon was *ever* reasonable. While he could part with the rings, he didn't want to lose the armor.

The standing silence between he and Daphne stagnated. She, still refusing to acknowledge his presence even with a slight glance, kept her gaze straightaway.

Roble knew it was best if he remained silent. He needed to choose his words more carefully. But the uneasiness he held concerning Daphne's true motives prevented him from doing so.

"But you don't have the proof the Shadowfae caused the flood, do you?" Roble asked.

Daphne turned her head slightly. Her eyes darkened as she regarded him. Blue sparks crackling on her fingertips, but he kept his eyes locked with hers, even though doing so meant could be considered a challenge.

A sheen glazed her eyes like a thin layer of blue frost. A chill jolted through him, and he fought hard not to look away from her frozen pools of misery. Her captivating gaze was luring, and she was trying to lull him with a form of hypnosis. He broke eye contact.

She laughed softly like the whispering of a hummingbird's wings, which echoed inside his mind; laughter meant only for him to hear. His jaw tightened because he sensed her arrogant triumph and the dominance of her power over him. He'd never been exposed to that type of drawing power, but he understood that she could, in the matter of minutes, force his mind into submission. Her capabilities were far more dangerous than he and the others credited her. She was the complete opposite of her sister. He doubted Portia recognized the drastic change in her sister's aura since the last time they were together.

After the ringing soft laughter faded, Daphne smiled.

"I've a sense of the dark power behind what caused that flood," Daphne said. "It's why I journey through the swamps the way I do to rejoin our kindred and restore Linden-hold."

"From my understanding of the Shadowfae, their numbers are broad and differ in many ways. Most are not evil, at least no more evil than some of the Seelie, but they are considered outsiders shunned by the Seelie, as they're not *pure* Fae," Roble said. "Does this coincide with the truth?"

Daphne nodded. "Yes."

"Aren't you and your sister part of the Unseelie Courts?" Roble asked.

"To some degree, yes."

"Some? Wouldn't it be either or?"

"Must we squabble over semantics?"

Roble shrugged. "Call it what you will. I only want to know why your near hatred stems toward an entire group of Fae, rather than narrowing it down to the rightful guilty party."

"Careful, Overlander," she hissed. Her eyes displayed a darkened pool and resembled swirling ink. "Don't meddle in the affairs that weigh no bearings on you. You've seen what happens to my enemies, or is your memory too short?"

"I'm not your enemy."

"Not yet," Daphne replied. "You seem determined to become one."

"No. I'm not against you. Before I stand beside you to defend your cause with my life and the lives of those dearest to me, I want proof the Shadowfae were responsible. You confess that you and Portia are Unseelie. Why then would the Shadowfae, who are Unseelie, want to cause you great harm?"

"Because we favored bringing light into these shadowed swamps," Daphne replied. "Our understanding and use of magic is far stronger than theirs."

"So why do they oppose sunlight? They don't have to journey into your town."

"Their hideousness forms and features cause them to seek the shadows. They may have viewed us as a threat; not fully understanding our intentions. At no time did we ever seek to bless the entire swamp into fertile workable lands. That would only invite humans to further corrupt and distort what we had worked so hard to achieve. We only wanted *our* town that way," Daphne said.

"Did you ever express that to them?" Roble asked.

She frowned. "We were never offered the chance."

"So, in return, you've no intention to seek a peaceful negotiation?"

Daphne sighed angrily. Roble feared he'd far crossed the line with her. "Why do you continue to prod and poke questions at a tender place in my heart and mind? At the moment, I've set my attention on traveling to protect you and your party. Must you evoke my hospitality? Do you wish to seek to have my wrath turned toward you?"

"That isn't my intention," Roble replied.

Daphne's jaw tightened. Rather than continue their conversation, she stepped onto the raft and turned away from him.

Roble had been snubbed by people in the Overlands, and Daphne's reaction was quite the same. So, they disagreed, but that didn't mean he was angry with her. He wasn't making accusations, but she probably took it as such.

His words had nearly provoked her to attack. The sparks on her fingertips were an involuntary warning. Somehow, she managed to keep herself in check. It'd hardly serve her purpose to kill a Dragon Skull Knight in the presence of a peaceful hamlet and in view of her sister.

What troubled Roble was how Portia had convinced herself and the townsfolk that she could never brood over her inner rage or direct bad thoughts toward another without shortening her life. Daphne's approach and outlook was the opposite. She held no reservations about starting a war against those might be innocent of her charges. The manner in which she had destroyed the Saurians and their mage proved her strength.

He wished he could examine the anatomy of the magically electrocuted Saurians, but they didn't have time. The rafts were ready to depart. He'd only worsen his stance with Daphne by taking the time to investigate.

After his conversation with Daphne, he wondered if she viewed him as an enemy because they didn't see eye-to-eye about the Shadowfae. He didn't any have ground for counterarguments anyway, since he had only recently learned about their courts.

Roble glanced at Portia, who was carrying on an enlightened conversation with Shawndirea. Both held partial smiles. Shawndirea met his gaze and her smile broadened. A warmth washed through him, filled with comfort and joy.

Fate's direction for individuals was often unpredictable. Roble believed Shawndirea was destined to have found him and they should be together. But

Fate was often cruel as well by taking precious blessings from those who received them. He hoped the confrontation with Lez'minx didn't cost them far more than Roble's refusal of the rings. By the end of the next day, they'd all know. His gut twisted from worry.

CHAPTER 53

*L*ehrling waited at the side of the raft for Collette.

Collette hugged and kissed her mother, several elderly women, and embraced other friends and family members. Her captivating smile brightened the otherwise gray, damp misery shrouding Dagger's Tears. She seemed the only shining light in the overcast morning.

On the lodge balcony, her father sat scowling on a broken barstool. Hatred heated his eyes. His disdain wasn't particularly aimed at any of them. This was his general disposition. If Collette noticed him, she never acknowledged it.

Lehrling pitied her father more for his bitter heart than for his physical disfigurements.

Jaux was blessed with an incredible daughter and a good wife, but his bitterness blinded him to what blessings he still possessed.

Seeing the excitement on Collette's face thrilled Lehrling and she was finally leaving the dismal hamlet, but he feared her haste might cost her or someone else in their party a premature death.

He glanced from Collette to Roble. Roble stood on the river's bank talking to Daphne.

Regret tightened Lehrling's chest and seeped into his mind for taking a stand against Roble's sound advice to leave Collette in Dagger's Tears and return for her at a later date.

Roble's advice was in Collette's best interests. Perhaps Lehrling's heart was too soft. Seeing the hurt and brokenness on Collette's face and in her eyes was more than Lehrling could handle. He believed he might never see Collette again, if she didn't leave with them.

236

She loathed her inability to venture outside the borders of Dagger's Tears and should she be denied the opportunity Lehrling feared her disappointment might make her harm herself or set out on her own. Or when Lehrling returned for her, she might have nothing to do with him, feeling scorned. Either way, he'd lose her.

While Lehrling couldn't predict they'd eventually marry, his heart hoped they might. Despite their age difference, he'd never meet another woman with her warm generosity and kindness. He scolded himself, "You're an old fool."

Perhaps it was time to consider retiring his sword and living his final years on a small farmstead, gardening and raising sheep. Riding was become harder on his aging bones and younger knights were more effective in defending the crown.

He could train and mentor young squires for knighthood. But he wanted a wife and children after all these empty years as a knight.

He released a tired sigh. Collette gave her final goodbyes to friends and family. Some gave her small gifts. While they talked, he couldn't get past spouting his stubborn words at Roble.

Lehrling worried his firm challenge might have damaged his friendship with Roble. Even though he didn't know Roble all that well, he didn't want a wedge driven between them. Roble was strong-minded and determined to defend the helpless. He already served Hoffnung's crown quite well.

Roble was much younger than Lehrling. Lehrling didn't know how deep a grudge Roble might harbor when slighted, but if threatened, Roble was quick to use weapons without a second thought.

Roble didn't seem threatened by Lehrling in the slightest. Instead, he downplayed Lehrling in a semi-mocking manner by stating Lehrling wasn't a challenge should they take up arms against one another. While Lehrling could've argued that in sword-to-sword combat he'd have been the victor, Lehrling couldn't get close enough to Roble to sword fight. Roble possessed the greatest advantage with the use of his throwing knives. No swordsman was a match against Roble's precision.

Lehrling wanted to right the wrong he'd committed against Roble in public. Lehrling would thoroughly apologize in private at the first opportunity. Until then, he prayed Roble might forgive him.

While Lehrling watched others ready the rafts, his focus turned to Geowren and what had become of his fellow Dragon Skull Knight. His best friend and mentor had stood upon this bank not too long ago.

Was Geowren still alive? If so, Lehrling needed Geowren's assistance more now than ever. Lehrling and Roble could use Geowren's fighting skills when they approached Lez'minx.

He wondered why Geowren decided to travel south toward Misthalls. Perhaps Geowren's information was a ruse to throw others off his trail? A lie sometimes benefited one in harrowing situations. If Geowren lied because his life was in danger and he were on the run, it was justifiable.

Collette took his calloused hand into hers, snatching his mind from Geowren's possible fate.

"Are you ready, my love?" She beamed a smile.

He smiled with uncertainty, and squeezed her hand. His eyes studied hers, but he was unable to determine if her words were meant to appease those of Dagger's Tears or if she looked at him with the same hope in their future. She didn't hesitate in grabbing his hand, no quiver or distaste in her voice, and no deceit was seen in her eyes. A strange sensation rushed to his heart. His stomach twisted with excitement.

Her smile soothed Lehrling, and her grip on his hand didn't waver. Her actions were genuine and not for display to those around them.

After they stepped onto the raft, he read the happiness Collette's friends and family held for her. He forced a smile realizing his responsibility to protect her. He didn't want her to become collateral damage, due to his self-ishness and shortsightedness to satisfy her desires of leaving Dagger's Tears behind. He hoped he could protect her.

CHAPTER 54

*S*hawndirea watched Roble speaking to Daphne from the corner of her eye while she talked to Portia. Despite the distance between them, Shawndirea discerned Daphne's rising anger.

Why did Roble always find ways to chaff others? While she didn't believe it was always intentional, he did it more often than not. He pried for information to fully understand a person's motives. But in Aetheaon, actions didn't dictate intent. Actions weren't synonymous with someone's reasoning. He delved for knowledge because he was cursed by his duties as a *scientist*—his apparent obsession in the Overlands—but in Aetheaon, this wasn't the proper way to resolve problems.

In spite of his inquisitiveness, she never wanted him to quash his want for discovery.

Portia continued talking about Daphne and how thrilled she was to see her sister again and soon their brother.

Shawndirea graciously smiled and nodded, but added little to the conversation. At the rapid rate Portia spoke, she didn't really want any added input from Shawndirea. Portia gushed about the revived hope of reestablishing Linden-hold without considering the cost the folks of Dagger's Tears suffered by her absence.

While Portia talked, Shawndirea's thoughts reflected on the dark pool and her deep sleep. The voice told her to accept who she truly was. It wasn't a dream or a nightmare or a delusion. She had been taken merely to have her attention focused in a new direction—a direction she'd have never taken due to the distractions in her life.

Although she didn't know, nor could she properly discern whom had spoken to her, the voice radiated a familiarity she was unable to explain. For some reason, she sensed she knew the being that pointed her toward the proper path. She only wished he'd revealed his name or something jarred her memories enough to dislodge it.

Secrets. Why must secrets be kept?

Portia droned on.

After Shawndirea had awakened, something else was revealed to her, but she couldn't tell Roble, although she needed to. But the last thing Roble needed was another distraction.

Distractions set forth unforeseen dangers. She wanted to tell him, but based on prior confrontations Roble had experienced, she forbade herself from telling him. She ached inside to keep any secret from him, but withholding this one hurt her most of all.

Merla and Cora joined Portia and Shawndirea. Tears welled in the two halflings' eyes.

Portia stopped speaking when she glanced at them. "My dears … what is wrong?"

Shawndirea cocked a brow. *Has she no clue?* Was Portia so self-absorbed that she didn't see how attached those in Dagger's Tears were to her?

"We need you to stay," Merla said.

"No," Portia replied, shaking her head. "I've happily served my purpose in Dagger's Tears."

"You can't leave us," Cora said. "You mustn't."

"I've taught you which herbs to use for different healing potions and the proper way to make poultices with blessed mud, herbs, and oils. You can readily take my place," Portia said with a smile.

"No," Merla said. "Your presence offers us more than the healing abilities you perform. You're the light within this drab hamlet. Without you, our hope perishes."

"That's—"

Dolan stormed to them and stopped. He huffed. His eyes narrowed with anger. "What's this I hear that you're leaving Dagger's Tears?"

Portia explained her reasons for leaving.

"Unacceptable!" he said. His chest rose and his hands formed tight little fists. "If ever a place has needed you, it's here. Not off on some delusional trip, hoping to find a lost city that probably no longer exists. Believe me, after our exile, we looked for a place of unity and hope. A place we could call home. At first, we thought it was the Glades of Sorrow, but our town was attacked and decimated. We packed up and settled Dagger's Tears. You joined us. We received you as family. One of our own. Last night we suffered another attack."

"And you wish to leave us," Cora said, wiping away tears. "Who's going to stop them when they return and you're gone?"

For a moment, Portia was a loss for words. Her eyes viewed them with pity. "I—I don't—"

"Bah!" Dolan said, frowning and waving her off. "You're no different than those we placed our trust in years ago."

"Believe me," Portia said, "I'm not leaving to cause you harm or to leave you vulnerable."

"Yet, you are!" Dolan spat.

"What if I return for you—"

"What if?" Dolan said. "What if? We-e-l-l, what if *I* were the height of a human? Huh? What if I could walk on water or fly like a bat? None of these are possible, nor will they ever be. What if's are generally spoken about things that won't happen. If you're leaving us with an empty promise, I won't bank on it. It won't happen. We won't ever see you again."

"Dolan," Cora said, shaking her head. "Don't be rude."

"Perhaps we should gather sugar-coated mushrooms and make a delightful loaf, eh?" Dolan said. "I'm tired of others letting us down and leaving us to fend for ourselves."

Portia's eyes widened. "I never realized the degree of your bitterness, Dolan. I'm quite surprised."

Merla frowned. "You *never* noticed before?"

"I ignore his childish outbursts," Portia replied.

Dolan sighed and looked at Cora and then at Merla. "This leaves only one thing for us to do."

"What's that?" Cora asked.

"We travel with them," Dolan replied.

"You cannot—" Portia said.

Dolan pointed a stern finger at her. "We can and we *will*."

"You don't realize the dangers," Portia said.

"We saw *real* dangers last night. Had your sister not fried those lizard fiends like fritters, we'd all be dead," Dolan said.

"I tried," Portia said.

"Save it!" Dolan said, holding his palm up. "You need our protection as much as we need yours."

"There's not enough room," Portia said.

Dolan laughed heartily. "Not enough room? For four halflings? We fit into the tiniest of places. No one will notice."

"Shawndirea," Portia said, "please explain to them?"

Shawndirea shook her head. "We've no time. Roble's motioning that it's time for us to get aboard."

CHAPTER 55

Roble handed the last small crate of supplies to a hooded dryad, carefully watching where he stood in the mud. Standing in one spot too long was dangerous. The muck stuck to his boots and held fast, trying to pull him down. But moving was also hazardous. He didn't want to slip and lose a leg to one of the massive turtles beneath the water.

Even though the turtles weren't visible, streams of air bubbles popped on the water's surface. The bubbles when the turtles exhaled or when their claws disturbed the river bottom.

Roble stepped back, and his foot slipped on the slick mud. He almost fell but was caught from behind. Strong hands held him upright, preventing Roble from landing on his back and getting stuck.

"Thought you could use a hand," Lehrling said with a smile. "Or maybe a *couple* of hands."

Roble halfway laughed, nodded, and then slapped a firm hand on Lehrling's shoulder. "Thanks."

Roble walked to the top of the bank without glancing at Lehrling and laughed with a tinge of embarrassment.

"Roble," Daphne said. "You and Lehrling need to load your horses onto the second raft."

"We can ride," Roble said.

Daphne shook her head. "No. You'll never keep up with us."

"There's a path alongside the river," Roble said, pointing.

"It's an uneven path that often leads away from the river due to small tributaries and fallen trees. You must ride *with* us. Otherwise, you'll arrive several days after us. We won't wait for you."

Roble shrugged. "Can this raft support two large horses?"

"They're built soundly and support far more weight than most small ships. Dryads understand our strengths and limitations when it comes to woodworking," she replied.

Shawndirea frowned. "I thought dryads couldn't harm a tree."

Daphne leveled an even stare. "We didn't. The lumber composing these two rafts came from a human logging yard after they rampaged an Elven forest. The spirits of the trees were gone. We wept and blessed each board used in these rafts. These vessels, though small, are far sturdier than any ship in Hoffnung's navy. They're a tribute to the former dryads who possessed the wood."

Shawndirea wiped away a tear. "That must've been devastating for you."

"No less than you weaving a cloak from butterfly wings," Daphne replied.

Fresh tears welled in Shawndirea's eyes at the thought of such a monstrosity.

Daphne returned her stoic attention to Roble. "The raft will safely carry your horses."

Roble looked at Lehrling. They went to retrieve their horses.

Dolan, Cora, and Merla hurried their stubby legs to the river's edge. Portia walked briskly behind them, scolding them under her breath.

"What seems to be the problem?" Daphne asked.

"These three wish to travel with us," Portia replied.

"Nonsense," Daphne said.

"Try and stop us," Dolan said, leaping onto the second raft where Roble and Lehrling were leading their horses.

Cora and Merla didn't hesitate to follow.

"Do you understand how ludicrous your actions are?" Daphne asked.

"*What* I understand is that we're going," Dolan said.

"As am I," Rufus said from behind Dolan.

"Suit yourself." Daphne glanced at an agitated Aqese. "If we need to lighten the load, toss them overboard first. Use them as bait if necessary."

Aqese nodded and grinned at Dolan.

"Bait?" Dolan's face creased with anger.

Rufus' face tightened and his eyes grew fierce. He started around Dolan, but Dolan shook his head and placed a gentle hand on Rufus' shoulder.

"It be as it is anywhere we travel," Dolan said. "Because of our size, other races think us inefficient."

"Isn't right," Rufus said in a harsh whisper.

"No, it's not. But it means we must work harder to prove our worth."

CHAPTER 56

*E*ight agonizing hours later, Roble was physically and mentally exhausted. The muddy river occasionally curved into shallower bends without a consistent current.

In the shallowest sections of the river, everyone—including Daphne and Portia—got off and pulled the rafts until they reached deeper water. The raft with the horses was the hardest part. The horses couldn't be taken off the rafts or they risked a horse breaking its leg on the rocky river bottom. The best part of the journey was the lack of rain.

These shallow areas were darkened by thicker trees, hanging vines, and unusual curious reptiles. Strange ferns and orchids flourished on small islands of dirt and in the cracks of large trees. Were this place in the Overlands, Roble would've viewed this as unexplored paradise. But Aetheaon wasn't a place of serenity, especially not in these darker areas that housed creatures and magic wielders. Neither welcomed intruders into their abode.

Lehrling and Collette smacked biting flies and mosquitoes. Large red swollen bite marks covered their faces. Shawndirea spent most of her time zapping these nuisance insects with tiny blasts of heated light but they were too numerous to strike all of them.

Large butterflies with metallic-colored wings drifted on the slight breeze. Smaller butterflies puddled on the soggy river bank, feeding on minerals with their long tongues. Occasionally, a worn and weary butterfly drifted to Shawndirea to be have its tattered wings restored.

The darkened shroud produced by the thick canopy deceived fireflies into believing it was night. They glowed in the weeds and tree branches. The deception in the river's shallow pockets was its beauty, making one wish to cast aside fear to rest and relax. The occasional appearance of glowing eyes alerted them that they were being watched.

In spite of the humid, hot air, a chill shot down Roble's back. Someone or something was following them. He'd never gotten a full glimpse of these creatures with luminous eyes but their pursuit never lessened and their number seemed to increase the farther upriver the rafts drifted. These beasts coveted the shadows but didn't seem worried about letting Roble and his party know of their presence. Whatever they were, they were becoming bolder.

Shawndirea sat on his shoulder, occasionally whispering her concerns about being watched by the Shadowfae.

Daphne sensed these stalkers as well but remained quiet. Her companions, Aqese and Kilwese, each controlled a rudder of the two flat rafts. The small sails caught the slight breeze and drifted near a sandy wide shoreline. Jutting up from the sand were ancient broken pillars.

Daphne motioned toward the sandbar. "We stay the night here."

"In these ruins?" Lehrling asked. "Out in the open?"

She flicked her narrowed gaze at him. "Yes."

"Where are we?" Roble asked.

"The Ruins of Evendusk," she replied.

"Who lived here?" Lehrling asked.

"Dark Elves." She stood in silence for several long moments, studying the writing on the cracked, broken pillars rising from the sand. "They lived here several centuries ago. From what historians have written, the city was once a prosperous one."

"What caused its demise?" Lehrling asked.

Daphne shrugged. "Your guess is as good as mine. The historians who studied the city never determined the actual reason for its demise."

"You know we're being followed, correct?" Roble asked.

"Yes. I'm aware. Their more curious than anything else," Daphne replied. "Had they wanted to attack, they'd have already done so. But be prepared, in any case. Don't let down your guard."

Dolan's fearful eyes searched the shadowy trees on the opposite bank. Cora and Merla held small bows with tiny arrows that were more likely to infuriate any creature they shot rather than kill it. They were too nervous to step off the raft onto the bank. He took a deep breath, trying to muster his courage.

Rufus stood upright, crossed his arms in an attempt to look bold, but his eyes displayed his nervousness. He glanced with uncertainty at Dolan.

"This ... this doesn't look like a safe place to spend the night," Dolan said.

"We'll not find a more suitable place for camp before night overshadows us," Daphne said, "Do you want to drift on the river during the darkest hours of night?"

"Not particularly," he replied.

"You were warned to stay behind," Portia said. "It was *your* stubborn decision to travel with us."

Partially angered by the reminder, Dolan leapt from the raft onto the pebbled sandbar. A snarl formed on his lips and he huffed, eyeing the opposite shore lined with thick trees and snaky coiled, leafy vines. Ferns and dense brush filled the area between the tree trunks. He stood with his boots partway sunken in the sand and gripped his bow firmly.

Aqese and Kilwese pulled the rafts onto the small pebbled beach and then helped Lehrling and Roble unload the horses. Afterwards, they slung their quivers over their shoulders and readied their bows, standing near the rafts and watching the opposite river bank.

Lehrling walked his horse to a fallen pillar. He pointed at the dark shadowed recess against a hillside above the sandbar. "There's an opening above us."

Bones and skulls littered the sandbar beneath the opening.

Roble flicked his gaze at Daphne. "We're not alone. Someone still lives in the tunnel."

"Or something," she replied softly.

"And that doesn't concern you?"

"It does, but whatever lives inside most likely will prevent what has followed us from crossing the river. It's a fair tradeoff," Daphne said, looking toward the dark opening. "We could send the halflings in to investigate."

"Hey!" Dolan said, snarling.

"I jest, Dolan," Daphne said in a bland monotone that held no humor. "Let's gather driftwood and build ourselves a large fire. We split the nightwatch into three shifts, each with two individuals. Come morning, we continue upriver. We should be less than four hours away, unless we hit more shallow points."

"That requires *surviving* the night," Dolan said.

"Quite accurate evaluation, halfling," Daphne said. "All the more reason to remain vigilant. Which shift do you intend to keep watch?"

"I doubt I'll sleep a wink," he replied.

"All the better!" Portia said, smiling.

Roble shook his head. "Lehrling, come with me. Let's go see what's in the opening."

"Are you mad?" Lehrling asked with a raised brow. Collette squeezed his hand.

"No. We need to know if it's a creature or goblins or Ratkin living there. If it's a wolf or bear, we've a stronger possibility of not being attacked. If it's the latter ... we'll get mobbed during the night."

Lehrling swallowed hard. "Or the moment we look into the opening. Perhaps we'd be safer waiting for *it* to emerge?"

Roble sighed. "We're knights for God's sake."

"Goddesses' sake," Lehrling said. He kissed Collette's forehead and released her hand. "I'll be right back."

Roble shrugged and walked to the worn sandy path that ascended at a forty-five degree angle and led to the opening. He couldn't discern the recent unidentifiable footsteps.

"Look, Roble," Lehrling said, following behind. "I've been meaning to … apologize for my behavior in Dagger's Tears. For opposing your opinion—"

"No need. I'm past it." Roble kept his attention on the opening and without glancing at Lehrling.

"Are you sure? Because if you're leading me up here to prove a point about my bravery—"

"What's to prove? You're a Dragon Skull Knight, chosen by the King. He'd never chosen you if you weren't worthy."

"Don't mock me, Roble."

Roble turned at the top of the path and headed to the opening. Cool air that reeked of death flowed from the hole. "I'm not mocking you. What makes you think that?"

"This. Leading me up here in front of our party and Collette."

"You've nothing to prove. You've already won Collette's heart. She's held your hand during the journey and her eyes reveal her affection."

"Roble!" Lehrling said in a harsh whisper. "While I'm much older and more experienced than you, I still regard you as a better warrior. I'm actually learning *more* from you than you are from me."

"Better?" Roble laughed. "Why? *I'm* the fool who refused to listen to Shawndirea about these rings and got us into this mess to begin with."

"I'd have done the same thing. Any man would," Lehrling said. "With your enchanted armor, I'd have wondered what benefits the rings offered, too. Any knight from any kingdom would have tested the power of the rings."

"Is that so?"

Lehrling nodded. "Yes. When you fight mages or wizards, swords and axes are of no value. That's why Dwarves engrave runes into their weapons? Some tattoo runic symbols onto their faces, hands, and bodies. Dwarves cannot wield magic, but they readily defend themselves against it. So, if this is a public test, leading me here—"

"Lehrling, I'd never deliberately place you into harm's way, and I'd certainly never embarrass you in front of Collette."

"What are you doing, Roble?" Shawndirea asked, flying up behind him.

"*He* wants to find out what's in the opening," Lehrling said.

Roble said, "I simply want to know what's living here."

Lehrling shook his head. "Ratkin or goblins *might* be inside … *he* says."

"Is that so?" Shawndirea asked.

"Yes."

"If it's Ratkin or goblins, do you think it wise that only the *two* of you face them? Either could rip you to shreds before you could defend yourselves. Most likely, it's not goblins though."

"No?" Roble asked.

Shawndirea shook her head. "No. Goblins were driven out of Aetheaon and eradicated by Dwarven warriors. They never occupied swamps, either."

"She's right, Roble," Lehrling said. "I've heard many a bard's tale about the Dwarves final battle against the goblins. Many noble Dwarves died that day, but the goblins' slaughter remains a legendary tale."

"Did you ever consider that straggling goblins might have retreated into the swamps?" Roble asked.

"No. Swamps are not their … habitat," Shawndirea replied. "That's a word scientists use, right?"

Roble suppressed a grin. "Yes. My point is people change and adapt. I did. Maybe surviving goblins did, too?"

"Humans adapt to most anything," Shawndirea said sharply. "Other races do not. You'd never move a city of Elves into the heart of the desert. You'd never enslave Saurians and successfully move them from the swamps. They'd die. Goblins live in mountains."

"One less hostile creature for us to worry about then," Roble said.

Shawndirea sighed. "Your curiosity is a death wish."

"No, it's not," Roble said. "I assure you that I want to live a long life."

"You've an odd way of expressing that," she replied.

Roble's brow tightened as he processed her words. He nodded. "Perhaps. But I'd rather be the one surprising potential enemies than getting surprised by them."

"Either way doesn't allow longevity," she said. "Ratkin or goblins … hold no surprise. They react with hostility. They swarm intruders in a frenzy."

A roaring rhythm echoed from inside the opening.

"What's that?" Lehrling asked.

"It's not an animal," Shawndirea said softly.

"Then let's see," Roble said.

CHAPTER 57

*R*oble stepped into the shadowed recess of the hillside. "We need some light. Lehrling, do you see something we could light to use for a torch?"

"All I see are large dried bones. Do those burn?"

"They might," he replied. "We can try."

"Light draws too much attention," Shawndirea said.

"I can't see in total darkness," Roble said.

She sighed. "I meant *firelight*."

Shawndirea focused on her hands momentarily. Soft greenish light encircled them, offering enough light for them to see the crude pathway.

"This path doesn't seem like what an advanced city would have used for an entranceway."

"It wasn't," Shawndirea replied.

"How do you know?"

"From what I can tell, this path was bored through the city's outer wall after it fell."

Water splashed heavily against rocks farther ahead.

"A waterfall?" Roble asked, placing his hand against a tarnished marble pillar that held compacted soil and rock into place.

"Sounds like it," she replied.

Lehrling followed them. "I smell smoke."

"As do I," Roble said. "It's faint but carries on the sour air."

Revealed by the greenish glow on Shawndirea's hands were more bones, a few reptilian shriveled hides, but no discarded weapons.

Roble knelt and studied the long intact skeletal remains that were longer than he was tall. The long narrow jawbone held numerous teeth. "This is a skeleton of a crocodile."

Lehrling leaned down. "What's that exactly?"

Roble gave a quick explanation.

"Never heard of such a thing. They must be tasty creatures, as there are a lot of their remains," he said.

"Apparently so, but these creatures didn't crawl up from the river," Roble said.

"Maybe something brought them up from the river?" Lehrling asked.

"No. If these were in the river, we'd have seen them."

"Then how did they get here?"

"I don't know," Roble said. "In my world, they're aggressive hunters. They rest on the shorelines and when they're in the water, their eyes crest above the water. Nothing like that was in the river."

She said, "Roble's right. These bones aren't from creatures in Aetheaon."

"What's that mean?" Lehrling asked.

"I sense a rift in the realm barrier nearby," she said.

"Is that why Evendusk fell?" Roble asked.

In the greenish glow of her hands, her eyes peered into his. "Not through this rift. It's not large enough for an army to pass through."

"It's more recent than when Evendusk fell, too," Daphne said, standing behind Lehrling.

Lehrling clutched his chest and let out a brief shout. "Heavens, priestess! Announce yourself instead of sneaking up behind us!"

"Sorry," she said, "but Portia and I felt the magical tug of the rift and thought it best that we venture inside to warn you. It's good Shawndirea senses these things as well."

"Does the rift lead back to my world?" Roble asked.

"It's difficult to know without crossing through," Shawndirea said.

"Something I'd not advise," Daphne said. "It's far too risky, as the rift could close."

"Close?" Lehrling asked. His hand tightened on the hilt of his sword.

"It's true," Shawndirea said.

"Apparently Evendusk lies on a realm barrier, which means different rifts might have occurred over time," Portia said. "The realm wall might be too thin in this area."

"Something resides in these ruins," Roble said. "Why else would so many skeletal remains be along this pathway."

"Maybe," Daphne said, "Or maybe not. It's possible one of those creatures passed through one rift and something else came through a different one and feasted upon it."

"A double rift?" Shawndirea asked.

"That, or the two are superimposed," she replied.

"That's even more dangerous," Shawndirea said.

In the greenish glow of Shawndirea's light, Portia's eyes widened. "Shh! We're not alone."

Lehrling slid his blade from its sheath. Roble pulled two daggers free of his belt. Lehrling looked at Roble. "Did you hear something?"

"All I hear is the water splashing," Roble replied. "Did you hear anything other than that, Shawndirea?"

She placed her index finger against her lips and nodded. She flitted to his shoulder and whispered, "What we've heard isn't a physical sound, but rather an attempt to enter our minds, to locate and determine who and what we are."

"Roble," Lehrling said, "we should retreat to the river bank. *Now.*"

"I'm afraid it's much too late for that," Daphne said. "They know we're here. Anything less than an immediate confrontation is death."

CHAPTER 58

Roble glanced at Daphne, uncertain of what he should do. In the pale green orb of light that encircled Shawndirea, Daphne's face was grim. She stiffened, almost like petrified wood.

"Protect your minds," she whispered into Roble's mind.

The words weren't audible and her lips never moved. She was speaking telepathically to him. He wondered if she did the same with the others since she said, '*minds*'.

He gave a side-glance to Shawndirea and she placed a gentle hand to his cheek. "We're dealing with psionic beings."

Daphne issued a harsh glance at Shawndirea.

Silence! Daphne's voice rang inside Roble's head. Lehrling shook his head, placing his hands against his ears. The voice boomed and echoed, leaving a ringing sensation in Roble's ears as though Daphne shrilled the word aloud at her highest octave.

Roble tried to focus his thoughts toward Daphne, but he didn't know if she could detect his words like he had heard hers. "*What should we do?*"

"*Don't retreat*," she replied. "*Advance toward the waterfall*."

He was inclined to believe that following her command was suicidal. Fleeing, as Lehrling suggested, seemed the best option, given the present circumstances.

Lehrling looked into Roble's eyes. His brow furrowed. He whispered, "How am I hearing you inside my head?"

Portia grabbed Lehrling's arm tightly and turned him toward her. She flung her thoughts into his mind, "*Think your thoughts. We can hear you. Speaking aloud allows them to locate us faster.*"

Lehrling frowned but obeyed. "*How is this possible?*"

"A spell hangs over this narrow passageway," Daphne said, *"which allows intelligent beings to converse or read the thoughts of others. A delicate but rare type of spell, but quite beneficial whenever a group of thieves or invaders enter into a city and wish to refrain from physically voicing their conversations. However, in our case, using this form of telepathy is the deadlier, sharper side of a two-edged sword."*

"Why?" Roble and Lehrling asked at the same time.

"The more we speak, the faster they pinpoint our location. So move onward. Try to not phrase thoughts in your minds."

"That's impossible," Lehrling said.

"Yes, it's a horrible flaw for humans," Daphne replied. *"But try."*

Roble gripped the hilts of his throwing knives. For people not to think or question things in their minds was impossible. Human minds constantly deliberated about something, even when one didn't want to. The brain activity sought understanding, even during sleep, which was why people dreamed. Nightmares often held some truth as well, causing fear to awaken one.

Bright light shone ahead at the end of the path, meaning the exit was close. Under normal circumstances the light would've been inviting, but Roble feared the sudden light indicated they were getting close to where the inhabitants dwelled.

Lehrling took a sharp breath and held it. The subtle sounds of their breathing and their least adjusting movements seemed amplified. The longer they stood on the path, the more Roble felt exposed. He was reminded of a paralyzing nightmare from his childhood where an unknown entity had seen him. He wanted to run, but he couldn't walk or run. Instead, he fell to the ground, trying to crawl away.

"Go!" Daphne said.

Roble started to step forward but his leg felt heavy. He studied the edges of the carved tunnel in the glow of the light shining in. He didn't see any enemies, but he *felt* their presence. The sensation wasn't come from one being, but many.

In the same way he expressed his thoughts to Shawndirea and his friends, he felt others, strangers, feeling for him. It was similar to how bats used echolocation to hone in on insects to capture their prey.

"Move!" Daphne said.

Roble took a cumbersome step forward and slapped his hand against the earthen wall to steady himself. Pebbles and dirt spilled to the ground.

"You okay?" Shawndirea asked.

Roble nodded and attempted to take another step.

He didn't like not knowing what type of creatures they were about to encounter. Since he entered Aetheaon, he'd seen plenty of unusual species. The first monster he crossed paths with was in Devils Den and should've been enough of a deterrent to convince him to stay in the Overlands. Adaptation for survival was difficult by staying with Shawndirea, but his love for her and his distaste for the Overlands led him to abandon his previous life. Permanently returning to the Overlands wasn't an option.

His next step forward was easier. He took stealthily steps down the narrow tunnel. If he accidentally crossed into a rift, he wondered where he'd end up. *Which was more dangerous? he wondered. Stepping through a rift or facing the creatures with the ability to read their minds?*

"The rift is more dangerous," Daphne said.

Roble's face heated, remembering that anything he thought could be heard by his group. No secrets hung between them if revealed in their minds.

He listened with his mind, attempting to read the thoughts of the others. Only Lehrling's fearful thoughts and deep concern for their lives bellowed. Portia, Daphne, and Shawndirea were absent of thought or they had successfully shielded their thoughts. Using magic might allow them better protection, and since they weren't human, they were better able to control their thoughts.

The rushing waterfall became louder, and the light brightened. The air moistened with a richness of earth and minerals.

Roble stopped at the end of the carved-out tunnel, which overlooked a stone-tiled floor eight feet below where they stood. Large bright Elven glow-stones rested atop the pillars surrounding the water pool. Descending wasn't impossible but required a bit of careful footwork, so as to not plummet head-first onto the floor below.

Eight pillars surrounded the water pool. The Elven glowstones cast a yellowish-white hue like pleasant sunlight and washed across the massive room. The underground waterfall spilled from the rocks above. Strangely, the pool capturing the cascading water didn't overflow.

Four carved, marble statues of robed figures with swords and shields stood equally apart and encircled the pillars. The hoods shrouded what race had once lived in this city, but based on Woodnog's statues, Roble sensed they had been Elves. The architecture was phenomenal and displayed the majestic nature of the civilization now absent from Evendusk. Everything was buried, not only in ruins, but in mystery.

The quarters where they stood were former gardens. Thick leafy vines coiled around the pillars and partway up the statues. The glowstones blessed plant growth. Several vines draped with large colorful flowers. Others held heavy seedpods.

With the lighting and the access to fresh water, the place was still habitable, and yet, it remained abandoned for more than a century. That was except for whatever had killed and feasted on those foolish enough to enter the ruins. Curious treasure-hunters most likely met their demise.

No large carnivorous creatures were visible from Roble's vantage point.

The only activity were tiny moths flitting from flower to flower and flashing fireflies.

Daphne moved to Roble's right. She stood and gazed on the lit area below.

Roble gave her a side-glance. "What now?"

Confusion furrowed her brow. Her eyes searched the pillars and statues. After several minutes of silence, she finally said, "I'm not certain."

Lehrling lowered his sword and shook his head. "It seems too peaceful."

"I know," Daphne replied. "That's the deception. Be alert. We're being watched."

CHAPTER 59

*R*oble agreed with Lehrling about the peaceful solace surrounding these gardens. Were it not for the piles of white bones lining the walls, the falls and the pool would be tranquil. It was impossible to ignore the savagery of the violent deaths unseen enemies had enacted on their prey.

The telepathic reaches from creatures were extending their silent, mind-searching tendrils and softly brushed the edge of his thoughts. These feathery filaments slithering to find him weren't from Portia, Daphne, or Shawndirea. He clearly recognized their non-spoken thoughts when they spoke to his mind.

The mind-reachers in these ruins seemed to probe blindly. And even though no physical evidence of these dwellers was seen, they were here.

Somewhere.

Lehrling's hand gripped Roble's shoulder with a harsh squeeze. He turned Roble and then pointed at the corner of the dirt ceiling behind the waterfall. Fearful gasping breaths escaped Lehrling's open mouth. Lehrling acted like he wanted to speak or scream, but his obvious terror silenced him.

Narrow eyes reflected silver in the glow of the Elven glowstones. Two overly large insect-like creatures clung to the ceiling. Their bodies were flat like beetles but their mandibles were fierce, long, and sharper than a serrated blade. Several dagger-pointed edges lined the inside of the mandibles. With their massive size, their strength could pierce the strongest armors. His sharpest dagger or Lehrling's short sword probably couldn't penetrate the exoskeleton of these insect horrors.

A unrecognizable voice crept into Roble's mind. *"Caution, I give thee, or your fate is like those who've entered before you."*

"Anyone else hearing this?" Roble asked in his thoughts.

"Yes," Shawndirea, Daphne, and Portia replied.

"We don't take threats lightly," Roble thought.

"I offer no harm," the voice replied.

"Who are you?" Daphne asked.

"First, tell me how many are in your group?"

Roble studied the areas around the pillars and the waterfall, but still he couldn't see anyone. *"Why should we give you that information? It grants you an advantage."*

"Don't be a fool," the voice replied. *"I wish to aid your escape. Nothing more and nothing less."*

"Like those who killed before us?" Roble asked.

"Like you," the voice said, *"they wished to argue* instead *of listen."*

"The beetles on the ceiling ... Are they yours or perhaps you're one of them?"

"I've no part of them. They're what killed the ones that entered our gardens. Unless you heed my warning, they'll feast on you."

"Your gardens?" Shawndirea asked. *"You're a resident of Evendusk?"*

"Yes."

Shawndirea exchanged glances with Daphne.

Daphne shook her head. *"Impossible."*

"It's true. I'm the last voice of my people."

"Then reveal yourself," Roble said.

"I cannot. The moment I become visible, we all die. Now, yield to me your trust."

Roble shook his head. *"My trust's more precious than gold. I don't freely give it."*

"Fool!" the voice said. *"You're the foolish warrior standing on the ledge, slightly ahead of the others."*

"I'm a knight, but hardly a fool," Roble replied.

Seated at his ear, Shawndirea snickered. His face heated, as he glanced at the rings on his fingers.

"Sorry," she whispered before kissing his cheek. "I couldn't help it."

The telepathy voice continued, *"Warriors use brute force far more often than commonsense. Why do you think so many have died here? Warriors' ears are deaf to the soundest advice."*

"If the beetles are responsible for the piles of bones, commonsense hardly comes into play. Insects are incapable of negotiation," Roble replied. *"Extermination is the best solution."*

"You imply that's possible with your metal weapons," the voice said.

"Yes."

The hidden speaker's roaring laughter echoed in their heads. *"Your ignorance truly reigns above your rationality."*

"How so?" Roble asked.

"Their carapaces are harder than any metal the best smith might use. Your weapons can't penetrate their shells. They've no physical weakness or vulnerability a warrior can find. Hundreds who have tried before you and failed."

"There's always an exception," Roble replied.

"Tell that to the ghosts of those who died before you."

"Roble," Lehrling whispered. *"We should retreat."*

"Retreat?" Laughter echoed in their heads again. *"In a matter of seconds, the tunnel behind you will be filled with those beetles. They've surrounded you while you've wasted time talking to me."*

"So, you set us up?" Roble asked.

"Not at all. I asked a simple question and you refused to answer and still you squabble. The blame falls on yourself. I could've helped. Instead, you debate. Still think you're not *a foolish warrior?"*

Roble took a sharp breath. Anger overshadowed him. He glanced over his shoulder into the darkened tunnel. Clicking sounds echoed in the corridor, which could only be the leg sheaths of the scurrying beetles running in their direction.

"Metal weapons are useless," the voice said. *"Did you not notice? No swords or metal armor lie on the floor. Don't waste your time looking. Time's a fleeting commodity. No metal's here except for what you've brought inside. There's a reason for that."*

"And what would that be?" Roble asked.

"The beetles' produce an acid that erodes metal. Are you ready to tell me how many are in your group, or do you wish to be reduced to piles of bone?"

"What difference does that make now?" Roble asked.

"See? No rationality. Your stubbornness will be your death."

"There are five of us," Shawndirea said aloud.

Roble felt the heat of her angered glare directed at him.

"Finally, a voice of reasoning." His voice held a tone of relief and a slight sigh.

"Why's that important?" Daphne asked.

"Because I only read the minds of two men. The foolish one and the coward standing beside him. I sensed others capable of blocking my mental probing, so some of you work magic?"

"Yes."

"How many have this ability?"

"Three," Shawndirea replied.

"Three? That's good. Perhaps it's enough."

"Enough for what?" Roble asked.

"Get off that ledge, if you wish to live," the voice said.

"Who are you?" Roble asked.

"Is a name important at this moment?"

"You said that you'd—"

"*Still* you argue. Sephar'ris is my name. Let's hope you've not wasted so much time that my name will be the one you hear."

CHAPTER 60

Roble stepped off the edge of the bored tunnel and dropped onto a narrow rock jutting from the wall. Shawndirea flew from his shoulder and hovered above him. In flight, she was the only one safe from the beetles.

The rock Roble stood upon was supported by the top of a broken pillar that once served as a buttress for the ceiling. He reached toward Lehrling, offering his hand. Lehrling stooped and clasped it.

From the tunnel came the high-pitched hungry shrills of massive hurtling insects. Their hard exoskeletons clattered against one another as they fought and scurried to reach their prey.

"Jump!" Roble shouted to Lehrling, still clutching his Lehrling's hand. Lehrling closed his fearful eyes, mouthed a prayer, and took what was an actual leap of faith.

Lehrling landed on the narrow top of the rock beside Roble, but his footing wasn't sound. He teetered to the right, his boots slipped, and his weight yanked Roble with him. Lehrling completely missed the pillar's broken edge, which could have provided him adequate footing.

Roble's free hand slid along the edge of the cracked wall, until he frantically gripped a thick root. He held fast, struggling not to lessen his grip with either hand. Lehrling's dead weight became more difficult to hold with Lehrling helplessly flailing his free arm and adding further strain to Roble's right arm and shoulder. Lehrling blindly grabbed for a solid object to steady himself, but nothing was within his reach.

"Plant your feet against the pillar," Roble groaned.

Lehrling straightened his legs and placed his feet against the pillar, but slick wet moss prevented his boots from steadying his balance.

Roble looked at the tunnel opening, hoping Portia or Daphne might notice his peril and offer assistance. Instead, Daphne grabbed Portia by the hand and turned her sister to face the scuttling giant beetles rushing to the edge of the opening. The sisters raised their free hands, chanted in a strange language, and a flickering fiery wall roared into a gate of hellish heat across the tunnel.

Several beetles squealed, their armored legs clattered like slamming steel shields, and their fire-engulfed bodies barreled past Daphne and Portia. Covered with flames, the beetles crashed on the marble-tiled floor below. The passing heat of their blazing bodies nearly scorched the side of Roble's face. Shawndirea thrust a bolt of icy air to lessen the fire's effect since he lacked a protective helm. His armor absorbed the flaming heat from the neck down. At least he was spared the flames, but he continued struggling to hold Lehrling.

The dying beetles crashed to the floor, landing on their backs. Their burning legs and antennae curled, growing tighter and crisper until death froze them. Regardless of how tough their exoskeletons were, fire was their greatest weakness. Their insides boiled from the intense heat.

Roble pulled the root harder, trying to maintain his footing. The strain of holding Lehrling free weight was overbearing. Matters would've been worse if Lehrling wore plate or steel instead of leather.

"Hold on, Lehrling," Roble groaned.

Using the root for leverage, Roble pressed his chin to his chest and pulled. Pain stung like needles in his shoulders and arms. He worried he was near dislocating his shoulder, but he refused to surrender to the pain.

Although the fall to the floor wasn't far enough to *kill* Lehrling, but landing wrong could break Lehrling's legs or back or neck. Such injuries could immobilize him. Being deep in the swamp made getting him outside the ruins and the swamp quite difficult.

After several weak attempts, Lehrling placed his hand into a narrow crevice. He gripped the rough rocks and pulled himself up enough to position his feet in a large crack in the pillar. The strain in Roble's arms and shoulders lessened.

Roble helped Lehrling secure better footing before Lehrling dove forward and landed on his stomach. He clung to the rock with his free hand.

Roble released the root and Lehrling's hand. He waited a few minutes to let the pain subside. After catching his breath, he turned and placed his back against the rock wall. While resting, he scanned the ceiling near the waterfall where the other large beetles clung. They were gone. Had the fire frightened them? Perhaps.

No longer using telepathy, Sephar'ris said, "Well done. You killed at least three of them."

"Show yourself," Roble said in between panting.

"I cannot. Not yet."

"Why not?"

Sephar'ris didn't reply.

The fire wall Daphne and Portia created filled the inside of the tunnel. The outer air pressure from where they had entered sucked the flames all the way through the corridor to the outside.

"If any beetles were in the tunnel, the fire has destroyed them. At least we have a safe passage out," Daphne said. "As for you, Sephar'ris, reveal yourself, if you wish further aid from us."

"I tell you the truth. I cannot. For if I do, all of you die with me."

Short of breath, Roble said, "All of the beetles are dead or have retreated."

"Although daunting, the beetles aren't what I fear the most," Sephar'ris said.

"What causes you greater fear?" Daphne asked.

"The rifts," he replied.

"We sensed a rift," Shawndirea said. "Actually, we thought we sensed more than one."

"There are at *least* three," he said. "Perhaps more."

"What abnormality do they have that troubles you?"

"You don't understand."

"Then explain it?" Roble said, angrily rising to his feet.

"Warrior—"

"Knight," Roble seethed.

"Knight, I can *not* speak logically with you."

"And why is that?"

"Because warr—*knights* are not led by logic."

"I'd be happy to debate that," Roble said.

"I'm certain you would!" Sephar'ris shouted. "Again, *proving* my point."

Even though Sephar'ris spoke aloud, the high ceiling caused his voice to echo, making it impossible to pinpoint his exact position.

Sephar'ris sighed. "Warriors use aggressive brute strength to get what they want. Like now, your anger indicates—"

"My anger," Roble said, "stems from the fact that we almost lost our lives. I've little patience to put up with your charade—"

"Charade?" Sephar'ris said in an abrupt tone. "I assure you this is no charade."

"Then—"

"Don't make demands of me," Sephar'ris replied. "Or I'll simply cease talking and leave you to your demise. You've yet to witness the real danger in this place. Without further assistance from me, you'll trigger what guards these portals and you'll die. Simple as that."

Roble crossed his arms and tried to suppress his anger. "My apologies. Please shed more light on this."

Sephar'ris kept silent for the better part of a minute. "The reason no one before you lived as long as you have is because a warrior led them to their deaths. Every ... single ... time. The warriors believed their muscle could defeat everything before them. None killed any of the flesh-eating insects. Perhaps you, warrior, will let that seep into your thickened skull. You didn't kill the dead beetles on the floor. The mages, or whatever they are, used their magic to destroy them. Not you or your weapons."

"I realize that," Roble said. "No need to hammer the point. But I'm not as thick-skulled as you'd think. Skip the prattling and get to the point."

"*Roble!*" Shawndirea hissed in a firm whisper.

Silence hung between them for several minutes, until Roble exchanged glances with Lehrling and then Shawndirea. Both shrugged.

"Enough of this," Roble said, grabbing the large root and preparing to climb up to the opening where Portia and Daphne stood. "Let's leave this place."

"Wait," Sephar'ris said in a softer tone. "Perhaps I've been too hasty in my judgments, based upon all those who've blatantly ignored my warnings in the past. But I plead to those who wield magic. Please offer your power to release me."

"What must we do?" Daphne asked.

Shawndirea flew to the broken pillar where Roble and Lehrling stood.

"Repair the rifts."

Shawndirea frowned. "Repair them?"

"Yes."

Shawndirea glanced toward Daphne. The two exchanged puzzled expressions.

"Do you know where they are?" Daphne asked.

"They overlap above the water pool," Sephar'ris replied. "And are hidden inside the waterfall."

"How many?"

"Two I'm certain of, but a third rift emerges between the two on occasion."

"We don't possess enough power to seal these rifts. Since they're so close together," Daphne replied.

"You must try," he replied in a weak voice mixed with sorrow. "It's the only way I can be freed."

"What do you know about the rifts?" Portia asked.

"If they're not sealed, chaos will emerge in full force. Nothing will prevent worser things from entering our realm."

"And you know this how?" Roble asked.

"Because I witnessed how it occurred."

"You know why the rifts overlap?" Roble asked. He offered his hand to help Daphne step down onto the top of the broken pillar.

Lehrling had already climbed down the thick ivy vines encircling the pillar and waited to help Daphne and Portia to the floor.

"Yes," Sephar'ris replied.

"How long have these rifts existed in Evendusk?" Daphne asked, turning in the direction of the water pool.

"The formation of the rifts were the downfall of Evendusk," he said solemnly.

"Several rifts materializing so closely together couldn't occur naturally," Daphne said. "I've never encountered the combination of rifts before. I've heard of a double rift only once. These inside the waterfall didn't occur on their own, did they?"

"No. She'zist and her coven performed rituals at an altar where the water pool now sets. They bent edges of different realm barriers until they weakened. They formed narrow rift slits that allowed us to pass into different realms and others from those realms could come to us." Sephar'ris' voice broke. "Their hope was to increase our power by forming alliances with civilizations in other realms, but that didn't happen. Instead, we were invaded, costing thousands to die in our city."

"What happened?" Lehrling asked.

"None of the realms She'zist connected to held peaceful races. All were hostile. They entered too swiftly for us to defend ourselves."

Shawndirea flew closer to the waterfall, studied it for several moments, and then darted back to where Roble and Lehrling stood. "She didn't intentionally open more than one rift at a time, did she?"

"She never intended for more than one to be open at a time. She *thought* she could open and close them at will. But she discovered that while they had each been easy to open," Sephar'ris said. "They were quite difficult to close."

Roble frowned. "Why didn't she seal them?"

"She tried. But as you can see, she failed. Forming and opening the rifts was too easy, which was suspicious. Closing them was an *impossible* task."

"Why?" Roble asked.

"She and her coven formed a circle around the rift column when the first invasions came. They died first. They didn't have time to set a spell into place or react. Monsters came through first, killed the witches, and then retreated into the rifts. Then came the soldiers to kill the rest of us."

"How'd you survive?" Lehrling asked.

Sephar'ris ignored the question. "Those of us farther into the city who held magical abilities summoned to close the rifts. We, too, failed. After plundering came from three different races, the portals became heavily guarded. The beetles you encountered were the current guardians. Perhaps the last."

"Why would they be the last?" Roble asked.

"What's left for them to take?" Sephar'ris asked. "They've destroyed everything we held sacred. What valuable gems and precious metals we possessed were taken through the rifts. All that's left of our city are these ruins. Hulls of shops, houses, lodges, and the palace are in shambles. The beetles guarded the rifts to prevent anyone on this side from invading their realms."

"What races passed through into Evendusk?" Daphne asked.

"Goblins were one. The others ... I've never seen before."

"Goblins?" Lehrling said in surprise. "Did they return through the rifts?"

"No. They resided here for a short time. Then they left our city and dispersed into Aetheaon."

"So what opposition do we face once we try to seal the rifts?" Daphne asked.

"No one knows," Sephar'ris replied. "I imagine other monsters lie in wait should anyone tamper with the rifts."

"You want *us* to seal the rifts?" Roble asked.

"Not *you*, obviously, since you cannot wield magic."

"I'm aware," Roble said angrily. "But if Evendusk's witch coven was unable to seal the rifts, what makes you believe these three can succeed?"

"Four," Sephar'ris said. "I'll assist with my magic."

"Four?" Roble said. "Against whatever else might come through the portals? That's too great a risk."

"Not as risky as it was a few days ago," he said.

"And why's that?"

"A stranger came into this garden, apparently drawn to the rifts. He was a dark sorcerer unlike any I've ever seen. The depth of his evil power astounds me." Sephar'ris's voice quaked. "Before he arrived, I wasn't the only voice warning others about the portals. Three of my brethren hid with me. This man, or *demon*, I should say, sucked their spirits into himself. Their essence, though pure, he took and tarnished by adjoining them to his soul."

"That's possible?" Roble whispered.

Shawndirea nodded.

"Why did he spare you?" Roble asked.

"A question I've mulled over for days," Sephar'ris said softly. "Perhaps he left me as a witness? To alert others? I simply do not know."

Daphne frowned and walked closer to the water pool. "Do you know this wizard's name? Was it Tyrann?"

"No," he replied. "Tyrann I'd have recognized, as I crossed paths with him long ago before the formation of the Black Chasm. This was a darker wizard with an evilness far greater than Tyrann. Tyrann never leaves the City of Mortel. Even you should know this."

Daphne nodded. "Any idea who this was?"

"Mors ... that's what one minion called him. He arrived in a black carriage with a horse from the abyss."

Roble and Lehrling exchanged troubled glances.

"You know of him?" Sephar'ris asked.

Roble nodded. "Yes. He's the Plague-bringer. He destroyed most of Glacier Ridge. He has raised armies of undead and even a dead dragon. He's a necromancer."

"I realize his power. He's still adding numbers to his army. When he left Evendusk, he called to life more than a thousand of our dead to serve him. Those we revered in life are now fallen as his undead."

"A thousand?" Roble said, shaking his head. "If that many left, they'd have been an obvious path. No such evidence disturbs the tunnel we entered or the garden grounds."

"Indeed not," Sephar'ris said. "With power of his magnitude, he formed a portal from the rifts and ushered them through."

"Did he leave with them?" Daphne asked.

"No. Not through the rift portal. He closed it soon after they departed. None of the guardians opposed him."

"He sent the army through?" Roble said. "To where?"

"I've no idea. After they went through, he got onto the black carriage and a magical whirlwind carried him away."

Roble looked at Daphne. "Where do you think he sent them?"

"The possibilities are endless, Roble. Perhaps he has them suspended somewhere to release at another time."

"He can do that?" Lehrling asked.

"Yes. As a necromancer that has Death following him, he's able to suspend resurrections at will. Frightening to comprehend." Daphne wrung her hands with worry. "If one could predict his first major attack, we could attempt a counterattack against him. As it is, he's building an army too massive to count."

"Can you seal these portals?" Roble asked.

"Let me consult with my sister and Shawndirea."

CHAPTER 62

Roble scanned the ruined structures in Evendusk's gardens. The tarnished architecture made him wish he could have seen this city's former glory.

After much deliberation with Portia and Shawndirea, Daphne finally said, "There's the slight chance we can mend the rifts by bending them into one combined corner. Doing so prevents the rifts from being usable, which stops any further invasions into these ruins. But, we need a sacrifice. One pure in heart, mind, and soul. Performing such a sacrifice requires dark sorcery that none of us are willing to do."

"We have no other options?" Roble asked. "These rifts must be closed so Mors cannot manipulate them for his cause."

"I agree," Lehrling said, stepping closer. "There must be another way."

Shawndirea looked into Roble's eyes. "We've no other way to seal these planar rifts. Should we only close one, the other two will be triggered. All three must be sealed at once. Otherwise, more guardians will attack."

"I volunteer," Sephar'ris said softly.

Roble and the others frowned and looked in the direction of Sephar'ris' voice. For the first time, he didn't use echoes to distort his location. He was closer than what they expected.

"What?" Roble asked.

"Sacrifice me," Sephar'ris replied. "It's the only solution to seal the portals."

Lehrling looked puzzled. "Why are you willing to do this without much thought?"

"For as long as I care to remember, I've offered warning after warning to those who've entered Evendusk. My warnings were never heeded. Hundreds of treasure-seekers have lost their lives."

"You did all you could. You're not responsible for their fates," Shawndirea said.

"Perhaps not, but the weight and toll is more than I wish to bear. Sealing the rifts prevents further deaths. At least more deaths caused by the creatures guarding the rifts."

Lehrling's brow furrowed. "But you're the last survivor of Evendusk. You know the truth and legends of your city. Why not be an orator to tell the history of your city to visitors since you're the sole survivor?"

"That's not entirely true," Sephar'ris said.

"What isn't?" Roble asked.

"Me being the last survivor."

"Aren't you?" Lehrling asked. "You said that Mors took the souls of your other comrades."

"That did occur," Sephar'ris said. "But my words weren't phrased properly."

Daphne's eyes narrowed. "What do you mean?"

Sephar'ris materialized in front of them. They gasped.

He said, "I didn't survive."

"You're a ghost?" Roble asked.

"Yes," Sephar'ris replied. "I'm not the last survivor, per se. I'm the last living *voice*. My essence is a purity you'll never find in the living. I remained, along with my brethren, to warn the living of the dangers residing in our gardens."

Roble glanced at Daphne. "Can a spirit even be sacrificed?"

Before Daphne replied, Sephar'ris said, "I'm part of Evendusk, so it's vital you use my essence to thread these rift barriers shut. Nothing else can achieve such a feat."

Roble stared in disbelief at Sephar'ris. The pale figure hovered several inches off the tarnished tiles. If Sephar'ris' image mirrored his living appearance, he must have died in his mid to late twenties. The cowl he wore didn't cover his bearded chin and his sleeves concealed his hands. His face still looked human in his transparent form.

The hem of his robe hid his feet. The pendant of his necklace flickered silver in the light, making his eyes glow oddly.

Daphne sighed. "He's right, Roble. Sacrificing himself in spirit form could bind the three rifts into one corner, and block the passage from any side. He'd become the tethered anchor, sealing them shut forevermore. No blood would be shed, so it wouldn't be dark sorcery."

Roble said, "You're fine being imprisoned forever, Sephar'ris?"

"My sacrifice won't be imprisonment at all," he replied. "It'd be my honor to seal these rifts and preserve what's left of Evendusk. I'll forever become the guardian of the city."

"Your bold sacrifice impresses me," Roble said. "I'm curious, though, what more could be done to ensure we lessen Mors' power before his final confrontation."

"What confrontation?" Sephar'ris asked.

"He's been gathering a massive undead army in Aetheaon to conquer all the kingdoms. He's preparing for war. Few of the living will lie down. The majority will fight."

"The bloodshed will be massive," Lehrling said.

"With these rifts sealed," Roble replied, "will that prevent Mors from accessing the armies he sent through the rift?"

"Only if he tried to summon them through these rifts," Daphne said. "He could still pull them through a different portal."

"Does he have such power?" Roble asked.

"I don't know," Daphne replied.

"No, he doesn't," Sephar'ris said.

"And you know this, how?" Portia asked.

"He has the power to raise the dead," Sephar'ris replied. "The only reason he could use these rifts was because they were already open. He manipulated the guardians into attacking each other. While they fought, Mors commanded his demon minions to kill the guardians. He cannot create portals. I pray Roble is right. Shutting the portals prevents Mors from using Evendusk's former residents from becoming pawns in Mors' undead army."

Shawndirea glanced at Portia and then to Daphne. "Then we use our magic to shut these rifts?"

Portia and Daphne nodded.

"A final word of warning," Sephar'ris said. He looked at Roble. "Once their incantation begins, expect to be attacked from the guardians."

"Didn't Mors destroy them?" Lehrling said.

"Yes," Sephar'ris replied. "However, Mors might have placed some of his minions inside the portals to protect them. Be prepared."

Roble nodded.

Sephar'ris said, "May the gods and goddesses protect you."

CHAPTER 63

Roble pulled two sharp daggers from sheaths on the back of his belt. The blades' edges gleamed silver in the bright glow of the Elfstones. He stood opposite Lehrling at the water pool. Lehrling appeared nervous with his short sword drawn. Sephar'ris hovered outside the waterfall above the pool.

Roble watched the splashing waterfall that vanished into the water pool. Being this close, the rift was evident. The water should have been splashing off the pool, but it poured through an unseen hole. He'd have thought it an illusion had he not learned magic was real. The rift inside Devils Den where he crossed into Aetheaon with Shawndirea was hidden deep inside the cavern. He wondered where this rift opened and if it was in the Overlands. Most likely not, given the monsters Sephar'ris mentioned.

For someone to unexpectedly step through a rift, Roble understood how that might drive a person insane. In that situation, his sanity might have fled, too, but Shawndirea had informed him beforehand, so his mind was prepared to cross realms.

Daphne took a pouch of reddish brown grains from inside her robe. While walking a circle around the water pool, she poured the red grains, enclosing Shawndirea and Portia inside the circle with her. After the circle was complete, the three stood equal distances apart and faced the water pool.

Sephar'ris faced Roble and then glanced to everyone else. "May the richest blessings be bestowed upon each of you after you leave Evendusk. I offer my gratitude for what you've done for me today."

Daphne, Portia, and Shawndirea raised their hands and began chanting with their eyes closed. Seconds later, a cool air rushed through the city tunnels. The temperature plummeted.

Roble held the hilts of his daggers. He wasn't certain what to expect. The fear in Lehrling's eyes indicated he didn't either. Roble wished other knights and warriors stood with them. He didn't like their current odds, especially when they weren't sure how many guardians might emerge from the portals.

His gaze flicked to Shawndirea. Her eyes were closed. She was encapsulated by the growing circle of protection and drawing her magic from the earth. He wished he could have consulted with her privately beforehand to lessen his apprehension and to express his love for her one last time; in case the results ended catastrophically.

Unseen waves of energy flowed. The hairs on the back of his neck stiffened. A tingling sensation ran down his spine and sent chill bumps across his extremities. The increasing force pulsated.

Roble readied the daggers and attempted to step forward but the magic barrier of the protective circle pushed him back. The air thickened. Any movements he made were sluggish like trying to run through chest-deep water.

The reddish brown grains Daphne spread to form the circle levitated and swirled, forming a wall around them. Fear caused Roble to tremble.

The rising wall was enclosing Shawndirea and the sisters inside *with* the portals, which meant that anything coming out of the portals would attack them directly. He and Lehrling could not intervene, as they had been instructed.

Roble struggled to run but his legs weighed heavy like steel anchors. He screamed to warn Shawndirea but his words were silenced. No sound came from his mouth, though he shouted fiercely.

Overcome by concern and possible betrayal, he glanced at Lehrling. Lehrling stood petrified, watching the floating reddish-brown grains disperse tiny green sprouts that rapidly extended leaves and grew, weaving together like a magical curtain of vines. The vines serpentined, knitting and meshing together, and bit by bit, his view of Shawndirea was being blocked.

How could he and Lehrling protect them when Daphne prevented them from entering the circle? She never gave any forewarning that she was going to build a barrier that prevented he and Lehrling from entering.

Movement from behind Lehrling captured Roble's attention. He shouted, "Run!"

Lehrling didn't hear Roble's desperate cry, nor did it echo in Roble's ear.

Roble faced Lehrling and pushed against the invisible force holding him in place. He didn't know whether this resistance was from the magic circle or an unseen entity lurking in the shadowed ruins. Had Sephar'ris deceived them?

He had no time to ponder and little time to react.

Roble leaned forward, lowered his head, and pushed against the viscous air. Every muscle ached for the short distance he moved.

Lehrling looked from the circular ivy wall and gazed into Roble's eyes. He read the panic on Roble's face, and Lehrling turned to watch a giant beetle drop from the ceiling. The thick atmosphere slowed its descent.

Lehrling pushed off his left foot, trying to dive to the side, but instead of a rapid fall to the ground, he hung in the air, momentarily cradled, while steadily descending like a fallen leaf drifts softly to the forest floor.

They seemed suspended inside a gel that hampered all movement. The beetle was helpless and maneuvered from what was its attempted attack but it, too, seemed confused by the sudden thickening air. Time was somehow lapsing, but that gave he and Lehrling no real advantage. Instead it prolonged their defense or their need to flee.

Lehrling drifted to the ground while Roble pushed his body through the invisible viscous medium. He gained several steps but the strain on his entire body was sapping his strength. His inability to inhale enough oxygen was also depleting him making him lightheaded and dizzy. His vision blurred, darkened, and his heartbeat hammered inside his head. He'd be unconscious in seconds if he couldn't alleviate the massive strain taxing his body.

Roble's lungs ached from the drowning sensation pressing against his chest. To survive, he did the only thing he could and that was to stop fighting his way through the gel-like barrier.

A blinding light gleamed inside the vine-enclosed circle where Shawndirea stood. Fighting to breathe, he realized he was helpless to defend her or himself. Gasping, Roble watched the gardens darkening in spite of the light. His knees buckled, everything spun in slow motion, and he fell backwards with little more speed than a falling feather. The frightening sensation shrouding him was similar to the atmosphere in the Black Chasm, except that the air wasn't poisonous. It was simply too thick to breathe in adequately.

Roble was falling into suspended animation. At least, that's how he viewed it. Everything on the outside of the protective circle moved painstakingly slow, enough to challenge the most tenacious monk's inner patience.

Was Daphne to blame for the pausing of time?

By the time Roble fell seated on the floor, Lehrling was lying on his side, his eyes lazily staring at Roble. No pain reflected in his eyes, but the heaviness of his eyelids meant he was fighting sleep or possibly death, if he couldn't breathe.

The maddening bright light inside the tall cylindrical vine wall flashed. Tiny rays escaped through narrow slits in the foliage. The light prevented Roble from seeing the activities that occurred inside the circle.

The large beetle finally hit the floor and skidded across the rock. It landed on its back, lifeless, with its legs curled in death.

Roble wanted to push himself to his feet to check on Lehrling, but the invisible force held him down. With the exception of the dead beetle, no other insects or attackers revealed themselves ... yet. Since everything moved in slow motion, it was difficult to determine. Should observers be cloaked by invisibility, dangers still existed.

Roble wondered whether their magical circle was capable of preventing guardians from emerging from the rifts and attacking them. Their combined power was strong enough to incapacitate him and Lehrling. Hopefully, the rifts had melded enough to prevent further attacks.

Still gripping his daggers, he raised his hands in a defensive manner. That's when his heart nearly froze. The gems in his rings flickered and brightened. Shawndirea's spell no longer clouded them. He didn't understand why, but he assumed her full attention and her magical attunement were needed to keep their protective circle intact while they sealed the rifts. With her spell broken, Lez'minx could use the rings again.

The gemstones glowed brighter, sending a tingling sensation through Roble's fingers and up his forearms. The thick air around him melted, and he could move freely. He took several deep breaths before pushing himself to his feet.

Lehrling's heavy eyes closed. Roble took a cautious step toward his friend, expecting the viscous wall to hamper his movements, but the invisible barrier retreated. He hurried and helped Lehrling sit up.

Lehrling panted, frowned, and rubbed his forehead.

"What's happening?" Lehrling asked.

Roble shrugged.

For the first time since the magical ivy cylinder enveloped Shawndirea, Portia, and Daphne, Roble could hear. Their voices chanted in a language with a soothing melody. The blinding light inside the protective circle hummed steadily but at a slight undertone. The sound of the waterfall was gone.

"You okay?" Roble asked, offering his hand to help Lehrling stand.

Lehrling nodded. "I am now. I couldn't breathe."

Roble pulled Lehrling to his feet. "Me, either."

Lehrling's eyes widened. "Your rings."

Roble nodded. "I know."

"Are there no guardians?"

"We've no way to know," Roble replied. "Daphne hedged us on the outside of their circle. If anything emerges, we've no way to intervene."

"The beetle—"

Roble shook his head. "No. It was here before they began the incantation."

"No," Lehrling said, pointing. "It's moving."

CHAPTER 64

*R*oble looked at the beetle lying on its back. Its legs twitched and it rocked back and forth on its curved shell, attempting to right itself. Roble rushed at it with one dagger raised above his head.

The blade couldn't penetrate the beetle's thick chitin exoskeleton. He never really expected it to. With the beetle lying on its back, its most vulnerable spot was exposed. Between the head and the thorax were soft connecting muscles not covered by chitin, which allowed the insect flexibility.

Roble brought down the blade, plunging it into the tender muscles. The beetle shrieked and its legs writhed and thrashed. Because the beetle was enormous, the dagger didn't severe the head from its body. Roble yanked the blade free and stabbed repeatedly, until only a narrow strip of muscle attached the head to the thorax.

Green liquid oozed from the severed muscles and dripped, forming a growing pool on the floor. The beetle wasn't completely dead, but it was dying. Even if it flipped over, it couldn't effectively use its mandibles to attack. Any further movements would most likely detach its head.

"Do you see any other beetles?" Roble asked.

They scanned the ceilings and the shadowed edges of the walls.

Lehrling shook his head. "No."

Roble turned his hands and studied the glowing gems set in his rings. "Now, what to do about these?"

"How'd they become active again?" Lehrling asked, stepping closer.

"I'm not certain," Roble replied. "But, once the stones activated, the choking air around us thinned and allowed us to move and breathe again."

"You think Lez'minx is protecting you?" Lehrling frowned.

"It would seem that way."

"I shouldn't," a voice said.

Lehrling and Roble stared at the dying beetle from where the voice came. They exchanged troubled glances.

The beetle's lobbing head craned. Its giant obsidian eyes shimmered while examining them. For a moment, Roble and Lehrling's reflections were visible. The sheen resembled a mirror but the illusion soon faded. The glassy dark eyes glowed and ignited like flickering fire. The voice continued, "I should've just watched you breathe your last breaths and die."

"Then why didn't you?" Roble asked, holding his daggers.

"I've need of you."

"Lez'minx?" Roble said.

Lehrling gasped. His hand rested on the hilt of his sword without hesitation.

"Aye, tis me, though not in the most prominent vessel," he replied. "It suffices for now."

"I want freed of these rings you've given me," Roble said firmly.

"For what reason?"

"I'll be enslaved to no one."

"Enslaved? Is that how you view the rings? That they've *somehow* enslaved you to me?"

"Haven't they? I see no alternative."

The beetle shuttered. "What harm have I caused you? Can you tell me one thing I've ever done to inflict hurt upon you? No, you cannot. But, I *have* rescued you twice."

"And yet, upon our last conversation, you threatened to kill Shawndirea, my wife," Roble replied, unable to calm the anger in his voice.

"Simple words spoken in mere moments of haste," Lez'minx replied. "I assure you I've no intention of seeing her or you harmed. There's no reason for why we cannot skirt past such remarks."

"Your words aren't easily forgotten. I won't dismiss them from my memory, ever."

"Overlanders savor grudges," Lez'minx said. "Much like those in Aetheaon. My apologies. I've every intention of seeing you and her prosper."

"For a price," Roble said.

"And what price is that?" Lez'minx asked.

"Servitude."

"You've mistaken my intent. I can offer you anything you desire. There's no limits to the power and wealth you could have."

"By serving you? No. I'm not interested."

"I've only asked that you meet with me at my temple and hear my proposal."

"Your temple?" Roble laughed.

"Why does that amuse you?"

"Because I know your true real identity. You're *not* a god or a demigod. You don't *have* a temple. A shrine you've built to flatter yourself, perhaps, but it's not a temple. You've no devoted worshippers."

"Humor me then, Roble. How did you find this ... *incorrect* information?"

Lehrling opened his mouth to speak, but Roble shook his head, and motioned with his hand for Lehrling to remain silent.

"I have secrets," Roble said, "just like you have secrets."

"You're in the Ruins of Evendusk, so you seek to find me," Lez'minx said. "That impresses me."

"Don't expect my adoration once we find you," Roble said. "That's not my objective."

"Do you not fear what I'm capable of doing?"

"Why should I fear what you might otherwise do anyway?" Roble asked. "You use guile and threats to have others obey your demands. Just to enlighten you, that's not worshippers. Those are victims fearful of your bullying demeanor."

"Do recall how I killed a few dozen Shadowfae in the blink of an flickering wisp."

"Yes. I witnessed the unnecessary slaughter. You've created a vast number of enemies within the Shadowfae because you murdered them. Consider the repercussions."

"You're taking their side, Overlander?"

"No. But your rings make them assume I'm under your hold so I'm their enemy as well. I'm not vested in your underhanded affairs or your agendas."

"Understand something. I protected you and Shawndirea when Dirk set about to imprison her."

"That somehow grants you my loyalty?"

"Shouldn't it?"

Roble said, "Your conceit for how the realm should behold you holds far more vanity than a god would ever display."

"You're right," Lez'minx said. "Most gods wouldn't tolerate your belligerent and defiant attitude. Perhaps I should kill you now?"

Shrills echoed from inside the protective circle where Shawndirea, Portia, and Daphne continued chanting.

"What was that?" Lez'minx asked. "I sense a great magical binding force. What's happening?"

"Nothing that concerns you," Roble replied, pressing the rings against his dark armor.

"What's Shawndirea up to?" Lez'minx asked. "Seems she's channeling a powerful spell."

"You're making assumptions, which means you're not omniscient. Kind of kills your boast of being a god, doesn't it?"

"Whatever she's doing allowed her spell on the rings to be broken. For something to require that much of her attention—"

Roble frowned. "It doesn't concern you."

"You *might* need my assistance," Lez'minx said in a near desperate tone.

"I'll take my chances," Roble replied. He looked at Lehrling. "Use your sword and severe the beetle's head from its body."

Lehrling nodded, drawing his short sword. He brought the sword up over his head, and decapitated the beetle. The ricochet clashed like two heavy swords striking one another. Lehrling winced from the jarring pain. "Will that stop him from speaking?"

Roble shrugged. "Perhaps for now. I need some thick mud or clay to cover these stones until Shawndirea's able to recast the spell."

Lehrling scraped clay from the wall with the tip of his sword. He rubbed a thick glob over each stone.

The pure white light inside the ivy cylinder ignited upward like a thick laser. Lehrling and Roble shielded their eyes. The light slowly dimmed and they glanced at the circle.

Dried, crumbled leaves from the brittle ivy vines dropped to the floor. The crisp vines bent under their own weight and dissolved into red dust.

Shawndirea's wings drooped. She sat on her knees, leaning forward while balancing herself with her hands. Sweat streaked her face. She panted with her eyes closed, trying to regain her composure.

Roble rushed to her. "Are you okay?"

She offered a slight nod. "Give me a few minutes."

"Sure."

Afraid to touch or move her until she was stronger, he looked where the waterfall had been. Instead of a waterfall, a column of white crystal rose from the water pool to the ceiling, shimmering like wet ice. No water dripped down the sides. Sephar'ris' image was visible about midway up the crystal.

Portia stretched prostrate on the floor. Shallow breaths escaped her narrow mouth. Daphne lay outstretched beside her. Neither attempted to rise. Soft groans rumbled in their throats.

"Not to alarm anyone," Roble said, "but Shawndirea's spell to block Lez'minx's view through the rings has been broken."

Daphne's and Portia's eyes flicked open. They gazed in his direction but were too tired to raise their heads.

"You're certain of this?" Daphne asked.

"He spoke to Lehrling and I just moments before your incantation ended."

Shawndirea gasped and looked at his rings.

"Then he knows we're with you?" Portia asked.

"He questioned what was happening, but he couldn't see you because of the thick ivy," Roble replied.

Daphne sighed and pushed herself into a seated position. "We've not much time. I hope we've not lost the element of surprise. As long as he doesn't know Portia and I are with you, we still maintain the advantage."

CHAPTER 65

Fifteen minutes passed before Roble offered his hand to Shawndirea. Though weary, she stepped onto his palm, placed her fingers to her temples, and winced.

The white crystal column around Sephar'ris' pulsed. Energy beamed outward, much like the healing stones Daphne used destroying the Saurians.

"Are you okay?" Roble asked.

"I'm fine. Drained is all," she replied.

Daphne stepped closer to Roble, examined his rings, and offered a weak smile. "Good. You did the right thing by covering these rings with clay. Perhaps in a few hours, Shawndirea will have enough strength to recast her spell over them."

Shawndirea nodded. "It shouldn't take that long. My strength is returning faster than I expected."

Daphne smiled and nodded. "That's due to Sephar'ris' blessing, spilling from his essence in the light."

"How soon can you cast a new spell over the rings?" Roble asked.

Shawndirea straightened and arched her back. Her wings no longer drooped and the color returned to her face. "Maybe fifteen minutes. Did he know what we were doing?"

"He asked," Roble replied. "But, he knows where we are."

"He knows we're in Evendusk?" Portia asked.

Roble and Lehrling nodded.

Portia glanced at Daphne and then to Roble. "Are you certain he didn't see us?"

Roble said, "With the ivy wall and bright light, I don't think he could. He fished for information, but I didn't give any. Instead, I pointed out that since he didn't know, it meant he couldn't be a god."

"I'm sure that went over well," Daphne said with a shrewd grin.

Roble shrugged. "Yeah. He threatened my life."

"Our brother mustn't know that we are with you," Daphne said. "Shawndirea, allow Portia and I to assist you with the incantation. Rather than simply block him, we should track his whereabouts. We want to find him before he finds us."

"You plan to kill him?" Lehrling asked.

"That's probably what he'll expect us to do," Daphne said.

"Is that your intention?" Roble asked.

Daphne wiped sweat from her brow and forced a smile. "Let us worry about the confrontation. You figure out how you'll negotiate to free yourself of those rings. For the moment, we need to gather everyone inside the ruins where they'll be safer."

Shawndirea gazed at the crystal pillar that enclosed Sephar'ris. Brightness set in his frozen eyes and a content smile widened on his face. "He's at peace."

"He served the purpose he wanted," Daphne replied. "He'll forever be a part of Evendusk, as a true guardian binding the three rifts together."

Lehrling eyed the crude broken pillar that led to the tunnel where they had entered Evendusk. "We should get the others, but I cannot possibly scale that wall. At least not by myself. Is there another entrance?"

Roble eyed the stone street from the crystal pillar to the far wall where the street once led. Large fallen rocks blocked the road, which was probably why others burrowed a new tunnel to get into the ruins. "The main passage collapsed years ago."

"I'll go inform the others," Shawndirea said.

Roble glanced at Daphne. "Are all the beetles in the tunnel dead?"

"It's doubtful any survived the fire," she replied. "It's doubtful any *thing* survived it."

*S*hawndirea glided through the smoke-filled tunnel, passing over several charred beetle carapaces. The lingering aroma of the burnt insects was a nauseating smell that forced her to cover her nose.

Moss and mushrooms clinging to the rocks were shriveled into black crispy plant matter. The slightest vibrations from her delicate wings caused these plant remnants to dissolve into ash and drift to the tunnel floor.

The degree of heat from the fire Daphne and Portia had created was beyond her comprehension. She had seen dryads' power in the past, but nothing like this. What confused her was recalling Daphne's rebuke to remind Portia where their magical power came from. Dryads drew their magic from the forests. The problem was that the crude tunnel didn't feed any trees. No thick roots cut into the tunnel, either.

Dryads used their power to protect their trees but none possessed the ability to deforest an area. Dryads perished when the trees they were linked to died.

The wall of fire spell was instant without any prior preparation by Daphne or Portia. The fire wasn't a single wall that closed off one end. The roaring fire blazed through the entire tunnel, singeing and killing anything in its path. Shawndirea had never met a dryad with the ability to cast fire spells because fire destroyed forests, and was an unwelcomed element for dryads to use.

She wondered about Lez'minx and why Daphne and Portia despised him enough to want to kill him. What had he done to scorn them? Daphne kept denying her murderous intent, but her eyes betrayed her. Her facial expressions revealed her lies.

Roble seemed to have noticed this, too, which was why he pressed Daphne for further information. Daphne avoided giving a direct answer. What did they intend to do to Lez'minx and why?

Those were questions she doubted she'd get answered until after Lez'minx was dead, provided that was Daphne's true intent. His premature death would leave Roble with the dilemma of the bound rings. While Lez'minx's spell probably ended with his death, Daphne had created enough doubt that the spell wouldn't dissolve. They couldn't risk taking that chance.

Roble needed to persuade Lez'minx to release him from the rings *before* Daphne and Portia confronted their brother and possibly killed him. Daphne seemed worried about Lez'minx finding out about her and Portia before they arrived, which explained their need for secrecy. They needed the element of surprise. Did that mean he was stronger than them?

Faint light appeared about ten yards from the mouth of the tunnel that overlooked the river's edge. She increased her speed until she noticed a charred body on the floor. She dipped slightly and hovered while examining the scorched body. They never passed a corpse on their way through. All they had seen were the bones of victims.

After a brief inspection, Shawndirea assumed the corpse was one of Daphne's party that paddled a raft. But a closer look revealed the bones were of a little person and *not* a dryad. His death wasn't intentional, as neither Daphne nor Portia had any idea he was in the tunnel.

Tears crested in her eyes. The severity of the burns prevented her from determining which halfling it was.

"You must claim your rite and accept the power of who you truly are," a voice whispered inside her mind.

Shawndirea stiffened and then she flitted toward the tunnel entrance.

"Don't flee," he said. "Power and authority await you."

She recognized the male's voice from her deep sleep. What disturbed her was she remembered this same voice from when she was a child.

Chills shot through her.

"Have you not discovered the change in your magic since you crossed the in-between?"

"I have gone mad," Shawndirea whispered, placing her hands to her temple.

"Not mad. *Enlightened.* There's a grand difference."

"Until you reveal to me who you are, you're only a figment of my troubled mind," she replied.

"Your place is not with the human—"

"Roble's my husband. Nothing changes that. I chose him and he has chosen me."

"He's in danger for as long as he stays with you."

"I can protect him," she said.

"Can you?"

"Yes. I'm confident that I can. He trusts me."

"Trusts you?" A slight chuckle rumbled inside her mind. "And yet, you've not told him everything about you, now have you?"

Shawndirea took a sharp breath and bit her tongue. How did he know her mind and her secrets?

"I know all about you," he said.

"Who are you?"

A gentle rumble of laughter rang in her ears and slowly faded.

She peered down the dark tunnel. Roble and the rest of their group were approaching in the shadows. She tried to push the thoughts from her mind to regain her composure.

Daphne paused where Shawndirea hovered. In the darkness, Daphne noticed the scorched body beneath the faery's glow. "Who is this?"

Shawndirea fought tears. "I—I'm not certain."

Lehrling carried a flaming torch and stopped where Daphne and Shawndirea were on the tunnel path. His voice choked. "It's one of the halflings?"

"Yes," Daphne replied.

"Oh, no," Portia said, placing a hand over her mouth. "What have we done?"

"We protected ourselves," Daphne replied. "That's what we did. Sometimes, casualties occur."

Portia's eyes narrowed. "To you these halflings are nothing. But for me, they're my friends."

"They were warned," Daphne said with coldness.

"Warned?"

"I told them to remain in Dagger's Tears," Daphne said. "Did I not?"

Portia glared.

"Sister, you know as well as I that none of us had any idea one of them followed us into the tunnel," Daphne said.

Tears trailed down Portia's cheeks.

"I'm sorry," Daphne said. The coldness faded in her voice and genuine remorse weighed her features. "I hate that this has happened. I do. But understand its death would've been far worse had one of those giant beetles attacked."

"It?" Portia said. "He or she has a name."

"I phrased my words poorly," Daphne said. "Please forgive me."

Portia knelt beside the smoldering body. The charred blistered flesh prevented them from identifying which halfling had died.

"It's regrettable," Roble said.

Portia gasped, then whimpered softly, walking toward the tunnel exit.

"It was unforeseeable," Daphne said, shaking her head. "We barely had time to defend ourselves from the beetles' attack. We didn't have time to think—"

"We know," Shawndirea said. She rose in the air and darted to catch up with Portia.

Roble glanced from the dead halfling's body and looked into Daphne's tear-filled eyes. She possessed no hardened exterior, and for the first time, she revealed deep passion not shown before. Perhaps her tragic losses caused her to shield herself by displaying a calloused look toward those around her. Sudden regret crashed through her facade. "None of us blame you."

"I fear that's not true," Daphne replied. "Portia will never forgive me."

"What you did saved our lives," Roble said.

"Indeed," Lehrling said, unable to hide his sadness. "Accidents happen."

Roble nodded. "The last thing I'd have ever suspected was for any of them to follow us."

"I know," Daphne said. "Yet, I cannot relinquish my guilt."

Roble took her hand. "Come on. We need to get back to the others."

She accepted his hand and nodded. He half expected her to pull away from his grip. Her cold skin was odd with little bumps and grooves similar to tree bark. Though cold, a flux of energy flowed through her skin and provided a tickling sensation as her power massaged against his flesh. The odd sensation was pleasant.

"Perhaps I've misjudged you," Daphne said.

"I know I have you," Roble replied.

"Is that so?"

He nodded. "Yes."

"You probably saw me for what I wanted you to see, but in truth, my heart isn't petrified."

"I'm beginning to see that," he replied with a grin.

Her lips formed a quick grin, which disappeared in the blink of an eye. "I envy Shawndirea."

"Why is that?" Roble asked.

"She sacrificed her right to the throne of Elvendale because of how much she loves you. Despite you being a human, she looked deeper. I somewhat see what has drawn her to you. You're not like other humans in Aetheaon, and certainly not like other Overlanders I've encountered."

"No, he's certainly not," Lehrling said.

Daphne smiled. "I've a feeling there's a reason she sought you in the Overlands, and fate has everything to do with you being in Aetheaon. It's no accident you're here. That's perhaps the reason my brother wishes to control you. He must've sensed that when you obtained your armor. When our paths cross his tomorrow, you'll be freed of those rings, and he'll release you from all future obligations."

"Mind if I ask what he did to make you hate him as thoroughly as you do?" Roble asked.

"That's a story for another day," Daphne replied.

CHAPTER 67

Using the light from Lehrling's torch to guide him, Roble led the way to the tunnel entrance. At the mouth of the tunnel stood small the shadowed outlines of the halflings.

"Have you seen Rufus?" Dolan asked. "He left us some time ago to examine the cave and see that you were all right."

Merla nodded. "We became concerned after the blaze of fire spewed out of the tunnel."

"Is a dragon in there?" Cora asked.

Shawndirea regarded them and her eyes filled with tears.

"No dragon," Daphne said. Her voice cracked when she attempted to say more, so she looked away.

"What happened?" Dolan asked. His face tightened with fear. "Is he okay?"

Lehrling lowered the torch and looked down.

"He is ... not," Portia said.

Cora and Merla gasped.

"What happened?" Dolan asked, peering into the dark tunnel. "He's dead?"

Daphne nodded. "I'm afraid so."

Dolan sniffled. "How'd he die?"

"The fire," Daphne replied.

"No dragon? Then explain that fiery explosion. We felt the heat near the river bank," Dolan said. "If no dragon, magic must've caused the fire's creation?"

"Yes," Daphne said with remorse. "My sister and I cast a fire spell."

The three halflings' eyes hollowed in disbelief. Their attention turned to Portia who stood wringing her hands.

Anger narrowed Dolan's gaze. His voice became harsh. "You killed Rufus?

Your magic, you said, was *always* for healing others. And yet, you killed our friend and brother."

Portia closed her eyes. Tears spilled and ran down her cheeks. "The spell was made in haste to protect us."

"It didn't protect *him*," Dolan said through gritted teeth. "Now, did it?"

"In all fairness," Roble said, "they didn't know Rufus was in the tunnel."

Dolan pointed a stern finger. "You keep out of this, Overlander. All was well until you and Lehrling and Daphne came to Dagger's Tears. Portia would never have done such a thing without her sister."

"None of us knew Rufus was in the tunnel," Roble said. "Had the fire not killed him instantly, he'd have died a painful, much slower death."

Dolan pulled a dagger. The blade reflected in the torchlight. "I said for you to keep out of this!"

"Careful," Roble said, sliding a hand over a throwing dagger.

"As I recall," Daphne said. Her remorse faded and anger coated her words. "You were all told to remain in Dagger's Tears, were you not?"

Balls of red flames rose on her hands. Portia withered and cringed at the sight of the fire.

Shawndirea shook her head. Her fingertips glowed green. She glared at Daphne. "No! No one else needs to die!"

"That depends upon Dolan," Daphne said. "Put the blade away."

Dolan watched the flames dance on Daphne's hands. His eyes seemed to entertain that he still wanted to attack.

Cora placed a hand on his cheek. "What's done is done, Dolan. We don't want to lose you, too. Let's … let's go get Rufus' corpse."

Dolan brushed her hand away and glared at Daphne. His hand tightened on the dagger's hilt as though he might attack. "Magic can't protect you from everything."

"Dolan," Cora whispered. "Don't make us lose you, too."

"Not today, you won't lose me at her hand," Dolan said. "I won't give her the pleasure of killing another of us. Hers is coming. She has no remorse for our loss."

"That … isn't true," Daphne said.

Dolan rammed his dagger into its sheath and pushed his way past Roble and the others.

"Allow me to help," Roble said.

"Do us no favors," Dolan replied.

"Here," Lehrling said, offering Dolan the torch. "You'll need this. It's mighty dark inside."

Dolan paused for a moment, staring into the flame. He shrugged and nodded, and then he took the torch from Lehrling. "Thanks."

Cora and Merla followed Dolan, weeping and wailing.

Daphne watched the three halfings walk away. "What happened was not done purposely," she said. "I hope you search your hearts and understand that. I would never use magic—"

"Be gone," Dolan said. "Let us concern ourselves with the loss of our brother."

Nightfall darkened the already dark sandy river bank as Roble and his friends left the entrance and made their way down the narrow pathway to join the dryads near the river's edge.

Daphne joined Aqese and Ki'wese at the supplies and the horses. A small fire flickered atop the sand-covered pebbles. Before she said anything, she glanced at the tunnel and shook her head.

"Nothing I do will ever make this right," Daphne said.

"What's wrong?" Aqese asked.

Daphne's eyes narrowed. "Why'd you allow one of the halflings to follow us?"

"They were to watch out for themselves," he replied in an even tone. "You were quite adamant that they were on their own."

A wash of various emotions crossed her face. She turned toward Roble. "I knew I should have *made* them stay at Dagger's Tears. Now, I've more enemies to contend with."

"Rufus' death wasn't your fault," Roble said.

Lehrling nodded. "I agree."

Collette wrapped her arms around him.

"I appreciate that," she said. "But your opinions on the matter won't alter Dolan's hatred toward me."

"Anger is sometimes part of the grieving process," Roble said.

"He's more than angry. He'll seek vengeance. I saw it in his eyes. I know the look, as it's beamed from my eyes for decades."

Shawndirea landed atop Roble's left shoulder. "Once he's had time to process the situation, he'll settle down and his anger will lessen."

Portia shook her head. "If it were Cora or Merla, that might be true. But Dolan … Dolan is different. He designated himself as their leader after their exile. He feels responsible for them. With Rufus' death, he's not only angry with you, Daphne, but he's angry with himself."

"While that may be," she replied, "the last thing we need is further contention before we confront Lez'minx."

"It's best we sort through that elsewhere," Ki'wese said, pointing toward the river. "We cannot camp alongside the river. It's too dangerous."

On the other bank, curious eyes glowed within the darkness of the scrubby brush and the bent leafy trees. As Roble had expected for some time during their journey, they were being watched and followed.

Daphne noticed the eyes and nodded. "We're much safer inside the ruins, since the dangers are gone."

Ki'wese said, "We take only the necessities."

"What about the horses?" Lehrling said.

"We can't leave them here," Roble said. "They won't survive the night."

Daphne regarded the tunnel entrance with a look of horror. She seemed uncomfortable returning to the tunnel, especially since Dolan was inside with Rufus' remains. Reluctantly, she walked with them to the sandy trail.

Daphne and Portia had cleared the tunnel, killing everything inside, which unfortunately included Rufus. While Roble didn't exactly fear Dolan, he knew one thing for certain. None of them would get a moment of sleep tonight, as no one could predict Dolan's actions.

CHAPTER 68

etting the two horses to follow the jutted narrow pathway up to the tunnel entrance wasn't easy, but they managed to coax them there.

At Roble's suggestion, they built a fire inside the mouth of the tunnel instead of going back to the gardens. They needed to watch the river and prevent their rafts from being stolen. If anything swam or flew across the river, Roble and the others held a vantage point.

Roble thought it odd that the eyes of these watchers glowed in the absence of light. Normally, nocturnal animals' eyes were only visible in the reflection of the light. He kept reminding himself that *normal* in Aetheaon was different than his former home.

Aqese tended the fire while the rest of the group divided and sat with their backs against the wall. Not only did they need to watch unknown enemies, they needed to keep their eyes on Dolan.

Dolan was unstable and angered. On occasion, grief turned to violent vengeance when someone blamed another for a loved one's death. Grief clouded one's judgment. Even though Dolan wasn't visible, his anger and rage were hotter than their campfire.

Daphne kept her focus directed to where Dolan and the halflings were.

The echoes of Cora and Merla sobbing down the tunnel was haunting, but not nearly as troubling as the half broken expression on Daphne's face.

From the moment Roble first encountered Daphne, she remained stoic with a frozen aura until Rufus' unfortunate death. He understood that she blamed herself. He'd worry more if she didn't. But her rigid persona was gone and that also bothered him, especially since they'd confront Lez'minx the next day. They couldn't afford her to be distracted.

Daphne was shaken. Shaken meant she was weaker. Something Lez'minx

291

would capitalize on when things got nasty. Portia noticed her sister's turmoil and embraced her. Daphne whispered apologies.

Collette leaned her head against Lehrling's shoulder. Her eyes were heavy. She was closer to sleep than any of the rest of them. Lehrling's gaze fixed upon the fire. A slight smile curled on his lips as Collette intertwined her fingers with his. Roble recognized the glee of new love, and he thought it a shame that Lehrling and Collette couldn't have a more picturesque setting. Such a time and place might be weeks away or never occur, depending on how things transpired with Lez'minx.

Cora and Merla stopped their wailful cries. The tunnel grew quiet except for the soft crackling fire.

"What happened?" Roble whispered to Shawndirea.

"How should I know? Perhaps their grieving is over for now?"

"Or their wall of fire missed a beetle?"

She shook her head. "Doubtful. The halflings are coming our direction."

A flickering light glowed farther down the tunnel and grew as they approached. Cora held the torch, leading the way, while Dolan held Rufus' burnt body over his shoulder. Merla wiped tears from her eyes.

Dolan stood at the fire and his serious stare passed to each of them and then fixated on Daphne. His evident anger and his elongated shadow made him more intimidating as if he had grown several feet taller.

"We ask that you use your fire to turn the remainder of his body to ash." Dolan carefully set Rufus' charred, blistered body at the edge of the fire. "Might as well complete the process so we can set his ashes adrift on the river in the morning."

Lehrling winced at the sickening sound of the blistered flesh rupturing as it touched the floor. Collette gasped and pressed her face against Lehrling's chest, hiding her eyes and covering her nose to escape the smell.

"Dolan," Daphne said. "His death was not—"

"He's at peace," Dolan said. "Let's leave it at that."

Portia said, "Don't let your anger overshadow the truth. We barely had time to use the spell we chose to defend ourselves."

"And if we all had died," Daphne said, "where'd that have left the rest of you?"

"So sacrificing *him* to save yourselves—" Dolan said.

"He *wasn't* a sacrifice," Daphne said. Her eyes narrowed with fiery fury. Her brief weakening of her countenance mended, returning to her normal nonchalant expression. "We didn't know he was foolish enough to have entered the tunnel."

The rigid Daphne had returned. As she rose, Dolan took a step back in fear.

"His death was not deliberate," Daphne said, "but if you wish to continue your accusations, perhaps I can show you exactly what a *deliberate* death is. Do you still wish to challenge me?"

Dolan's lips tightened and his eyes darkened. His hand rested on the hilt of his dagger but his fingers were lax. The uncertainty in his eyes indicated his fear was greater than his need for revenge.

"Wait!" Roble said, rising.

"Overlander," Dolan said, "this does *not* concern you!"

"You're right. It doesn't," Roble replied. "But it does concern whether you live or not to see another day. Before you allow your emotions to direct you through Death's door, you should know that Daphne didn't kill Rufus."

Everyone's surprised gaze turned to him in an instant.

"Don't lie to spare her guilt," Dolan said.

"I'm not lying. I've no reason to spare her the agony of remorse if she actually killed him."

"She cast the wall of fire spell," Dolan said. His face tightened with fury. Spittle sprayed from his lips. "She even admitted as much."

"As did Portia," Roble said. "Do you wish to kill her, too?"

Dolan shook his head. "The wall of fire spell was Daphne's doing, not Portia's. Portia only yielded assistance and Daphne funneled Portia's magic. I doubt Portia even knew what spell Daphne planned to use."

"Yes. None of us deny what spell Daphne used, Dolan, but Rufus was *already* dead before any magic was dispelled," Roble replied.

Daphne looked surprised.

"What makes you think that?" Dolan asked.

Roble walked to Rufus' body and knelt beside it. He pointed at dark grooves that carved deep into both sides of the halfling's abdominal region. "These wounds were inflicted by one of those giant beetles. Rufus died before the flames ever filled the tunnel."

Dolan knelt and studied the wounds. He pressed his fingers against the side of the wound and pushed the flap of raw skin aside. Clear ooze and dark blood leaked from the gaping hole The deep wound almost resembled a curved blade of a sharp sword. "You sure?"

Roble nodded. "Even the blistering caused by the fire couldn't hide them. Did you see any hulls of the beetles' shells."

"We saw one," Dolan said.

"They were massive insects," Cora said, sniffling. "At first, we thought the shell was a chest plate."

"Those beetles were why Daphne and Portia cast the fire spell," Roble said. "There were more inside the ruins, too. Most likely, Rufus was attacked by one that dropped from the ceiling."

Cora and Merla looked at the tunnel's ceiling.

Dolan released the flap of skin to cover the puncture wound in Rufus' side. He glanced at Daphne and offered a slight bow. "My apologies. My judgment was in haste. I'd never have seen these puncture marks had the Overlander not pointed them out."

Daphne weighed his words for a few moments in silence. "Your reaction is understandable, Dolan. My attitude was brash toward you at Dagger's Tears when I had insisted you and your party remain behind. Regardless of my words then, I'd have done everything within my power to have saved Rufus from the beetle had I known he was there. I hope you recognize this as the truth."

"As would I," Portia said. "And you know this."

Dolan nodded slowly. His eyes teared. "We've lost so many of our kind."

"As have we," Daphne said. "I fully recognize the pain that toils within you. Portia and I will do as you request with Rufus' remains. I wish we could've intervened and protected him, rather than learning of his demise."

Cora wiped a tear from her cheek. "Thank you."

Aqese and Ki'wese stood and gently lifted Rufus' remains and carried his corpse outside the tunnel entrance.

After they returned, Roble said, "Tomorrow may prove more treacherous than today. We need to sleep. I'll keep the first watch."

Daphne smiled. "Your offer is appreciated, but Aqese and Ki'wese will stand guard outside. Portia and I will watch this end. None of the beetles should have survived, but we're better equipped at destroying them than you. You need your rest. You must be sharp-witted when we find Lez'minx. A tired mind is more susceptible to the cunning tricks he will attempt to confuse you with tomorrow."

CHAPTER 69

*M*orning came quickly.

Roble could have sworn he'd just closed his eyes when Ki'wese shook his shoulder until his eyes opened. Roble eased into a sitting position, blinked, and looked around until his eyes were able to focus clearly. Several seconds passed before he remembered they'd camped in the tunnel above the river.

"Sleep doesn't put off the inevitable," Daphne said with a slight smile. "Lez'minx awaits."

Ki'wese turned a large hunk of meat on the spit above the fire. Juices dripped from the caramel-colored meat into the flames. The smell was similar to bacon. His stomach growled with hunger.

Lehrling sat against the cave wall with a big portion of meat in his hand. He cheeks bulged as he chewed a bite larger than his mouth could handle. He smiled with juice dribbling from the sides of his lips.

Roble grinned. "That must be good. What are you eating?"

Ki'wese said, "Wild boar. Several were rooting on the riverbank this morning. Help yourself."

Roble rose and walked to the fire. At Ki'wese's feet lay the massive head of the three-eyed boar. Its black twisted tusks could've shredded through the flesh of any animal or leather armor.

"Where's everyone at?" Roble asked. Only he, Ki'wese, and Lehrling sat at the tunnel entrance.

"Daphne, Portia, and Shawndirea are searching for herbs," Ki'wese replied. "The halflings are scattering the ashes of Rufus along the river."

"By themselves?" Roble said.

"No. Aqese is with them, so they're safe, if that's what worries you."

"And Collette?" Roble asked, glancing at Lehrling.

Lehrling forced down his large bite and then cleared his throat. "She's helping Shawndirea find herbs, and hopes to find fresh fruit."

Ki'wese laughed. "Less chance of that occurring."

Roble grinned, turned toward the spit, and peeled off a thick piece of boar meat. As he devoured it, he couldn't avert his attention from the interesting patterns on Ki'wese's skin. From a distance, one might mistake the markings for tattoos. Up close, though, the dark lines were exactly like the tree rings on a stump.

"What troubles your mind?" Ki'wese asked.

Roble realized he had been staring too long. "My apologies. Those patterns on your skin are fascinating."

"Why's that?"

Roble shrugged. "The lines ... they remind me of tree rings."

Ki'wese studied Roble for several seconds. His curiosity turned to disgust and he frowned. "So were you a destroyer of trees, like other humans?"

"No. But most any human from the Overlands has seen woodgrain."

"Which is why the majority of dryads fled your realm to reside in ours or others. Overlanders are the most destructive beings I've witnessed. They've no regard for the sanctity of forests, rivers, or seas. I'm surprised your kind has survived for as long as they have."

"I'm not like them," Roble said.

Ki'wese looked intently into Roble's eyes and gave a solemn nod. "I detect that to be true. Shawndirea would never have chosen you as her husband if you were like other Overlanders."

Lehrling chuckled.

Ki'wese flicked his gaze at Lehrling. "Something amusing?"

"Their first encounter wasn't as romantic as—"

Roble glared at Lehrling. "Now's not the time."

Lehrling's eyes widened. "You're right. I'm sorry."

"Once you've finished eating," Ki'wese said, rising, "put out the fire. I need to find Aqese and prepare the rafts. We need to carry them over the shallow pocket in the river before loading the horses. Eat your fill. It'll be a while before our next meal. Let's hope this isn't the last."

Ki'wese left the tunnel and descended the narrow path.

CHAPTER 70

*A*fter a half hour of carrying the two rafts over the rocky, shallow section of the river and reloading the supplies and horses, Roble wiped sweat from his brow.

His weakened knees shook. Shawndirea slept on Bleys' saddlebag. She said little after they had returned with stuffed pouches with various herb leaves. She still looked drained. He worried she might not be physically and mentally ready to draw upon her magic for battle.

Should the circumstance ever arise, he'd give his life for hers. She'd do the same for him, as she truly loved him. At the moment, she could hardly defend herself. She didn't have the necessary energy to protect the two of them, though she'd try. Sealing the rifts had sapped her. The procedure had weakened all of them, including Lehrling and himself.

After Rufus died, the halflings mourned their loss. Their eyes revealed their hurt. Their zeal was gone. Grief weighted their minds.

Roble stared at his rings and then at the river's bend ahead. In a few hours, their journey of finding Lez'minx would finally be over, provided he was where Daphne predicted he was hiding. For Roble, this meeting was more like hunting prey rather than seeking an affable conversation with an enemy. He intended, one way or the other, to be freed from the rings' binding. He saw nothing less than a major confrontation. He'd protest Lez'minx's demands and Lez'minx probably would refute Roble's arguments. Roble understood he held no advantage in the fight but hoped whatever threat Daphne and Portia presented was enough to sway Lez'minx to release Roble.

Exhausted, Lehrling lay on the raft with his back resting against a wooden crate. His eyes were closed and Collette lay pressed against him, deep in sleep.

Apprehension tightened Roble's stomach since he held no foreknowledge of how the final outcome would end. He'd always regret bringing Shawndirea and Lehrling into this battle. Both insisted he not go alone. Retracing the journey they'd traveled thus far, he'd have never gotten here alive. Not by himself. He'd have been lost days earlier.

Yet, the more Roble thought about their journey, the more he questioned whether Lez'minx purposely directed them along a path that he had chosen and none of their encounters were by chance. After all, Lez'minx had rescued them twice, thus attempting to somehow cement a false friendship between Roble and him, using the situations to persuade Roble's loyalty to make Roble think he needed Lez'minx.

In some ways, Roble was tempted to accept at least part of Lez'minx's terms, if only to save Lehrling, Shawndirea, and the others traveling with him from certain death.

Being a stranger in Aetheaon, Roble thought it was beneficial to have advantages over unexpected enemies. Deep down, he knew he couldn't blindly offer and submissively give his allegiance to someone that would control his actions; especially after Daphne and Portia had revealed Lez'minx's mischievous nature.

Roble didn't know Lez'minx's scheme, but if worse came to worst, he hoped Lehrling and Shawndirea would be spared.

While deep in thought and watching the muddy river, Daphne slipped up alongside him.

"Do you see it?" she asked.

"What?" Roble replied.

"The branches of the Great Tree," she said, pointing.

He followed the direction of her finger and looked into the dim, woven canopy of long, crooked tree branches that reached from one side of the river to the other. Mist and fog rose on the river, drifting upwards. Roble took a sharp breath and held it as the faint outline of the Great Tree's rugged, gnarled branches slowly materialized into view.

The massive branches forked outward and upward like giant arms wide enough for horse carriages to travel like roadways. Some branches disappeared into the heavy overcast sky.

Roble had never seen tree branches as wide and long as these. Yet, that was all he could see of the tree. The branches. The trunk was still far beyond sight, hidden in the mist. The tree defied all feasible traits possible for any tree species. As heavy as these branches were and as far as they stretched from the trunk, it didn't seem possible. The weight alone should've snapped them from the trunk, or they should've rotted. It was almost magical ...

Roble shook his head. It *was* magic. Nothing else explained the phenomenon.

Blinks of red, yellow, and emerald lights flashed from fireflies drifting through the mist. Frogs bellowed and peeped along the marshy edge of the river. The strange cries of birds echoed and blended together.

"Spectacular?" Daphne asked.

Roble's eyes flicked to meet hers. "Beyond spectacular. Why would anyone choose to leave?"

Daphne smiled and motioned to get Aqese's attention. "Pull the rafts to the shore and tie them. We walk the remaining distance to better ensure our brother doesn't see our arrival."

"What about the horses?" Roble asked.

"They stay aboard the rafts. With all the underbrush, they'd be more a hindrance than a help," she replied.

Roble leaned down and shook Lehrling's shoulder. Lehrling's eyes opened in surprise. "We're here."

"Saggy-nook?" Lehrling eased up and rubbed his eyes. "So soon?"

"She told us it wasn't much farther," he replied.

Lehrling nodded. "I know. I hoped I had longer to sleep."

Collette pulled away from Lehrling, stretched, and yawned. She stared at the closest tree branch in disbelief.

Dolan, Merla, and Cora helped paddle the raft to the riverbank.

"How close does the river flow to the tree's trunk?" Roble asked.

Daphne said, "The river bends well before we could ever see the Ruins of Saggy-nook. From past experiences, if we don't go ashore now, we won't have another chance, as the river becomes rapid and jagged rocks prevent our rafts from reaching the shore."

Lehrling stood, arched his back, and groaned. He clasped a firm hand on Roble's shoulder and smiled. "These old bones insist this is my last arduous journey, friend."

"Let's hope it's not the last journey for each of us," Daphne said with a firm stare.

Lehrling's smile retreated. "I didn't mean it like *that.*"

"Is Shawndirea okay?" Daphne asked, peering closer to the faery.

"She's slept since we left the ruins," Roble replied. "But I don't think it's severe like before."

"It's best you wake her," Daphne said. "None of us can afford to be mentally unguarded."

"We need her insight," Portia said. "She might detect what we cannot. She's attuned differently."

Roble nodded.

Aqese looped a long rope around a tree root and tied the raft while Ki'wese did the same on the second raft.

Roble nudged Shawndirea. She opened her eyes, blinked, and then smiled at him.

"How do you feel?" he asked.

She stood and expanded her wings. "Rested. Why?"

"We're here."

"I figured as much."

"Shh!" Daphne said, placing her index finger to her lips.

All the sounds of nature grew deadly silent.

"That was impressive," Roble said.

Daphne glared and whispered, "They weren't responding to me."

"Then what?" Collette asked.

Daphne glanced toward Portia. "Runefel is nearby. Do you sense him?"

Portia nodded. "Yes."

"Shield your mind, sister. The same goes for Shawndirea, Aqese, and Ki'wese. Our brother mustn't know we're here."

"Lez'minx?" Lehrling whispered.

Daphne nodded. "Now, please, keep silent. He mustn't know we're here."

Shawndirea frowned. Her eyes searched the trees and the canopy. "I sense a powerful force."

"I told you," Daphne said. "Our brother—"

Shawndirea shook her head. "It's not your brother I sense. I recognize his power, but this … this isn't him."

Portia's brow raised in question, as did Daphne's.

"It's probably the magical aura of the tree," Daphne said. "Portia and I are akin to it."

"Yes," Portia said. The mossy hair on her arms stood slightly and bent in the gentle flow of the breeze. "Its power is stimulating."

"No, I feel that, but the stronger sensation isn't the tree, and it's not Lez'minx," Shawndirea said.

A troubled expression tightened Portia's brow. "I sense what she speaks of now. Do you, sister?"

"Unfortunately … yes," she replied.

The halflings looked at the riverbank with apprehension.

Aqese extended his hand to Daphne to help her step on a massive tree root to get to the riverbank. She accepted. On the bank, she looked at Dolan. "You three remain behind with the horses."

Dolan shook his head. "We didn't take this journey to be onlookers. We came to fight with you and in Rufus' honor."

Daphne regarded him with renewed respect.

"Very well, but only if you remain silent and comply with our advice," Daphne replied.

Dolan gave a firm nod.

Roble gripped Aqese's hand and stepped from the raft. Their determined eyes met with mutual coldness, not for one another, but each knowing their mission. While each held different reasons, it'd soon end.

Roble stood on the giant tree root. A surge of energy jolted his feet and moved upward through his calves. This energy was magical. He stepped off the root onto the sandy bank.

Once Roble's feet were steadfast, Aqese clasped Roble's shoulder and nodded his appreciation with a slight grin. The already dim forest and river grew darker, colder. The slight misting rain stopped, and for several long moments, complete silence enveloped them.

"Be on guard," Shawndirea whispered to Roble. "We're *not* alone."

CHAPTER 71

*R*oble slid two throwing knives from his belt and held the blades, ready to fling them in an instant.

Ki'wese used a machete-like blade to slice a path through the thick dead brush. No evident path lay before them. Unlike the other areas of the swamp, the ground was almost dry. The sandy soil was undisturbed by any previous footprints.

Other than the thick, meandering roots of the Great Tree, all the smaller brush and bramble were dead and shriveled. The larger trees seemed healthy but their leaves were a dull greenish-yellow.

Roble reasoned that had these plants been alive, Ki'wese wouldn't be cutting a path through them; not since he was a dryad.

"Why's all the scrub brush dead?" Roble whispered.

Shawndirea shrugged. "I do not know."

Daphne whispered into his mind. *"The Great Tree is consuming the life of its neighboring plants."*

"Why?"

"A possibility for reasons comes to mind," she replied. *"The tree may be diseased and dying; thus, she's drawing sustenance to maintain her life. Or someone's pooling and siphoning too much of her magic for ill-gotten gain, which could also kill her. Either way, she's forced to sap the surrounding plants. My guess is the latter. Runefel has been steadily draining her magical well for his own greedy pursuit. To kill dozens of the Shadowfae days ago required a lot of magic, if no blood sacrifices were performed concurrently."*

Whispering sounds rasped in the darkened tree branches overhead. Fast-moving creatures zipped from tree to tree beyond their view in the canopy.

They were cloaked by magic to be invisible or simply moved too swiftly for Roble to see.

Whatever they were, their interest seemed to be observing Roble and his party, but the creatures remained reluctant to approach or allow themselves to be seen.

"*What are they?*" Roble asked.

"*At this point, it's difficult to know. Being this close to a tree filled with magic, we're liable to come in contact with almost anything,*" she replied.

"*Don't forget,*" Portia said, "*when she and I were children, we witnessed a lot of carnage from those obsessed to obtain more magical power or trying to claim the tree for their own.*"

"*Which means,*" Daphne said, "*we might encounter skirmishes or be attacked before we even find Runefel.*"

"*I'm aware,*" Roble said. "*What makes you think he's been successful at laying claim to the Great Tree's essence?*"

"*To kill a couple dozen Shadowfae assassins from halfway across the swamps, means he has access to magic that exceeds his knowledge and abilities,*" Daphne said. "*Even I and Portia combining our strengths could not do such a feat without an enormous magical boost. This tree feeds upon its surroundings to maintain its essence, as you called it. But the height of the energy issuing outward stimulates any of us with the ability to cast spells. The closer we get, the more overwhelming this sensation becomes. Should we become giddy and act unusual, you need to know, it's because of this outpouring of magic flowing through us.*"

"*Giddy?*" Lehrling asked.

Daphne nodded. "*The energy flux is more than we can handle until we acclimate.*"

"*If that's the case,*" Roble said, "*why do so many try to murder others to obtain—*"

"*That has to do with the intention of one's heart,*" Daphne said. "*Lust and greed are negative attributes that become magnified the closer one gets to the tree's trunk. But those must be prominent inner traits to begin with. Obsession overtakes their reasoning. They don't care who they hurt or kill. Portia and I never sought magic due to lust and greed. As children, we fed modestly from the tree's magic resources. Runefel—*"

"Shh!" Shawndirea placed her index finger to her lips and nodded to the right of the path Ki'wese was cutting.

Ki'wese lowered his blade and everyone grew silent. "What is it?"

"Listen," Shawndirea whispered.

The thumping rhythm was faint but grew steadier and a bit louder.

"What's that?" Roble asked.

Lehrling's brow rose. His eyes narrowed as he cocked his head to listen. With a gasp of recognition, he whispered, "Orc war drums?"

Portia glanced at Daphne with apprehension. "Orcs?"

"I've only heard their war drums once before," Lehrling said. "That was half my lifetime ago, during my first voyage on the seas as a Dragon Skull Knight soon after King Erik christened me into the Order. The sound of Orc drums is unmistakable, even after all these years."

"Where did you encounter Orcs?" Roble asked.

"Cinder Isles at the outskirts of the Ashen Sea."

Portia looked at Lehrling. "So are these Orcs planning to go into battle? Is this a battlecry?"

Lehrling shrugged. "Battlecry? No. Probably not. They might be signaling a warning to others of their arrival. I don't rightly know. I only heard the drums as our ship sailed past the isles. From what I know of the Orcs, a battlecry is their loud roars before they rush and remove your head with an axe."

Daphne swallowed hard. "It can't be Orcs. Not in the middle of Woodnog Swamps."

Shawndirea nodded. "I think it is."

"Why would they be here?" Lehrling asked.

"The ruins was probably once their city," Daphne said. "Though it's merely our speculation based on the carvings."

"How'd they get this far from the river?" Roble asked. "The only trail is the one Ki'wese's. No one's taken this direction for many years."

Daphne nodded. "Yes, that's true. Another inlet is farther upriver. I chose to stop here to lessen our chance of being seen, which seems to have been a good choice, given that the Orcs arrived before us."

"What now?" Ki'wese asked.

Daphne looked at Roble. "What do you wish to do? Do you want to turn back and hope for another time to confront Runefel, or do we take our chances and hope for the best?"

"What do you wish to do?" Roble asked.

"Portia and I will continue to the Great Tree," she said. "Our agenda doesn't change. We cannot allow ourselves to be veered off our path. It's time Runefel understands he must answer for his misdeeds."

Lehrling frowned and shook his head. "We're no match to fight Orcs. Even a small band of Orcs could destroy us."

Dolan considered what Lehrling had said, cleared his throat, and in spite of his nervous demeanor, he said, "Cora, Merla, and I are going to the tree."

Lehrling glanced at him in surprise.

Roble looked at Ki'wese. "Keep clearing a path. As for Lehrling, Shawndirea, and Collette, they—"

"I'm going," Shawndirea said.

"As am I," Lehrling said, rubbing an index finger across his silver Dragon Skull pendant. He gave an uneasy glance at Collette. "At best, the Orcs are most likely a scouting group sent from one of their ships elsewhere. That doesn't make them any less deadly, just less to deal with."

"My guess is they're not here for the magic tree," Roble said.

"No," Daphne said. "Most likely not, and that might make them even more dangerous."

"In what sense?" Roble asked.

"If this had once been their land and city, perhaps they wish to reclaim it," she replied. "In which case, *anyone* they encounter becomes their enemy."

CHAPTER 72

One the drumbeats became louder, Roble placed a hand on Ki'wese's shoulder and asked him to stop clearing the path. He feared the sharp blade hacking the dead brush branches might catch the Orcs' attention. Despite the faint whispering of the razor-edged machete, dead leaves and twigs rattled and crunched.

Pushing their way through the thick, dead underbrush would not be an easy endeavor. The sharp barbs on some branches clung to their leather armor and cloth robes. More a hindrance than dangerous, these brambles and barbs slowed their forward progress.

The winged creatures in the canopy darted out of sight but their interest in following Roble and the others continued.

Roble pushed aside the final two dead branches, which opened to a clearing. The earthy ground vanished beneath aged tile stone. Sprigs of dead weeds stood in the cracks and grooves of the tiles.

To their left, a giant gnarled tree root snaked toward the Great Tree. Ruins of stone walls were stacked in jagged piles. Over time, the weather and the huge roots carved way through the stone barriers.

The height of the root stood higher than Roble's six-foot stature, causing him to stare in awe at the towering tree in the distance. No wonder the soil was bone-dry and the underbrush beyond the broken wall was dead. For the tree to sustain itself, it needed a vast amount of nutrients, and it claimed whatever sustenance necessary to survive.

Even though Roble and his party arrived at the clearing, the Orcs were not seen. The hollow, deep thudding drums remained steady, and were closer, but where the Orcs had positioned themselves was a mystery.

"Careful," Shawndirea said. "They've probably concealed themselves at a higher vantage point."

Roble nodded.

"There," Daphne said, rushing to his side and placing a gentle hand upon his shoulder. She pointed. "There, in that crevice of the trunk, near the old door opening of the higher level."

Six Orcs partially dressed in sleeveless, dark metal plate armor were seated around a small glowing fire that produced no smoke. A seventh Orc stood with a decorative staff raised in his right hand. He wore dark robes and chanted while two of the seated Orcs beat the constant rhythm on the drums.

Roble marveled at their massive size. They were three times his width with huge biceps, thick chests, shoulders, and backs. They needed no weapons to tear his limbs from his body. Their blackish-green skin and their dark armor concealed them against the backdrop of the tree's mossy bark.

Regardless of their size, Roble guessed they were swift on their feet. He contemplated turning back. Had it not been for his damned curiosity, he probably would have. Before he whispered his fear to Daphne, the standing Orc stopped chanting, opened his eyes, and stared in their direction.

Lehrling mumbled curses under his breath, as Roble did inside his mind. They stiffened in silent horror when the seated Orcs turned and noticed them. There was no retreating now. To run made them prey to the Orcs. But standing their ground against the Orcs certainly ensured quick deaths, but Roble hoped a peaceful resolution could be achieved.

The shaman spoke a word in a language Roble had never heard voiced in Aetheaon, but its meaning was clear to the six seated Orcs. Staring at Roble and his group, the Orcs growled.

Roble succumbed to intense fear unlike anything he'd ever experienced before. The Orcs were much larger than the Vykings with thicker muscles. A throwing dagger probably wouldn't pierce an Orc's skin.

"Don't run," Daphne said, "and don't show any fear."

"That's easy for you to say."

"I'm quite frightened," she replied.

"You hide it well," Roble said.

She gave him an even side-glance. No laughter tugged at the edges of her mouth or lightened her glare. She was more serious than any other time they had spoken.

"Of course, you've hidden all your emotions quite well," he said.

The six Orcs slid their hands upon the thick hilts of their double-sided axes and heavy hammers that lay on the ground beside them. They rose to their feet more fluidly than Roble could've done. He guessed they stood over eight feet in height. The metal of their weapons scraped against the stone floor while they dragged them to themselves.

For some reason, their strange orange-yellow eyes fixated on Roble. Their thick, heavy brows tightened. They expressed rage in their low rumbling growls that could make a lion flinch.

Veins snaked down the Orcs' arms while they held their heavy weapons. Each giant axe and warhammer probably weighed more than Roble. They turned the axes in their hands with ease as though they were tinker toys.

Roble thought of several odd epitaphs for his gravestone, some of which he thought humorous, but he never said them aloud.

Daphne spoke aloud in a language he didn't understand, which captured the shaman's attention. His intense facial features weakened. The anger in his gaze turned to curiosity and sudden interest. The six warriors turned their attention toward the shaman, awaiting his reply.

"She told them that we wish them peace and blessings and that our battle is not with them," Portia whispered to Roble.

"You think they're open for peaceful coexistence?" Roble asked.

"Depends," Daphne said.

"On what exactly," Roble whispered.

"How much they hate humans," she replied.

Roble exchanged glances with Lehrling, who appeared more nervous than ever.

The Orc shaman set the end of his staff onto the stone floor and made a motion in the air with his left hand. The six warrior Orcs nodded with disappointment, and slowly sheathed their weapons.

"That's a good sign, right?" Lehrling asked.

"It would appear so," Roble said.

"For now," Daphne whispered.

The shaman walked away from the smokeless fire and ambled his way to Daphne with the menacing six warriors following behind. As they came closer, Roble noticed that several of the Orcs had suffered injuries; some more severe than others. A line of drying blood crusted from a hole in one's left side and flowed down the upper part of his thigh.

The shape and depth of the wound could be best explained in that the Orc must have been stabbed with a sharp-tipped spear or a pike. A dagger or most short swords probably couldn't have pierced his thick skin. With the amount of dried blood, the puncture wound had been deep, but the Orc walked without the slightest hint of pain, which might have been hidden by his harsh scowl. Less severe lacerations covered the other Orcs on their faces, muscled arms, and exposed chests.

Thick yellow tusks protruded from their mouths. Some of the large tusks were sharp and even the broken ones were frightening to behold.

The shaman spoke to Daphne as he approached. After several minutes of bantering, Roble soon understood what they were saying, and the shaman's name was Uksen. He marveled that the words in this unusual language made sense. The only explanation for this odd understanding was that someone had cast a translation spell, making it possible for them to understand one another. Or, had the Great Tree allowed it?

"We are the last survivors of our fleet," Uksen said. "We set sail to return to Cinder Isles when Vykings attacked us. We lost several ships, and our Chief's son, Borgess, was one of the casualties. Our vessel caught the swell of high waves and strong storm winds forced us to the shoreline of Aetheaon."

"How did you come so far inland?" Daphne asked.

Uksen took a deep breath and sighed. His weary eyes were troubled. "Our ancestors once ruled these swamps. Where this tree stands was once our greatest city, Nozord."

"I see," Daphne said. "My sister and I have believed this for years. We thought Orcs occupied this city, but we couldn't read the language carved into stones."

"Yet, you speak it?" Roble asked.

Uksen leveled a harsh, imitating stare at Roble. Roble cringed. "She speaks our modern language, human. *Not* our ancient one that's carved into our monuments."

Roble offered a humble nod and eased back a few steps, trying to present submissiveness to avoid a heated confrontation. Uksen, like the other Orcs, looked easy to offend. Roble doubted any of them were capable of smiling. Their aged wrinkles creased deeper frowns and indicated they growled in anger a lot. He didn't want to be on the receiving end of their wrath.

Strange tattoos were carved into Uksen's face. His nose, cheek, and chin were pierced with bones. His earlobes drooped from the weight of heavy gold rings. The other six Orcs' body art resembled Uksen. He wore a headdress that flowed down his back with large dark feathers. The greenish-black skin of his face made his yellowish-orange eyes gleam brighter.

When he exhaled, the huff through his nose was a rough snort. His large tusks made breathing more difficult.

"What is it you seek?" Daphne asked.

"The staff I carried was destroyed in our battle against the Vykings. Without it, my power has weakened. Legend tells that our greatest shaman ancestor, Thull, is buried in these ruins. I seek his staff. It's an artifact that would enhance my magical abilities. As you can see, some of us are in need of healing," Uksen said.

Daphne looked confused. "Thull?"

"Yes," Uksen said in an raspy tone.

Shawndirea stood on Roble's shoulder and cleared her throat. "You'll not find any remnants of Thull in Nozord."

Uksen flicked his gaze at her. "Why not?"

"Mors summoned him from the dead and used him and his power to fight at the Battle of Hoffnung," she replied.

Uksen snorted. His voice lowered to a gravelly growl. "Who is this ... *Mors*?"

"He's a necromancer," Roble said. "Thull ... his skeleton was destroyed during the battle."

Uksen growled and ground his tusks. The other Orcs replied with the same aggression. "Where do we find Mors?"

"He's known as the Plague-bringer. He comes and goes, vanishing in a magical whirlwind," Roble said. "He's building an army to destroy all the major cities and rule over Aetheaon."

"He's your enemy?" Uksen asked.

Roble nodded. "Yes."

Determination set in Uksen's eyes and his thick jaw hardened. "Since he desecrated Thull, he's our enemy, too. Since he's your enemy that makes us allies. We'll hunt him and once he's found, we stand by your side in battle. What he's done can never be forgiven. Not in this life or in the lives hereafter."

Roble started to offer his thanks but the injured Orc toppled forward, clutched the deep wound in his side, and collapsed at Uksen's feet. His comrades formed a circle around him and knelt. Uksen inspected the wound. He looked at Daphne and shook his head. "Without the staff, our hope to heal him and ourselves is gone."

Daphne gave a reassuring smile. "Not necessarily."

CHAPTER 73

*R*oble stepped away from the Orcs to stand beside Lehrling, Collette, and the halflings while Shawndirea, Portia, and Daphne attuned their magic to heal the injured Orc.

In disbelief, he watched the Orcs, a mighty and yet frightening race. He marveled at the strangeness and wonder of this race. From their reputation of a hostile, war-seeking people, he was surprised at the shaman's quickness to ally themselves against Mors, but thankful to have the giant warriors on their side.

A glowing dome enclosed around the injured Orc, Uksen, Shawndirea, and the dryad sisters. Warmth radiated from the magical bubble for several minutes. The injured Orc opened his eyes and sat up with a horrifying growl of surprise, ready to attack. Uksen placed a gentle hand on the Orc's shoulder, offering words of assurance that all was well.

But not all was well.

After the healing dome vanished, Shawndirea dropped and crumpled to the ground, curling into a fetal position. Roble ran to her. She appeared lifeless. With tender care, he eased her over onto her back. She opened her weakened eyes.

"What happened?" Roble asked. "Are you okay?"

She offered a slight nod. "Fatigued. That's all."

He placed his hand beside her, and she crawled upon his palm and collapsed again. She snored softly.

"Why are you still so weak?" Roble whispered.

Daphne's eyes expressed her concern. "Especially here, near the Great Tree? She didn't have any reason to draw from her magic when the tree's essence abounds like an overflowing river."

"We're in your debt," Uksen said. "How can we assist you?"

Daphne looked into Roble's eyes for a moment and then turned to Uksen. "We came to Nozord to find my brother. Our confrontation might prove difficult and dangerous."

Uksen thought for several moments. "We've not encountered anyone. Though we've not been here long."

"He wouldn't be on the outskirts," Daphne said. "He'd be on the other side, where the pools and fountains are."

"We could scout the gardens," Uksen said in a deep rumbled voice. "Should we find him, we'll restrain him and bring him to you."

"It's not that easy," Portia said. "His sorcery is strong."

Uksen chuckled and the other Orcs bellowed laughter. "Perhaps. But our trinkets and weapons resist and repel evil sorceries."

"We appreciate your help then," Daphne said.

Uksen turned his gaze to Roble and Lehrling. He frowned. "I recognize your dragon pendants. You're Dragon Skull Knights serving Hoffnung's king?"

"Queen Taube, now," Lehrling said.

"And Erik? What of him?" Uksen asked.

Lehrling summarized King Erik's disappearance and the possibility of his most likely, unfortunate death.

Uksen's saddened eyes looked at the broken tile floor. He shook his head. "He was always generous in his trades with the Cinder Isles. We wondered of his absence for quite some time."

Lehrling's brow rose in surprise. "He ventured to Cinder Isles?"

"Periodically."

"That's odd," Lehrling said.

"Why?" Uksen asked.

"It's odd that he'd venture to your isle without our Order," Lehrling said.

"Can a king not venture to wherever he wishes?"

"Of course. Usually, though, such travels … it's just odd that he'd put himself and our kingdom at risk."

"You perceive us as a threat?" Uksen asked.

"I recall only one voyage where I and other Dragon Skull Knights sailed within sight of Cinder Isles," Lehrling said. "We heard your war drums."

"Was Hoffnung's crest upon the sails?"

"Of course."

"Then the sound you heard was most likely a welcoming hail."

"We sailed past," Lehrling said.

"I see. Perhaps the others with you didn't share his unbiased attitude?"

"That may be."

Uksen shrugged. "King Erik never came alone. He was always well guarded. He's the only human king we viewed as non-hostile to our people.

Hoffnung has never been viewed as our enemy." He offered a smile that appeared shrewd due to his large tusks. "You and I may talk further at another time. For now, let us see if we can find the one you seek. What is his name?"

Daphne said, "Runefel ... But he has deceived Roble and Lehrling into calling him, Lez'minx."

"If he is here," Uksen said, "we shall find him."

CHAPTER 74

A half hour later, Roble sat against the mighty root of the Great Tree with Shawndirea curled on his palm. Like before, she was unresponsive, deep in sleep, and he feared for her life.

Daphne came and sat beside him. "She's not awakened?"

Roble shook his head. "No. Any idea why this has occurred again?"

Dolan and the other halflings studied the carved markings in the stone wall and the floor without words. Their overshadowing gloom remained evident. Collette and Lehrling sat lost in conversation nearby.

Everyone was drained from the long journey, especially Shawndirea.

Roble peered up the Great Tree's trunk, unable to estimate how tall the massive tree was. Dismal clouds and a low curtain of fog hampered his vision.

Portia joined Roble and Daphne. Her interest was also on Shawndirea's well-being.

"When we cast the healing spell together," Daphne said to Portia, "did you sense anything amiss that might've somehow afflicted Shawndirea?"

Portia shook her head. "No."

"Neither did I," Daphne sighed. "Her collapse makes no sense."

"I know," Portia said. "Magical essence abounds all around us. The overflowing well of magic should flow through her. The spell shouldn't have drained her. It simply *couldn't* have."

"Something has," Roble said.

"Someone or something inhibits her magic. That's obvious. It's almost as though she becomes ill after she casts a spell. A curse, perhaps?"

"You've never experienced this before?" Roble asked.

Daphne and Portia shook their heads.

"Here?" Daphne said. "Never."

"I should've known it was you! I sensed that familiar, aggravating feeling from years ago. I thought you died ages ago!"

Daphne turned in the direction of Lez'minx's voice. In a harsh tone, she replied, "You should be so fortunate."

Everyone's attention turned to Lez'minx's shouting. Roble was stunned to see a strange creature roped and tied and being dragged by two Orcs. He wasn't like Portia or Daphne at all. Despite his much smaller size, he possessed incredible strength in his ability to resist their tugging.

"Is this the one you seek?" Uksen asked.

Roble, Lehrling, and the halflings stared at Daphne and Portia with obvious confusion as they awaited their answer.

Daphne and Portia rose and nodded.

"You never mentioned he was a goat-boy," Uksen said.

"Goat-boy!" Lez'minx glared.

Daphne appeared agitated when she stared at Lez'minx. But Portia responded with an affectionate smile.

Roble expected Lez'minx to look like his sisters, but he was nothing like them. He wasn't a god, but he certainly looked like what most people in the Overlands would consider a demon. From the waist down, his muscled legs were covered with thick coarse hair. His cloven feet dug in the ground, making it difficult for the Orcs to pull him along, in spite of their great strength.

His red hair flowed in neat, twisted strands down to his shoulders. His radiant face might be considered handsome with his neatly trimmed beard and mustache, if one ignored other aspects. Two goatlike horns protruded and curled backwards on his forehead.

Lez'minx was a satyr.

When Lez'minx's eyes met Daphne's, his resistance in following the Orcs lessened. Fear widened his strange eyes. He flicked his gaze rapidly from one person to the next, almost as if he might be trying to find a quick route of escape.

"I never imagined our reunion would require such forcefulness," Lez'minx said. His voice was smoother than warm honey, revealing no bitterness or hostility. "If you wished to talk, you could've asked, without the escorts and ropes. Ya not still into that sort of—"

"You'll not escape us so easily this time," Daphne said with sheer coldness.

Roble involuntarily shivered, as chills shot down his back.

Uksen walked to Daphne and held a crooked staff and a small harp. "We took these from him."

"You keep the staff," she said.

Uksen studied the staff for a few moments before acquiescing a slight nod.

"That's mine," Lez'minx said in a sweet tone. "It'll do you no good, green-skin. It's not attuned to you. You've no use for it, so give it back."

Uksen's brow furrowed. He turned and faced Lez'minx, offering the staff for a moment before anger narrowed his eyes and he gripped the staff tighter. "Sneaky. Trying to seduce my mind with the gentleness of your words? Do so again and find your tongue over there."

A grin spread on Lez'minx's face. "Keep the staff, greenskin, and the longer you hold it, the more you'll be willing to do my bidding. Ask Roble."

Uksen took the staff in both hands and bent it.

"No!" Lez'minx said. "Daphne don't allow him to break it!"

Daphne ignored his protest and cast her glance at Roble. "State your piece before Portia and I enact our justice."

Lez'minx's mouth dropped. Portia's brow furrowed with uneasiness.

Roble frowned and strode toward Lez'minx. When Lez'minx fought against the two ropes tied around his neck and attempted to break free, the two Orcs tightened their hold on the restraints. One Orc's massive hand wrapped around Lez'minx's neck.

"You must free me, Roble," Lez'minx said in a choked voice. He stared with the purest sincerity. "I beg you."

"Remove your spell on these rings. I want them off and to have no further ties to you. I've no idea what your sisters plan to do to you, but before they seek revenge, break the spell," Roble said. "Free me."

Lez'minx fought the Orc's grip, stretched his neck, and looked past Roble. He whispered, "Revenge? So it's true? What do they plan to do?"

"You need to ask them, not me."

Lez'minx closed his eyes and mumbled a few words.

"What'd you do?" Roble asked.

"I've blocked their ability to hear us talk."

"Why?"

"Because you need to learn the truth. I've done nothing to them. *Ever.*"

"Again, an argument you need to discuss with them."

Lez'minx's eyes shifted nervously. He noticed Shawndirea in Roble's hand. "Your faery … she's injured?"

Roble looked at Shawndirea's curled form. "I—I don't know what's wrong."

"It wasn't my doing," Lez'minx said. "I swear it. I kept my word—"

"Just remove the rings," Roble said.

"Haven't I done more to protect than harm you? I've never caused you harm," Lez'minx said. His eyes shimmered and his tone held soft musical rhythm.

"Just—"

"Don't be so hasty to disregard the truth, my dear Roble," Lez'minx said. "I never meant any ill will. I saved your lives. That's worth something."

Roble's jaw tightened. As much as he despised Lez'minx for the rings, he felt a tinge of pity for Lez'minx and wanted to help him. Surely, it had something to do with Lez'minx being a satyr. "While appreciated, I refuse to ignore your deceit to spy on us without our consent. That violates trust on so many levels. You should've told me that was a price for wearing the rings."

"A price? Yes, everything has a price, or haven't you figured that out yet?" Lez'minx whispered. "If you'd known what benefited me from your wearing the rings, would you have worn the rings?"

"No, I wouldn't be wearing them at all. I'd have destroyed them."

"Fair enough. Look, I didn't cause Shawndirea's sickness," Lez'minx said. "You must believe me."

"You threatened her life," Roble replied. "Can't you see why I'll always doubt your denial?"

"Yes. I'll remove the rings," Lez'minx said with genuine fear, "if you'll do one thing for me?"

"I didn't come here to bargain," Roble said. "Remove these rings."

"They're going to kill me, aren't they?" Lez'minx asked.

"I don't know their intent. They've not told me."

"What *do* you know?"

"I've the feeling that whatever they've planned does not bode well for you," Roble replied.

"Do you know their reasons?"

Roble shook his head. "No. That's something they've not told me, either."

Lez'minx kept his gaze focused on Daphne and Portia. He was stalling.

"What are you waiting for?" Roble asked, frustrated.

"The second I remove the rings, they're going to kill me."

"If that's their intention, they're going to do it anyway. That much I know. They insisted I confront you first, or the chance I have to get them removed was gone."

Lez'minx nodded. "I see. Did they give any hints as to why they wish to kill me?"

"They've never said they were going to *kill* you."

"Well, harm me then? Keep me prisoner for their wanton needs?"

"Your sisters have—"

Lez'minx frowned. His eyes bore into Roble's. He whispered, "They're *not* my sisters."

Roble's eyes widened. "That's what they told us."

"And you believe them?" Lez'minx asked, rolling his eyes. He huffed. "Of course you would, Overlander. You believed I was a god, after all. Gullible."

"They're *not* your sisters?"

"No ... Do I *look* anything like them? That, in itself, should leave nothing to question."

"They're quite insistent. I questioned the possibility when I saw that you're a satyr."

"Yet, you have doubts?"

"Not anymore."

"That's good. Then perhaps now you can better determine what their true intention is. They want me dead," Lez'minx said.

"For what reason?"

"For being jilted?"

"Jilted?"

"Surely, even an Overlander understands the reputation of a satyr? I understand we're *legends* and lore in your realm."

Roble nodded. "You used your charm on them? Why? They're dryads."

"Half-dryads. That doesn't matter what they are. Their attraction toward me was, well, strange nonetheless, but we developed a different, special type of bond. *They* pursued me and not the other way around. I never charmed them, as you put it. Later, I wanted to leave, to move on, but they used their nature spells to prevent my escape. That is, until the great flood. During their distraction to stay alive, I managed to escape their tendrils."

"You caused the flood?" Roble asked.

Lez'minx shook his head. "No, but I know who did. And I'll *never* divulge that information, so don't bother asking."

"Why did you pretend to be a god?"

"Why not?" he replied. He shrugged and a snarl curled on his lips. "Overlanders know no differently. My kind have always been pranksters."

"That's another reason why it's hard to believe anything you tell me."

Lez'minx offered a genuine smile. "I understand that. Hopefully, you can detect my truthfulness right now, as my life is most likely in jeopardy. You seem a rational person. One capable of discerning the intentions others have."

"If that's what you believe about me, why'd you bother deceiving me about who and what you are?"

"You took Bausch's armor," Lez'minx said. "Another way my magic saved you and Shawndirea's lives. Bausch never paid homage to me for the armor. Once I discovered what happened to Bausch, I used the opportunity to beguile you since you're an Overlander. I shouldn't have, but had it worked, I'd have another servant to work through. To your credit, you're far wiser than the majority of Overlanders who've entered our realm. Most don't survive six months."

Roble frowned. "I've no idea their intentions, but I'll find out before we leave you with them."

"And if they wish my death?"

Roble shrugged. "They'd need a good reason."

"So you would defend me?"

"I didn't say that. But since they've been lying about their relationship to you, I won't allow your death if I can prevent it. I don't know how much I can protect you since I know no magic."

"Very well," Lez'minx said with a huff. "Turn your hands palmside down so I can see the gemstones in the rings."

"Any tricks," Daphne said, still from a distance. "And the Orcs will slit your throat, Runefel."

"My name is Lez'minx!" Anger flared his nostrils. Then, he cringed and whispered, "They can hear us now."

Daphne said, "All the same, you've been warned."

His anger turned to indignation. "Best you remember who has the greater power between us, Daphne."

"That's why Portia has come with me."

Portia's brow creased with confusion as she glanced at Daphne in regard to the statement.

Lez'minx took a deep breath. His eyes softened as he looked into Roble's. "No tricks. I swear it. I realize it's too late to gain your trust, but I hope you believe what I've said."

Roble recognized the depth of Lez'minx's hostility toward Daphne, and if the satyr wasn't bound with ropes, he'd probably attack her.

Lez'minx sighed. "Turn your hands."

Roble gently placed Shawndirea into the crook of his left arm and turned his hands where the gemstones were visible.

Lez'minx's throat rasped. He cleared his throat and spat green snot on each ring. "There."

Roble leveled an even stare and his jaw tightened. His hands tightened into fists.

"Easy. It's not an insult. It's the only way to inactivate my binding spells so you can remove the rings," Lez'minx said in a soft whisper. "Don't be skeptical. Without my spit, no other wizard or mage could undo the spell."

Roble looked at the glob of snot on the gemstones. His stomach turned.

"You only have a few minutes to take them off or you'll wear them forever."

Despite the acrid taste at the back of Roble's throat at the thought of touching the green spittle. For all Roble knew, this could be a test or it might be the satyr's twisted sense of humor.

Before Roble twisted the rings, he studied Lez'minx's eyes. A hint of eager laughter brightened the satyr's eyes. If anyone could witness the gleam in a jester's eyes before he unveiled his folly, Lez'minx gaze mirrored it. For a moment, Roble expected Lez'minx to burst into laughter, but he remained in utter silence.

"Go on," Lez'minx said. "What're you waiting for?"

"If this is an underhanded—"

"Where's your trust?"

"In you? That's already been established," Roble said.

"Why be like that?"

"With all you've done?"

Lez'minx's eyes narrowed. "In time, you'll understand that, although I schemed, I was never your enemy. But the longer you tarry, the more I believe you really don't want to break these bonds between us. It's fine if you don't, as I will continue to protect you. For small favors, of course."

Roble's jaw tightened. He twisted the left ring without any resistance and slipped it off his finger. He did the same with the other ring.

"See?" Lez'minx said, beaming a smile.

Roble stared at the two rings covered in viscous green slime, dropped them on the old tile floor, and crushed them under the heel of his boot.

"Hey!" Lez'minx said. "Do you realize how long it took me to craft those?"

Daphne and Portia stepped to each side of Roble. They took the ropes from the two Orcs, nodded their appreciation, and faced Lez'minx.

"Brother, it's been a long time," Daphne said.

Desperation set in Lez'minx's eyes. He looked at Roble.

"What are you going to do with him?" Roble asked.

"Your business with him has ended," Daphne said. "It's best you attend to Shawndirea."

"No, your charade ends now," Roble said. "Privately, if you wish, or I can tell everyone what this is actually all about."

Daphne's eyes glowed fiery red. Her face withered. "Don't threaten me, Overlander. You haven't your faery to protect you. And if you stand in our way, you might lose her, too."

"He has me," Lez'minx said.

"And," a voice thundered from a large branch of the Great Tree. The sky darkened. "He has us!"

CHAPTER 75

*S*hawndirea drifted, lower and lower, and deeper into the strange black, purple abyss. She didn't struggle to prevent her fall, as she didn't fear the place like the first time she entered the deep sleep.

Although she held no fear, she was confused, wondering what had drawn her consciousness into this unusual endless place again.

"Did you decide?" the male voice asked.

"About?"

"Which Court you serve?"

"I'm Seelie," she replied. "Nothing changes that."

"Your actions have changed far more than you realize," he replied. "You'll *never* be recognized as pure Seelie any longer. You know the reasons why."

"Then why bother asking?"

"Because I wanted to know if you've thought about the repercussions of your actions."

"I have."

"And?"

"Nothing has changed."

"Nothing?"

"No," she replied. "If sent back in time, I'd do everything the same. No changes. No remorse."

"Then *awaken*! Now!"

CHAPTER 76

*R*oble stood between Lez'minx and Daphne. Their anger and resentment toward one another was postponed. Their attention was drawn to the shimmering glints of silvery wings descending from the tree's canopy.

Sudden darkness shrouded the ruins on the outskirts of the Great Tree, making it impossible to get a clear view of the hovering creatures. The winged creatures that were following them decided to reveal themselves.

Shawndirea opened her eyes and shook her head. She pushed herself to her feet and looked upward.

"What have you done?" Daphne whispered to Roble.

Roble didn't reply. His attention was on the higher levels of the tree. A bright orb intensified. He didn't know what was occurring. Shawndirea took to flight and landed on his shoulder. She pressed herself against his cheek.

Roble said. "Are you okay?"

"Yes."

"What happened?"

"Now's not the time," she replied. Facing Lehrling and the others, she whispered, "Whatever you do, don't pull any weapons, or you're dead."

Uksen spoke commands in his orcish language. The other Orcs nodded and crossed their hulkish arms to show they held no weapons.

"What are these creatures?" Roble asked, as the bright orb lowered like a falling bubble.

"We're about to find out," Shawndirea replied.

"Oberon," Lez'minx whispered. He crouched behind Roble to hide.

When the orb hovered less than fifteen feet above the stone floor, an assembly of a hundred or more armored faeries formed a large circle with their swords drawn. Another circle of faeries hovered above them with loaded crossbows and long bows.

"Oberon?" Shawndirea asked. Her eyes brightened and she gasped. She flitted to the stone floor and knelt.

Daphne, Portia, and the other dryads knelt, keeping their gazes fixated on the floor.

King Oberon's feet touched a high knot of a massive tree root. The bubble surrounding him vanished.

Roble stared at Oberon in awe. Several seconds passed before he realized he had stopped breathing.

"Bow, you fool!" Shawndirea whispered harshly.

Roble dropped to both knees without a second's thought. His eyes met Oberon's. A jolt of electrical energy surged through Roble's body but still he couldn't look away.

At Roble's side, Lez'minx lie prostrate and sobbed heavily, whispering his confessions to King Oberon.

Horns protruded from the King's head. His eyes radiated a regalness unlike Roble had seen in other royal leaders' eyes. His countenance was solemn. Without speaking, he commanded fear, respect, and honor.

Even the Orcs lowered into bows. Lehrling and Collette clung to one another, bowing with apprehension. The halflings cowered, blubbering sobs not quite as loudly as Lez'minx's.

Oberon's great presence was so overpowering that Roble wondered why Oberon bothered with an armed entourage. When Orcs even offered submission without resistance, Roble doubted any enemy could draw a weapon to attack.

Roble couldn't explain the mixed emotions rushing through him. The pit of his stomach twisted with excitement. His heart hammered in his chest, and he was so overcome by the intense supernatural energy that he became light-headed. Tears flowed for no explainable reason.

"Court has come to order," a female said from the shadows. A few seconds later, she marched past Roble and his party, stopped at the base of the massive root on which Oberon stood, and then she faced the crowd.

"Court?" Daphne whispered.

"Siophra?" Shawndirea said softly.

"You know her?" Roble asked.

"She's the Unseelie Queen."

"Order!" Siophra said through tight teeth. Her opal eyes pierced the gloom and fixated on Lez'minx's sobbing form.

"What atrocities have made it worth summoning me to this realm, Siophra?" Oberon asked in a stern tone.

"Your servant," she said, pointing at Lez'minx.

"What has he done this time?"

"He murdered twenty-six Shadowfae renegades," she replied. Her eyes blazed her fury at Lez'minx.

"What do you say of this, Runefel?" King Oberon asked.

"He goes by Lez'minx now," Daphne said.

Siophra flicked her gaze at Daphne. Venom coated her words. "One word more from you and you'll be petrified kindling."

Daphne pressed her face to the cracked floor tile.

The air surrounding them turned icy cold.

Oberon shook his head. "Lez'minx? Why the name change? Still trying to hide?"

"Hide? Yes. But not from you," he replied.

"Then from whom?" Oberon asked.

"The two dryads, Daphne and Portia."

"I suppose there's no reason to entertain why?" Oberon chuckled.

"No."

"Your brother, Pan, has thought you dead for quite some time," Oberon said. "He believed the massive flood you requested from him to wash through the swamps had killed you along with the others. He has carried heavy grief ever since. He'll be relieved to learn that you're still alive."

"I'll happily speak with him and explain," Lez'minx said.

"Don't be so quick to think your actions are forgiven," Oberon said. "Why did you kill the Shadowfae?"

"They were going to kill Roble. They planned to kidnap his fair wife, Shawndirea, so they could overthrow Elvendale's throne."

Oberon glanced at Siophra. "What do you know of this?"

Siophra's hardened gaze became suddenly troubled. She turned toward Oberon. "This is the first I've heard of this."

"Shawndirea," Oberon said. "Is his statement true?"

Shawndirea stood and nodded. "It is how Lez'minx describes."

"Who's the leader of this rebellion?" Oberon asked.

"That's something I wish to know, too," Siophra said icily.

"My cousin, Dirk," she replied.

"Dirk?" Oberon said. He frowned and stared off into the distance.

"He's Seelie," Siophra seethed. "What ... How'd he get Unseelie to follow him?"

"It would seem," Oberon said, looking at Siophra, "that you've not keep a tight watch on your own."

"I know precisely—" Siophra began.

"Careful," Oberon said, interrupting. "Lest you incriminate yourself further."

"Incriminate myself?" the Queen said. Her brow furrowed.

Oberon shifted his feet. Anger thundered in his voice. "You called them *renegades*, did you not? And if so, why haven't you dealt with them well before now? There's only one reason I can think for why you haven't. You wish to see Queen Istrell's throne taken by the Unseelie."

Siophra's mouth gaped. "That's not true!"

"So you knew nothing about this plot?" Oberon asked.

"Nothing at all," Siophra said, shaking her head. "I swear it."

Oberon studied her intently for several long moments. Siophra met his gaze and knelt to one knee, quaking.

"What became of Dirk?" Oberon asked, turning his attention to Lez'minx again.

"He fled," Lez'minx said.

"You let him escape?"

"I offered to kill him for Shawndirea since he threatened to take her, but she declined," Lez'minx said.

"She declined because you offered to do it in return for her allegiance," Roble said.

Shawndirea cast a harsh stare at him.

"Is what the Overlander said, true?" Oberon asked.

Lez'minx shuddered. "Yes. That's what I offered."

"I should strike you dead," Oberon said, drawing his sword.

"No, Your Highness, please," Lez'minx said.

"He's not the only guilty one here," Siophra said. "The Overlander killed one of the Shadowfae, too."

Oberon's jaw tightened. "Did he now?"

"To be fair," Roble said.

"Don't question my fairness," Oberon replied.

"I'm not, but in my defense, the dagger I threw was intended for Dirk. I nicked him, but the dagger flew past him and struck one of the Shadowfae. My intention was to kill Dirk."

Oberon smiled. "Interesting. You'd kill Dirk without hesitation?"

"He threatened my wife," Roble replied.

"Shawndirea?"

Roble nodded.

"Your wife!" Siophra spat.

"She is."

Perplexed, Siophra looked at Shawndirea. "How could you betray your own mother and the Seelie Court? Don't think I'll usher a welcome to you in my Courts."

"Have I made such a request?" Shawndirea said through gritted teeth. "I'm still Seelie."

"No, you're not!" Siophra said. Her face contorted from bitterness. "And you're not one of us, either! I won't allow it! I'll see you dead first!"

"Careful, Siophra," Oberon said. "That's my daughter you're threatening."

Siophra's hand went over her heart. Her mouth dropped and her eyes widened. Her knees buckled. She looked faint.

Confused, Roble glanced at Shawndirea. She was the mirrored, shocked image of Siophra.

Siophra said, "Wait a minute. *She's* your daughter?"

Oberon smiled. "Yes. Istrell and I considered marriage long ago, when she carried Shawndirea inside her. But my duties across the realms requires too much time. We decided against marriage."

Shawndirea swallowed hard. Tears formed in her eyes. "I thought I recognized your voice … Wait, you've been talking to me during those deep sleeps. That was you, wasn't it?"

"Yes," Oberon said. "Over the decades, I've spoken to you in your dreams. I've whispered my blessings to you on the moonbeams gracing your room at night. I've visited your mother's palace many times and watched you grow. I brought you many gifts, but you probably don't remember."

Tears spilled down her cheeks. "You … you called yourself Beron?"

"Yes." Oberon's face glowed as he smiled. "You were always so elegant and graceful. I knew you were destined for greatness. So many times I wanted to reveal who I was, but then I'd need to explain why I couldn't be around."

"You approve of her marrying an Overlander?" Siophra asked.

"No, I don't," Oberon said.

"I can't do as you asked in my dream," Shawndirea said. "I'll *not* annul my marriage to Roble."

"I no longer ask that of you. Not after learning his strength and integrity. For an Overlander, it's obvious how much he loves you, and that he's willing to give his life to protect you at all costs. That's rare in any realm. But why have you kept secrets from him?"

"Secrets?" Roble said, glancing at her.

Oberon said, "Tell him. The time's long overdue."

"Here? Now?" she said. "I think—"

"No," Oberon said. "If it's privacy you think you need, you've had more than adequate amounts of opportunities before. *Now's* the appropriate time."

Shawndirea sighed. She lifted her hands upward, chanted a beautiful melody, and shifted from her faery form into her human height. She walked to Roble, took his hands into hers, and then she placed them upon her stomach.

"We're going to have our first child," she said. Tears flowed down her cheeks. "A son, I think."

Tears crested in Roble's eyes and spilled. "A son?"

She nodded.

Roble grinned, pulled her into his arms, and embraced her. Lehrling stood nearby wiping his eyes with one hand while his other arm hugged Collette.

Siophra faced Oberon. "Has the court session come to a close with this … *good* news?"

"No," Oberon said. "I'm afraid not. I must dispense proper punishments. The Orcs are free to leave to set up camp or sail downriver. Everyone else must stay."

CHAPTER 77

Roble held Shawndirea while the Orcs walked past. Uksen handed the staff to Lez'minx, but a few seconds later, Siophra took the staff away.

"How long have you known you were pregnant?" Roble asked.

"Before we left our home to come here," she replied.

"Why didn't you tell me?"

"You'd have protested my traveling with you; worse than you already had."

"Of course I would've. Or I wouldn't have gone."

"Confronting Lez'minx was a necessity," Shawndirea said. "Had we not found him, he would've eventually found us. He knew our every move."

Roble stared into her sparkling, emerald eyes. "All this journey, I thought you resented me because of the rings. At times, I felt like you hated me."

"I was never happy for your shortsighted action. I'm sorry for lashing out at you so much during this journey. I think it's because of my pregnancy," she said.

Oberon walked to them. Six faery guards with swords and shields formed a semi-circle behind the King. Every other guard kept a fierce, protective gaze at those around Oberon. Their weapons were drawn.

Oberon said, "Your pregnancy with a human was also a reason for why you kept falling into deep sleep. Your body was adjusting. The good thing about delving into your subconscious was that I could talk with you."

"Father, I wish you'd have told me years ago who you really were," Shawndirea said.

"As do I," Oberon said. "But we have time to catch up. I hope to spend time with you and him as well."

Shawndirea said, "I can't believe my mother kept this a secret for so long."

Oberon chuckled. "She has her reasons, but mostly she did it to keep you safe."

"Safe?"

Oberon nodded. "I have enemies in each realm where faeries abide. Some worse than others, and some of my heirs have been killed or taken for ransom. The less you tell others of your lineage, the safer you remain."

Roble regarded Oberon for several moments. Shawndirea's eyes were the same color as her father's. "Will our baby be okay since he's half human?"

"Your child should be perfectly fine. Shawndirea suffers the toil alone. The further along she becomes, the less she'll succumb to those deep sleeps. As to whether your child will be attuned to magical abilities or not, no one can say. Your child's physical traits may be human and faery. Your children will be recognized by most as Unseelie. Istrell will not be pleased."

Sadness claimed Shawndirea's eyes, which burdened Roble. No matter the differences between her and her mother, he didn't like the thought of their children being spurned by immediate family.

Oberon's face became grim. "Now, if you'll excuse me, order needs restored."

Oberon took to flight and returned to his vantage point atop the giant tree root.

"Shawndirea, my dear daughter," Oberon said. "Because of your marriage to Roble and because your children will not be pure Seelie, you cannot rule over Elvendale, even if your mother offers you the rite. Siophra has made it clear that she won't welcome you into her Courts. Perhaps this is due to your contention with Istrell?"

In shame, Siophra lowered her gaze and nodded. "This is true."

"Even though Shawndirea's nothing like Istrell?" Oberon asked.

"I perceive Shawndirea is nothing like her mother, but should I invite her into my Courts, the tension between Elvendale and the Unseelie Courts would magnify. If you've a hint of Istrell's stubborn behavior, Oberon, you know I speak the truth."

Oberon laughed. "I remember quite well. That was another reason for why I couldn't see the marriage working. No offense, Shawndirea."

"None taken. I cannot think of a time when my mother placed others before her. I doubt she ever has. I've never been free of her bitter contention, even as a child. I've always thought that if ever she smiled, her face might shatter," Shawndirea said in a serious tone without the slightest hint of amusement.

Siophra reared back her head and laughed a high shrill until tears formed in her eyes. After she composed herself, she wiped away tears and looked at Shawndirea. "I'm truly sorry. I shouldn't laugh at your expense."

"No need to apologize," Shawndirea said. "I'm not laughing because I meant what I said."

Siophra released a long sigh. The sudden laughter made her countenance glow. "I'm tempted to invite you into my Courts solely to irritate her."

"No," Oberon said, shaking his head. "There's been too much contention between the two courts. It's time that a truce mends the two, and I think I have a way to do that."

"How?" Siophra said.

"My blood flows in Shawndirea's veins, which makes her royalty, regardless of Istrell. Shawndirea deserves a throne to rule from," Oberon said.

Shawndirea shook her head. "No. It's not what I want. I'll not have it. I'm content being the Butterfly Queen."

"As I've told you before, that's nothing more than a title. No throne comes with those duties."

"I understand and I'm content with that."

"No," Oberon said. "I've need of your counseling to bring balance and order between the Seelie and Unseelie Courts."

Siophra eyed the King shrewdly. "What do you have in mind?"

"Do tell," Shawndirea said, placing her nervous hand into Roble's.

"You've already renounced your ties to the Seelie throne in Elvendale, and due to possible retaliation from your mother, you cannot be accepted into the Unseelie Courts. You're a faery without a home or a proper Court. The best resolution is for you to rule over the In-between and have Courts set up for you to govern."

"Splendid idea!" Siophra said, clasping her hands together.

"Father, no," Shawndirea said. "This isn't what I want."

"It's not what you want, but it's what you and your children *need.*"

"Where would we reside? I have no armies," Shawndirea said.

"All of that will be established. I'll provide an army from a different realm, one that is neutral between the two Courts in Aetheaon. They'll obey all you command, and make certain you and your family are protected at all costs."

"Roble and I have urgent matters to attend to now with the Plague-bringer trying to destroy all the kingdoms in Aetheaon. We've no time—"

"Your residence in the In-between won't occur immediately," Oberon said. "It takes time to build a castle. Once established, you'll have an army. Your children will be properly trained, educated, and protected. As Queen you'll oversee the new kingdom, and you'll be the mediator between your mother and Queen Siophra."

Shawndirea squeezed Roble's hand.

Roble looked into her uncertain eyes. He smiled and kissed her forehead.

She smiled. "This was never part of my plan when I sought to find you."

"I know."

"You're okay with *this?*"

"From what I've witnessed the past few weeks, and knowing your mother firsthand, your father's right. Someone needs to negotiate between the two courts."

"I don't think I'm the suitable choice," she said.

"Why not?"

"My mother's liable to resent me even more."

"You're the most qualified choice. I'll speak with your mother before I leave Aetheaon and draw up a treaty between Elvendale and the Unseelie Courts," Oberon said.

"Do you really believe she'd sign such a treaty?" Shawndirea asked.

"She'd be foolish to reject, especially since Dirk wishes her dead."

"To the Heavens," Shawndirea said, placing a hand over her mouth. "Do tell her that Feather is a pawn under Dirk's control."

"She'll be informed," Oberon said. "Do you accept?"

Shawndirea nodded.

"Good. Next order is what to do with Lez'minx," Oberon said.

Lez'minx trembled and made his way to stand at the foot of the massive root. He tucked his bearded chin and averted direct eye contact with Oberon. His thick bent horns hid his gaze as he stared at the floor.

Oberon frowned and looked at Queen Siophra. "How many Shadowfae did Lez'minx kill?"

"Twenty-five. Roble killed the twenty-sixth," she replied.

Oberon nodded. "What punishment do you wish enacted upon Roble?"

Roble's hand tightened around Shawndirea's. He never expected his fate played into the punishments.

"None," Queen Siophra replied. "I detected the sincerity in Roble's actions. He didn't intentionally strike the Shadowfae faery. I've no doubt that he intended to kill Dirk instead."

"Noted," Oberon said. "And Lez'minx?"

Siophra studied the satyr for over a half minute. "He's your servant, and since he's Pan's brother, I accept whatever punishment you deem fitting."

"Very well," Oberon said. He eyed Lez'minx. "Are you ready to accept your fate?"

"Yes, Your Highness," Lez'minx said, nervously meeting Oberon's gaze. He bleated and clamped a hand over his mouth. "Apologies."

"Queen Siophra, Lez'minx is your servant for a quarter of a century, doing whatever unpleasant menial duties you'd have him do. His magic will be stripped from him during the next twenty-five years; one year for every Shadowfae's life he took. Had they not been renegade faeries, the punishment would be even harsher."

Queen Siophra nodded her acceptance. "I accept your decision."

"As for you," King Oberon said, pointing a stern finger at Daphne. "You threatened my daughter's life and—"

"I had no idea she was your daughter," Daphne said. "I beg your forgiveness … and hers."

"Whether she was my daughter or not, isn't what matters. You deceived the Dragon Skull Knights into believing Lez'minx was your brother, when that's the furtherest from the truth. The plan to use your magic to harm one of my servants because you felt spurned is misuse in its most abhorrent manner." Oberon formed a white orb on his right palm and blew into it. Icy snowflakes gusted toward Daphne, freezing her into place. Her appendages hardened and splintered. The sheer look of terror remained etched in her face.

Oberon directed his gaze at Portia and the two male dryads. "Let this be a warning. I'm under the impression she deceived all of you with her true intentions as well. Is this correct?"

"She tricked me," Portia said, clasping her hands together while sitting on her knees. "She's nothing like she was ages ago. She darkened and uses dark magic. Her intentions toward Lez'minx until several minutes before you appeared was unknown to me. Ki'wese and Aqese? I don't know about them."

Aqese said, "We sailed the rafts. Nothing more. She told us she wanted to gather those who had once lived in Linden-hold before the flood. We didn't know Daphne, other than by recognition when she first requested our aid."

Oberon stared firmly at Portia, as though he read her thoughts and intentions. A bag appeared in his hand and he tossed it before her. "Return to Dagger's Tears with the halflings, Portia. Plant these tree seeds in your hamlet so you no longer drain your strength when casting magic. Ki'wese and Aqese may stay at Dagger's Tears if they desire."

"What about us?" Roble asked.

"After a feast, some wine, and a good night's sleep, I'll have you escorted outside of Woodnog Swamps. Where is your destination?"

"The City of Woodnog," Shawndirea said.

Oberon waved his hand and a large banquet table materialized near the Great Tree's trunk. "Eat your fill. The table never goes bare, and the wine-skins never empty."

Roble's mouth watered. After days of eating dried jerky, he was pleased to see another great meal.

Oberon held his hand out at Roble. On his palm were the two rings that Roble had crushed underfoot. "You forgot these."

Roble eyed the rings suspiciously. "No. I don't want them."

Oberon smiled. "Runefel's spell no longer enchants them. Mine do, however."

"What sort of spell?" Roble asked.

"Shawndirea carries my grandchild," Oberon said. "I wish to be alerted when it's time for the birth. To send word to me, have Shawndirea kiss each stone. You'll find over time that more enchants the rings than that. But nothing obtrusive or controlling. Take care of my daughter."

Roble swallowed hard and nodded. "I will."

"Roble," Lehrling said. "Look."

Swooping downward was a blue raven and it lighted upon Lehrling's hand.

"There's something tied to its leg," Shawndirea said.

Lehrling untied the parchment and unrolled it. "It's a message from Zauber. He has issued summons for all the Dragon Skull Knights to rendezvous at a hollow near Barrier Pass on the outskirts of Woodnog."

"Not until after we eat," Roble said.

Lehrling laughed. "I agree. And a night's sleep to boot won't delay us much longer."

CHAPTER 78

"And that's how we got back to Woodnog," Roble said, sitting at the campfire and taking a freshly poured tankard of stout from Dwiskter. "It's a shame we had not met Oberon *before* we went into the swamps."

Shawndirea smiled.

Boldair stoked the campfire with a long stick. "That be a mighty fine, and yet, quite a *long* story, if I have me say. Tell me, Overlander, you've a knack for storytelling. Perhaps, secretly, you desire to be a bard? Maybe you're part Dwarf?"

Roble's face reddened, and he shook his head. "No."

Dwiskter laughed, slapped his knee, and elbowed Drucis. "An Overlander bard! Can ye imagine?"

Drucis downed his tankard. "I don't know. If he happened to tell us tales of things in his own realm, nobody'd believe it, and dat, Boldair, might make *his* tales more sought after than ye own!"

The smile drained from Boldair's face and Dwiskter's laughter faded.

Zauber puffed his pipe and grinned, contently listening.

"You 'ave a point. Don't fill his head with silly ambitions. I still tell the best tales and have had the greater adventures," Boldair said.

"No arguments from me," Roble said.

Boldair looked at Lehrling. "And where's your lady? Dis Collette? I didn't see her riding with you. Parted ways, so soon?"

Lehrling sipped his stout and shook his head. "No. Due to the dangers we might face with the Plague-bringer, I requested King Oberon to send her with an escort to Woodnog where she'll hopefully be safer."

"Dat's a good idea," Boldair said. "I'm not certain if we should head into the Woodnog early tomorrow or wait another day to recuperate from all this stout. We'll 'ave horrid headaches on the morrow."

"Aye!" Drucis said.

"Tis a shame," Zauber said, running his hand through his long beard, "that your father couldn't aid us in this battle, Shawndirea."

"The battle isn't his. That's what he said," she replied.

"While I suppose that's true, we could use all the help we can find," Zauber said.

"Still no word from other Dragon Skull Knights?" Lehrling asked.

"No ravens. No word," Zauber said with a smile. "But we mustn't allow hope to die."

"Hope never dies," a deep voice said from the dark pathway that cut through the trees. "And a Dragon Skull Knight never yields."

Lehrling stood at the campfire. His eyes widened in surprise. "Do my eyes deceive me? Praise be to the Goddesses. Geowren?"

"Aye, ol' friend," Geowren said with a broad grin. He dismounted and was fiercely embraced by Lehrling.

"I feared you were dead," Lehrling said, patting Geowren's back hard. "It's been so long."

"You should've taken the journey with me, as I requested. I hope your wait for Bausch was worth it?"

Sadness filled Lehrling's eyes. "Sadly, no. He's no longer with us. Killed by Vykings."

"I see. I'm sorry for your loss. I know how fond you were of him, as though he were your own son," Geowren said, looking Lehrling in the eyes and clasping his hands on Lehrling's shoulders. Geowren looked at the Dragon Skull pendant on Roble's armor with question. "Who is this? A new one to the Order?"

Lehrling introduced them and explained briefly how Roble had found Bausch and then saved Lehrling's life.

"An Overlander, eh?" Geowren frowned. "I suppose since King Erik's absence, they're recruiting anyone? Even Dwarves?"

Boldair turned with fierceness in his eyes. "Aye, we were chosen by Lady Dawn because of our valor at the Battle of Hoffnung. I don't recall *you* splitting Vyking skulls with us."

"I didn't mean to offend," Geowren said with a sly smile. "But, I was in the battle with all of you. Just in disguise."

"Likely story," Drucis said.

"Call it into question if you want," Geowren said, "but I came through the sewers with several warriors of my own. We captured two Vykings, and let's just say that despite the rumors, you *can* torture them enough to get answers. I'm closer to finding King Erik than ever before, but not before we destroy the Plague-bringer for good."

"Several warriors?" Boldair said. "And what of their fates? Are they alive to corroborate your story?"

Geowren nodded toward the dark trees behind them. "Look for yourself."

Boldair turned to see four weary travelers. One woman wearing cloth, and three men dressed in leather armor.

"Ask them whatever you like," Geowren said.

Boldair turned his attention to poking the fire a bit more, a bit harder.

"We've one other in our group, but he's currently stealing an item that'll prove most useful in our battle ahead," Geowren said. "Perhaps you know him? Crukas?"

"The thief!" Dwiskter said. "Why would you trust—"

"Perhaps I should've said that we *hired* him for a purpose," Geowren said. "He must fulfill the duty to get the gold. His bonus is whatever valuables he finds while stealing the item. No gold upfront, so we're at no loss should he fail."

"Bah!" Dwiskter said. "You can never trust a thief, *especially* Crukas, the master thief."

"You've news that King Erik is alive? We found where you had been in Polderholm. And the magical portal. Tell us what you discovered," Lehrling said.

Geowren combed his thick black beard with his fingers and laughed heartily. "That's a long story, as long-winded as the one the Overlander told, and one that'd require many tankards and half a roasted wild boar to pry it from my mouth."

"Then you're in luck!" Boldair said. Excitement rang in his voice. "We've got plenty of both. While I cannot speak for all the others, I'm always keen on hearing new stories."

Drucis and Dwiskter rolled their eyes.

"Yes. Every word," Lehrling said in awe. "Please, tell us what you've discovered."

"Before you begin," Zauber said. "Answer one question for me."

"Certainly," Geowren said.

"Does this long story give us helpful information in finding a way to defeat Mors?"

"It does."

"Then, please," Zauber said, waving a permissive hand. He puffed his long pipe with an intent frown creasing his brow and a sly grin. "Proceed."

AUTHOR'S NOTE

Thank you for purchasing this novel. If you enjoyed this book, please check out my website and join my mailing list at www.leonarddhilleyii.com to receive a free digital copy of Forrest Wollinsky: Vampire Hunter.

If you could also take a moment and leave a review, it is greatly appreciated!

Blessings to you and yours.

ACKNOWLEDGMENTS

A special thank you to KC Riley-Gyer for the extra set of eyes to catch my mistakes, and her friendship from the opposite of the earth.

ABOUT THE AUTHOR

Leonard D. Hilley II grew up a quiet, shy kid with an inquisitive mind. Learning to read at an early age, he fell in love with books. He read every book he could get his hands on and stacks of dark comics about ghosts, monsters, and creepy things that stalk the night.

Like a lot of boys, he caught beetles, wooly bears, butterflies, and had an ant farm. When he was ten, his interests in science increased even more after seeing a professor's insect collection. Soon he set out on his quest to build his own collection. He also learned to rear butterflies and moths to obtain perfect specimens. He learned botany, gardening, and set his goal to become an entomologist.

At eleven, he saw Star Wars. His imagination soared. Soon after, he discovered Roger Zelazny's Chronicles of Amber. Six months later, he had written the first draft of a novel. A novel he later discarded, but the characters stuck with him. Years later, these characters came to life in Shawndirea, which Hilley intended to be a novella for Devils Den. The characters, however, refused to be ignored and took the opportunity to unveil Aetheaon in their first epic fantasy. Lady Squire: Dawn's Ascension was quick to follow.

Shawndirea was Hilley's farewell to butterfly collecting, and those who have read the novel understand why. He has taken Ray Bradbury's advice to heart: "Follow the characters." He does. He follows, listens, and take notes—often never knowing where they're going to take him, but he's never been disappointed in the results.

Hilley earned a B.S. in Biology and an MFA in Creative Writing to combine his love of science and writing.

Sci-fi Titles: Predators of Darkness: Aftermath, Beyond the Darkness, The Game of Pawns, Death's Valley, The Deimos Virus.

Epic Fantasy: Shawndirea (Aetheaon Chronicles: Book One), Lady Squire (Aetheaon Chronicles: Book Two), Frosthammer (Aetheaon Chronicles: Book Three), Shadowfae (Aetheaon Chronicles: Book Four), and Devils Den.

UF/PR: Succubus: Shadows of the Beast (Nocturnal Trinity Series: Book

One), Raven (Nocturnal Trinity Series: Book Two), A Touch of the Familiar (Nocturnal Trinity Series: Book Three)

YA UF/Paranormal: Forrest Wollinsky Vampire Hunter; Forrest Wollinsky: Blood Mists of London; Forrest Wollinsky: Predestined Crossroads.